MW00772814

BURIED DEEP

AND OTHER STORIES

BURIED DEEP

AND OTHER STORIES

NAOMI NOVIK

NEW YORK

Copyright © 2024 by Temeraire LLC

All rights reserved.

Published in the United States by Del Rey, an imprint of Random House, a division of Penguin Random House LLC, New York.

DEL REY and the CIRCLE colophon are registered trademarks of Penguin Random House LLC.

The following stories have been previously published:
"Araminta, or, The Wreck of the *Amphidrake*" in *Fast Ships, Black Sails,* edited by Ann & Jeff VanderMeer (San Francisco: Night Shade, 2008)
"Vici" in *The Dragon Book: Magical Tales from the Masters of Modern Fantasy,* edited by Jack Dann and Gardner Dozois (New York: Ace, 2009)
"Buried Deep" in *The Mythic Dream,* edited by Dominik Parisien & Navah Wolfe (New York: Saga Press, 2019)
"Spinning Silver" in *The Starlit Wood: New Fairy Tales,* edited by Dominik Parisien & Navah Wolfe (New York: Saga Press, 2016)
"Commonplaces" in *The Improbable Adventures of Sherlock Holmes,* edited by John Joseph Adams (San Francisco: Night Shade, 2009)
"Seven" in *Unfettered III: New Tales by Masters of Fantasy,* edited by Shawn Speakman (Battle Ground, Wash.: Grim Oak Press, 2018)
"Blessings" in *Uncanny Magazine,* Issue 22, May/June 2018
"Lord Dunsany's Teapot" in *The Thackery T. Lambshead Cabinet of Curiosities,* edited by Ann & Jeff VanderMeer (New York: Harper Voyager, 2011)
"Seven Years from Home" in *Warriors,* edited by George R. R. Martin & Gardner Dozois (New York: Tor, 2010)
"Dragons & Decorum" in *Golden Age and Other Stories,* by Naomi Novik (Burton, Mich.: Subterranean Press, 2017)
"Castle Coeurlieu" in *Unfettered II: New Tales by Masters of Fantasy,* edited by Shawn Speakman (Auburn, Wash.: Grim Oak Press, 2016)

LIBRARY OF CONGRESS CATALOGING-IN-PUBLICATION DATA
Names: Novik, Naomi, author.
Title: Buried deep and other stories / Naomi Novik.
Description: First edition. | New York: Del Rey, 2024. |
Identifiers: LCCN 2024023252 (print) | LCCN 2024023253 (ebook) |
ISBN 9780593600351 (hardcover) | ISBN 9780593600368 (ebook)
Subjects: LCGFT: Fantasy fiction. | Short stories.
Classification: LCC PS3614.O93 B87 2024 (print) |
LCC PS3614.O93 (ebook) | DDC 813/.6—dc23/eng/20240523
LC record available at https://lccn.loc.gov/2024023252
LC ebook record available at https://lccn.loc.gov/2024023253

Printed in the United States of America on acid-free paper

randomhousebooks.com

1 2 3 4 5 6 7 8 9

First Edition

Book design by Susan Turner

CONTENTS

AUTHOR'S NOTE

I feel the need to warn you that this book is full of lies. Not the stories; the stories are as true as I could make them when I wrote them, but the introductions. When I'm finished writing something, it leaves me; if I tell you anything about these stories, the chances are extremely good that I made it up when an editor or an interviewer asked me, months or years after I wrote the actual story, and now I misremember it as what I was thinking at the time, or it's what I think of them now, reading them again at a distance in some cases of decades.

The real truth is that only the stories themselves can tell you what I was thinking. If I could put one of them into a few neat and tidy paragraphs, I wouldn't have bothered to write a story. There are no shortcuts in the Labyrinth.

So I *have* written introductions for these stories, but I invite you to ignore them, or to think of them as just that, introductions, as if we were at a party together and I had to leave but before I went I wanted to haphazardly introduce you to a good friend of mine that I thought you might get on with, by telling you something sort of vaguely interesting about them, and then disappearing, and after I've gone the friend might lean over and say, "Actually, that was all wrong, let me tell you the truth," and you should believe them and not me.

And after you have read them, your opinion will be at least as good as mine. Books don't have any pretense of living on their own, part of their magic. If you put the book down and go to the other room for a snack, the book will not go on without you; I've written these words and other people have edited them and formatted them and put them down on paper, but we've come as far as we can go, and the rest of the journey is yours, if you choose to lend them your eyes and your brain to live in for a little while.

Naomi

BURIED DEEP
AND OTHER STORIES

ARAMINTA, OR, THE WRECK OF THE *AMPHIDRAKE*

My house growing up was full of words; my mother read widely. She had a specific taste in romance novels: thin and smooth, to be drunk up like a glass of wine in the evening and the empties taken back to the used bookstore in large bags to exchange for a case of new ones, or ones that had been read long enough ago to be good to taste all over again.

The Regencies were my favorites; Heyer of course, but almost any would do, except I had violent feelings about the ones that were wrong, by which I meant the ones where the characters were modern people playing dress-up in diaphanous muslins and riding in carriages, just pretending. Because I was interested in the rules, so inviolate and so obvious to the characters themselves, these people living inside narrow boxes, especially the women—in the short length of these books, their world couldn't be more real and complicated, so instead they had to believe in the rules, inhabit them, or else it didn't feel right. And I didn't mind if they cheated, but they had to be clever about it.

So this is a Regency story: about a world with a different set of rules, and a very good cheater.

LADY ARAMINTA WAS SEEN OFF FROM THE DOCKS AT Chenstowe-on-Sea with great ceremony if not much affection by her assembled family. She departed in the company of not one but two maids, a hired eunuch swordsman, and an experienced professional chaperone with the Eye of Horus branded upon her forehead, to keep watch at night while the other two were closed.

Sad to say these precautions were not entirely unnecessary. Lady Araminta—the possessor of several other, more notable names besides, here omitted for discretion—had been caught twice trying to climb out her window, and once in her father's library, reading a spellbook. On this last occasion she had fortunately been discovered by the butler, a reliable servant of fifteen years, so the matter was hushed up; but it had decided her fate.

Her father's senior wife informed her husband she refused to pay for the formal presentation to the Court necessary for Araminta to make her debut. "I have five girls to see established besides her," Lady D— said, "and I cannot have them ruined by the antics which are certain to follow."

(Lest this be imagined the fruits of an unfair preference, it will be as well to note here that Araminta was in fact the natural daughter of her Ladyship, and the others in question her daughters-in-marriage, rather than the reverse.)

"It has been too long," Lady D— continued, severely, "and she is spoilt beyond redemption."

Lord D— hung his head: he felt all the guilt of the situation, and deserved to. As a youth, he had vowed never to offer prayers to foreign deities such as Juno; and out of obstinacy he had refused to recant, so it had taken three wives and fourteen years to acquire the necessary son. Even then the boy had proven rather a disappointment: sickly and slight, and as he grew older preferring of all things literature to the manly arts of fencing or shooting, or even sorcery, which would at least have been respectable.

"But it is rather messy," young Avery said, apologetic but unmoving, even at the age of seven: he *had* inherited the family trait of obstinacy, in full measure. It is never wise to offend foreign deities, no matter how many good old-fashioned British fairies one might have invited to the wedding.

Meanwhile Araminta, the eldest, had long shown more aptitude for riding and shooting than for the cooler arts, and had a distressing tendency to gamble. Where her mother would have seen these inappropriate tendencies nipped in the bud, Lord D—, himself a notable sportsman, had selfishly indulged the girl: he liked to have company hunting when he was required at home to do his duty to his wives— and with three, he was required more often than not.

"It is not too much to ask that at least one of my offspring not embarrass me on the field," had been one of his favorite remarks, when chastised; so while her peers were entering into society as polished young ladies, beginning their study of banking or medicine, Lady Araminta was confirmed only as a sportswoman of excessive skill, with all the unfortunate results heretofore described.

Something of course had to be done, so a match was hastily arranged with the colonial branch of a similarly exalted line. The rumors she had already excited precluded an acceptable marriage at home, but young men of good birth, having gone overseas to seek a better fortune than a second son's portion, often had some difficulty acquiring suitable wives.

In those days, the journey took nearly six months, and was fraught with considerable dangers: storms and pirates both patrolled the shipping lanes; leviathans regularly pulled down ships, mistaking them for whales; and strange fevers and lunacies thrived amid the undersea forests of the Shallow Sea, where ships might find themselves becalmed for months above the overgrown ruins of the Drowned Lands.

Naturally Lady Araminta was sent off with every consideration for her safety. The *Bluegill* was a sleek modern vessel, named for the long, brightly painted iron spikes studded in a ridge down her keel to fend off the leviathans, and armed with no fewer than ten cannon. The cabin had three locks upon the door, the eunuch lay upon the threshold outside, the maids slept to either side of Araminta in the large bed, the chaperone had a cot at the foot; and as the last refuge of virtue she had been provided at hideous expense with a Tiresian amulet.

She was given no instruction for the last, either in its use or in how it would act to preserve the virtue in question, and only told with great emphasis to always keep it in its box and put it on only if the worst should threaten—the worst having been described to her rather hazily by Lady D—, who felt suspiciously that Araminta already knew a good deal too much of such things.

There were not many tears in evidence at the leave-taking, except from Lady Ginevra, the next-oldest, who felt it was her sisterly duty to weep, though privately delighted at the chance of advancing her own debut a year. Araminta herself shed none; only said, "Well, good-bye," and went aboard unrepentant, having unbeknownst to all concealed a sword, a very fine pair of dueling pistols, and a most inappropriate grimoire in her dower chest during the upheaval of the packing. She was not very sorry to be leaving home. She was tired of being always lectured, and the colonies seemed to her a hopeful destination: a young man who had gone out to make his fortune, she thought, could not be quite so much a stuffed-shirt.

AFTER ALL THE PREPARATIONS AND warnings, the journey seemed to her so uneventful as to be tiresome: one day after another altered only by the degree of the blowing wind, until they came to the Drowned Lands and the wind died overhead. She enjoyed looking over the railing for the first few days, at the pale white gleam of marble and masonry which could yet be glimpsed in places, when the sailors gave her a bit of spell-light to cast down below.

"There's nowt to see, though, miss," the master said in fatherly tones, while she peered hopefully. Only the occasional shark, or sometimes one of the enormous sea-spiders, clambering over the ruined towers with their long spindly red legs, but that was all—no gleam of lost treasure, no sparks of ancient magic. "There's no treasure to be had here, not without a first-rate sorcerer to raise it up for you."

She sighed, and insisted instead on being taught how to climb the rigging, much to the disgust of the sailors. "Not like having a *proper* woman on board," more than one might be heard quietly muttering.

Araminta was not perturbed, save by the increasing difficulty in coaxing interesting lessons from them. She resorted after a while to the privacy of her cabin, where through snatched moments she learned enough magic to hide the grimoire behind an illusion of *The Wealth of Nations,* so she might read it publicly and no-one the wiser. The Tiresian amulet she saved for last, and tried quietly in the middle of the night, hidden from the third eye beneath the bedcovers while the chaperone, Mrs. Penulki, snored. Araminta was taken aback by the results, which were immediate, and took it off again straightaway, but discovering that the effects reversed themselves with equal speed, after a moment an adventurous spirit overcame her first hesitation, and she decided on making a more thorough trial. The maids on either side of her, at first rather startled, were persuaded with only a little difficulty to participate. (It must be admitted they were somewhat young and flighty creatures, and already overawed by their noble charge.)

Two slow months they spent crossing the dead shallow water, all their sails spread hopefully, and occasionally putting men over the side in boats to row them into one faint bit of current or another. All the crew cheered the night the first storm broke, a great roaring tumult that washed the windows of Araminta's high stern cabin with foam and left both of the maids moaning weakly in the water-closet. Mrs. Penulki firmly refused to entertain the possibility that Araminta might go outside for a breath of fresh air, even when the storm had at last died down, so she spent a stuffy, restless night and woke with the changing of the watch.

She lay on her back listening to the footsteps slapping against the wood, the creak of rope and sail. And then she was listening only to an unfamiliar silence, loud in its way as the thunder; no cheerful cursing, not a snatch of morning song or clatter of breakfast.

She pushed her maids until they woke and let her climb out to hurry into her clothes. Outside, the sailors on deck were standing silent and unmoving at their ropes and tackle, as if preserved in wax, all of them watching Captain Rel-lowe. He was in the bows, with his long-glass to his eye, aimed out to port. The dark tangled mass of storm-clouds yet receded away from them, a thin gray curtain dropped across half the stage of the horizon. The smooth curve of the ocean bowed away to either side, unbroken.

He put down the glass. "Mr. Willis, all hands to make sail, north-northwest. And go to quarters," he added, even as the master cupped his hands around his mouth to bellow orders.

The hands burst into frantic activity, running past her; below she could hear their curses as they ran the ship's guns up into their places, to the complaint of the creaking wheels. "Milady, you will go inside," Captain Rellowe said, crossing before her to the quarterdeck, none of his usual awkward smiles and scraping; he did not even lift his hat.

"Oh, what is it?" Liesl, one of the maids, said, gasping, as Araminta came back in.

"Pirates, I expect," Araminta said, tugging her enormously heavy dower chest out from under the bed. "Oh, what good will wailing do? *Help* me."

The other ship emerged from the rain-curtain shortly, and became plainly visible out the windows of Araminta's stern cabin. It was a considerable heavier vessel, with a sharp-nosed aggressive bow that plowed the waves into a neat furrow, and no hull-spikes at all: instead her hull was painted a vile greenly color, with white markings like teeth also painted around.

Liesl and Helia both moaned and clutched at one another. "I will die before you are taken," Molloy, the eunuch, informed Araminta.

"Precious little difference it will be to me, if I am taken straightaway after," she said practically, and did not look up from her rummaging. "Go speak to one of those fellows outside: we must all have breeches, and shirts."

The chaperone made some stifled noises of protest, which Araminta ignored, and which were silenced by the emergence of the pistols and the sword.

The jewels and the trinkets were buried amid the linen and silk gowns, well bundled in cloth against temptation for straying eyes, so they were nearly impossible to fetch out again. The amulet in particular, nothing more than a tiny nondescript silver drachma on a thin chain, would have been nearly impossible to find if Araminta had not previously tucked it with care into the very back corner. It was just as well, she reflected, glancing up to see how the pirate vessel came on, that boredom had driven her to experimentation.

FROM THE QUARTERDECK, CAPTAIN RELLOWE, too, watched the ship coming up on their heels; his glass was good enough to show him the pirates' faces, lean and hungry and grinning. He was a good merchant captain; he had wriggled out of more than one net, but this one drew taut as a clean line drawn from his stern to her bows. The once-longed-for steady wind blew into his sails with no sign of dying, feeding the chase still better.

Amphidrake was the pirate's name, blazoned in yellow, and she was a fast ship, if rigged a little slapdash and dirty. Her hull at least was clean, he noted bitterly, mentally counting the knots he was losing to his own hull-spikes. Not one ship in a thousand met a leviathan, in season, and cannon saw them safe as often as not; but spikes the owners would have, and after the crossing of the Shallow Sea, they would surely by now be tangled with great streamers of kelp, to say nothing of barnacles and algae.

(The storm, of course, would have washed away any kelp; but the spikes made as satisfying a target to blame as any, and preferable to considering that perhaps it had not been wise to hold so very close to the regular sea-lanes, even though it was late in the season.)

In any event, the pirate would catch the *Bluegill* well before the hour of twilight, which might otherwise have given them a chance to slip away; and every man aboard knew it. Rellowe did not like to hear the mortal hush that had settled over his ship, nor to feel the eyes pinned upon his back. They could not expect miracles of him, he would have liked to tell them roundly; but of course he could say nothing so disheartening.

The *Amphidrake* gained rapidly. The bo'sun's mates began taking around the grog, and the bo'sun himself the cat, to encourage the men. The hand-axes and cutlasses and pistols were laid down along the rail, waiting.

"Mr. Gilpin," Captain Rellowe said, with a beckon to his first mate, and in undertone said to him, "Will you be so good as to ask the ladies if, for their protection, they would object to putting on male dress?"

"Already asked-for, sir, themselves," Gilpin said, in a strange, stifled tone, his eyes darting meaningfully to the side, and Rellowe turning found himself facing a young man, with Lady Araminta's long black curls pulled back into a queue.

Rellowe stared, and then looked away, and then looked at her head—*his* head—and then glanced downward again, and then involuntarily a little lower—and then away again. He did not know how to look. It was no trick of dress; the shirt was open too loose for that, the very line of the jaw was different, and the waist.

Of course one heard of such devices, but generally only under intimate circumstances, or as the subject of rude jokes. Rellowe (if he had ever thought of such things at all) had vaguely imagined some sort of more caricaturish alteration; he had not gone very far in studies of sorcery himself. In reality, the line between lady and lord was distressingly thin. Araminta transformed had a sword, and two pistols, and a voice only a little high to be a tenor, in which she informed him, "I should like to be of use, sir, if you please."

He meant of course to refuse, vocally, and have her removed to the medical orlop, if necessary by force; and so he should have done, if only the *Amphidrake* had not in that very moment fired her bow-chasers, an early warning-shot, and painfully lucky had taken off an alarming section of the quarterdeck rail.

All went into confusion, and he had no thought for anything but keeping the men from panic. Three men only had been hit—and those by little more than splinters—but a drop of blood spilled was enough to spark the built-up store of terror. The mates had been too free with the grog, and now the lash had less effect: a good many of the men had to be thrust bodily back into their places, or pricked with sword-point, and if Araminta joined in the effort, Rellowe managed not to see.

ARAMINTA WAS PERFECTLY HAPPY, HERSELF; it had not yet occurred to her they might lose. The ship had been very expensive, and the cannon seemed in excellent repair to her eye: bright brass and ebony polished, with fresh paint. Of course there was a personal danger, while she was on-deck, but high spirits made light of that, and she had never balked at a fence yet.

"You cannot mean to be a coward in front of all these other stout fellows," she sternly told one sailor, a scrawny underfed gaol-rat attempting to creep away down the forward ladderway, and helped him back to the rail with a boot at his back end.

The crash of cannon-fire was glorious, one blast after another, and then one whistling by overhead plowed into the mizzenmast. Splinters went flaying skin in all directions, blood in bright arterial spray hot and startling. Araminta reached up and touched her cheek, surprised, and looked down at the bo'sun, staring glassy-eyed back at her, dead at her feet. Her shirt was striped collar to waist with a long sash of red blood.

She did not take it very badly; she had done a great deal of hunting, and stern lecturing from her father had cured her of any tendency to be missish, even when in at the kill. Elves, of course, were much smaller, and with their claws and pointed teeth inhuman, but near enough she was not tempted in the present moment either to swoon or to be inconveniently ill, unlike one small midshipman noisily vomiting upon the deck nearby.

Above her head, the splintered mizzen creaked, moaned, and toppled: the sails making hollow thumping noises like drum skins as it came down, entangling the mainmast. Araminta was buried beneath a choking weight of canvas, stinking with slush. The ship's way was checked so abruptly, she could feel the griping through the boards while she struggled to force her way out through the thick smothering folds. All was muffled beneath the sailcloth—screams, pistol-shots all distant—and then for a moment Captain Rellowe's voice rose bellowing over the fray, "Fire!"

But their own cannon spoke only with stuttering, choked voices. Before they had even quite finished, a second tremendous broadside roar thundered out in answer, one ball after another pounding into them so the *Bluegill* shook like a withered old rattle-plant. Splinters rained against the canvas, a shushing noise, and at last with a tremendous heave Araminta managed to buy enough room to draw her sword and cut a long tear to escape through.

Pirates were leaping across the boards: grappling hooks clawed onto whatever was left of the rail, and wide planks thrust out to make narrow bridges. The deck was awash in blood and wreckage, of the ship and of men, torn limbs and corpses underfoot.

"Parley," Captain Rellowe was calling out, a shrill and unbecoming note in his voice, without much hope: and across the boards on the deck of the other ship, the pirate captain only laughed.

"Late for that now, Captain," he called back. "No, it's to the Drowned Lands for all of you," cheerful and clear as a bell over the water. He was a splendid-looking fellow, six feet tall in an expansive coat of wool dyed priest's-crimson, with lace cuffs and gold braid. It was indeed the notorious Weedle, who had once taken fourteen prizes in a single season, and made hostage Lord Tan Cader's eldest son.

Inexperience was not, in Araminta's case, a synonym for foolishness; defeat was now writ too plainly across the deck for her to mistake it. Molloy, staggering over to her, grasped her arm: he had a gash torn across the forehead and his own sword was wet with blood. She shook him off and shot one pirate leaping towards them. "Come with me, quickly," she ordered, and turning dashed into the cabin again. The maids, terrified, were clinging to one another huddled by the window, with Mrs. Penulki pale and clutching a dagger in front of them.

"Your Ladyship, you may not go out again," the chaperone said, her voice trembling.

"All of you hide in the water-closet, and do not make a sound if anyone should come in," Araminta said, digging into the dower chest again. She pulled out the great long strand of pearls, her mother's parting gift, and wrapped it around her waist, hidden beneath her sash. She took out also the gold watch, meant to be presented at the betrothal ceremony, and shut and locked the chest. "Bring that, Molloy," she said, and dashing back outside pointed at Weedle, and taking a deep breath whispered, "Parley, or I will throw it overboard. *Dacet.*"

The charm leapt from her lips, and she saw him start and look about suspiciously, as the words curled into his ears. She waved her handkerchief until his eyes fixed on her, and pointed to the chest which Molloy held at the ship's rail.

Pirate captains as a class are generally alive to their best advantage. The value of a ship bound for the colonies, laden with boughten goods, might be ten thousand sovereigns, of which not more than a quarter might be realized. But a dower chest might hold such a sum alone, or twice that, in jewels and silks more easily exchanged for gold. Weedle was not unwilling to be put to the little difficulty of negotiation to secure it, when they might finish putting the sword to the survivors afterwards.

"I should tell you at once, it is cursed," Araminta said, "so if anyone but me should open it, everything inside will turn to dust." It was not, of course. Such curses were extremely expensive, and dangerous besides, as an unwitting maid might accidentally ruin all the contents. Fortunately, the bluff would be rather risky to disprove. "There is a Fidelity charm inside, intended for my bride," she added, by way of explaining such a measure.

Weedle scowled a little, and a good deal more when she resolutely refused to open it, even with a dagger at her throat. "No," she said. "I will go with you, and you may take me to Kingsport, and when you have let me off at the docks, I will open it for you there. And I dare say my family will send a ransom too, if you let Captain Rellowe go and inform them," she added, raising her voice for the benefit of the listening pirates, "so you will all be better off than if you had taken the ship."

The better to emphasize her point, she had handed around the gold watch, and the pirates were all murmuring over it, imagining the chest full to the brim of such jewels. Weedle liked a little more blood in an engagement—the fewer men to share the rewards with after—but for consolation, there was not only the contents of the chest, but what they augured for the value of the ransom.

"What do you say, lads? Shall we give the young gentleman his passage?" he called, and tossed the watch out over their heads, to be snatched for and scrambled after, as they chorused agreement.

"Lord Aramin, I must protest," Captain Rellowe said, resentfully. With the swords sheathed, his mind already began to anticipate the whispers of censure to come, what indignant retribution her family might take. But he had scarcely any alternative; exposing her to rape and murder would certainly be no better, and, after all, he could only be censured if he were alive for it, which was some improvement. So he stood by, burdened with an ashamed sense of relief, as she crossed with unpardonable calm to the pirate ship and the chest trundled over carefully behind her.

The *Amphidrake* sailed away to the south; the *Bluegill* limped on the rest of her way to New Jericho, there to be received with many exclamations of horror and dismay. The family of Lady Araminta's fiancé (whose name let discretion also elide) sent an agent to Kingsport at once; followed by others from her own family.

They waited one month and then two, but the *Amphidrake* never put in. Word eventually came that the ship had been seen instead at port in Redhook Island. It was assumed, for everyone's comfort, that the pirates had yielded to temptation and tried the chest early, and then disposed of a still-disguised Lady Araminta for tricking them.

Now that there was no danger of her rescue, she was much lionized; but for a little while only. She had been most heroic, but it would have been much more decorous to die, ideally on her own dagger. Also, both the maids had been discovered, shortly after their arrival in port, to be increasing.

Her fiancé made the appropriate offerings and, after a decent period of mourning, married a young lady of far less exalted birth, with a reputation for shrewd investing, and a particularly fine hand in the ledger-book. Lord D— gave prayers at the River Waye; his wives lit a candle in Quensington Tower and put her death-date in the family book. A quiet discreet settlement was made upon the maids, and the short affair of her life was laid to rest.

◦　◦　◦

THE REPORT, HOWEVER, WAS QUITE wrong; the *Amphidrake* had not put in at Redhook Island, or at Kingsport either, for the simple reason that she had struck on shoals, three weeks before, and sunk to the bottom of the ocean.

AS THE *BLUEGILL* SAILED AWAY, stripped of all but a little food and water, Captain Weedle escorted Lady Araminta and the dower chest to his own cabin. She accepted the courtesy quite unconsciously, but he did not leave it to her, and instead seated himself at the elegant dining table with every appearance of intending to stay. She stared a little, and recollected her disguise, and suddenly realized that she was about to be ruined.

One might think this understanding was a little late in coming, but Araminta had generally considered the laws of etiquette as the rules of the chase, and divided them into categories: those which everyone broke, all the time; those which one could not break without being frowned at; and those which caused one to be quietly and permanently left out of every future invitation to the field. Caught browsing a spellbook was in the very limits of the second category; a bit of quiet fun with a lady friend in the first; but a night alone in the company of an unmarried gentleman was very firmly in the last.

"You aren't married, are you?" she inquired, not with much hope; she was fairly certain that in any case, a hypothetical Mrs. Weedle a thousand sea-miles distant was not the sort of protection Lady D— would ever consider acceptable for a daughter's reputation, magic amulet or no.

Weedle's face assumed a cast of melancholy, and he said, "I am not."

He was the by-blow of an officer of the Navy and a dockside lady of the West Indies sufficiently shrewd to have secured a vow on the hearth before yielding; accordingly he had been given a place aboard his father's ship at a young age. He had gifts, and might well have made a respectable career, but he had been taken too much into society by his father, and while of an impressionable age had fallen in love with a lady of birth considerably beyond his own.

He had presence enough to appeal to the maiden, but her family forbade him the house as soon as they realized his presumption. She in turn laughed with astonishment at his suggestion of an elopement, adding to this injury the insult of drawing him a brutal chart of their expected circumstances and income, five years out, without her dowry.

In a fit of pride and oppression, he had vowed that in five years' time he would be richer than her father or dead; and belatedly realized he had put himself into a very nasty situation, if any god had happened to be listening. One could never be sure. He was at the time only eighteen, several years from his own ship and the chance of substantial prize-money, if he should ever get either; and the lady's father was exceptionally rich.

Pirate ships were rather more open to the advancement of a clever lad, and there was no Navy taking the lion's share of any prize, or inconveniently ordering one into convoy duty. He deserted, changed his name, and in six months' time was third mate on the *Amphidrake* under the vicious

Captain Egg, when that gentleman met his end untimely from too much expensive brandy and heatstroke.

A little scuffling had ensued among the officers, and Weedle had regretfully been forced to kill the first and second mates when they had tried to assert their claims on grounds of seniority; he was particularly sorry for the second mate, who had been an excellent navigator, and a drinking-companion.

With nothing to lose, Weedle had gone on cheerful and reckless, and now six years later he was alive, exceptionally rich himself, and not very sorry for the turn his life had taken, though he still liked to see himself a tragic figure. "I am not married," he repeated, and sighed, deeply.

He would not have minded in the least to be asked for the whole tale, but Araminta was too much concerned with her own circumstances to care at all about his. She did not mind at all about being ruined for its own sake, and so had forgotten to consider it, in the crisis. But she cared very much to be caught at it, and locked up in a temple the rest of her days, never allowed to do anything but make aspirin or do up accounts for widowers; *that* was not to be borne. She sighed in her own turn, and sat down upon the lid of the chest.

Weedle misunderstood the sigh, and poured her a glass of wine. "Come, sir, there is no need to be afraid, I assure you," he said, with worldly sympathy. "You will come to no harm under my protection, and soon you will be reunited with your friends."

"Oh, yes," she said, unenthusiastically. She was very sorry she had ever mentioned a ransom. "Thank you," she said, politely, and took the wine.

For consolation, it was excellent wine, and an excellent
dinner: Weedle was pleased for an excuse to show away his
ability to entertain in grand style, and Araminta discovered
she was uncommonly hungry. She put away a truly astonishing amount of beef and soused hog's face and mince pie,
none of which she had ever been allowed, of course; and she
found she could drink three glasses of wine instead of the
two which were ordinarily her limit.

By the time the servants cleared away the pudding, she
was in too much charity with the world to be anxious. She
had worked out several schemes for slipping away, if the pirates should indeed deliver her to her family; and the pearls
around her waist, concealed, were a great comfort. She had
meant them to pay her passage home, if she were not ran-
somed; now they would give her the start of an independence. And, best of all, if she were ruined, she need never
worry about it again: she might jettison the whole tedious
set of restrictions, which she felt was worth nearly every
other pain.

And Weedle did not seem to be such a bad fellow, after
all; her father's highest requirements for a man had always
been that he should be a good host, and show to advantage
upon a horse, and play a decent hand at the card-table. She
thoughtfully eyed Weedle's leg, encased snugly in his silk
knee-breeches and white stockings. It certainly did not need
the aid of padding, and if his long curling black hair was a
little extravagant, his height and his shoulders rescued that
and the red coat from vulgarity. Fine eyes, and fine teeth;
nothing not to like, at all.

So it was with renewed complacency of spirit she offered Weedle a toast, and gratified his vanity by saying sin-

cerely, "That was the best dinner I ever ate. Shall we have a round of aughts and sixes?"

He was a little surprised to find his miserable young prisoner already so cheerful: ordinarily, it required a greater investment of patience and liquor, and a show of cool, lordly kindness, to settle a delicate young nobleman's nerves and impress upon him his host's generosity and masterful nature. But Weedle was not at all unwilling to congratulate himself on an early success, and began at once to calculate just how much sooner he might encompass his designs upon Lord Aramin's virtue. Ordinarily he allowed a week; perhaps, he thought judiciously, three days would do, in the present case.

Meanwhile, Araminta, who had spent the last several months housed in a cabin over the sailors' berth, and was already familiar with the means of consolation men found at sea, added, "Winner has first go, after?" and tilted her head towards the bed.

Taken aback, Weedle stared, acquiesced doubtfully, and picked up his cards with a faintly injured sense that the world was failing to arrange itself according to expectations. The sentiment was not soon overcome; Araminta was very good at aughts and sixes.

ARAMINTA LIKED TO BE ON *Amphidrake* very well. The pirates, most of them deserters from the Navy or the merchant marine, were not very different from the sailors on the *Bluegill*. But they did not know she was a woman, so no-one batted an eye if she wished to learn how to reef and make sail, and navigate by the stars. Instead they pronounced her a good sport and full of pluck, and began to pull their fore-locks when she walked past, to show they did not hold it against her for being a nobleman.

Weedle was excellent company in most respects, if occasionally inclined to what Araminta considered inappropriate extremes of sensibility. Whistling while a man was being flogged at the grating could only be called insensitive; and on the other hand, finding one of the ship's kittens curled up dead in the corner of the cabin was not an occasion for mourning, but for throwing it out the window, and having the ship's boys swab the floor.

She enjoyed her food a great deal, and was adding muscle and inches of height at what anyone might have considered a remarkable rate at her age. She began to be concerned, a little, what would happen if she were to take off the amulet, particularly when she began to sprout a beard; but as she was certainly not going to do any such thing amidst a pack of pirates, she put it out of her mind and learned to shave.

The future loomed alarmingly for other reasons entirely. If only they had gone directly to Kingsport, Araminta had hoped they should arrive before the ransom, and she might slip away somehow while the men went on carouse with their winnings. But Weedle meant to try and break his personal record of fourteen prizes, and so he was staying out as long as possible.

"I am sure," she tried, "that they are already there. If you do not go directly, they will not wait forever: surely they will decide that I am dead, and that is why you do not come." She did not consider this a possibility at all: she envisioned nightly a horde of chaperones waiting at the docks, all of them with Horus-eyes glaring at her, and holding a heap of chains.

"I must endure the risk," Weedle said, "of your extended company," with a dangerously sentimental look in his eye: worse and worse. Araminta decidedly did not mean to spend the rest of her days as a pirate captain's paramour, no matter how splendidly muscled his thighs were, although she depressed herself by considering that it might yet be preferable to a life with the Holy Sisters of The Sangreal.

She was perhaps inappropriately relieved, then, when a shriek of "Leviathan" went up, the next morning; and she dashed out to the deck on Weedle's heels. Now surely he should have to turn about and put in to port, she thought, not realizing they were already caught, until she tripped over the translucent tendril lying over the deck.

She pulled herself up and looked over the side. The leviathan's vast, pulsating, domelike mass was directly beneath the ship and enveloping her hull, glowing phosphorescent blue around the edges and wobbling softly like an aspic jelly. A few half-digested bones floated naked inside that transparent body, leftovers of a whale's ribcage. A faint whitish froth was already forming around the ship, at the waterline, as the leviathan's acid ate into the wood.

The men were firing pistols at it, and hacking at the tough, rubbery tendrils, without much effect. The leviathan leisurely threw over a few more, and a tip struck one of the pirates; he arched his back and dropped his hand-axe, mouth opening in a silent, frozen scream. The tendril looped half a dozen times around him, quick as lightning, and lifted him up and over the side, drawing him down and into the mass of the leviathan's body. His eyes stared up through the green murk, full of horror and quite alive: Araminta saw them slowly blink even as he was swallowed up into the jelly.

She snatched for a sword herself, and began to help chop away, ducking involuntarily as more of the thin limbs came up, balletic and graceful, to lace over the deck. Thankfully they did nothing once they were there other than to cling on, if one did not touch the glistening pink tips.

"Leave off, you damned lubbers," Weedle was shouting. "Make sail! All hands to make sail—"

He was standing at the wheel. Araminta joined the rush for the rope lines, and shortly they were making nine knots in the direction of the wind, back towards the Drowned Lands. It was a sorry speed, by the *Amphidrake*'s usual standards; the leviathan dragging from below worse than ten thousand barnacles. It did not even seem particularly incommoded by their movement, and kept throwing over more arms; an acrid smell, like woodsmoke and poison, rose from the sides. The men had nearly all gone to huddle down below, out of reach of the tendrils. Weedle held the wheel with one arm, and an oar with the other, which he used to beat off any that came at him.

Araminta seized his long-glass and climbed up to the crow's-nest to go looking out: she could see clearly where the water changed color and the gorgeous blue-green began, the shipping lanes visible as broad bands of darker blue running through the Shallow Sea. The wind was moderately high, and everywhere she looked there seemed to be a little froth of cresting waves, useless; until at last she glimpsed in the distance a steady bank of white: a reef, or some land near enough the surface to make a breakwater; and she thought even a little green behind it: an island, maybe.

A fist of tendrils had wrapped around the mast since she had gone up, poisonous tips waving hopefully: there would be no climbing down now. She used the whisper-charm to tell Weedle the way: south by southeast, and then she grimly clung on to the swinging nest as he drove them towards the shoals.

WHAT WAS LEFT OF THE leviathan, a vile gelatinous mess stinking all the way to the shore, bobbed gently up and down with the waves breaking on the shoals, pinned atop the rocks along with what was left of the *Amphidrake*. This was not very much but a section of the quarterdeck, the roof of the cabin, and, unluckily, the top twelve feet of her mainmast, with the black skull flag gaily flying, planted neatly in a noxious mound of jelly.

The wreckage had so far survived three rainstorms. The survivors gazed at it dismally from the shore, and concocted increasingly desperate and unlikely schemes for tearing away, burning, or explaining the flag, on the arrival of a Navy patrol—these being regular enough, along the nearby shipping lanes, to make a rescue eventual, rather than unlikely.

"And then they put out the yard-arm, and string us all up one by one," the bo'sun Mr. Ribb said, morbidly.

"If so," Araminta snapped, losing patience with all of them, "at least it is better than being et up by the leviathan, and we may as well not sit here on the shore and moan."

This was directed pointedly at Weedle, bitter and slumped under a palm tree. He had not been in the least inclined to go down with his ship, although he secretly felt he ought to have done, and it was hard to find that his unromantic escape had only bought him a few weeks of life and an ignominious death.

Araminta did not herself need to worry about hanging, but she was not much less unhappy, being perfectly certain the Navy would take her directly back to her family, under such guard as would make escape impossible. Nevertheless, she was not inclined to only eat coconuts and throw stones at monkeys and complain all day.

The island was an old, old mountaintop, furred with thick green vegetation, and nearly all cliffs rising directly from the ocean. Where the shoals had blocked the full force of the waves, a small natural harbor had developed, and the narrow strip of white sand which had given them shelter. Climbing up to the cliff walls to either side, Araminta could look down into the glass-clear water and see the mountainside dropping down and away, far away, and in a few places even the bleached gray spears of drowned trees below.

They had found the ruins of an old walkway, back in the jungle, while hunting: smooth uneven bricks of creamy white stone which led up and into the island's interior; but none of the men wanted to follow it. "That's the Drowned Ones' work," they said, with shudders of dismay, and made various superstitious gestures, and refused even to let her go alone.

But after three days and a rainstorm had gone by, leaving the black flag as securely planted as ever, hanging loomed ever larger; and when Araminta again tried to persuade them, a few agreed to go along.

The walkway wound narrowly up the mountainside, pausing occasionally at small niches carved into the rock face, mossy remnants of statues squatting inside. The road was steep, and in places they had to climb on hands and feet with nothing more than narrow ledges for footholds. Araminta did not like to think how difficult a pilgrimage it might have been, three thousand years ago, before the Drowning, when the trail would have begun at the mountain's base and not near its summit. The men flinched at every niche; but nothing happened as they climbed, except that they got dust in their noses, and sneezed a great deal, and Jem Gorey was stung by a wasp.

The trail ended at a shrine, perched precarious and delicate atop the very summit; two massive sculpted lion-women sprawled at the gate, the fine detail of their heavy breasts and beards still perfectly preserved, so many years gone. The roof of the shrine stood some twenty feet in the air, on delicate columns not as thick as Araminta's wrist, each one the elongated graceful figure of a woman, and filmy drapery hung from the rafters still, billowing in great sheets of clean white. An altar of white stone stood in the center, and upon it a wide platter of shining silver.

"Wind goddess," Mr. Ribb said, gloomily. "Wind goddess for sure; we'll get no use here. Don't you be an ass, Porlock," he added, cutting that sailor a hard look. "As much as a man's life is worth, go poking into there."

"I'll just nip in," Porlock said, his eyes on the silver platter, and set his foot on the first stair of the gate.

The lion-women stirred, and cracked ebony-black eyes, and turned to look at him. He recoiled, or tried to: his foot would not come off the stair. "Help, fellows!" he cried, desperately. "Take my arm, heave—"

No one went anywhere near him. With a grinding noise like millstones, the lion-women rose up onto their massive paws and came leisurely towards him. Taking either one an arm, they tore him in two quite effortlessly; and then tore the parts in two again.

The other men fled, scattering back down the mountainside, as the lion-women turned their heads to look them over. Araminta alone did not flee, but waited until the others had run away. The living statues settled themselves back into their places, but they kept their eyes open and fixed on her, watchfully.

She debated with herself a while; she had read enough stories to know the dangers. She did not care to become a permanent resident, forced to tend the shrine forever; and it might not be only men who were punished for the temerity to enter. But she had also read enough to know that Juno was related to the wind goddess: the lion-women had become her servants, in the old Roman temples, and some destiny was plainly at work here, the still-working punishment for her father's insolence. And if she was too much of a coward to make it good, then surely she would deserve nothing more than to be shut up in a quiet temple all the rest of her days.

"All right," she said at last, aloud, and reaching up to her neck, she took off the amulet.

She was braced to find herself abruptly back in her own former body, a good deal smaller; but the alteration was as mild as before. She looked down at her arms, and her legs: the same new length, and still heavy with muscle; she had lost none of the weight she had gained, or the height. Breasts swelled out beneath her shirt, her hips and waist had negotiated the exchange of an inch or two between themselves, and her face when she touched it felt a little different—the beard was gone, she noted gratefully—but that was all.

The guardians peered at her doubtfully when she came up the stairs. They did get up, as she came inside, and paced after her all the way to the altar, occasionally leaning forward for a suspicious sniff. She unwound the strand of pearls from around her waist and poured the whole length of it rattling into the offering-dish, a heap of opalescence and silver.

The lion-women went back to their places, satisfied. The hangings rose and shuddered in a sudden gust of wind, and the goddess spoke: a fine gift, and a long time since anyone had come to worship; what did Araminta want?

It was not like Midwinter Feast, where the medium was taken over and told fortunes; or like church services at Lammas tide. The goddess of the Drowned Ones spoke rather matter-of-factly, and there was no real sound at all, only the wind rising and falling over the thrumming hangings. But Araminta understood perfectly, and understood also that her prepared answers were all wrong. The goddess was not offering a little favor, a charm to hide her or a key to unlock chains, or even a way off the island; the goddess was asking a question, and the question had to be answered truly.

Easier to say what Araminta did not want: to go home and be put in a convent, to go on to the colonies and be married. Not to be a prisoner, or a fine lady, or a captain's lover, or a man in disguise forever; not, she added, that it was not entertaining enough now and then. But what she really wanted, she told the goddess, was to be a captain herself, of her own life; and free.

A fine wish, the goddess said, for a fine gift. Take one of those pearls, and go down and throw it in the ocean.

Araminta took a pearl out of the dish: it came easily off the strand. She went down the narrow walkway, down to the shore, and past all the men staring at her and crossing themselves in alarm, and she threw the pearl into the clear blue waters of the natural harbor.

For a moment, nothing happened; then a sudden foaming overtook the surface of the water, white as milk. With a roar of parting waves and a shudder, the *Amphidrake* came rising from the deep in all her shattered pieces, seaweed and ocean spilling away. Her ribs and keel showed through the gaps in her half-eaten hull for a moment, and then the foam was climbing up her sides, and leaving gleaming unbroken pearl behind. The decks were rebuilt in smooth white wood; tall slim masts, carved in the shapes of women, climbed up one after another, and vast white sails unfurled in a wind that came out of nowhere, and teased them gently full.

The foam subsided to the water, and solidified into a narrow dock of pearl, running to shore to meet her. Araminta turned to look a rather dazed Weedle in the face.

"This is my ship," she said, "and you and all your men are welcome, if you would rather take service with me than wait for the Navy."

She pulled her hair back from her head, and tied it with a thread from her shirt; and she stepped out onto the dock. She was nearly at the ship when Weedle came out onto the dock at last, and called, "Aramin!" after her.

She turned and smiled at him, a flashing smile. "Araminta," she said, and went aboard.

"*Araminta, or, The Wreck of the* Amphidrake," *first appeared in* Fast Ships, Black Sails *by Night Shade Books in 2008. This fabulous anthology is a collection of pirate stories edited by Jeff and Ann VanderMeer.*

AFTER HOURS

As I was writing the Scholomance trilogy, I felt very strongly even from early on that it was ultimately the story of El and Orion and their friends fighting to make a world where other stories could happen: stories that they would have liked to imagine for themselves. Here's one of those stories.

I T WAS DIFFICULT ENOUGH TO GO CREEPING PAST JAYNE'S bed, slow and quiet to keep from waking her, that Beata closed the door behind her with a sense of triumph. The feeling carried her a little way down the dark corridor, but by the time she had passed even a few doors, she unwillingly began to think that perhaps sneaking out hadn't been such a good idea. It had seemed much more reasonable at dinnertime in the bright cafeteria than it did now, with the skinny little ghost mushroom in her hand barely casting a shine on the walls, and a faint soft *drip drip drip* of water going somewhere and everywhere at once, and all the dorm room doors shut up tight on either side.

The handbook the school had sent to all of them before induction was so frantic about everything—don't ever climb the stairs alone, don't ever go to the bathroom alone, death lurks for you in every corner, ward your cafeteria table every time you eat, ward your library seat, ward all your projects, ward your *head* when you walk to class, ward ward ward ward ward, and if you don't, here are the thousand kinds of terrible maleficaria that will find you and eat you right away. "Why am I going to this place?" she had asked, looking up from it with horror at Mama and Baba Danka and Baba Jadwiga, all reading over her shoulders.

"Don't worry," Mama said. "It won't be like this. They only haven't changed the warnings yet, since the Calling. They want you to keep your guard up, that's all."

Her only other choice was to do what Baba Danka had done for Mama, and what Baba Jadwiga had done for Baba Danka, and Baba Jadwiga's own mother for her: to lie down and be put to sleep, down in the deep cave where they and the babas before them had all slept, until she woke up seven years later in all her power and a mind and body she didn't remember. And when Beata said she didn't think that sounded so bad next to going away to this awful school, they all shook their heads again, and said that it wasn't safe anymore.

Since the Calling, there weren't so many maleficaria wandering around, but the worst ones, the maw-mouths, those were hungry and hunting all the more. One had come to their little cottage six months ago, and they'd only got away because the krasnoludki had warned them just in time to run out through the back door. The maw-mouth had stayed in the cottage for a week, disappointed and hoping they would come back, poking itself into every pocket and cranny of the house, devouring every last crumb out of Baba Danka's cupboards and sucking all the mana out of all their things and knocking them over, so when it finally gave up and went away, and they went in, almost everything was smashed or broken or fallen into dust.

It had gone into the cave, too. There was nothing in there for it to smash, and the mana there wasn't the kind that it could suck out, but they'd seen the path of its passage in the dust. And a sleeper couldn't be moved.

But the handbook had still made the school sound almost as bad, and Beata had privately been skeptical that Mama knew what she was talking about. The Scholomance had never been a choice for them before: they were poor witches in a poor country, and none of them had ever even visited an enclave. They had lived quietly in the old ways instead, doing the deep magic that most maleficaria didn't sniff out, almost never meeting another witch. The babas still went on about it for half an hour every time before and after Beata went on the bus to meet Krystyna, how amazing and wonderful it was that she could have *a friend,* and they sounded anxious the whole time, as though they were trying to convince themselves it was all right and safe for her to go and be together with another witch girl, even if they were only going to the café or the shopping center with mundanes everywhere.

It was only Krystyna who had finally convinced her to go. Krystyna was from Szczecin, and her father had gone to the Scholomance. "It *was* like this," she said, going over the handbook. "But it's much better now, since the Calling. Of course you have to come! We'll be allies, and help each other. It'll be all right."

And it *was* all right. It turned out that no one listened to the handbook at all. Not even the enclavers with mana to spare followed half the rules. Yes, if you were going down to the workshop on a Monday morning, some company was a good idea; a sophomore from Warsaw had told Krystyna that she should put aside some mana all year, so when it was late in the term, she could make a shield or an early-warning spell, just in case there was a stray digester or a little mimic hiding somewhere. But that was all. There were no striga or caranya or leszy or anything else truly terrible.

One of the other freshmen told her that the big mals didn't get in past something called the gatekeeper, which wasn't mentioned in the handbook at all. Someone in her

Maleficaria Studies class, which everyone mostly used for study hall, said it was a wizard that the enclaves had hired to guard the school, which didn't feel right to Beata; how could you *pay* someone to do a job like that? None of the freshmen she knew had seen such a person. Someone else said they'd heard it was a new special warding that had been installed, at great expense. That also didn't feel right; why wouldn't they have done it sooner? But she didn't know what *was* right, then.

It was like the Calling itself: there were so many stories going around about it that even a witch couldn't be sure what had really happened. They knew that it *had* happened; even in the forest they'd heard the song, distantly, and they'd heard the old savage leszy who lived deep in the woods and sometimes stole children go crashing away towards it, and he had never come back. Baba Jadwiga had told the krasno-ludki to go hide in their burrows and gave them soft wax to stuff in their ears to save them from it. But they didn't know who had done it, or how, or why. Mama said it was so big a thing, and so many different tales were traveling through so many mouths, that it would be a while longer before even the babas would be able to winnow out the true ones: they needed a few more years listening to all the stories, shaking the sieve and letting the wind carry away the chaff, before they could work out the truth.

Beata wasn't sure which story was true about the gate-keeper, either. Perhaps it was a little bit of all of them. The Calling had killed so many mals that they weren't around to come in here, and the warding kept out the maw-mouths, and maybe there was a wizard hired to maintain the ward-ing? But the real way people got hurt in school wasn't maleficaria, it was getting their own spells wrong, or blowing themselves up or poisoning themselves with mistakes so stupid that the babas would have died of shame themselves if Beata had made one. So she had stopped worrying very much.

The rules about curfew were the only ones that everyone did still follow, even the seniors. Everyone agreed it was still dangerous, that the mals came in at night and the wards didn't get them right away. Anyway it was hard to be out after curfew: all the lights went out, and there were alarms if you tried to go into someone *else's* room. That was supposedly to keep people from wandering the halls too late—and hooking up, of course.

It also stopped people from changing rooms. Beata would have changed rooms the day after induction herself if she could have. Someone else would have taken Jayne in a minute. Someone *stupid.* She knew very well that the babas would be sighing if they could hear her thoughts. *You should keep trying to make friends, Beatko; she's meant to be good for you,* Mama would have said. The handbook *had* told them that much, about the new way the school worked: *You and your roommate have been matched through a complex working designed by five master incanters, based on affinity alignment, personal compatibility, and divination,* only that was nonsense too, like all the rest of it. Or not exactly nonsense: *she* had clearly been meant to be very good for *Jayne.*

She remembered with a sense of betrayal how excited she had been at first to meet her roommate: a friend who might be from somewhere halfway around the world— places so far away from the forest that they might as well have been on the moon. She'd been holding her breath, wondering how it was going to happen, how it would feel, when the rough stone walls of the cave had just melted away into the dull metal walls of her skinny new dormitory room, and across from her was a girl with three whole bags at her feet and a shiny power-sharer on her wrist.

Krystyna had *congratulated* her, when they found each other at dinner, after Beata had introduced her to Jayne, even though Jayne had only said, "Hey," very shortly, and had gone away to go eat with the other freshmen from her own enclave, and hadn't invited them or even just Beata to come along. But everyone she'd eaten with herself—Krystyna and her own roommate Huilang from Singapore, who spoke English and Chinese and *six* other languages, including Russian, which Krystyna had studied at school—and another boy Janusz from Poznan and his roommate Maceo, who was an artificer from Spain—assured her enviously that everyone hoped for an enclave roommate. They had so many magic artifacts, they knew so many exciting modern spells, their parents could afford to buy them extra weight allowance. "Maybe she'll even invite you in someday!" Krystyna had said, with excitement. Beata had been privately dubious about the idea: Szczecin seemed so big and noisy to her, what would *Chicago* be like? But they had still made it feel like winning a prize, an unexpected door opening into a whole different world.

But then she'd gone back to her room after dinner and found Jayne unpacking not just the three bags she'd brought but two *more* bags that one of the seniors from her enclave had left behind to be passed down to her. Her things were strewn everywhere, and some of them she'd actually put away on *Beata's* bookcase and in a drawer of her dresser—

the *top* drawer, even! Jayne had only said over her shoulder, insincerely, "You don't mind, do you? It looked like there was room. You can borrow things sometimes."

"But I do mind!" Beata said. She hadn't meant it very angrily at the time: she'd been a little bit annoyed that Jayne hadn't asked, but she'd still been persuaded by everyone else to think herself *lucky,* and it *did* look like there was room, because she had used almost all her own weight allowance to bring the big bag of dirt and the parts for the big wooden drawer to hold it, and that would go under her bed. She even meant to *explain* to Jayne that she was going to need the room: the big drawer would be for growing her grzybki, but she was going to need the bookshelves to dry them, and the dresser drawers to store them.

But before she could say anything more, Jayne had straightened up and turned round, folding her arms over her chest, and said coldly, "I'm the daughter of Dominus Warren of Chicago. Are you *sure* you mind?"

Beata had stared at her, and then she'd said, "I'm a witch from the Crooked Forest. Whatever you leave where it doesn't belong will all turn to dust by morning," and thumbed her nose and spat to make it so. Jayne had stared at her and laughed rudely and said, "Oh, *right*," and made a show of casting a shield spell over all her things, and then the next morning she woke Beata up with a scream because of course the curse had worked, and it had crumbled everything that Jayne hadn't put away properly, and that wasn't just the little statue that she'd left deliberately on Beata's bookcase but also the clothes she'd left untidily on the chair and the book she'd dropped on the floor and the notebook and pens she'd left scattered on her desk.

"What are you, some kind of *idiot*?" Jayne had yelled at her. "That was a *warding* statue, you moron! It was strong enough to protect our whole room!"

"How is that *me* being an idiot? You shouldn't have left it where it didn't belong," Beata said coldly back. "The curse doesn't go away, either, if you don't know *that* much."

"*What?*" Jayne had shrieked, and she hadn't wanted to believe it until the single sheet of paper she left out that night was dust the next morning, too.

Then she'd gone whining to one of the seniors from her enclave, who had come up to their room and put on a pair of strange glasses and looked at Jayne and her things and said, "Wow, that's *crazy*," and asked Beata, "How did you even *do* that?"

Beata shrugged. "She *asked* for it." That was how curses worked, at least honest curses. Baba Jadwiga would have twisted her ear all the way off if she'd tried to curse someone who *hadn't* asked for it, or more than they deserved, but you couldn't be stupidly rude to a witch and not expect something a little bad to happen. It wasn't even a real curse to have to be *neat*.

"Consent magic, right," the senior had said, nodding.

"I did *not*!" Jayne said furiously. "That is a total *lie*!"

"Uh-huh, sure," the senior said; he was waving his hands around through the air as if he was seeing something there. "I can see the lines of it. You're the one running it."

"What?" Jayne said.

"You're the one powering it," the senior said. "You did something that let her in, and the spell's hooked up to you now. I wouldn't mess with it until you get home over Christmas and get the senior healers to look at it. You're not getting rid of this thing without a major intervention, and if you do something wrong, it might screw up that anima brace you've got."

"You've got to be *kidding* me," Jayne said.

The boy took off the glasses and shrugged. "Up to you. Don't say I didn't warn you," and walked out.

Jayne glared at Beata and hissed, "You are going to be *sorry* for this," and stormed out.

Beata had felt rather pleased with herself then, too, but only for a very short time. Because Jayne might have to keep her things in order now, but that didn't hurt her, and *she* had told all the other enclave students that Beata could curse them if they said anything rude to her, so they weren't rude to her, but none of them would talk to her, either. And the enclave students were the ones who had all the spare things and all the spare mana.

The handbook had also said they could bring only one little sack in with them, only fifteen kilos, and Beata had said, "But it's impossible to bring everything for a whole year!" Krystyna had explained to her that you had to bring lots of one especially good thing instead, and then trade. So after talking it over with Mama and the babas, Beata had decided that the best thing for her to do was to bring what she needed to grow mushrooms, which didn't need any light, and which she could usually persuade to do interesting things, with only a drop or two of some potion to feed to them. She had shown Krystyna a few of them, and Krystyna had enthusiastically agreed that they would be excellent.

But now almost no one would trade with her for them. They weren't something you *had* to have, usually. That wasn't what mushrooms were good for. For instance she could easily grow a mushroom that would turn into a comfortable small hut to sleep in for a night, if you threw it down in the woods; she could grow a mushroom that would make you beautiful as the spring for an hour, if you cut it up and mixed it with water and put it in your hair. But there wasn't much call for things of that sort in the Scholomance.

She had been hoping to be given some useful potion recipes in alchemy class, which she could then use to grow many mushrooms that would do the same thing, and then she would trade those mushrooms. But her very first assignment was for a *euphoric elixir,* which she was shocked to be given: it was not quite like being told to make opium, but not very far off it either. She could have grown and sold an entire drawerful of *those* mushrooms very easily, but she knew very well what the babas and Mama would have said; it would be unhealthy and dangerous for anyone to take.

Unless, as she learned a few days later, looking in the library for anything useful to do with it, the person who was to take it had a wounded anima, which was not a thing Beata had ever heard of, but seemed to be something that could happen in a bad accident with magic, to someone unshielded standing too close. For such a person, the power of the elixir would instead go to strengthen the anima, and they wouldn't feel drunk or high at all.

As it happened, the only person in the entire school who had such an injury was Jayne, who needed to take a dose of such a potion once every week. And she wasn't good enough at alchemy to brew it herself, so she had to pay other people to make it for her, which was very expensive, and that was the reason her parents had spent a fortune in mana, even by their standards, to get her to school with so much extra weight allowance, so she would have so much to trade.

It made Beata almost wild with anger when she found out and realized that *this* was why she'd been assigned Jayne as a roommate: Jayne was meant to get what she needed at a bargain price, and *she* was meant to be humbly grateful for being paid that bargain price, which would see her through school in modest comfort.

But without it, she was already in modest *discomfort,* and it was getting worse. She had to wash out one of her two pairs of underwear and socks every night, so they would be dry by the end of the next day, and they were wearing out quickly. She was glad she had listened to Baba Danka and brought two good linen dresses for clothing, which she could also sleep in, and they were standing up to the rinsing better, but they were still getting stained and dingy, because her laundry spell needed eucalyptus leaves, and she could get no more. She had run out of toothpaste and her pen had run out of ink, and two days ago her soap had slipped out of her hand in the shower and broken into five pieces, all but one of which had gone down straight down the drain. And she could have *made* herself more toothpaste and ink and soap, but she couldn't trade for any of the ingredients.

Meanwhile Jayne had plenty of everything, even friends—or followers as Beata thought of them. She'd acquired a small group of girls who weren't from an enclave themselves and desperately wanted to be, and they would come over to the room in the evenings to play cards before curfew, all of them snacking on treats that Jayne provided and laughing and agreeing with everything she said, wearing nice clean clothes and ignoring their schoolwork, and carefully not looking over at Beata.

And yesterday, to break the camel's back, Beata had been given a choice of three new assignments, in her alchemy class: one was to make a *different* kind of euphoric elixir, just as useless to her, and either of the other two would have been wonderful—a potion for making you very good at math for a little while, and a good stomach-cooling antidote—if only she could have gotten the ingredients.

"What if you sold her just the first one you made?" Krystyna suggested tentatively. "Then you could buy the supplies."

"I'm not going to go and beg her to buy from me," Beata said. "Anyway she won't. She can buy *one* potion from anyone else as easily as me. It's only important to her if I sell to her all the time."

"You really don't want to make the second euphoric, though," Huilang said. "If you choose to do two assignments in a row like that, the school will start specializing you. You'll be getting nothing but euphoric elixirs from now on."

There were many supplies provided in the laboratories, of course, but the seniors and juniors went to the supply cabinets first thing in the morning, on their way upstairs to breakfast, and took everything valuable. By the time freshmen came in the afternoons, what was left was only good enough for simple and basic potions. "So I must go right away, when it has been freshly restocked, before anyone else has gone," Beata said.

"You can't beat the older students to the supply, even if

you go first thing and skip breakfast," Janusz said. "And if any of them are there, they'll take anything good you've found."

"Then I'll go *before* first thing," Beata said. "When do the cabinets restock?"

"At midnight, probably," Maceo said. "It's always easier to move things in and out of space at the day's edge. But you can't go to the labs in the middle of the night."

"Why not?" Beata said, coolly. "I'm not afraid of a little dark."

They were all very dubious about the idea, and not even Krystyna would agree to go with her. "I don't think this is very smart," she said nervously, and Huilang was even more unsympathetic. "Not even seniors go out after curfew," she said. "You're going to get yourself killed."

"*Has* anyone got themselves killed going out after curfew, since the Calling?" Beata asked.

"No, because *no one goes out after curfew*," Huilang said. "You don't even have to do it. All you need to do is make a reasonable deal with your roommate, which you should do anyway."

"And what is this reasonable deal that you think she is going to give me, if I promise to grow her medicine for all four years?" Beata said.

"Why don't *I* ask for you?" Krystyna suggested. "Maybe she wants to make up, too. It's been almost a month, it's not good to hold grudges," and everyone else backed her up firmly, until Beata—very grudgingly—agreed.

She didn't watch as Krystyna went across the cafeteria to speak to Jayne, who was sitting at a table with other Chicago enclave freshmen and even three sophomores. It was behind her back anyway, but she saw it on Maceo's and Huilang's faces, even before Krystyna came back, her lips pressed tight and a red flush in her face, which was so smiling and warm usually. "No," she said, sitting down again. "She won't agree."

"She wouldn't make a deal at *all?*" Huilang said dubiously.

Krystyna said, "I won't repeat it, what she offered," so shortly that Beata knew it must have been something outrageous, to make Krystyna not only refuse it for her, but get really angry.

"I'm going, then," Beata said, feeling her own face heat with anger. "I'm going tonight."

"Okay," Maceo said abruptly. "I'll go with you, for half of the supplies. I'll be able to trade them for better materials in the shop," he added, when they looked at him.

Huilang said with a sigh, "No. You two will split forty–forty. If you make it back, you'll give me ten percent, and five each to Krys and Janusz, and in exchange they'll each put in some mana and I'll cast you an inverted glamour, after dinner—the sort of thing that makes you less likely to be noticed. Then at least you'll have a *chance* not to get eaten," she added pointedly.

Beata might still have had a second or a third thought that night, except after dinner, Jayne swept back into the room with two of her toadies, and in front of them said to her, full of false sympathy, "Beata, I'm *so* sorry. I didn't realize you were having such a tough time. I told Krystyna, I've lined up a supply already, so I don't really need the elixir from you, but if it would make you feel better, you could go ahead and make it for me, and I'll see what I can do for you.

Do you need some new underwear? A pen, maybe? I can't make any *promises*, but just ask me for anything you really need."

Beata had never in her life before *wanted* to curse someone badly, with something wicked and dreadful. She had to close her mouth hard around the answer that wanted to come back out, *I hope you choke on every swallow and vomit as soon as you have it down,* and then she said, "A promise is only as good as the maker, so why would I want yours?" and turned her back to stare down at her desk, with the alchemy assignment laid out on top, the list of *optional ingredients* mocking her, and her resolution hardened to stone.

And so now here she was, crept out into the hallway, which was *very* dark, and not like the dark of the woods, after all—which was frightening but in its own way, a known and living way she'd grown up with, where something might come out of the night and devour you, but if it did, your bones would go into the ground, and flowers would grow. Here it was the dark of being a thing in the wrong place, soft and vulnerable and fallen between the turning wheels of a machine, like one of the poor little hedgehogs that tried to cross the road and were flattened by cars into useless pulp.

But nothing leapt out at her, and she got a little of her courage back by the time she saw Maceo's light coming the other way to meet her at the top of the nearest stairwell between their rooms. He was walking very slow and careful as well, putting his feet down softly one at a time. His floating light was a little thing the size of a coin, made of thin circles of wood fanned out into a ball with a small twist of straw inside glowing like the filament of a bulb.

The only thing he said was, "Are you sure?" in a whisper,

at the top of the stairs, and she nodded back, because at that moment she was again. She wasn't certain why they were whispering, when it seemed there was nothing around to overhear, but it felt like the right thing to do. They *were* the little hedgehogs, creeping through the dark; they didn't want anything to see them, to know that they were out here.

They started together down the stairs, each of them holding on to the railing with one hand, taking turns going first. It seemed to take a very long time. Beata was almost ready to say they'd missed the entrance to the sophomores' floor, even though she was sure they hadn't, when finally they turned around another flight and saw it below them. Maceo let out an explosive breath of relief when he saw the opening, as if he'd also started to wonder.

But as they came closer to it, their steps slowed; without saying anything, they both stopped still halfway up the flight. The opening was darker than the darkness on the stairs: they could just make out the edges of the next flight going on down, but the mouth of the dormitory area was pitch black. Maceo's hand came groping for hers, and she moved the little mushroom into her other hand and gripped back. Neither of them moved. She thought of turning around and going back upstairs, but somehow that seemed even worse: putting their backs to that darkness.

She leaned in and whispered to his ear, "No light." She had brought her second dress tied up around her waist like an apron, to use for carrying the supplies back. She didn't have any other bag. She tucked the ghost mushroom inside it until the light was completely gone from view, and took hold of the railing. After a moment, Maceo nodded, and he took his small light out of the air and turned it off.

The dark swallowed them up in a single gulp. His hand was still in hers. Slowly, Beata slid her toes along the step, over the edge, and down to the next one. Maceo was moving next to her the same careful slow way. She almost didn't know him, she thought suddenly. She knew his family had a garden of orange trees, because he had told them so a few days ago when there had been a bowl of oranges in the cafeteria line, small wizened half-ripe oranges. He had traded to get one and then he'd cut it up and poured a few sugar packets on the slices, and left them the rest of the meal until the end and shared them around, sour and bitter and sweet all at once, the orange taste bright and strong. After he'd eaten, he'd put his head down on the table buried in his arms for a little while without talking.

Other than that, she knew he liked football and computer games, although that seemed to be what came in every box called *boy* that she had met here in school, and he worked very hard on his projects and had helped Krystyna, who was in one of his shop classes, with hers, and she knew that he had agreed to come downstairs with her because he wanted better materials than he could get. Beata had only been glad before that he'd offered, but now she wondered why he was really doing it, after all.

She couldn't ask him now. She only held on to his hand as together they slowly crept down one step after another, feeling their way in the dark, until they reached the open air of the landing. Then they had to cross it, blind. They were gripping on to each other so tight it almost hurt. Beata couldn't hear Maceo breathing. She was breathing as quiet as she could herself, too, her mouth open, slow slow slow. Her hand was out groping and she was sliding her feet slowly over the floor. She thought she'd come to the edge of the next step twice before she actually reached it, and when she found it at last, she checked three times, running the underside of her foot along the edge, before she believed again, and then she tugged Maceo over until her hand found the handrail: almost three feet to the side, that was how far they'd drifted over.

They went down the whole next flight still in the dark, still groping, and the one after that, and then they finally stopped and just stood in the dark, listening hard, until finally Beata let go of his hand and took out her little ghost mushroom again. They kept going down with just that bit of light. Maceo changed places with her, so he could hold the railing while she held the light and they could keep holding hands. After they went around another turn in the stairs, they sped up some more, until they were going as fast as they could without actually running, one foot hurrying over another, panting, until Maceo jerked to a stop and Beata realized the next opening was right there: they'd made it down to the second floor—the level for the juniors and the laboratory.

They couldn't put out the light again, because they were going out into the hallway. But for some reason it didn't feel as dreadful as the other landing. Beata tried to persuade herself that they'd only been stricken with fear, for no reason. She didn't believe it, though. She didn't like to think about going back past that landing in the dark again. She wondered if maybe they could just stay down here instead; maybe they could find some safe corner, a quiet place to hide in, until the lights came back on in the morning.

The nearest supply room was still far away, and it seemed

to be even farther than it was. The time dragged, and her feet were aching as if she'd walked the whole day. Maceo was tired too; he sighed softly, next to her, and then at last they reached the next corridor junction, and Beata knew the supply room was only two doors down from there.

The door wasn't locked. Maceo turned the knob and opened it, and Beata drew a deep sharp breath of wonder. She'd come to the supply room more than a dozen times since the start of the term. It was a small cramped room with barely enough space for five people to stand in it at the same time, and when there were ten people in it at once the way there usually were, everybody was elbowing and shoving against each other to get a hand into any of the bins that still had anything in them, low dusty bins labeled with *marigold petals* and *baking soda* and *dried oak leaves* and *salt,* and all of it crushed and much worse than what she would have found in Baba Danka's cupboards. All the bins above them had always just been empty and blank.

Now the whole room, floor to ceiling, was crammed full. The bin of *moonglow pollen* was shining a faint pink radiance upwards that fought with the flickering blue of *incendiary powder* a few rows above. There were a hundred ingredients she'd never even heard of, and some of almost everything that she ever had: a row of metals, the bins heaped with *silver dust* and *iridium flakes* and *titanium shavings;* a basket of tiny bottles filled with things like *argonet blood* and *bristlecone sap.* Beata couldn't even start to grab, she only stood letting her eyes roam over all of it, less in greed than in wonder: she felt like she'd gone for a walk in the woods to gather some herbs and had stumbled on the house built of gingerbread and candy that Mama had always warned her about.

"Wow," Maceo said, almost under his breath. "All right. Okay." He sounded a little dizzy himself, as if his head was spinning also. He turned and got one of the plastic sacks out of the box by the door and shook it open, and then he held the mouth wide and started putting it over the bin of powdered diamonds, as if he meant to tip the whole thing in.

"Wait," Beata said in a sharp whisper, catching for his wrist. "No. We can't just grab and grab."

Maceo eyed her as if she'd said something odd. "That's . . . why we came?"

Beata shook her head with absolute and iron certainty. She didn't know many incantations or recipes, she didn't have a bag of artifice, but she'd been taught in stories, and she recognized the lesson of the one she was standing in right now. "This isn't all for us," she said. "We were clever and brave, but we mustn't be greedy. What are you working on? What is it that you want to make, that you can't make?"

Maceo was silent a moment, and then he said, almost as if he was ashamed, "A guitar."

"A magic instrument?" Beata said, taken aback. "But that's too hard! I thought even seniors can't make one, most of them."

"No, not—I just want to *use* magic, to help make a guitar," he said. "I couldn't bring mine. It was just too heavy, even if I used it instead of a bag and stuffed things in. My parents wouldn't let me. But I found instructions in the library to make one . . ." He trailed off.

"Just to play?" Beata said a little wonderingly, and he

nodded, and she was even more sure, then; Maceo also hadn't come just to grab and be rich, he'd come for something he *needed*. "What do you need to make it?"

"Wood, mostly," he said. "But it has to be special thin aged wood, and I'll need a junior to lend me some time on the better tools."

"All right," Beata said. "Take as much as you need to trade for that. And I'll take the supplies for my potions, and we'll find something good for the others."

Maceo paused, but then slowly he put the bin back on the shelf, and just took two scoops of the diamond dust, and then another sack with three scoops of gelatinous steel; meanwhile Beata got the ingredients off her list, none of them so special and rare, only a few beads of hematite and a small chunk of pyrite, for the math potion, and for the cooling potion she took pink salt and grey salt, a small bag of cedar shavings, and ten preserved luna moth wings. And for Huilang and Krystyna and Janusz, she took one small bag each of powdered jewels: star sapphire, opal, and citrine.

But after she put the last scoop in and closed the bin, she noticed a tiny jar standing on the shelf half hidden behind it, with a scrap of linen cloth in it wrapped around something, and in very small print it was labeled in Polish, *kwiat paproci*. Beata caught her breath and reached for it, and then stopped herself just before she touched it.

Maceo had finished gathering his things, and saw her staring; he came over and whispered, "What is it?"

"It's *fern flower*," she said.

There were so many fairy tales and stories about it, but Beata knew a true one, her family's own story. "Here she found it, my baba's baba's mother," Baba Jadwiga had told them all, with ceremony, every summer on the shortest night of the year, when they'd come to give thanks in the cave. "Growing from a cleft in this very stone. She was only a girl, lost in the woods. She found it in innocence and ate it, and slept until she woke seven years later, a woman and a witch. This way the gift of magic first came into her blood, and it has stayed with us ever since."

Beata had always loved the story. She knew most wizards would have scoffed, and told her there was no spell or magic that could turn a mundane into a wizard, but she knew it was true anyway. Finding magic, finding a thing of magic, while you were still young enough to truly believe, could open the door, and then if you had some little gift as well, a powerful magic could awaken it to bloom. Like the fern flower itself, bursting out of the ordinary.

She could only imagine the magic you could do with such a thing. She wouldn't try on her own. She would save it and take it home with her when the summer came; Baba Jadwiga would know the right thing to do with it. It was all wrong for it to even be here in a jar on a shelf, waiting for some student to snatch it up and throw it into some ordinary potion. Her hand was reaching back for it, without quite deciding, and then Maceo put his hand out on *her* wrist.

"You're right," he said softly. "You were right the first time. If we take too many things—valuable things—we'll be noticed. The spell Huilang made for us isn't that strong. If it's something very powerful, if it has mana of its own . . ."

He didn't need to finish. They'd both felt it, the thing in the corridors, the thing they'd crept quietly past. A thing that had only just barely not noticed them, because they'd been as careful and quiet as they could, as hidden as they could;

because they were only freshmen, still mostly children, their pockets empty of real power. She looked away from him and stared at the jar once more, her stomach clenching with longing, but he was right, and she was right. It wasn't fern flower, not really, not for her. For her it was the gingerbread, glazed with sugar, inviting her to take a big poisonous bite. It wouldn't even be here in the morning, surely. Real fern flower wouldn't come to anyone on a shelf, in a jar.

She closed her longing hand up into a fist and turned her back on the jar. She stuffed all the other sacks into her spare dress and tied it up around her waist again. They tip-toed back out of the supply room, and before Beata could suggest it, Maceo whispered to her, "Maybe we could just hide in a laboratory until morning?"

She nodded urgently. They went to the laboratory just next door and crawled under one of the tables together, hud-dled up, shoulder to shoulder. Beata put her head down against her knees. She was glad they couldn't talk. She be-lieved they'd done the right thing, but she also wanted to weep. She knew real fern flower wouldn't come on a shelf, but she also felt sure she would never find it again, either. It wouldn't come a second time, in one life, and she would wonder about it forever, if she *had* made the right choice.

Maceo stiffened next to her, and Beata lifted her head and shifted just two fingers apart from each other on her closed fist, to let out the least sliver of light. He had his head up; he was listening. "Did you hear something?" she whis-pered, carefully just in his ear, as quiet as possible, and then she heard it herself: a faint sound coming from the supply room next door. They were both frozen, holding their breath;

it came again. Something was *in* there, moving the bins around. Beata looked at Maceo, and he looked back at her. In the ghost light his eyes were so wide there was white around them.

They didn't need to talk to ask each other the question: stay and keep hiding, or try to run? They didn't need to talk to answer it: whatever was in there had *followed* them, followed a scent or a trail they'd left without knowing, and if it had followed them to the supply room, it could follow them *here*—

Maceo grabbed her hand and they both got up as softly as they could and crept to the door, slow and soft. When his hand found the doorframe, Beata closed her hand over the ghost mushroom's light, and he slowly and carefully opened the door, and they went out into the corridor. The sound from the supply room was so much louder in the hall, like something was dragging the bins around, knocking things over, and then Beata realized she could see Maceo's face and the walls of the hallway, because there was a *light* inside, a thin line of it visible just around the frame of the door. They both stood staring at it, and then there was a loud clattering crash, and Beata heard a hissed "Shit!" on the other side.

"Someone else?" Maceo said, blankly, but that was ridiculous; unless someone else had known that they were going and had *followed* them, using them as a stalking horse to clear the way—and then as soon as she'd thought of that, Beata knew who it was. She let go of Maceo's hand and yanked open the door and found the faintly glowing outline of a cloaked person kneeling on the floor trying to scoop up moonglow powder dust: they'd emptied the bin into a sack, the same way Maceo had been going to, and it had burst all over them and the floor.

Beata took another step and grabbed off the hood, and the magic of the cloak broke; Jayne was there staring up at them. "Oh, you stupid cowardly—" Beata said, and then Maceo grabbed for her hand through the door and said, "Run! *Run!*"

Jayne came running after them as they flew down the corridor together, with the horrible sound on their heels: a raspy slithering, something heavy and scaled skimming back and forth over the metal floor. It was coming quicker than they could run, getting louder even as they were panting, and there was a pale greenish fog gathering behind them, coming on ahead of it, flowing as fast as a running stream. It was catching up to Jayne, who was trying frantically to shake her cloak clean even as she ran, beating at the material with her hands. But the moonglow was clinging on to it. It was bright enough that they didn't need any other light to see where they were going, and neither did the thing behind them. Maceo looked back over his shoulder and looked at Beata, and jerked his head sideways a little: he wanted to go down the next corridor junction, and try to get away from Jayne.

Beata wanted to also. Jayne wasn't *with* them, and that had been her own choice. She'd deliberately sneaked down after them, letting them bear all the risk while she hid in safety, and then she'd drawn the maleficaria down on them all, being even more selfish and greedy. But behind them Jayne's breath was coming in sobbing gasps, terrified, and if they ran away and left her to draw the beast away—the way she had meant to do to them—she would *die;* she would be torn apart and eaten alive by one of those horrible things in the handbook that Beata had stopped believing in. But now she had to believe in all of them, and all of them were back there, every nightmare of teeth and rending claws and murder.

So when they came to the next junction, instead Beata turned and threw the one other mushroom she had with her, to land just behind Jayne. She wasn't even sure if it would work at all; she knew that it *wouldn't* if she'd thrown it on a sidewalk or a metal ramp, anything that men had made. But when it landed in the green mist, it swelled up just as if she'd thrown it in the woods, into a little mushroom house that filled up the whole corridor, the roof squashing up against the ceiling with a noise of tinkling glass as it smashed one of the overhead lights, the walls bulging through the doors of two laboratories on either side. Jayne staggered to a halt next to them, all of them gulping desperately for a few breaths, and Beata said to her, "Throw it that way! Down that hall, as far as you can!"

"Are you insane? It's a cloak of—" Jayne started, and Maceo snapped at her, "Don't come after us if you're keeping it!" and ran again, the opposite way. Beata ran after him, and a moment later Jayne was behind her, without the cloak, and the scattered pale traces of moonglow fading off her skin. Another moment went, and they heard the squelching and muffled noises of the little mushroom hut being torn apart behind them, awful noises that sounded like the rending of flesh.

The cloak gained them another handful of moments: the maleficaria went down the other corridor at first, and they heard the fabric shredding. When Beata risked a quick glance back, the last of the moonglow outlined a shape that shouldn't have been possible, the misty gas condensing into a solid hunched thing like a monstrous snake with a long coiling tail but also a head and shoulders that swelled out into four arms, or maybe six; two of them at least were holding up the cloak to its head, so it could sniff at it. And then it dropped the cloak and slithered around, and came on after them.

They were already running as desperately fast as they could. Maceo was out in front; he had his little light in his own fist, almost all closed in, but Beata didn't need to see; she could hear Jayne neck and neck alongside her, panting. The floor was striking hard against her pounding feet with every step, going through her body, and then she heard Maceo give a gasp and he all but slammed into a wall straight ahead, half bouncing off it and skidding a little as he scrambled to go around another turn. With the warning, they managed to turn more smoothly, and catch up to him, and they were running all three of them in a row, filling the corridor.

His light had flown out of his hand and was flying along with them, too bright: they could see too much. The green mist was gone, but the snake-creature was now a terrible solid beast behind them, getting closer and closer. Jayne looked around at it once, and then gasped out, "Scream! Scream as loud as you can! On three!" and counted, and all together they did scream, and the thing recoiled, hissing, giving them a little more space. But then Maceo said something that sounded like he was swearing, and swerved again in desperation, away from a *dead end* of the corridor looming up, and into a laboratory room: there wasn't anywhere else to go.

They slammed the door behind them and threw tables down to barricade it, but they knew it wasn't going to hold for long. Maceo sent his light darting around over the whole room, looking for another way out. "The vent, the vent!" Jayne said, and they ran over and climbed up onto the table beneath it, and then all screamed together as the snake-creature struck into the door from the other side, so hard that its talons came through the surface like push-pins, and tore it out whole before it came hunching into the room, more horrible to look at in the light, too real and clear, a cobra head stretched wide with two enormous elongated eyes at the top, slitted and green, and its mouth almost toothless and opening on a gullet lined with pale white sharp bones, big enough to just shove you whole down its throat, with six arms too dreadfully like the arms of a *person,* enormous and bulging, except the taloned hands with thick claws.

It hissed again in distaste when they screamed, but it didn't recoil again. It came slithering at them across the room, mouth wide, arms reaching, and Beata couldn't think of anything to do. They couldn't reach the vent, she had nothing to throw, there was nothing they could do, they'd used everything they had that was any use—

And they'd needed everything, they'd had to do everything, because its claws were not quite a hand's-width distance away from Jayne's arm when it jerked suddenly to a halt and began thrashing wildly as it was dragged away from them, a crackle of golden light lashing back and forth around its body. The hissing grew loud enough to almost be a shriek, and then the snake-creature simply came *apart,* arms and scales and head and body almost tearing away from each other and somehow—collapsing backwards, the whole maleficaria sinking in on itself and shriveling down and then only—*gone,* vanished entirely, as if something else had swallowed *it* whole. They all clutched at each other as the footsteps came through the door behind it, and stared frozen down at the new terror, all the worse because it looked exactly like a *human being,* an ordinary man with silver-gold hair and a young face, who looked up at them and said, "Hey, it's a bad idea to be out after curfew," in mild tones.

Then Jayne gave a small gasp and said, "Oh my god, you're Orion Lake," and sank down on the table on her knees and burst into tears.

"Uh, yeah," the man said, sounding a little perplexed. "Are you hurt?"

"No?" Beata said, uncertainly, darting a look at Maceo, who was staring wide-eyed down at the man—who wasn't really that old, she realized: he didn't look much older than the seniors. He was even dressed up nicely, in a buttoned-down shirt and a pair of trousers, as if he were going out dancing or to a restaurant.

"Okay, well, maybe get back to your rooms," the man said, with a wave, and then Jayne said, "Wait! Wait, Mr. Lake—" and scrambled down. "You can just call me Orion," the man said, and she gulped and said, "Can—can you take us back to the freshman dorms? We got lost."

"Oh, sure, come on," he said, easily.

"Who is he?" Maceo whispered, as they shakily crept after him, down the hall.

"The gatekeeper," Jayne whispered back. "Orion Lake. He's Domina Lake's son, from New York."

It wasn't much of an answer; what was someone like that doing *here*? Jayne could only shrug, helpless. Orion walked openly through the middle of the corridor, a light orb gliding alongside him; he even *whistled* as he went, and poked his head into the rooms they passed as if he wasn't the least bit afraid of anything at all that might jump out at him, and once while he was looking in one of the labs, something *did* jump out of the one across the way, not at him but at Maceo, who was on that side. Beata didn't even get to see what it was; she saw the movement and drew breath to yell, and before she could let it out, Orion had whipped around, and the leaping thing was the one that shrieked instead; it was torn apart and gone so quick it might never have been there at all.

"Figures it would be good hunting tonight," Orion said afterwards, in a rueful tone, looking down at his shirt, which had a thin rip in it where the mal had tried to claw at him; his skin underneath it didn't look hurt at all.

The climb back up seemed much quicker than the way down. Maybe it was only because Orion was with them, his own hair catching the light of his orb, glowing brilliant silver-white with an edge of gold that almost seemed to outline his skin as well, if you looked at him out of the corner of your eyes. The landing at the sophomore level was only an ordinary stair landing, and when he brought them out into the main corridor of the freshman dorms, they were just—at the bus stop a short walk from home, nothing to be afraid of at all.

"Okay, I've got to get going," Orion said, glancing down at his watch. "Don't come out again during curfew. The wards have to open for supplies overnight; that's the best chance for the big mals to get upstairs. And I wasn't going to do my rounds until late tonight. You're lucky I heard you screaming down the pipes."

"Yes," Beata said. "We were lucky. Thank you," with all her heart, and Maceo and Jayne echoed it, and then he waved and went strolling back into the stairwell and on downwards, leaving them shaky underneath Maceo's floating light.

They all just stood there together for a moment. Beata didn't quite want to separate yet, and it seemed neither did the others. "We could walk you back," Jayne said, after a moment, vaguely in Maceo's direction; she was looking away down the hallway and avoiding their gaze.

Maceo looked at Beata. "Yes," she said. They walked him together to his room, and then finally he waved to them and went inside, and the two of them walked back to their room, in the watery light of Beata's slightly crushed ghost mushroom. They went inside and put on all the lights in the room. Jayne sat down on her bed and put her face in her hands and cried a little more, and Beata untied her spare dress and unpacked her supplies onto her bookcase in a neat row, and then she got into her bed and pulled all the covers up around her into a tight little ball because she was shivering-cold, and she couldn't help thinking about how it *had* been, how the school had been, before; all the impossible demands the handbook had made, which of course all really only meant *be lucky, be very lucky,* and how it felt, knowing that they'd had to *be lucky,* to live.

Her shivers calmed, after a while, and she began to feel warm again. Jayne had stopped crying by then. When Beata sighed a little, and put an arm out to get the cup of water next to her bed, Jayne said, without looking at her, "I guess you don't need it anymore, but if you wanted, I'd go halves— between what it costs you and what I'm paying." And then, before Beata could say anything, she amended quickly, "Two-thirds."

She was trying very hard to sound as though she didn't care much, one way or another. But after all, whatever she was paying was enough that *she'd* been willing to sneak out, after curfew, for the chance to stuff bags full of moonglow and diamonds. Instead of having to take help, from someone she didn't like, who didn't like her.

Beata asked abruptly, "How did it happen?"

Jayne was silent so long that Beata thought she wouldn't say, but then she shrugged, still without looking up, and said in an offhand way, "They were trying to open another gateway, from Chicago to Santa Barbara, and the binding on our end slipped loose during the opening ceremony. A lot of people got killed, and my dad . . . he wasn't right next to it, but he had to—he had to shunt the damage into his anima. He couldn't cast anymore."

"But what does that have to do with," Beata began, confused, and then stopped talking, a dreadful tightness in her throat.

Jayne said with a tone of defiance, that refused pity, "Usually it grows back, for little kids. They thought it would be fine by the time I went to school. It has, mostly. It'll be okay by the time I'm a senior." If she wore some sort of magical brace; if she took a potion, once a week, that she had to pay for; if she lived so long. If she was lucky.

None of that excused the way Jayne had acted. No one had made her be rude, and hateful, and selfish, and greedy. Except someone had; her father had. And that wasn't Beata's *fault,* but it was a story she'd also been taught: the story her family had thought she wasn't in anymore; the story that had saved all of them. Because Beata had been told, as a little girl, that after she woke up in the cave with life and magic and power, saved from hungry monsters, she would still have to pay for that luck. Maybe not in a day, or a year, but someday, she'd find someone—the honest boy or the virtuous girl, the spoiled princess or the dreaming fool, the children lost in the woods—who needed *help,* the help of a witch of the Crooked Forest, to put their feet back on the right path. A night of shining beauty to meet the right match, for a girl whose stepmother was using her like a servant; a handful of beans that grew so well that they filled a whole garden plot and fed an entire family: that was the sort of thing that she'd have to think of and arrange, a story for her to make come out right.

Or a good sharp curse or two, to cure that spoiled princess of bad manners and greed, and then to find a way to lift the *real* curse upon her.

Beata took a deep breath and said, "We'll go to the lab together on Saturday. I'll teach you to make the potion, and then I can give you the mushrooms for nothing more, when you need them. They only need some water and scraps from the cafeteria. You'll help me take care of them."

Jayne jerked her head up to stare as if she thought Beata was—lying, or making fun of her. "Why would you—" she said, and stopped halfway, caught between the fear of the answer and not knowing.

"If magic knows you'll pay, sometimes it comes in advance," Beata said. "And this is how I'll pay, for the luck we had tonight. Because it was wicked, what they did to you," she added, "so as much as I can, I'll set it right," and Jayne flinched and curled in on herself; she put her head down against her knees and wrapped her arms around them and began crying again, perhaps because no one else had ever admitted it. Not even she herself, saying *it'll be okay,* as if time alone could make something like this whole. Her father had chosen to do harm to her, for his own sake; others had helped him, and then they'd told her that it was all right. Surely that was why she'd thought it was decent to say *I'm the daughter of the Dominus* and then expect people to give way to anything she wanted, even if anyone could see it was unjust and wrong.

Beata still felt a lingering grudge of resentment in her belly: she had still been put here to help Jayne, to help set Jayne's story right, as if it mattered more than her own, and Jayne had been lucky tonight, too. But it was only a small mean thought, next to what had been done to her, so after a moment, Beata pushed herself out of her nest of blankets and went over and sat down next to Jayne on her bed, and put her arm around her bowed thin shoulders. "We'll make you well," she said. "There will be a way."

Jayne bobbed her head up and down in a nod without raising it and whispered, muffled and wet, "I'm sorry. I'm *sorry.*"

Beata sighed. But it did feel good to hear that, at least. "I forgive you," she said. "You should tell Maceo, too, though."

"I will," Jayne said, and then still without looking up, she reached out a hand and groped for Beata's, and put something small and soft inside it, and said, "I thought you were just being stupid," and Beata looked down and put her other hand over her mouth, swallowing down a shriek, tears coming to her own eyes: it was the little scrap of linen, tied with a single thread, that had been inside the jar, and even in her palm she could feel a faint glowing warmth starting to come through the fabric from the fern flower, a gift of magic and of hope, that grew only in impossible places.

VICI

I'd vaguely had the idea for some time that in the Temeraire universe, the Western tradition of taming dragons began in Roman times. Then one of my friends became a fan of the TV series Rome *and sold me on it; after watching an episode and reading Plutarch's* Life of Antony—*as close as you can get to reading a gossip magazine straight from the streets of ancient Rome—I knew that he'd absolutely been the one to start it, and it didn't go well for him at all. Or perhaps you could say that it went very well indeed.*

WELL, ANTONIUS," THE MAGISTRATE SAID, "you are without question a licentious and disreputable young man. You have disgraced a noble patrician name and sullied your character in the lowest of pursuits, and we have received testimony that you are not only a drunkard and a gambler—but an outright murderer as well."

With an opening like that, the old vulture was sending him to the block for sure. Antony shrugged, philosophically; he'd known it was unlikely his family could have scraped together enough of a bribe to get him let go. Claudius's family was a damn sight richer than his; and in any case he could hardly imagine his stepfather going to the trouble.

"Have you anything to say for yourself?" the magistrate said.

"He was a tedious bastard?" Antony offered, cheerfully.

The magistrate scowled at him. "Your debts stand at nearly two hundred fifty talents—"

"Really?" Antony interrupted. "Are you sure? Gods, I had no idea. Where *does* the money go?"

Tapping his fingers, the magistrate said, "Do you know, I would dearly love to send you to the arena. It is certainly no less than you deserve."

"The son of a senator of Rome?" Antony said, in mock appall. "They'd have *you* on the block, next."

"I imagine these circumstances might be considered mitigating," the magistrate said. "However, your family has petitioned for mercy most persuasively, so you have an alternative."

Well, that was promising. "And that is?" he said.

The magistrate told him.

"Are you out of your mind?" Antony said. "How is that mercy? It's twelve men to kill a dragon, even if it's small."

"They did not petition for your life," the magistrate said patiently. "*That* would have been considerably more expensive. Dragon-slaying is an honorable death, and generally quick, from my understanding; and will legally clear your debts. Unless you would prefer to commit suicide?" he inquired.

Dragons could be killed, guards might be bribed to let you slip away, but a sword in your own belly was final. "No, thanks anyway," Antony said. "So where's the beast? Am I off to Germanica to meet my doom, or is it Gaul?"

"You're not even leaving Italy," the magistrate said, already back to scribbling in his books, the heartless bugger. "The creature came down from the north a week ago with all its hoard and set itself up just over the upper reaches of the Tiber, not far from Placentia."

Antony frowned. "Did you say its *hoard*?"

"Oh yes. Quite remarkable, from all reports. If you do kill it, you may be able to pay off even your debts, extraordinary as they are."

As if he'd waste perfectly good gold in the hand on anything that stupid. "Just how old a beast are we talking about, exactly?"

The magistrate snorted. "We sent a man to count its teeth, but he seems to be doing it from inside the creature's belly. A good four to six elephantweight from local reports, if that helps you."

"Discord gnaw your entrails," Antony said. "You can't possibly expect me to kill the thing alone."

"No," the magistrate agreed, "but the dragon hunter division of the ninth is two weeks' march away, and the populace is getting restless in the meantime. It will be as well to make a gesture." He looked up again. "You will be escorted there by a personal guard provided by Fulvius Claudius Sullius's family. Do you care to reconsider?"

"Discord gnaw *my* entrails," Antony said, bitterly.

ALL RIGHT, NOW THIS WAS getting damned unreasonable. "It breathes *fire*?" Antony said. The nearest valley was a blackened ruin, orchard trees and houses charred into lumps. A trail of debris led away into the hills, where a thin line of smoke rose steadily into the air.

"Looks like," Addo, the head of the guards, said, more enthusiastically than was decent. Anyone would've thought Antony had won *all* the man's drinking money last night, instead of just half. There hadn't even been a chance to use it to buy a whore for a last romp.

The guards marched Antony down to the mouth of the ravine—the only way in or out, because the gods had forsaken him—and took off the chains. "Change your mind?" Addo said, smirking, while the other two held out the shield and spear. "It's not too late to run onto it, instead."

"Kiss my arse." Antony took the arms and threw the man his purse. "Spill a little blood on the altar of Mars for me, and have a drink in my memory," he said, "and I'll see you all in Hell."

They grinned and saluted him. Antony stopped around the first curve of the ravine and waited a while, then glanced back, but the unnaturally dedicated *pedicatores* were sitting there, dicing without a care in the world.

All right; nothing for it. He went on into the ravine.

It got hotter the further in he went. His spear-grip was soaked with sweat by the last curve, and then he was at the end, waves of heat like a bath-furnace shimmering out to meet him. The dragon was sleeping in the ravine, and *merda sancta*, the thing was the size of a granary. It was a muddy sort of green with a scattering of paler green stripes and spots and spines, not like what he'd expected; there was even one big piebald patch of pale green splotchy on its muzzle. More importantly, its back rose up nearly to the height of the ravine walls, and its head looked bigger than a wagon-cart.

The dragon snuffled a little in its nose and then grumbled, shifting. Pebbles rained down from the sides of the ravine walls and pattered against its hide of scales lapped upon scales, with the enameled look of turtle-shell. There was a stack of bones heaped neatly in a corner, stripped clean—and behind that a ragged cave in the cliff wall, silver winking where some of the coin had spilled out of the mouth, much good would it do him.

"Sweet Venus, you've left me high and dry *this* time," Antony said, almost with a laugh. He didn't see how even a proper company would manage this beast. Its neck alone looked ten cubits long, more than any spear could reach. And breathing fire—

No sense in dragging the thing out. He tossed aside his useless shield—a piece of wood against this monster, a joke—and took a step towards the dragon but the shield clattering against the ravine wall startled the creature. It jerked its head up and hissed, squinty-eyed, and Antony froze. Noble resignation be damned; he plastered himself back against the rock face as the dragon heaved itself up to its feet.

It took two steps past him, stretching out its head with spikes bristling to sniff suspiciously at the shield. The thing filled nearly all the ravine. Its side was scarcely arm's length from him, scales rising and falling with breath, and sweat was already breaking out upon his face from the fantastic heat: like walking down the road in midsummer with a heavy load and no water.

The shoulder joint where the foreleg met the body was directly before his face. Antony stared at it. Right in the armpit, like some sort of hideous goiter, there was a great swollen bulge where the scales had been spread out and stretched thin. It was vaguely translucent and the flesh around it gone puffy.

The dragon was still busy with the shield, nosing at it and rattling it against the rock. Antony shrugged, fatalistically, and taking hold of the butt of his spear with both hands took a lunge at the vulnerable spot, aiming as best he could for the center of the body.

The softened flesh yielded so easily the spear sank in

until both his hands were up against the flesh. Pus and blood spurted over him, stinking to high heaven, and the dragon reared up howling, lifting him his height again off the ground before the spear ripped back out of its side and he came down heavily. Antony hit the ground and crawled towards the wall choking and spitting while rocks and dust came down on him. "Holy Juno!" he yelled, cowering, as one boulder the size of a horse smashed into the ground not a handspan from his head.

He rolled and tucked himself up against the wall and wiped his face, staring up in awe while the beast went on bellowing and thrashing from side to side above, gouts of flame spilling from its jaws. Blood was jetting from the ragged tear in its side like a fountain, buckets of it, running in a thick black stream through the ravine dust. Even as he watched, the dragon's head started to sag in jerks: down and pulled back up, down again, and down, and then its hind-quarters gave out under it. It crashed slowly to the ground with a last long hiss of air squeezing out of its lungs, and the head fell to the ground with a thump and lolled away.

Antony lay there staring at it a while. Then he shoved away most of the rocks on him and dragged up to his feet, swaying, and limped to stand over the gaping, cloudy-eyed head. A little smoke still trailed from its jaws, a quenched fire.

"Sweet, most gracious, blessed, gentle Venus," he said, looking up, "I'll never doubt your love again."

He picked up his spear and staggered down the ravine in his blood-soaked clothing and found the guards all standing and frozen, clutching their swords. They stared at him as if

he were a demon. "No need to worry," Antony said, cheerfully. "None of it's mine. Any of you have a drink? My mouth
is unspeakably foul."

"WHAT IN STINKING HADES IS that?" Secundus said, as the
third of the guards came out of the cave staggering under an
enormous load: a smooth-sided oval boulder.

"It's an egg, you bleeding *capupeditum*," Addo said.
"Bash it into a bloody rock."

"Stop there, you damned fools. It stands to reason it's
worth something," Antony said. "Put it in the cart."

They'd salvaged the cart from the wreckage of the village
and lined it with torn sacking, and to prove the gods loved
him, even found a couple of sealed wine jars in a cellar. "Fellows," Antony said, spilling a libation to Venus while the
guards loaded up the last of the treasure, "pull some cups
out of that. Tomorrow we're going to buy every whore in
Rome. But tonight, we're going to drink ourselves blind."

They cheered him, grinning, and didn't look too long at
the heap of coin and jewels in the cart. He wasn't fooled;
they'd have cut his throat and been halfway to Gaul by
now, if they hadn't been worried about the spear he'd kept
securely in his hand, the one stained black with dragon
blood.

That was all right. He could drink any eight men under
the table in unwatered wine.

He left the three of them snoring in the dirt and whistled as the mules plodded down the road, quickly: they were
all too happy to be leaving the dragon-corpse behind. Or
most of it, anyway: he'd spent the afternoon hacking off the

dragon's head. It sat on top of the mound of treasure now, teeth overlapping the lower jaw as it gradually sagged in on itself. It stank, but it made an excellent moral impression when he drove into the next town over.

THE REALLY ASTONISHING THING WAS that now, when he had more gold than water, he didn't need to pay for anything. Men quarreled for the right to buy him a drink and whores let him have it for free. He couldn't even lose it gambling: every time he sat down at the tables, his dice always came up winners.

He bought a house in the best part of the city, right next to that pompous windbag Cato on one side and Claudius's uncle on the other, and threw parties that ran dusk until dawn. For the daylight hours, he filled the courtyard with a menagerie of wild animals: a lion and a giraffe that growled and snorted at each other from the opposite ends where they were chained up, and even a hippopotamus that some Nubian dealer brought him.

He had the dragon skull mounted in the center of the yard and set the egg in front of it. No one would buy the damn thing, so that was all he could do with it. "Fifty sesterces to take it off your hands," the arena manager said, after one look at the egg and the skull together.

"What?" Antony said. "I'm not going to pay *you*. I could just smash the thing."

The manager shrugged. "You don't know how far along it is. Could be it's old enough to live a while. They come out ready to fight," he added. "Last time we did a hatching, it killed six men."

"And how many damned tickets did it sell?" Antony said, but the bastard was unmoved.

It made a good centerpiece, anyway, and it was always entertaining to mention the arena manager's story to one of his guests when they were leaning against the egg and patting the shell, and watching how quickly they scuttled away. Personally, Antony thought it was just as likely the thing was dead; it had been sitting there nearly six months now, and not a sign of cracking.

He on the other hand was starting to feel a little—well. Nonsensical to miss the days after he'd walked out of his stepfather's house for good, when some unlucky nights he'd had to wrestle three men in a street game for the coin to eat— since no one would give him so much as the end of a loaf of bread on credit—or even the handful of times he'd let some fat rich lecher paw at him just to get a bed for the night.

But there wasn't any juice in it anymore. A stolen jar of wine, after running through the streets ahead of the city cohorts for an hour, had tasted ten times as sweet as any he drank now, and all his old friends had turned into toadying dogs, who flattered him clumsily. The lion got loose and ate the giraffe, and then he had to get rid of the hippo after it started spraying shit everywhere, which began to feel like an omen. He'd actually picked up a book the other day: sure sign of desperation.

He tried even more dissipation: an orgy of two days and nights where no one was allowed to sleep, but it turned out even he had limits, and sometime in the second night he had found them. He spent the next three days lying in a dark room with his head pounding fit to burst. It was August, and the house felt like a baking-oven. His sheets were soaked through with sweat and he still couldn't bear to move.

He finally crawled out of his bed and let his slaves scrub and scrape him and put him into a robe—of Persian silk embroidered with gold, because he didn't own anything less gaudy anymore—and then he went out into the courtyard and collapsed on a divan underneath some orange trees. "No, Jupiter smite you all, get away from me and be quiet," he snarled at the slaves.

The lion lifted its head and snarled at him, in turn. Antony threw the wine jug at the animal and let himself collapse back against the divan, throwing an arm up over his eyes.

He slept again a while, and woke to someone nudging his leg. "I told you mange-ridden dogs to leave me the hell alone," he muttered.

The nudging withdrew for a moment. Then it came back again. "Sons of Dis, I'm going to have you flogged until you—" Antony began, rearing up, and stopped.

"Is there anything more to eat?" the dragon asked.

He stared at it. Its head was about level with his, and it blinked at him with enormous green eyes, slit-pupiled. It was mostly green, like the last one, except with blue spines. He looked past it into the courtyard. Bits and chunks of shell were littering the courtyard all over, and the lion— "Where the hell is the lion?" Antony said.

"I was hungry," the dragon said, unapologetically.

"You ate the lion?" Antony said, still half dazed, and then he stared at the dragon again. "You ate the *lion*," he repeated, in dawning wonder.

"Yes, and I would like some more food now," the dragon said.

"Hecate's teats, you can have anything you want," Antony said, already imagining the glorious spectacle of his next party. "Maracles!" he yelled. "Damn you, you lazy sodding bastard of a slave, fetch me some goats here! How the hell can you talk?" he demanded of the dragon.

"*You* can," the dragon pointed out, as if that explained anything.

Antony thought about it and shrugged. Maybe it did. He reached out tentatively to pat the dragon's neck. It felt sleek and soft as leather. "What a magnificent creature you are," he said. "We'll call you—Vincitatus."

IT TURNED OUT THAT VINCITATUS was a female, according to the very nervous master of Antony's stables, when the man could be dragged in to look at her. She obstinately refused to have her name changed, however, so Vincitatus it was, and Vici for short. She also demanded three goats a day, a side helping of something sweet, and jewelry, which didn't make her all that different from most of the other women of Antony's acquaintance. Everyone was terrified of her. Half of Antony's slaves ran away. Tradesmen wouldn't come to the house after he had them in to the courtyard, and neither would most of his friends.

It was magnificent.

Vici regarded the latest fleeing tradesman disapprovingly. "I didn't like that necklace anyway," she said. "Antony, I want to go flying."

"I've told you, my most darling one, some idiot guard

with a bow will shoot you," he said, peeling an orange; he had to do it for himself, since the house slaves had been bolting in packs until he promised they didn't have to come near her. "Don't worry, I'll have more room for you soon."

He'd had most of the statuary cleared out of the courtyard, but it wasn't going to do for long; she had already tripled in size, after two weeks. Fortunately, he'd worked out a splendid solution.

"Dominus," Maracles called nervously, from the house. "Cato is here."

"Splendid!" Antony called back. "Show him in. Cato, my good neighbor," he said, rising from the divan as the old man stopped short at the edge of the courtyard. "I thank you so deeply for coming. I would have come myself, but you see, the servants get so anxious when I leave her alone."

"I did not entirely credit the rumors, but I see you really have debauched yourself out of your mind at last," Cato said. "No, thank you, I will not come out; the beast can eat you, first, and then it will be so sozzled I can confidently expect to make my escape."

"I am not going to eat Antony," Vici said indignantly, and Cato stared at her.

"Maracles, bring Cato a chair, there," Antony said, sprawling back on the divan, and he stroked Vici's neck.

"I didn't know they could speak," Cato said.

"You should hear her recite the *Priapea,* there's a real ring to it," Antony said. "Now, why I asked you—"

"That poem is not very good," Vici said, interrupting. "I liked that one you were reading at your house better, about all the fighting."

"What?" Cato said.

"What?" Antony said.

"I heard it over the wall, yesterday," Vici said. "It was much more exciting, and," she added, "the language is more interesting. The other one is all just about fornicating and buggering, over and over, and I cannot tell any of the people in it apart."

Antony stared at her, feeling vaguely betrayed.

Cato snorted. "Well, Antony, if you are mad enough to keep a dragon, at least you have found one that has better taste than you do."

"Yes, she is most remarkable," Antony said, with gritted teeth. "But as you can see, we are getting a little cramped, so I'm afraid—"

"Do you know any others like that?" Vici asked Cato.

"What, I suppose you want me to recite Ennius's *Annals* for you here and now?" Cato said.

"Yes, please," she said, and settled herself comfortably.

"Er," Antony said. "Dearest heart—"

"Shh, I want to hear the poem," she said.

Cato looked rather taken aback, but then he looked at Antony—and smiled. And then the bastard started in on the whole damned thing.

Antony fell asleep somewhere after the first half hour and woke up again to find them discussing the meter or the symbolism or whatnot. Cato had even somehow talked the house servants into bringing him out a table and wine and bread and oil, which was more than they'd had the guts to bring out for *him* the last two weeks.

Antony stood up. "If we might resume our business," he said pointedly, with a glare in her direction.

Vincitatus did not take the hint. "Cato could stay to dinner."

"No, he could *not*," Antony said.

"So what was this proposition of yours, Antony?" Cato said.

"I want to buy your house," Antony said, flatly. He'd meant to come at it roundabout, and enjoy himself leading Cato into a full understanding of the situation, but at this point he was too irritated to be subtle.

"That house was built by my great-grandfather," Cato said. "I am certainly not going to sell it to you to be used for orgies."

Antony strolled over to the table and picked up a piece of bread to sop into the oil. Well, he could enjoy this, at least. "You might have difficulty finding any other buyer. Or any guests, for that matter, once word gets out."

Cato snorted. "On the contrary," he said. "I imagine the value will shortly be rising, as soon as you have gone."

"I'm afraid I don't have plans to go anywhere," Antony said.

"Oh, never fear," Cato said. "I think the Senate will make plans for you."

"Cato says there is a war going on in Gaul," Vincitatus put in. "Like in the poem. Wouldn't it be exciting to go see a war?"

"What?" Antony said.

"WELL, ANTONIUS," THE MAGISTRATE SAID, "I must congratulate you."

"For surviving the last sentence?" Antony said.

"No," the magistrate said. "For originality. I don't believe I have ever faced this particular offense before."

"There's no damned law against keeping a dragon!"

"There is now," the magistrate said. He looked down at his papers. "There is plainly no question of guilt in this case, it only remains what is to be done with the creature. The priests of the temple of Jupiter suggest that the beast would be most highly regarded as a sacrifice, if you can arrange the mechanics—"

"They can go bugger a herd of goats," Antony snarled. "I'll set her loose in the Forum, first—no. No, wait, I didn't mean that." He took a deep breath and summoned up a smile and leaned across the table. "I'm sure we can come to some arrangement."

"You don't have enough money for that even now," the magistrate said.

"Look," Antony said, "I'll take her to my villa at Sta-biae—" Seeing the eyebrow rising, he amended, "—or I'll buy an estate near Arminum. Plenty of room, she won't be a bother to anyone—"

"Until you run out of money or drink yourself to death," the magistrate said. "You do realize the creatures live a hundred years?"

"They do?" Antony said blankly.

"The evidence also informs me," the magistrate added, "that she is already longer than the dragon of Brundisium, which killed nearly half the company of the fourteenth legion."

"She's as quiet as a lamb?" Antony tried.

The magistrate just looked at him.

"Gaul?" Antony said.

"Gaul," the magistrate said.

"I HOPE YOU'RE HAPPY," HE said bitterly to Vincitatus as his servants joyfully packed his things, except for the few very unhappy ones he was taking along.

"Yes," she said, eating another goat.

He'd been ordered to leave at night, under guard, but when the escort showed up, wary soldiers in full armor and holding their spears, they discovered a new difficulty: she couldn't fit into the street anymore.

"All right, all right, no need to make a fuss," Antony said, waving her back into the courtyard. The house on the other side had only leaned over a little. "So she'll fly out to the Porta Aurelia and meet us on the other side."

"We're not letting the beast go spreading itself over the city," the centurion said. "It'll grab some lady off the street, or an honorable merchant."

He was for killing her right there and then, instead. Antony was for knocking him down, and did so. The soldiers pulled him off and shoved him up against the wall of the house, swords out.

Then Vincitatus put her head out, over the wall, and said, "I think I have worked out how to breathe fire, Antony. Would you like to see?"

The soldiers all let go and backed away hastily in horror.

"I thought you said you couldn't," Antony hissed, looking up at her; it had been a source of much disappointment to him.

"I can't," she said. "But I thought it would make them let

you go." She reached down and scooped him up off the street in one curled forehand, reached the other and picked up one of the squealing baggage-loaded pack mules. And then she leaped into the air.

"Oh, Jupiter eat your liver, you mad beast," Antony said, and clutched at her talons as the ground fell away whirling.

"See, is this not much nicer than trudging around on the ground?" she asked.

"Look out!" he yelled, as the temple of Saturn loomed up unexpectedly.

"Oh!" she said, and dodged. There was a faint crunch of breaking masonry behind them. "I'm sure that was a little loose anyway," she said, flapping hurriedly higher.

He had to admit it made for quicker traveling, and at least she'd taken the mule loaded with the gold. She hated to let him spend any of it, though, and in any case he had to land her half a mile off and walk if he wanted there to be anyone left to buy things from. Finally he lost patience and started setting her down with as much noise as she could manage right outside the nicest villa or farmhouse in sight, when they felt like a rest. Then he let her eat the cattle, and made himself at home in the completely abandoned house for the night.

That first night, sitting outside with a bowl of wine and a loaf of bread, he considered whether he should even bother going on to Gaul. He hadn't quite realized how damned *fast* it would be, traveling by air. "I suppose we could just keep on like this," he said to her idly. "They could chase us with one company after another for the rest of our days and never catch us."

"That doesn't sound right to me at all," she said. "One

could never have eggs, always flying around madly from one place to another. And I want to see the war."

Antony shrugged cheerfully and drank the rest of the wine. He was half looking forward to it himself. He thought he'd enjoy seeing the look on the general's face when he set down with a dragon in the yard and sent all the soldiers running like mice. Anyway it would be a damned sight harder to get laid if he were an outlaw with a dragon.

Two weeks later, they cleared the last alpine foothills and came into Gaul at last. And that was when Antony realized he didn't know the first damn thing about where the army even was.

He didn't expect some Gallic wife to tell him, either, so they flew around the countryside aimlessly for two weeks, raiding more farmhouses—inedible food, no decent wine, and once some crazy old woman hadn't left her home and nearly gutted him with a cooking knife. Antony fled hastily back out to Vincitatus, ducking hurled pots and imprecations, and they went back aloft in a rush.

"This is not a very nice country," Vincitatus said, critically examining the scrawny pig she had snatched. She ate it anyway and added, crunching, "And that is a strange cloud over there."

It was smoke, nine or ten pillars of it, and Antony had never expected to be glad to see a battlefield in all his life. His stepfather had threatened to send him to the borders often enough, and he'd run away from home as much to avoid that fate as anything else, nearly. He didn't mind a good fight, or bleeding a little in a good cause, but as far as he was concerned, that limited the occasions to whenever it might benefit himself.

The fighting was still going on, and the unmusical clanging reached them soon. Vincitatus picked up speed as she flew on towards it, and then picked up still more, until Antony was squinting his eyes to slits against the tearing wind, and he only belatedly realized she wasn't going towards the camp, or the rear of the lines; she was headed straight for the enemy.

"Wait, what are you—" he started, too late, as her sudden stooping dive ripped the breath out of his lungs. He clung on to the rope he'd tied around her neck, which now felt completely inadequate, and tried to plaster himself to her hide.

She roared furiously, and Antony had a small moment of satisfaction as he saw the shocked and horrified faces turning up towards them from the ground, on either side of the battle, and then she was ripping into the Gauls, claws tearing up furrows through the tightly packed horde of them.

She came to ground at the end of a run and whipped around, which sent him flying around to the underside of her neck, still clinging to the rope for a moment as he swung suspended. Then his numb fingers gave way and dumped him down to the ground, as she took off for another go. He staggered up, wobbling from one leg to the other, dizzy, and when he managed to get his feet under him, he stopped and stared: the entire Gaulish army was staring right back.

"Hades *me fellat*," Antony said. There were ten dead men lying down around him, where Vincitatus had shaken them off her claws. He grabbed a sword and a shield that was only a little cracked, and yelled after her, "Come back and get me out of here, you damned daughter of Etna!"

Vincitatus was rampaging through the army again, and

didn't give any sign she'd heard, or even that she'd noticed she'd lost him. Antony looked over his shoulder and put his back to a thick old tree and braced himself.

The Gauls weren't really what you'd call an army, more like a street gang taken to the woods, but their swords were damned sharp, and five of the barbarians came at him in a rush, howling at the top of their lungs. Antony kicked a broken helmet at one of them, another bit of flotsam from the dead, and as the others drew in he dropped into a crouch and stabbed his sword at their legs, keeping his own shield drawn up over his head.

Axes, of course they'd have bloody axes, he thought bitterly, as they thumped into the shield, but he managed to get one of them in the thigh, and another in the gut, and then he heaved himself up off the ground and pushed the three survivors back for a moment with a couple of wide swings, and grinned at them as he caught his breath. "Just like playing at soldiers on the Campus Martius, eh, fellows?" They just scowled at him, humorless *colei,* and they came on again.

He lost track of the time a little: his eyes were stinging with sweat, and his arm and his leg where they were bleeding. Then one of the men staggered and fell forward, an arrow sprouting out of his back. The other two looked around; Antony lunged forward and put his sword into the neck of one of them, and another arrow took down the last. Then, another one thumped into Antony's shield.

"Watch your blasted aim!" Antony yelled, and ducked behind the shelter of his tree as the Gauls went pounding away to either side of him, chased with arrows and dragon-roaring.

"Antony!" Vincitatus landed beside him, and batted away another couple of Gauls who were running by too closely. "There you are."

He stood a moment panting, and then he let his sword and shield drop and collapsed against her side.

"Why did you climb down without telling me?" she said reproachfully, peering down at him. "You might have been hurt."

He was too out of breath to do more than feebly wave his fist at her.

"I DON'T CARE IF JUPITER himself wants to see me," Antony said. "First I'm going to eat half a cow—yes, sweetness, you shall have the other half—and then I'm going to have a bath, and *then* I'll consider receiving visitors. If any of them are willing to come to me." He smiled pleasantly, and leaned back against Vincitatus's foreleg and patted one of her talons. The legionary looked uncertain, and backed even further away.

One thing to say for a battlefield, the slaves were cheap and a sight more cowed, and even if they were untrained and mostly useless, it didn't take that much skill to carry and fill a bath. Antony scrubbed under deluges of cold water and then sank with relief into the deep trough they'd found somewhere. "I could sleep for a week," he said, letting his eyes close.

"Mm," Vincitatus said drowsily, and belched behind him, the sound like a thundercloud. She'd gorged on two cavalry horses.

"You there, more wine," Antony said, vaguely snapping his fingers into the air.

"Allow me," a cool patrician voice said, and Antony opened his eyes and sat up when he saw the general's cloak.

"No, no." The man pushed him back down gently with a hand on his shoulder. "You look entirely too comfortable to be disturbed." The general was sitting on a chair his slaves had brought him, by the side of the tub; he poured wine for both of them, and waved the slaves off. "Now, then. I admired your very dramatic entrance, but it lacked something in the way of introduction."

Antony took the wine cup and raised it. "Marcus Antonius, at your command."

"Mm," the general said. He was not very well-favored: a narrow face, skinny neck, hairline in full retreat and headed for a rout. At least he had a good voice. "Grandson of the consul?"

"You have me," Antony said.

"Caius Julius, called Caesar," the general said, and tilted his head. Then he added, thoughtfully, "So we are cousins of a sort, on your mother's side."

"Oh, yes, warm family relations all around," Antony said, raising his eyebrows, aside from how Caesar's uncle had put that consul grandfather to death in the last round of civil war but one.

But Caesar met his dismissive look with an amused curl of his own mouth that said plainly he knew how absurd it was. "Why not?"

Antony gave a bark of laughter. "Why not, indeed," he said. "I had a letter for you, I believe, but unfortunately I left it in Rome. They've shipped us out to"—he waved a hand—"be of some use to you."

"Oh, you will be," Caesar said softly. "Tell me, have you ever thought of putting archers on her back?"

"Vici" was first printed in The Dragon Book: Magical Tales from the Masters of Modern Fantasy *by Penguin (Ace Books) in 2010.*

BURIED DEEP

I wrote this thinking about the Labyrinth, not in the sense of a synonym for a maze, with many branching paths, but Ariadne's dancing ground, the ancient pattern that pilgrims used to walk, the single road that winds incomprehensibly until it comes with a final turning to the conclusion. Our journey in time, where only one road can be taken, and the paths are pruned as we pass them; a journey towards truth and revelation, the journey to the story's end. The only way out is through.

THE LIE MINOS TOLD, WHICH NO ONE BELIEVED, AND no one was expected to believe, was that his youngest son had been shut up for the sake of the servants, whom he had begun brutalizing even as a babe. The lie everyone believed, and told in whispers, was that the queen had played the king false with a handsome guardsman, and he'd shut up the child to keep another man's son from any chance of inheriting his throne.

But Ariadne had been five years old, herself a late and unexpected child, when her even more unexpected brother had begun to grow under Pasiphae's heart, and she had been so very excited. Her other brothers were all grown men, big men, warriors; Minos's bull-strong sons, the court called them, her father's pride and irrelevant to her. Her sisters had been married off and gone before she was even born. And she had already been clever and good at creeping, so she'd been in the birthing room when the baby had come out bellowing, with the nubs of the horns still soft and rounded on his forehead, and her mother's attendants had begun to scream.

Minos had all of them put to death, along with three particularly handsome guardsmen with fair hair, to start the second lie and keep the secret. His secret, not her mother's. Everyone in all of Crete knew of the white bull the sea had sent him, and that Minos had bred it to his cattle instead of putting it to the knife the way the priests had wanted, but

Ariadne and her mother knew more than that: they knew that Minos had asked for a sacrifice, one great enough to mark him for the throne over his brothers, and the god had sent the bull for that purpose, to be given back to him, not kept. So it was Minos's fault, and not her mother's, but Pasiphae had paid for it, and so had her women, and Ariadne's little brother most of all.

Ariadne shouted at her mother the day her father's men came to take Minotaur away. "We could go to Grandfather!" she said; she was twelve, and her silent frightened brother was holding her hand tight and trying to stay hidden behind her, futile: he was a foot taller than her already, with the big cow-eyes large and dark and liquid on either side of his broad soft nose.

They lived with their mother and a few cowed servants— some of them *had* been killed, but by her father's orders, not by Minotaur—in a single tower perched on the edge of a green meadow in the hills far above Knossos. It had been built as a watchtower, to give warning of men coming from the sea. They could see for a long way from the windows of the narrow top story, all the way to the sea far below, glossy and deep, like her brother's eyes. Mother usually stayed in the more comfortable rooms below, but when she came up, she never looked at the sea, only the other way, down at the city: the red columns of the temple, and the people in the markets or thronging the streets to celebrate a festival, and her face was hard and bitter.

Father never came to them. But once a year, on Ariadne's birthday, someone came and took her down the long dusty hill to the palace, to be presented to him and to receive another heavy necklace of gold, each one growing with her, so that now she had seven of them, the smallest one close around her neck and the largest hanging over her growing breasts. A great dowry accumulating in chains, to apologize for her imprisonment.

It was the only apology Minos ever made. He avoided being alone with her; she was always taken in to him by a nurse or a maidservant, who warned her strictly not to ask her father to let her come and live in the palace, as if he wanted to pretend that he wasn't refusing her just because he told her no through someone else's mouth. But she wouldn't have asked, anyway. She didn't want to live in the palace, with her father and his lies, even before he'd sent men to take her brother away.

She had instead begun to worry about being taken away herself; she'd started to be old enough, that year, to understand that soon her father would begin to look for someone else to hold her chains. That was why she'd already thought of going to her grandfather: Pasiphae's father was Helios, the great lord of the easternmost city of Crete, the place where the sun rose, and a power in his own right, with a fortress that not even Minos's navy could have shattered.

But Pasiphae shook her head and said flatly to Ariadne, "You're old enough to stop being a fool. The king of Crete needs the sea god's favor. If the priests learn your father's lost it, they won't stop with *his* blood to buy it back. It'll be your brother on the altar, and me, and you as well, likely as not," and after she said that, Minotaur carefully pulled his big hand out of hers—he was only seven, but he'd already learned how easily he could hurt people, if he wasn't careful—and he put on the heavy wide-hooded cloak that Ariadne had sewn for him so they could go walking in the hills together at night, and then he went out to the waiting guards.

Minos had sent the Oreth to take him: his slave guards, warriors all bought from countries so far away that they had little hope of making a safe return. Their tongues had all been cut out. They were brutal men, hardened by their own misery and everything they saw in their work. They didn't fear death or the gods, or thought they didn't, and they would have cut off the head of a seven-year-old boy if her father told them to, much less put him into a prison. But when Minotaur came out a big silent hulk in his cloak, they all went still and afraid, even though they couldn't see his face, and their hands went to the hilts of their swords. After they shut the door in her face, and Ariadne ran upstairs to look out of the window, she saw them walking in a group ten paces ahead, not looking back at all. Minotaur was trudging after them alone, his head in the cloak bowed, following them to the door, which wasn't a door, only a hole in the earth.

She had watched them build the shrine all the last year, Minotaur peeking one eye out from behind a curtain next to her, both of them fascinated: it was the most interesting thing that had ever happened. First the priests had come to bless the site, and after them Daedalus, walking over the meadow for days marking the ground with long sticks left poking out. Then the digging began, which took a long time, because there were only six workmen on the whole project: four big slaves to dig the passage, twenty feet down into the ground, and two skilled ones to follow them, putting in the slabs of beautiful polished marble that came in on laden carts to make the floor and the walls.

The shape hadn't made any sense to her. The workmen had started in the very middle of the meadow, digging out the single round central chamber, and they even dug a well in the middle of it. She thought it would be the first room of many. But instead, from there they dug out a single circling passage, only one, with no rooms and no branching paths, that curved and folded back on itself like a bewildered snake that had lost sight of its own tail. They kept going and going digging in that one line, filling in one quarter of the circle after another, until they had honeycombed the whole meadow.

On moonlit nights sometimes Ariadne and Minotaur would sneak out and walk on the narrow dirt walls left between the passages, balancing with their arms stuck out on either side and the deep passages looming on either side. They couldn't run back and forth across the meadow anymore the way they had used to, because the winding passage covered the whole thing in an enormous circle, ripples spreading out from that central well. The walls were just wide enough that it wasn't *very* hard to balance for Ariadne's small feet, but it was just a little bit hard, enough that you had to pay attention to how you put your feet, one after the other. It was harder for Minotaur. He didn't eat, not since their mother had finally refused to nurse him anymore, to try and make him take food, but it didn't seem to matter. He was growing very big, and very quickly. By the time the men finished digging, he was teetering on the edges, having trouble not falling in.

She was waiting impatiently for the workmen to finish the last quarter of the circle, to see what they would do when the passage got to the end. The digging seemed like it had taken forever, and so much work. So she was sure it must be meant for a shrine to the god. She imagined steps coming up, and then flagstones being laid on top of the mysterious cellar, and pillars for some great temple. But when the workmen finished digging to the border of the great circle, the passage only stopped. They dug a very small circular room there just outside the rest of the maze, like an antechamber, and then they didn't do any more work the rest of that day, even though it was morning. They only sat down in the small bit of shade on the edge of the hillside with their tools scattered around them and drank from their jug of watered wine, watching the skilled workmen coming the rest of the way behind them.

The next day, the skilled workmen began to work back along the passageway towards the center, laying flat stones atop the passage to make a ceiling. The diggers followed them now, burying the stone under dirt from the enormous mound they had dug up out of the passages. They didn't leave anywhere for stairs to go down, only the one little round hole on the outside, above the antechamber, and the one big center hole in the middle. Ariadne was baffled. They had dug that whole enormous winding passage for nothing. Once it was buried, no one would even know it was there under the meadow. They weren't even marking the surface at all. By the time the men reached the middle again, there was already a thick furry coat of grass covering everything behind them: it was late spring, and the sky had been generous with both sunshine and rain.

Then yesterday, the final cart had come, hauled up from the city by a team of four big oxen, carrying two circular metal slabs braced on their sides, one big and one little, like coins for giants, and just the right size to fit over the two rooms. But they had been shrouded in sheets, so Ariadne still hadn't understood what the shrine was really for. But now the six workmen were standing by to put the big slab into the ground, and they had uncovered it, just barely visible in the coming light: a massive bronze disc covered with beaten gold, with a central hatch, engraved with the great head of the bull.

The Oreth led Minotaur to the waiting open hole. They went around to the far side and stood there watching him. The workmen drew back against the cart as he passed by. They had left a rope dangling down inside the hole. Minotaur stood on the edge looking down, and Ariadne gave a cry from the window, shouted, "Don't, don't!" but it worked the wrong way; his hood twitched, where his big ears underneath had twisted around to hear her, and then he sat down on the edge of the hole with his sandaled feet hanging over, and then he let himself down inside.

The workmen didn't move even after he vanished. Finally one of the Oreth made a sharp impatient gesture, and one of them went with dragging steps to the edge and then hurriedly pulled out the rope, hand over hand quickly, and backed away as soon as he could. Then they rolled the big golden seal to the edge and tipped it over carefully down to fit perfectly into the hole. Grass had already sprouted even at the edges. They hurriedly buried the seal all the way up to the edge of the central hatch. There was a narrow circular grating that went around the head of the bull, an opening for air.

The workers had already put the smaller seal over the anteroom. It also had a hatch in it, but unmarked. Ariadne watched from the tower while the Oreth opened the hatch and shoved all the workmen in, one after another, screaming for mercy and struggling and disappearing nevertheless, one after another, down into the dark, until the Oreth slammed the metal hatch back down on top of them, and turned the great locks. Six was a wrong number, and she wondered where Daedalus had gone; she hadn't seen him for the last week. A long time later, she heard that he'd fled by ship to Greece, abandoning his wife and son, just before the labyrinth had been finished. By then people were saying he was a sorcerer and the labyrinth was magic, but she knew that the only magical thing in it was her brother, her little brother, a piece of the god put down into the dark.

IN THE MORNING SHE OPENED her eyes and knew right away that Minotaur was gone. She got up and went to the window. The meadow was a smooth ordinary green meadow, the grass verdant and lush. Everything buried deep and silent, and only the two golden seals set into the earth, so low that in the dim light they were hidden in the grass, unless you knew where to look to catch a glimpse of gold.

Her mother had kept Ariadne inside all day yesterday, even after the Oreth had gone, but it was still early in the morning and no one else was awake. Her mother stayed up in the evenings, drinking wine, and after she went to bed, her two women finished whatever she had left, so they all slept late and heavily. Last night, her mother had opened a second jar of wine, leaving it almost unwatered, and she had poured Ariadne a glass. Ariadne had left it standing untouched on the table, along with her food.

She crept past the snoring women on the floor and her mother lying sprawled behind the thin curtains of her bed, and got outside without being stopped. She ran to the meadow, but she couldn't open the hatches herself, no matter how she turned the locks back and forth, no matter how she poked her fingers and branches into the cracks around it and strained. Either she didn't know the trick of the locks, or the doors were just too heavy. The metal was cold and slick with dew under her fingers as she struggled. Finally she gave up and she went to the central seal, to the narrow grating, and called through the dark opening.

But Minotaur couldn't answer her, if he was there: he couldn't speak. Once after a month of coaxing he'd tried to say something to her, and she'd woken up three days later in her bed, her ears and nose still crusted with dried blood. He'd refused even to try, after that. He might be somewhere wandering in that endless passage, alone in the dark, and not have heard her coming.

She fell silent, kneeling in the dirt by the seal, tears dripping off her face, and then she got up and went to the small seal, over the antechamber, and did her best to walk all over the meadow, stamping and jumping every so often, so that he'd hear her footsteps overhead, and know that she was there. And when she finally came back to the big seal in the center, she knelt there and talked to him until the sun was well up and her throat was dry, and then she stole back into the tower before anyone noticed she was gone. That day, and every day after. She crept out of her mother's tower in the hour of dawn, and she told Minotaur every day that she'd be back the next, so when at last she didn't come, he'd know that the chain around his neck was gone, and he could leave.

The third time she started to walk over the meadow, the grass suddenly began to wither just ahead of her toes, green blades curling in to form dusty yellow lines that she could see even in the early light. She stamped along between them, all the way until they brought her finally to the waiting center, and there she turned around and looked out over the meadow as the sun came up, and the yellow grass lines made an outline, faint but there, marking out the buried passageway underground.

After that, when she walked the path, she felt something moving beneath her feet: not quite a sound, not quite a vibration, but like heavy footfalls echoing against marble walls, deep within. So then she knew he was there, walking with her, the way they'd once walked together balancing over the walls. Only he had fallen inside, after all.

One week after they put Minotaur into the labyrinth, a priest came to dedicate the new shrine. It was only a young one, in a red robe, with a slightly younger acolyte leading a tired skinny bull for a sacrifice; the hill was a hot, steep walk up from the city. Minos had needed to give some excuse, for sending Daedalus and workmen up to dig and dig for months, but he didn't mean for the shrine to be important. It was meant to be forgotten. From the tower, Ariadne saw the priest and the acolyte come to the edge of the meadow, where they saw the pattern. They stood there staring, and they didn't kill the bull, after all. They went away instead.

The next day they came back, the young priest and two older ones. They stood beside the pattern for a long time, hesitating, as though they wanted to step onto it but didn't quite dare. Then they went away too, and the day after that they came back, the three priests, the acolyte leading the bull again and carrying water jugs dewed with moisture slung on his back, the high priest puffing along in his white robe with the red bands, and Minos himself with them. But this time they came in the early hours of the morning, before the sun was up, and Ariadne was still walking along the pattern to the seal. They saw her, and the young priest called out angrily, "What do you mean by this, girl? How dare you put your feet on the god's path. Do you think this is a dancing floor?"

She stopped and turned. The deep echoing was there under her feet; it stopped, too. The men were standing on the edge of the pattern, her father's face darkened, all of them waiting for her to cringe and apologize. She stood for a moment without moving. If she obeyed them, and came off, they would leave a priest here to watch over the labyrinth, so she could never come again. Minotaur would never know when they sent her away. There was a waiting beneath her feet, like the change in the light before rain came, even though the sun was coming up and lining the next mountains over with brilliance.

"It is for me," she said.

Her father said sharply, "Watch your tongue, girl," which meant now she was going to be whipped for impertinence. "Come here at once."

She took a breath and faced forward again and kept going along the path. "With your permission, I will bring her back," the young priest said to the king, to the high priest.

He untied his sandals before he came to get her. She saw him coming for her, cutting across the lines of the pattern, and then she had to turn her back on him to follow the next turn, one single foot's length along the pattern, and when she turned again with the following step, moving a little closer to the center, he wasn't there anymore. It wasn't a vanishing. There was only a moment when he was there, and then there was a moment when he wasn't, and all the moments in between those two moments were one moment, and endless.

The other men were still waiting impatiently. They were further away, and they were watching her; it took them a little longer to notice that he was gone. They looked around for him, confused at first, and then they looked at the empty sandals standing at the side of the pattern, and then they all drew back several steps from the labyrinth, and said nothing more. Ariadne kept going all the way to the seal, with thunder moving beneath her feet, and she knelt and said to the dark crack around the door, "I'm here."

They were still waiting when she came back to them. She could just have walked away, but she stayed on the pattern, and she didn't go quickly, letting the hot sun come up and bake them a little in their wigs and their crimped, oiled hair. Their robes were stained with growing dark patches of sweat when she came out finally, and stepped off the labyrinth.

She stood before them, and they looked at her, faces downturned and unsmiling, and then the high priest turned to her father and said, "She must be consecrated to the god," insistent, and her father's jaw tightened—thinking mostly, Ariadne knew, of all those heavy golden chains he'd put around her neck, his false apology, and how he wouldn't be able to use them and her to buy some lord's loyalty.

"I have to be back here tomorrow," she said.

They all paused and stared at her, and the high priest said, sternly, "My daughter, you will enter the temple—"

"I'm not your daughter," she interrupted. "I have to be here tomorrow morning. He'll be waiting for me."

The acolyte blurted, "Yidini?" meaning the young priest. His voice was ragged with desperation, but he flinched when the high priest gave him a hard narrowed look, and subsided; the other priests shifted uneasily, looking away from him.

Ariadne looked straight at her father and said, "Do you need me to say?" a threat, and even in his anger, his eyes darted to the labyrinth, to the gold seal on his hidden shame.

Minos was a clever man. He'd thought of one trick after another: to win the throne over his brothers, to keep it in his grasp, to build his wealth. And now he turned back to the high priest and said, "You will consecrate the tower as a temple, and my daughter will abide here, and tend the god's shrine, which he has chosen to favor."

Pasiphae went back to the palace in the city, gladly. Three women of the temple came to live with Ariadne instead. Reja, the eldest and a priestess, had a mouth whose corners turned down and plunged into dark hollows. Her hand often flinched when she taught Ariadne, as though she would have slapped a different novice, who wasn't the daughter of the king and the chosen of the god. When she came, she tried to make herself the mistress of the tower: she wanted to take the queen's room for herself, and put the rest of them together on the two higher floors.

Ariadne didn't do anything about it. She didn't see what she could do. The other women did what Reja told them.

That night they came upstairs with her, to the room where she had slept with Minotaur, and the two novices lay down on the big cot where he had slept. It was wide enough for both of them. Then they put out the candle, and even as Ariadne was falling asleep, one of the young women jerked up and said, "Who's there?" into the dark.

The other one sat up too. They both sat there shaking, and after a moment they scrambled up with all their bed-clothes and went creeping silently down the stairs, and they wouldn't come back upstairs even when Reja scolded them. Then she came up angry herself to accuse Ariadne of scaring them, and Ariadne sat up on her own cot and looked at her and said, "I didn't do anything. *You* lie down, if you want," and Reja stared at her, and then she went to the cot and lay down on it, on her back staring up into the dark with her angry frowning mouth, and then after a few moments she twitched, and twitched again, and then she got quickly up off the bed and stood in the middle of the room and looked down at Ariadne, who looked back at her, and then Reja said, in a very different voice, not angry, hushed, "Who slept in this room with you?"

The moon was outside, so she could see Reja's eyes, each one a small gleam in the dark, nothing like the deep shine of her brother's eyes, as if he hadn't ever been here at all. "His name is Minotaur," Ariadne said, defiantly. "He's under the hill now."

Reja was silent, and then she went downstairs and didn't scold the other priestesses anymore. The next morning she sat up when Ariadne went out, waking even though Ariadne was creeping out of habit, and she got up and followed her outside. She stood and watched her dance through the labyrinth all the way to the center, and when Ariadne came back out, Reja said, "I will show you how to pour the libations," and the rest of that day, Reja taught her with a jug of water, and then the next morning she was awake and waiting, before Ariadne went to the labyrinth, with a stoppered jug full of olive oil, deep-green and fragrant, from the first pressing. Ariadne took it. She carried it with her along the path, all the way to the seal, where she didn't follow the ritual. Instead she poured the oil all around the hatch, its locks, through the cracks, hoping to make it easier to open. But when she tried, it didn't help. The hatch was still too heavy for her. She couldn't even shift it a little bit in its groove. But as she knelt by the hatch with her fingers sore, unhappy and angry all over again, the seal beneath her moved a little, the whole hillside taking a deep sighing breath, and a little air came out of the grating from inside, full of the strong smell of the olive oil, fresh and bright, instead of the faint musty smell of earth.

It frustrated Reja that Ariadne wouldn't do the rituals properly, but she didn't scold her any more than she slapped her; she only grimly kept teaching her, one after another, the proper words and gestures for wine instead of oil, perfume instead of wine, as if hoping if she did it often enough, one day it would stick. Ariadne did the lessons, a little out of boredom and a little to be at peace with Reja, who managed things with ruthless efficiency and also sent the novices down to the city each day to bring something else to pour out, another bright living smell to send into the dark.

The acolyte who'd come up with the priests was set to guard them. There was nothing to guard them from, at least no danger that hadn't always been there, the last seven years while Ariadne had lived there with the queen and all her jewels, but the acolyte had seen something uncomfortable, and it was easier for the high priest and the king to forget about it if he wasn't around.

He wasn't allowed to stay with the women, of course; instead he had to build a hut to shelter in further down the hillside, and Reja kept a hawk's cold eye on him anytime he came up to their well for water, close enough to see the novices. The second day after they arrived, she paused in the prayer she was teaching Ariadne, and she got up and marched to a bush near where the trail down the mountain began. She pulled Nashu out of it by his ear and told him sharply if she caught him at it again, she would have him whipped out of the temple.

But he wasn't spying on the novices, even though they had their skirts hiked up around their waists, working on the garden. "I want to know where Yidini is!" he said, his voice wobbling up and down through a boy's soprano, and wrenched himself loose to take a step towards Ariadne, his fists clenched. "Where did you send him?"

She hadn't been sorry for the priest; to her, the priests were the ones who'd made her brother hide, who'd have put him to death. And Yidini had meant to drag her away. But she was sorry for Nashu, because someone he loved had been taken away and sent into the dark. She still couldn't help him, though, and when she said, "I don't know," he was angry, and he hated her for it.

He crept up the hill sometimes after that to watch her walking to the seal, in the dim early mornings. He hid in the bushes along the edge of the hill. Reja with her older eyes didn't catch him, but Ariadne knew he was there. She didn't say anything. There was something a little comforting in how much he cared; it meant she wasn't stupid for caring, either. She kept coming every day herself to pour the offerings down, a little bit of the mortal world, so her brother wouldn't disappear forever into the earth.

She wanted the days to change, sometimes; she had been afraid of being taken away, and now some small part of her wanted to go, wanted the life she'd avoided. She could still have had it. The golden chains sat in a locked chest in her room, the room where no one went but her, except hurriedly, in broad daylight, to sweep and clean. Her father, who had kept a bull the god had sent, would gladly have made some excuse for releasing her from the temple to buy a lord with her. And then her brother would melt back into the god like a little pond of water draining into a stream, and the vegetation would creep over the seals, and new grass would grow where the yellowed lines stood.

So she stayed.

The days did begin to change a little, over time. It was the poor hill folk who came first, the ones who couldn't afford to go to the temple in the city. They brought cups of milk, and an egg or two, and foraged greens. Once an anxious young man came with a lamb on a rope, and when Ariadne came out of the tower that morning, he was waiting on the edge of the labyrinth, and he knelt to her as if to the king and said, low, "My wife is giving birth soon, and the ewe died," a plea to turn aside the evil omen.

Reja looked at the lamb with greedy pleasure, thinking of the priest's portion, the best meat, and she said to Ariadne, "I'll show you how to make sacrifice," but Ariadne looked at the lamb with its wide uncertain liquid eyes, deep and brown, and said, "No." She took the rope and led the lamb with her through the passage to the seal. It butted at her as they went, bleating and trying to suck at her fingers, hungry, but she stayed on the track, and at the seal, she said, "There's a lamb here, if the god will take it to its mother, and let the shepherd's wife stay with her child up here," and then she took the rope off the lamb's neck, and rubbed the matted wool underneath it soft, and let the lamb go. It ran away from her bleating.

Reja and the shepherd were watching her from the edge of the labyrinth. It was like the last time: their faces didn't know that the lamb was gone at first, and then they looked around wanting to believe it had just run away, but there was nothing for it to have hidden behind on the bare hill, and then finally they had to understand that it was gone. The shepherd fell on his face, pressing his forehead into the dirt, and Reja drew back herself, staring, and then she knelt too, when Ariadne came out of the labyrinth.

Nashu was there, too. Later that afternoon, when Ariadne went down the hill to get some water, and she was alone, he came out of the bushes and stood staring at her with his face twisted up, and then he said, "Why Yidini? He was a true servant of the god! You could have sent that old fat priest."

Ariadne didn't bother trying to tell him she hadn't sent the young priest anywhere. She wasn't sure it was true, anyway. "Why would the god want an old fat priest?" she said instead, and Nashu was silent, and then he said, "Then I hate the god, if he took Yidini," defiantly.

"It's not worth your hating him," Ariadne said, after a
moment; she had to think it out for herself. "He doesn't
care."

Nashu glared at her. "Why does he care about *you*,
then?"

"He doesn't," she said slowly.

The next morning, she didn't dance. She only walked
straight to the center and knelt down by the seal and whispered, her throat tight, "It's all right if you want to go. You
don't have to stay for me. I'll be all right," because she hadn't
thought, before, that she was being selfish by holding on to
the little part of the god that could care about her, keeping
him there buried in the earth, instead of letting him go back
to the rest of himself.

There wasn't any answer. She left the labyrinth, walking
slowly with her head down, and went back into the tower,
where the two novices darted sideways looks at her, and
Reja determinedly looked at her directly and scolded her to
eat her supper of olives and bread and honey. That night,
Ariadne opened her eyes and looked over at the empty cot
across the room from her, and Minotaur was sitting there
looking at her. He was bigger than the last time she'd seen
him, much bigger: two feet taller than the biggest of the
Oreth, and his pale cream-ivory horns were wide and gleaming at the points, deadly. She knew she was dreaming, because he was too big. If he had really been there, she didn't
think she could have stood it. But when she sat up and
looked back at him, his eyes were still soft and liquid, and
she knew he didn't want to go back into the god, either. He
wanted to keep this piece of himself separate, this part that

could love her, for as long as he could. Even if he had to stay down there in the dark.

A RICH MAN FROM THE city sent a lamb, for the sake of *his* wife, but Ariadne told the slave who had brought it up the hill, "It's not a fair trade. Take it back."

The sweaty, thin boy stared at her and said uncertainly, "You don't want it?"

"A lamb doesn't mean the same thing to a rich man as a poor one," she said. "And if he cares, he should come himself."

So the boy went away, and two days later, the rich man did come himself: fat, even more sweaty despite the servants who had trailed him with fans and water jugs, and irritated. "What's this nonsense?" he said to Reja, complaining. "Now I had to come: my wife's father took it into his head that if I didn't, I'd as good as be killing her myself. And in this heat!"

Reja was going to be polite, because he was rich, and a nobleman, but Ariadne heard him and came down the stairs and out of the tower and said coldly, "You're asking for the god to put his hand into your life. Do you think that's a small matter? Go away again, if you don't want to be here."

The rich man scowled, but he said grudgingly, "Forgive me, Priestess," because he knew she was the king's daughter, and then he waved to the ass laden with rich gifts. "I have brought many fine offerings for the god."

The gifts were all for *her*, though: red and purple silks shot through with gold, a necklace, a box of coin, candied fruit. Ariadne shook her head in frustration as she looked over them, because there wasn't anything that she could send down into the dark; he hadn't even brought wine or perfume, because those weren't sophisticated enough: only a chest of sandalwood for her clothing and a luxurious loaf of dried cherries pressed with honey and nuts. There wasn't anything, but that was *his* fault, not his wife's, whose father had sent him to ask for her life, and Ariadne looked at his dripping, sweaty face, and said, "Come with me." She took him by the hand, and led him to the labyrinth, and said, "Stay on the path, and stay right behind me, no matter what."

It was the middle of the day. She'd already gone, that morning. But the deep thunder came soon under her feet: Minotaur had heard her. She heard the man's breathing go more and more ragged behind her, a faint whimpering deep in his throat. She didn't look back at him. The sun was hot on the crown of her dark hair, beating on her like a hammer, and the air over the golden seal shimmered. But the ground beneath her breathed coolness over her, and she kept dancing, all the way to the seal, and then she turned and the man went to his knees gasping, crouched over the seal, so wet with sweat that the drops were rolling off his earlobes and his nose and chin, his clothing soaked through.

"Take off your robes and squeeze out the sweat," she said, and he stripped down to his loincloth and wrung the robes like a woman getting clothing ready for drying, and the pungent sharp sweat trickled out of them and went into the grating, and the earth stirred beneath her.

She took him out after, back to his servants and his ass, and told him, "Now you can go back to your wife, and tell her and her father that you made a true offering to the god for her. And give the gifts to the people you meet on your way back home."

She didn't guess what that would do. It just sounded like the stories Reja taught her, of priests and oracles speaking, and Ariadne liked those, even as she knew that it wasn't anything like real priests, who needed offerings to live on and in exchange made a comforting show to distract men from death. But it worked, even if she hadn't meant it to work. The rich man went stumbling down the hill still full of terror, and pressed wealth into the hands of shepherds and a bewildered milkmaid and beggars in the street, and the whispers came down from the country folk and went in through the city gates with him, and after that even the city people said, *The god is there on the mountain, and the king's daughter is beloved of him.*

Reja didn't have to send the novices down to get offerings anymore. People came and brought them, often without any request attached. And a few fools came to see the god, because they didn't think it was real. Once it was a group of six drunken young noblemen whose fathers were too healthy and didn't give their sons enough work to do, and they showed up in the early hours shouting up at the tower windows that they wanted to speak with the god.

Ariadne was coming down anyway, because it was time; in summer the sun came early and quick. The drunken youths smiled at her, and one of them took her hand and bowed over it and said mournfully, putting it to his chest, "But you're too pretty to be locked up here with no lover but a buried god."

"He's my brother," Ariadne said. The young man was good looking, at least in the dim light, and she half liked the silliness, but Reja was at her shoulder, tense, afraid of something Ariadne had never had to fear before. That fear was trying to creep into her, telling her without words that she was a woman now, with breasts and her hair unbound, and fair game for drunk men who didn't believe in the god.

"Even worse!" the young man said. "Won't you have a drink with us? Here, we've the finest mead, brewed from my father's hives."

"It's time for me to go to the labyrinth," Ariadne said. "You can come if you want. You can bring it as an offering."

"Then lead on, and let me meet your brother!" the young man declared. "I'll show him a man worthy to court his sister!" His name was Staphos, and he kept smiling at her, and touching her hand. "Hurry and make the offering," he murmured to her as they walked. "I know what I want to ask the god for." His friends were singing, arm in arm with one another.

They were near the labyrinth when the bushes stirred, and Nashu came out and blurted, "Don't go in there with her!"

"Oh, so you *do* have some company up here!" one of the other youths said, gleefully, and Nashu said angrily, "I'm trying to save you! If you go with her, the god will take you," and they all started laughing, a drunken joyful noise, and Ariadne turned and took the jug of mead from Staphos and said, "He might. It's up to you if you want to come. Don't stray from the path, if you do," and she turned and put her foot on the path as the sun began to come up.

Staphos laughed again, and fell in behind her. The others came, too, singing a marching song and doing a mocking high-step behind her own dance, but the deep drumming echo rose beneath to meet them, and their song began to die away little by little. "Keep singing," she said, over her shoulder, but they kept fading out, until suddenly Staphos began a faint and wavering temple song, one Reja hadn't taught her, deep and chanted: one of the men's songs, probably. She felt that Minotaur heard it, and wanted to listen, and the deep echoes went quieter beneath them. Soon the young noblemen could sing it too, the repetition of the chant at least, which was only four syllables strung together in two different patterns.

They came to the seal, and Ariadne poured out the honey-strong mead, with all of them in a ring around her clutching hands and still singing. They followed her out again in silence, without singing, without saying a word. She stood on the hill watching them go down the trail in sunlight, and only then she noticed herself that Staphos wasn't with them anymore. She wasn't sure when he'd gone.

STAPHOS WASN'T A LAMB, OR even a young priest. He was the eldest son of one of her father's richer lords, and he'd been betrothed to the daughter of another. It made trouble below for her father, who wanted to make it someone else's trouble, as he always did. He sent a group of priests up to question her, one of them Staphos's cousin, and they questioned the novices, and Reja, and the acolytes also.

Nashu tried to get her into trouble, but he was too young and bad at lying. He told three different made-up grotesque stories about her butchering men on the seal, and then he gave up and told them that her brother the god lived under the hill, and she gave him offerings, and he took people who made her angry. And when the interrogating priest said, "Why my cousin?" Nashu blurted, "He tried to lie with her," which would have required the family to chisel Staphos's name off his tomb and cast him into the dark forever, if she had confirmed it.

But she was sorry about Staphos, so she told the priest, "He was only joking. The god wanted him, so the god took him. That's all I can tell you."

A messenger came two days later to summon her down to her father's palace. Ariadne didn't want to go. In her father's house, there would be guards and rooms with locked doors and lies shut up inside them, and if she said the wrong thing, she'd be shut up into one of them too. "I have to make the offering first," she said, and took a jar of oil out to the seal, and after she poured it down she said softly, "I have to go to the palace. I don't know if he'll let me come back."

The deep faint tremor lingered beneath her feet all the way to the labyrinth's end, and there it paused for a moment, and came on with her. The messenger and the escort of guards looked over their shoulders uneasily as they walked, and Reja, who had insisted on coming as chaperone, kept moving her lips silently in the formal chant to the god, and when they stopped for water, a few times, she knelt and prayed aloud, a prayer for mercy, while the soldiers opened and closed their hands around their hilts.

When Ariadne stepped onto the paved streets of Knossos, the sensation didn't disappear, but it receded deeper, muffled, and the soldiers relaxed in relief. They took her to the palace, and up another muffling flight of stairs into the higher chambers, until there was barely a faint echo lingering when the Oreth themselves took her the last of the way into the throne room, her father sitting with stern down-turned mouth in state, the high priest standing important beside the throne in robes, and both of them looking down at her from the height of the dais, so she had to look up at them. There was no one else in the room, only the Oreth on either side of her, and Minos said, "Daughter, two men have died at the god's shrine, under your hands. What have you to say of it?"

His voice bounced against the walls of the room, the heavy stone clad in marble: he knew how to pitch it to make the reverberations bright and loud, so his voice came at her from all sides, a whispering echo arriving a moment after the first sound reached her ears. But the floor under her swallowed the sound, and it fell away deadened.

"They didn't die under my hands," she said. "They went to the god. All *three* of them."

Her father's lips thinned, his hands closing around the gilded bull's-head ends of the arms of his throne, flexing. He looked at the Oreth around her, and then back at her, a warning, but he didn't need to worry. The high priest didn't care: he thought it was a shepherd, some poor man, someone who didn't matter. "It is not for you to decide who will go to the god, girl," he said to her.

"It's not for you, either," she said, without looking away from her father.

"You dare too far!" the high priest said, sharp and indignant, with a quick look at Minos, a demand.

"Strike her across the buttocks with the flat of your blade," Minos said, to the head of the Oreth, and the man drew his sword instantly and struck her with it, a hard painful shock that rolled through her body, up to her head and down in a tingle along her spine and back out through her legs, down, down into the ground, down into the ground where it began to echo back and forth, an echo that didn't die away, an echo that built a thunder-rumble far, far below that grew and grew until it came back up through the floor, and the room trembled all over, so the servant holding the tray of gilded cups stumbled, and the cups rang against each other, and the dewed jug of cool wine fell over and crashed to the ground, spilling green and pungent.

It died away slowly, but not all the way; the rumble was still there, close beneath her feet. The Oreth recoiled, stepping back from her. Her father's face was still and frozen, the high priest staring, and Ariadne finished breathing through the pain and looked up at them and said, "Tell him to hit me again if you want. But the god hits back harder. You *know* he does."

So she went back up the hill, and her father gave orders that no one was to go to the shrine, on pain of death. But it was too late. Minos told no one what had happened inside the throne room, and the high priest didn't either: he didn't want to be replaced by a high priestess. The Oreth couldn't tell anyone. But too many people had heard some story about the labyrinth by then, and too many of those had been waiting in the court with interest as the king's daughter, rumored beloved of the god, went in to face the king and the high priest. Her mother had sent someone to watch, and some of Staphos's family had come hoping to see her punished, and many others who only had nothing better to do had come to see if perhaps the god would perform some miracle in front of them, either because they hoped it would happen or because they were sure it wouldn't. And all those people were there when she went inside, and they were there when the whole palace shook, and they were there when she came out again alone, unpunished, and went back up the hill.

They lived with the shaking of the earth in Crete. The footsteps of the god, people called it, and when the god walked too heavily, he cast a long shadow of death. So people came to the shrine afterwards anyway, even though Minos forbade it. It was too much of a miracle, too big to be ignored. Minos himself understood that almost at once, just as soon as his temper cooled. He changed the command: no one was to go to the shrine until the festival of the god, in the spring. And then he sent his warships over the water, the fleet that his wealth and his cunning had built, filled with tall strong warriors fed on his fat cattle, with her eldest brother Androgeos in command.

The sails were white against the water as they sailed out over the dark shimmer of the water. Ariadne watched them out of the window until they vanished over the world's edge. Six months later they came back, without Androgeos, but with seven maidens and seven youths of Athens in his place, as tribute for the god. They came up the hill at dusk, at the head of a parade, a great noisy crowd of stamping feet and cheering: her father trying to make another lie, a new lie, a lie big enough to bury the god deep. And it might work: the god could hit harder, but he couldn't lie.

They stopped by the tower, and in front of the labyrinth erected a great platform for the king's throne, facing the other way, with Pasiphae and the high priest on either side. Ariadne sat silent and angry in a chair one step down from her mother, in a wine-red gown that her father had sent and insisted she wear: a gown for a princess instead of a priest-ess, with her chains of gold heavy upon her. The night came on, dark enough to hide the faint yellowed lines of grass with the glare of torches and feasting, singing and smoke that went up to the sky, not into the earth: a funeral for Andro-geos, and honor for the sacrifices, who were bunched up under guard on a dais next to her father's throne.

Minos rose and said, "May the god accept this tribute," with savage bitterness, tears on his face. Androgeos had been his eldest son. Pasiphae too had tears, but Ariadne was dry-eyed, still angry.

Then the Oreth came to take the sacrifices, the girls weeping softly and the youths trying not to look afraid, all except one: a young man with hair as bright as gold, strange among the others with their shining olive-black hair. Ariadne looked at him, and he really wasn't afraid. He stood and looked up at Minos, and his eyes weren't dark and deep like her brother's, but even in torchlight they were clear all the way through: the ocean on a calm day near the shore, shafts of sunshine streaming straight down to illuminate waves captured in pale sand, ripples on the ocean floor.

And the Oreth taking his arm had a second sword, a spare sword, thrust through his belt.

Ariadne stood up also, despite her mother's grasping hand, and said through a tight knot in her throat, afraid sud-denly, "I will lead them."

Minos only said, "Let it be done," and gave a nod to the leader of the Oreth, at his side.

She led the way through the cheering crowd and past the dais into the dark, groping her feet out one after another. The way felt strange to her, though she'd walked it every day for three years now. The night was a solid tunnel, the torches in the hands of the Oreth behind her only making small circles on the ground. She thought she had gone too far, that she'd missed it, and then she caught sight of the gold torch-light flickering over the golden seal.

The Oreth unlocked the hatch and heaved it open, two big men straining. The girls were weeping noisily now, crying protests, and one of the youths suddenly broke for it and tried to run, but one of the Oreth caught him roughly; he was a slim boy, and the Oreth was a head taller and gripped his arm in one hand, fingers easily meeting around the skinny limb, and held him.

"Have courage," the golden-haired one said to them, low and clear, his voice going out over them like wind stilling, and they quieted into a huddle. The captain of the Oreth was waiting with the sword in his hand, the spare sword, and he held it out, offering the hilt. The golden youth took it, grasping it easily. Ariadne stood, tense, waiting for a chance. She was only thinking that she had to warn Minotaur: she had to get to the seal and call to him, let him know that a golden-haired Athenian was coming, with a sword in his hand and the god looking out of his face with different eyes.

And then the Oreth looked at her—looked at her waiting on the other side of the hatch, and jerked his chin towards the dark hole, a command: *Go in.* Ariadne realized too late that she hadn't thought about her father, who had now buried a son he had wanted because of her, his daughter who knew his lies, who was held under the god's hand, so he couldn't strike her down.

She stood frozen on the edge of the dark, for a single blank moment. She could have run away: she was further away than the Athenian youth had been, and she could have fled into the dark, across the labyrinth. The god would take anyone chasing her, who tried to hurt her, surely. Surely. But if she ran, the golden Athenian boy would go down into the labyrinth. He would find her brother, her sleeping brother, and make a way for his friends to come out of the labyrinth at the other end: in the first light of morning they would come out, stained with her brother's blood, and there would be no more earthquakes, no piece of the god left under the hill, and the green grass would grow over the lines. Her father would reward him, call him blessed of the god, to have fought his way through the underworld. If Ariadne came back out with him, maybe Minos would even give the Athenian his own daughter to wife, and send him back to be a great lord in Athens, far away, where people wouldn't put her to death if she told them about her father's lies, because they wouldn't care at all.

She said instead, to the Oreth, "Come and help me down," and held her hands out to him across the dark hole. The man stood there a moment wary of her, his hand moving uneasily on the hilt of his sword. She remembered his face. He had helped to put the workmen down into this hatch. He had thrust them down roughly, pushing with his big arm and his sword held in his other hand, shoving them until they fell inside. He'd been ready to do that to her; he was ready to do it to the Athenians. He was slower to take a step to the edge, and reach out his hand to her. She gripped his hand and braced her foot against the far edge of the hole, and he let her down, kneeling to lower her into the dark, until her straining toes found the floor and she let go of his hand.

The torchlight made a golden circle of the hatch above. Inside there was only a cool dark, impenetrable. She could just make out the mouth of the passage, darkness on darkness, and a faint sense of the marble walls around her. There was a sluggish whisper of air coming out of it, like someone sighing faintly. She made herself start going, at once.

She heard the Athenians being pushed down behind her, cries and muted protests and soft weeping echoes, but worse than that footsteps, footsteps that she felt through the marble beneath her feet. She tried to run, for a little way, but she judged the distances wrong, and struck a wall before she expected it, ramming into stone with her forehead, although she'd thought she had a hand stretched out in front of her. She fell down hard, blinking away a dazzle that didn't belong, her eyes watering with the shock of pain.

But the dazzle wasn't just pain: a golden glow of light was coming down the hallway. The Oreth had given the Athenians one of the torches, too, along with the sword. They caught her, or nearly: she staggered up even as she saw them coming in a pack around the corner behind, staying close to their leader. She shut her eyes to keep the glare from getting into her eyes, and groped for the wall and went onward dancing instead, her stamping dance meant to wake her brother up, the dance her feet knew even in the dark.

That knowledge was what saved her. She kept her hand on the wall as she danced, along the familiar long curving stretch where the passage turned back outward, moving away from the center and back out to cross a great half circle from one quarter to the other, and halfway along it, the wall fell away suddenly and unexpected from beneath her fingers: another way to go, a branching in the path, where there shouldn't have been one. She kept going several curving steps past it on sheer habit, until her seeking fingers bumped against the wall on the other side of the opening, and only then stopped, shivering. The passage air was warm and moist around her, but out of the branching the air came spring-cool and brisk, a scent of olive oil and wine.

She made herself keep going, keep the dance going, and before she reached the next turning she heard the Athenians arguing behind her in the mainland tongue: which way to go, which way the wholesome air was coming from. And the footsteps seemed fewer, afterwards, as if some of them had gone the other way. Ariadne went on dancing, putting her feet down as quietly as she could. She passed another branching, another breath of clear air and freedom, even a hint of roast spring lamb, a smell of feasting. In the passage, the sense of something breathing was growing stronger: the slow rise and fall of enormous lungs. More of the Athenian footsteps fell off. Only a handful left behind her.

But she was coming closer. There was one more long curving, back into the last quarter. It wasn't far now to the seal, to the central chamber. When she passed another branching, a pungent waft of sweat came out of it, sweat and honeyed mead: a living, human smell, full of wanting and lust and strong liquor. On the other side, the thick air was so humid the walls were dewed with moisture, and they almost felt spongy, like the marble of a bathhouse worn into curves by years and bodies, next thing to flesh itself, yielding to an impossible pressure. Ariadne stood with just her very fingertips on the surface, her hand wanting to cringe away. She was afraid, so afraid. She wanted to turn around and run back to the torchlight flicker she could just see coming up from behind her. The god looking out of that golden youth's eyes wasn't the god down here. The god down here was the god in the dark, the god grown large and terrible, maybe too terrible to bear.

She remembered suddenly without remembering, a voice that burst into her ears and came out of her again, bloody. She still couldn't remember what it had said, but she remembered feeling it move through her like earthquake, cracking open fault lines. She felt a whisper of it moving through her now, finding its way.

She had been pleased when the god had shook the earth under her, so pleased when she'd seen fear on her father's face, looking out of the high priest. She'd liked it, walking back up the hill to the shrine that made her a priestess and a power, that spared her the fate of her sisters. She'd been angry, and she'd been brave, and she'd brought her brother one offering after another to distract him in his prison, but there was the one thing she hadn't done, the one thing bigger than all the others: she hadn't told. She'd told Reja, and she'd told Staphos, small whisperings at night in dark places, but when the priest had come asking questions, Staphos's cousin, the one who had asked her in the light of day, she hadn't told him what was in the labyrinth. She hadn't told the high priest, either the first time he'd come up beside her father or in the palace, the high priest who would have cast her whole family down if he'd believed her; she hadn't told the people in the square, when she'd come out of the king's palace with the earth trembling beneath her feet, and she hadn't told the people come up the hill reveling. Her brother, her little brother, had pulled his hand out of hers, and gone down into the dark to save her life, and she hadn't run down the hill shouting, begging a shepherd, a priest, a rich man for help.

So it was her lie, too. She was in the lie, and the lie was in her, and the lie couldn't go any further into the dark. If she kept holding on to the lie, she could only take this last branching. It wouldn't take her to death. It would go somewhere living and human, because there was no death for her in the labyrinth. Her brother wasn't angry with her. He didn't blame her. It wasn't her fault, and he loved her, and he would never hurt her.

Anyway, she knew where it went. She had watched them dig every inch of the passage out of the ground. There were no branches. The only magic in the labyrinth was what was in it. Her, and her choice. If she followed the branching, she would come to the chamber at the end: and it would be an empty chamber, with a stagnant well, and an open hatch above that she would be able to reach. There would be no one else there. It had been three years. Her bastard half brother had starved to death; his bones were somewhere in the passage, along with the bones of those poor workmen, and the priest, and Staphos, and soon the Athenians, who had all gotten confused and turned around in the dark. The lie would come up out of the ground with her and turn into that truth. And the people would see her come out of the ground, in the first light of morning, and they would kneel to her. Her father himself would kneel; he would make her high priestess, and she would have a voice that no woman had in Crete, and be safe and powerful, all her days.

She stood there, and then she turned around and waited while the torchlight came down the passage, until the last handful of Athenians came around. The golden one held the torch and the sword, and there were three others behind him, a young woman and two youths, all dark-haired, pale, shivering. They saw her and stopped. "Which way is it?" one of the dark-haired boys blurted, a little older than the others, and taller. "Tell us or we'll make you!"

"There's only one way," Ariadne said.

"There's a branching right there!" the girl said, a little shrill.

"No, there isn't," Ariadne said. She looked the golden-haired young man in the face. "There's only one way. The branching's in us, not in the labyrinth."

He looked back at her, his eyes clear and brilliant as jewels, but somehow familiar after all, and then he said, "Will you lead us?"

"Theseus!" the elder boy said. "Don't be a fool! The only way she'll lead you is straight into the maw of whatever thing they have penned up in here."

"Why would she help us?" the girl added. "Minos is her *father*, I heard them say so. Androgeos was her brother."

Then Theseus did pause, and looked at her. "Well?" he said, quietly. "Why would you show us the way?"

"I have another brother," Ariadne said. "And my father put him down here. If you'll help me get him out, get away with him, then I'll help you."

The other three Athenians wouldn't come. They stood at the branching, watching them go, holding the torch. The curve of the passageway swallowed them into the dark almost at once. Only Theseus came with her. She heard his footsteps following as she danced her way onward, finding the way with rhythm, the thick heavy damp smell ahead, a warm stink of sweat and musk, a breathing all around her, getting stronger, and then suddenly the wall slipped out from under her fingers, not into a branching but into a curving wall, and there was a little brightness ahead of her. Not much, only the glimmer of starlight seeping in through the tiny grating, which she could see in darker lines against the night sky overhead, and reflected in the still waters of the well.

"Minotaur," she said softly. "Minotaur, I'm here."

"Buried Deep" was originally published in The Mythic Dream, *an anthology from Saga Press exploring retellings of myths across cultures, published in 2019. Edited by Dominik Parisien and Navah Wolfe.*

SPINNING SILVER

I debated the most about including this story; space in a collection is limited for all sorts of practical publishing reasons, and I imagine many readers will be familiar with the novel version of this story, and there's so much overlap between the two. So I apologize to those who feel they're retreading familiar ground, but at the same time I felt that was what made it interesting to include: how with so much overlap, this remains a completely different story, that is also true.

I started this story thinking about my paternal grandmother, Chawa, a ferociously determined and cunning woman who kept two little children alive as a refugee alone in the Soviet Union during World War II, gleaning from fields and hustling without end; later in the Communist era she was caught smuggling gold for dollars, and had to bribe her way out of prison. Miryem isn't much like her, but this story is still about her, and it's not really a surprise that it twisted its way out of my grasp and started demanding to be told at much more length.

You can see many of the places here where the novel broke

out: the glimpses of Wanda and Irina and the tsar, and the line that told me that I had to write it: a power claimed and challenged and thrice carried out is true, *a piece of fairy logic that felt too right to me as soon as I wrote it, even though I knew at once that it was going to make more work for me.*

THE REAL STORY ISN'T HALF AS PRETTY AS THE ONE you've heard. The real story is, the miller's daughter with her long golden hair wants to catch a lord, a prince, a rich man's son, so she goes to the moneylender and borrows for a ring and a necklace and decks herself out for the festival. And she's beautiful enough, so the lord, the prince, the rich man's son notices her, and dances with her, and tumbles her in a quiet hayloft when the dancing is over, and afterward he goes home and marries the rich woman his family has picked out for him. Then the miller's disappointed daughter tells everyone that the moneylender's in league with the devil, and the village runs him out or maybe even stones him, so at least she gets to keep the jewels, and the blacksmith marries her before that first-born child comes along a little early.

Because that's what the story's really about: getting out of paying your debts. That's not how they tell it, but I knew. My father was a moneylender, you see.

He wasn't very good at it. If someone didn't pay him back on time, he never so much as mentioned it to them. Only if our cupboards were really bare, or our shoes were falling off our feet, and my mother spoke quietly with him after I was in bed: then he'd go, unhappy, and knock on a few doors, and make it sound like an apology when he asked for some of what they owed. And if there was money in the house and someone asked to borrow, he hated to say no, even if we didn't really have enough ourselves. So all his money, most of which had been my mother's money, her dowry, stayed in other people's houses. And everyone else liked it that way, even though they knew they ought to be ashamed of themselves, so they told the story often, even or especially when I could hear it.

My mother's father was a moneylender too, but he was a very good one. He lived in the city, twenty miles away. She often took me on visits, when she could afford to pay someone to let us ride along at the back of a cart or a sledge, five or six changes along the way. My grandmother would always have a new dress for me, plain but warm and well made, and she would feed me to bursting, and the last night before we left she would always make cheesecake, her cheesecake, which was baked golden on the outside and thick and white and crumbly inside and tasted just a little bit of apples, and she would make decorations with sweet golden raisins on the top. After I had slowly and lingeringly eaten every last bite of a slice wider than the palm of my hand, they would put me to bed in the warmest corner of the big, cozy sitting room near the fireplace, and my mother would sit next to her mother, and put her head on her shoulder, and not say anything, but when I was a little older and didn't fall asleep right away, I would see in the candlelight that both of them had a little wet track of tears down their faces.

We could have stayed. But we always went home, because we loved my father. He was terrible with money, but he was endlessly warm and gentle, and he tried to make his failure up to us: he spent nearly all of every day out in the cold woods hunting for food and firewood, and when he was indoors, there was nothing he wouldn't do to help my mother; no talk of woman's work in my house, and when we did go hungry, he went hungriest, and snuck food from his plate to ours. When he sat by the fire in the evenings, his hands were always working, whittling some new little toy for me or something for my mother, a decoration on a chair or a wooden spoon.

But winter was always bitter in our town, and every year seemed worse. The year I turned sixteen, the ground froze early, and cold, sharp winds blew out of the forest every day, it seemed, carrying whirls of stinging snow. Our house stood a little bit apart from the rest anyway, without other walls nearby to share in breaking the wind, and we grew thin and hungry and shivering. My father kept making his excuses, avoiding the work he couldn't bear to do. But even when my mother finally pressed him and he tried, he only came back with a scant handful of coins. It was midwinter, and everyone wanted to have something good on the table; something a little nice for the festival, their festival.

So they put my father off, and while their lights shone out on the snow and the smell of roasting meat slipped out of the cracks, at home my mother made thin cabbage soup and scrounged together used cooking oil to light the lamp for the first night of our own celebration, coughing as she worked: another deep chill had rolled in from the woods, and it crept through every crack and eave of our run-down little house.

By the eighth day, she was too tired from coughing to get out of bed. "She'll be all right soon," my father said, avoiding my eyes. "The cold will break."

He went out to gather some firewood. "Miryem," my mother said, hoarsely, and I took her a cup of weak tea with a scraping of honey, all I had to comfort her. She sipped a little and lay back on the pillows and said, "When the winter breaks, I want you to go to my father's house. He'll take you to my father's house."

I pressed my lips together hard, and then I kissed her forehead and told her to rest, and after she fell fitfully asleep, I went to the box next to the fireplace where my father kept his big ledger book. I took it out, and I took his worn pen out of its holder, and I mixed ink out of the ashes in the fireplace, and I made a list. A moneylender's daughter, even a bad moneylender, learns her figures. I wrote and figured and wrote and figured, interest and time broken up by the scattered payments—because my father had every one of those written down; he was as scrupulous in making sure he didn't cheat anyone as no one else was with him, and when I had my list finished, I took all the knitting out of my bag, put my shawl on, and went out into the cold morning.

I went to every house that owed us, and I banged on their doors: it was early, very early, because my mother's coughing had woken us in the dark. Everyone was still at home. So the men opened the doors and stared at me in surprise, and I looked them in their faces and said, cold and hard, "I've come to settle your account."

They tried to put me off, of course; some of them laughed at me. Some of them smiled and asked me to come inside and warm myself up, have a hot drink. I refused. I didn't want to be warmed. I stood on their doorsteps, and I brought out my list, and I told them how much they had borrowed, and what they had paid, and how much interest they owed besides.

They spluttered and argued and some of them shouted.

No one had ever shouted at me in my life: my mother with her quiet voice, my gentle father. But I found something bitter inside myself, something of winter blown into my heart: the sound of my mother coughing, and the memory of the story told too many times in the village square. I stayed in their doorways, and I didn't move. My numbers were true, and they and I knew it, and when they'd shouted themselves out, I said, "Do you have the money?"

They thought it was an opening. They said no, of course not; they didn't have such a sum.

"Then you'll pay me a little now, and again every week, until your debt is cleared," I said, "and pay interest on what you haven't paid, if you don't want me to send to my grandfather to bring the law into it."

Our town was small, and no one traveled very much. They knew my mother's father was rich, and lived in a great house in the city, and had loaned money to knights and once to a lord. So they gave me a little, grudgingly; only a few pennies in some houses, but every one of them gave me something, and I wrote down the numbers in front of them and told them I would see them next week. On my way home, I stopped in at Panova Lyudmila's house, who took in travelers when they stayed overnight. She didn't borrow money: she could have lent it too, except for charging interest. And if anyone in our town had been foolish enough to borrow from anyone but my father, who would let them pay as they liked or didn't. I didn't collect anything; from her I bought a pot of hot soup, with half a chicken in it, and three fresh eggs, and a bowl of honeycomb covered with a napkin.

My father had come back home before me; he was feeding the fire, and he looked up worried when I shouldered my way in. He stared at my arms full of food. I put it all down and I put the rest of the pennies and the handful of silver into the kettle next to our own hearth, and I gave him the list with the payments written on it, and then I turned to making my mother comfortable.

AFTER THAT, I WAS THE moneylender in our little town. And I was a good moneylender, and a lot of people owed us money, so very soon the straw of our floor was smooth boards of golden wood, and the cracks in our fireplace were chinked with good clay and our roof was thatched fresh, and my mother had a fur cloak to sleep under or to wear. She didn't like it at all, and neither did my father, who went outside and wept quietly to himself the day I brought the cloak home. The baker's wife had offered it to me in payment for the rest of her family's debt. It was beautiful; she'd brought it with her when she married, made of ermines her father had hunted in his lord's woods.

That part of the story turned out to be true: you have to be cruel to be a good moneylender. But I was ready to be as merciless with our neighbors as they'd been with my father. I didn't take firstborn children exactly, but one week, one of the peasant farmers had nothing to pay me with, not even a spare loaf of bread, and he cursed me with real desperation in his voice and said, "You can't suck blood from a stone."

I should have felt sorry for him, I suppose. My father would have, and my mother, but wrapped in my coldness, I felt only the danger of the moment. If I forgave him, took his excuses, next week everyone would have an excuse; I saw everything unraveling again from there.

Then the farmer's tall daughter came staggering in, a heavy gray kerchief over her head and a big heavy yoke across her shoulders, carrying two buckets of water, twice as much as I could manage when I went for water to the village well myself. I said, "Then your daughter will come work in my house to pay off the debt, three mornings this week and every week you can't pay," and I walked home pleased as a cat, and even danced a few steps to myself in the road, alone under the trees.

Her name was Wanda. She came silently to the house at dawn, three days a week, worked like an ox until midday, and left silently again; she kept her head down the entire time. She was very strong, and she took almost all the burden of the housework in just her three mornings. She carried water and chopped wood, and tended the small flock of hens we now had scratching in our yard, and watered the new goats and milked them, and scrubbed the floors and our hearth and all our pots, and I was well satisfied with my solution.

For the first time in my life, I heard my mother speak to my father in anger, in blame, as she hadn't even when she was cold and sick. "And you don't care for what it does to her?" I heard her cry out to him.

"What shall I say to her?" he cried back. "What shall I say? No, you shall starve; no, you shall go cold and you will wear rags?"

"If you had the coldness to do it yourself, you could be cold enough to let her do it," my mother said. "Our daughter, Josef!"

But when my father looked me in the face that night and tried to say something to me, the coldness in me met him and drove him back, just as it had when he'd met it in the village, asking for what he was owed.

So in desperation my mother took me away on a visit when the air warmed with spring and her cough finally went away, drowned in soup and honey. I didn't like to leave, but I did want to see my grandmother, and show her that her daughter wasn't sleeping cold and frozen, that her granddaughter didn't go like a beggar anymore; I wanted to visit without seeing her weep, for once. I went on my rounds one last time and told everyone as I did that I would add on extra interest for the weeks I was gone, unless they left their payments at our house while I was away.

Then we drove to my grandfather's house, but this time I hired our neighbor Oleg to take us all the way with his good horses and his big wagon, heaped with straw and blankets and jingling bells on the harness, with the fur cloak spread over all against the March wind. My grandmother came out, surprised, to meet us when we drew up to the house, and my mother went into her arms, silent and hiding her face. "Well, come in and warm up," my grandmother said, looking at the sledge and our good new wool dresses, trimmed with rabbit fur, and a golden button at the neck on mine, that had come out of the weaver's chest.

She sent me to take my grandfather fresh hot water in his study, so she could talk to my mother alone. My grandfather had rarely done more than grunt at me and look me up and down disapprovingly in the dresses my grandmother had bought. I don't know how I knew what he thought of my father, because I don't remember him ever having said a word about it, but I did know.

He looked me over this time out from under his bristling eyebrows and frowned. "Fur, now? And gold?"

I should say that I was properly brought up, and I knew better than to talk back to my own grandfather of all people, but I was already angry that my mother was upset, and that my grandmother wasn't pleased, and now to have him pick at me, him of all people. "Why shouldn't I have it, instead of someone who bought it with my father's money?" I said.

My grandfather was as surprised as you would expect to be spoken to like this by his granddaughter, but then he heard what I had said and frowned at me again. "Your father bought it for you, then?"

Loyalty and love stopped my mouth there, and I dropped my eyes and silently finished pouring the hot water into the samovar and changing out the tea. My grandfather didn't stop me going away, but by the next morning he knew the whole story somehow, that I'd taken over my father's work, and suddenly he was pleased with me, as he never had been before and no one else was.

He had two other daughters who had married better than my mother, to rich city men with good trades. None of them had given him a grandson who wanted to take up his business. In the city, there were enough of my people that we could be something other than a banker, or a farmer who grew his own food: there were enough people who would buy your goods, and there was a thriving market in our quarter.

"It's not seemly for a girl," my grandmother tried, but my grandfather snorted.

"Gold doesn't know the hand that holds it," he said, and

frowned at me, but in a pleased way. "You'll need servants," he told me. "One to start with, a good strong simple man or woman: can you find one?"

"Yes," I said, thinking of Wanda: she had nearly paid off her father's debt by now, but she was already used to coming, and in our town there wasn't much other chance for a poor farmer's daughter to earn a wage.

"Good. Don't go yourself to get the money," he said. "You send a servant, and if they want to argue, they come to you."

I nodded, and when we went home, he gave me a purse full of silver pennies to lend out, to towns near ours that hadn't any moneylender of their own. And when my mother and I came again in the winter for another visit, after the first snowfall, I brought it back full of gold to put into the bank, and my grandfather was proud of me.

They hadn't had guests over usually, when we were visiting, except my mother's sisters. I hadn't noticed before, but I noticed now, because suddenly the house was full of people coming to drink tea, to stay to dinner, lights and bustling dresses and laughing voices, and I met more city people in that one week than I had in all the visits before. "I don't believe in selling a sow's ear for a silk purse," my grandfather told me bluntly, when I asked him. "Your father couldn't dower you as the guests who come to this house would expect of my granddaughter, and I swore to your mother that I would never put more money in his pocket, to fall back out again."

I understood then why he hadn't wanted my grandmother buying dresses for me, as he'd thought, with fur and gold buttons on them. He wouldn't try to make a princess out of a miller's daughter with borrowed finery, and snare her a husband fool enough to be tricked by it, or who'd slip out of the bargain when he learned the truth.

It didn't make me angry; I liked him better for that cold, hard honesty, and it made me proud that now he did invite his guests, and even boasted of me to them, how I'd taken away a purse of silver and brought back one of gold.

But my grandmother kept her mouth pursed shut; my mother's was empty of smiles. I was angry at her again as we flew home in the warm sledge over the frozen roads. I had another purse of silver hidden deep under my own fur cloak, and three petticoats underneath my dress, and I didn't feel cold at all, but her face was tight and drawn.

"Would you rather we were still poor and hungry?" I burst out to her finally, the silence between us heavy in the midst of the dark woods, and she put her arms around me and kissed me and said, "My darling, my darling, I'm sorry," weeping a little.

"Sorry?" I said. "To be warm instead of cold? To be rich and comfortable? To have a daughter who can turn silver into gold?" I pushed away from her.

"To see you harden yourself like a stone, to make it so," she said. We didn't speak the rest of the way home.

I DIDN'T BELIEVE IN STORIES, even though we lived in the middle of one: our village had been cut out of the North Forest, a little too near the depths where they said the old ones lived, the Staryk. Children who ran playing in the woods would sometimes stumble across their road and come home with one of the pebbles that lined it: an unnaturally smooth pebble that shone in starlight, and got lost again very quickly no matter how much care you took with it. I saw them displayed in the village square a couple of times, but they only looked like smooth white pebbles, and I didn't think magic was needed to explain why children lost a rock again in short order.

You weren't supposed to ride through the woods dressed too fine, because they loved gold and gems and finery, but again, I didn't mean to be afraid of fairy lords when thieves would do just as well, to make it poor sense to go riding through a deep forest wearing all your jewels. If you found a grove full of red mushrooms with white spots, you were supposed to go back out again and stay well away, because that was one of their dancing rings, and if someone went missing in the woods they'd taken him or her, and once in a while someone would come staggering out of the forest, feverish, and claim to have seen one of them.

I never saw the road, or took any of it seriously, but the morning after my mother and I came back home, Wanda ran back inside, afraid, after she'd gone out to feed the chickens. "They've been outside the house!" was all she said, and she wouldn't go out again alone. My father took the iron poker from the fireplace and we all went out cautiously behind him, thinking there might be burglars or wolves, but there were only prints in the snow. Strange prints: a little like deer, but with claws at the end, and too large, the size of horses' hooves. They came right to the wall of the house, and then someone had climbed off the beast and looked through our window: someone wearing boots with a long pointed toe.

I wasn't stubborn about my disbelief, when I had footprints in snow to show me something strange had happened. If nothing else, no one anywhere near our town had boots that absurd, for fashion; only someone who didn't have to walk anywhere would have shoes like that. But there didn't seem to be anything to do about it, and they'd left, whoever they'd been. I told Wanda we'd hire her brother to come and guard the house during the night, mostly so she wouldn't be afraid and maybe leave her place, and then I put it out of my mind.

But the tracks were there again the next morning, though Sergey swore he'd been awake all night and hadn't heard a thing.

"If the Staryk haven't anything better to do but peer in at our windows, I suppose they can," I said out loud and clear, standing in the yard. "We're no fools to keep our gold in the house: it's in Grandfather's vault," which I hoped might be overheard and do some good whether it was an elf or a thief or someone trying to scare me.

It did something, anyway; that night as we sat at our work in the kitchen, my mother doing the fine sewing she loved, and I with my spindle, my father silently whittling with his head bowed, there was suddenly a banging at the door, a heavy thumping as though someone was knocking against the wood with something metal. Wanda sprang up from the kettle with a cry, and we all held still: it was a cold night, snow falling, and no one would come out at such an hour. The knocking came again, and then my father said, "Well, it's a polite devil, at least," and got up and went to the door.

When he opened it, no one was there, but there was a small bag sitting on the threshold. He stepped outside and looked around to one side and the other: no one anywhere in sight. Then he gingerly picked up the bag and brought it inside and put it on the table. We all gathered around it and stared as though it were a live coal that might at any moment set the whole house ablaze.

It was made of leather, white leather, but not dyed by any ordinary way I'd ever heard of: it looked as though it had always been white, all the way through. There wasn't a seam or stitch to be seen on its sides, and it clasped shut with a small lock made of silver. Finally, when no one else moved to touch it, I reached out and opened the clasp, and tipped out a few small silver coins, thin and flat and perfectly round, not enough to fill the hollow of my palm. Our house was full of warm firelight, but they shone coldly, as if they stood under the moon.

"It's very kind of them to make us such a present," my father said after a moment doubtfully, but we all knew the Staryk would never do such a thing. There were stories from other kingdoms farther south, of fairies who came with gifts, but not in ours. And then my mother drew a sharp breath and looked at me and said, low, "They want it turned into gold."

I suppose it was my own fault, bragging in the woods where they could hear me, but now I didn't know what to do. Moneylending isn't magic: I couldn't lend the coins out today and have the profit back tomorrow, and I didn't think they meant to wait a year or more for their return. Anyway, the reason I had brought in so much money so quickly was that my father had lent out all my mother's dowry over years and years, and everyone had kept the money so long they had built heaps of interest even at the little rate my father had charged them.

"We'll have to take the money from the bank," my mother said. There were six silver coins in the bag. I had put fourteen gold coins in the bank this last visit, and the city was only an eight-hour sleigh ride away when the snow was packed this hard. But I rebelled: I didn't mean to trade our gold, *my* gold, for fairy silver.

"I'll go to the city tomorrow," was all I said, but when I went, I didn't go to the bank. I slept that night in my grandfather's house, behind the thick walls of the quarter, and early the next morning, I went down to the market. I found a seat upon the temple steps while the sellers put out their stalls: everything from apples to hammers to jeweled belts, and I waited while the buyers slowly trickled in. I watched through the morning rush, and after it thinned out, I went to the stall of the jeweler who had been visited by the most people in drab clothes: I guessed they had to be servants from the rich people of the city.

The jeweler was a young man with spectacles and stubby but careful fingers, his beard trimmed short to stay out of his work; he was bent over an anvil in miniature, hammering out a disk of silver with his tiny tools, enormously precise. I stood watching him work for maybe half an hour before he sighed and said, "Yes?" with a faint hint of resignation, as though he'd hoped I would go away, instead of troubling him to do any business. But he seemed to know what he was about, so I brought out my pouch of silver coins and spilled them onto the black cloth he worked upon.

"It's not enough to buy anything here," he said, matter-of-factly, with barely a glance; he started to go back to his work, but then he frowned a little and turned around again.

He picked one coin up and peered at it closely, and turned it over in his fingers, and rubbed it between them, and then he put it down and stared at me. "Where did you get these?"

"They came from the Staryk, if you want to believe me," I said. "Can you make them into something? A bracelet or a ring?"

"I'll buy them from you," he offered.

"No, thank you," I said.

"To make them into a ring would cost you two gold coins," he said. "Or I'll buy them from you for five."

"I'll pay you one," I said firmly, "or if you like, you can sell the ring for me and keep half the profit," which was what I really wanted. "I have to give the Staryk back six gold coins in exchange."

He grumbled a little but finally agreed, which meant he thought he could sell it for a high enough price to make it worthwhile, and then he set about the work. He melted the silver over a hot little flame and ran it into a mold, a thick one made of iron, and when it had half cooled, he took it out with his leathered fingertips and etched a pattern into the surface, fanciful, full of leaves and branches.

It didn't take him long: the silver melted easily and cooled easily and took the pattern easily, and when it was done, the pattern seemed oddly to move and shift: it drew the eye and held it, and shone even in the midday sun. We looked down at it for a while, and then he said, "The duke will buy it," and sent his apprentice running into the city. A tall, imperious servant in velvet clothes and gold braid came back with the boy, making clear in every expression how annoyed he was by the interruption of his more important work, but even he stopped being annoyed when he saw the ring and held it on his palm.

The duke paid ten gold coins for the ring, so I put two in the bank, and six back into the little white pouch, and I climbed back into Oleg's sledge to go home that same evening. We flew through the snow and dark, the horse trotting quickly with only my weight in back. But in the woods the horse slowed, and then dropped to a walk, and then halted; I thought she just needed a rest, but she stood unmoving with her ears pricked up anxiously, warm breath gusting out of her nostrils. "Why are we stopping?" I asked, and Oleg didn't answer me: he slumped in his seat as though he slept.

The snow crunched behind me once and once again: something picking its way toward the sleigh from behind, step by heavy step. I swallowed and drew my cloak around me, and then I summoned up all the winter-cold courage I'd built inside me and turned around.

The Staryk didn't look so terribly strange at first; that was what made him truly terrible, as I kept looking and slowly his face became something inhuman, shaped out of ice and glass, and his eyes like silver knives. He had no beard and wore his white hair in a long braid down his back. His clothes, just like his purse, were all in white. He was riding a stag, but a stag larger than a draft horse, with antlers branched twelve times and hung with clear glass drops, and when it put out its red tongue to lick its muzzle, its teeth were sharp as a wolf's.

I wanted to quail, to cower; but I knew where that led. Instead I held my fur cloak tight at the throat with one hand against the chill that rolled off him, and with my other I held out the bag to him, in silence, as he came close to the sleigh.

He paused, eyeing me out of one silver-blue eye with his head turned sideways, like a bird. He put out his gloved hand and took the bag, and he opened it and poured the six gold coins out into the cup of his hand, the faint jingle loud in the silence around us. The coins looked warm and sun-bright against the white of his glove. He looked down at them and seemed vaguely disappointed, as though he was sorry I'd managed it; and then he put them away and the bag vanished somewhere beneath his own long cloak.

I called up all my courage and spoke, throwing my words against the hard, icy silence like a shell around us. "I'll need more than a day next time, if you want more of them changed," I said, a struggle to keep trembling out of my voice.

He lifted his head and stared at me, as though surprised I'd dared to speak to him, and then he wasn't there anymore; Oleg shook himself all over and chirruped to the horse, and we were trotting again. I fell back into the blankets, shivering. The tips of my fingers where I'd held out the purse were numbed and cold. I pulled off my gloves and tucked them underneath my arm to warm them up, wincing as they touched my skin.

ONE WEEK WENT BY, AND I began to forget about the Staryk, about all of it. We all did, the way one forgets dreams: you're trying to explain the story of it to someone and halfway through it's already running quicksilver out of your memory, too wrong and ill-fitting to keep in your mind. I didn't have any of the fairy silver left to prove the whole thing real, not even the little purse. Even that same night I'd come home, I hadn't been able to describe him to my anxious mother; I'd only been able to say, "It's all right, I gave him the gold," and then I'd fallen into bed. By morning I couldn't remember his face.

But Sunday night the knocking came again at the door, and I froze for a moment. I was standing already, about to fetch a dish of dried fruit from the pantry; with a lurch of my heart I went to the door and flung it open.

A burst of wind came growling through the house, as cold as if it had been shaved directly off the frozen crust of the snow. The Staryk hadn't abandoned a purse on the stoop this time: he stood waiting outside, all the more unearthly for the frame of wood around his sharp edges. I looked back into the house wildly, to see if they saw him also; but my father was bent over his whittling as though he hadn't even heard the door opening, and my mother was looking into the fire with a dreamy, vague look on her face. Wanda lay sleeping on her pallet already, and her brother had gone home three days before.

I turned back. The Staryk held another purse out to me, to the very border of the door, and spoke, a high, thin voice like wind whistling through the eaves. "Three days," he said.

I was afraid of him, of course; I wasn't a fool. But I had only believed in him for a week, and I had spent all my life learning to fear other things more: to be taken advantage of, used unfairly. "And what in return?" I blurted, putting my hands behind my back.

His eyes sharpened, and I regretted pressing him. "Thrice, mortal maiden," he said, in a rhythm almost like a song. "Thrice shall I come, and you shall turn silver to gold for my hands, or be changed into ice yourself."

I felt half ice already, chilled down to my bones. I swallowed. "And then?"

He laughed and said, "And then I will make you my queen, if you manage it," mockingly, and threw the purse down at my feet, jingling loud. When I looked back up from it, he was gone, and my mother behind me said, slow and struggling, as if it was an effort to speak, "Miryem, why are you keeping the door open? The cold's coming in."

I HAD NEVER FELT SORRY for the miller's daughter before, in the story: I'd been too sorry for my father, and myself. But who would really like it, after all, to be married to a king who'd as cheerfully have cut off your head if your dowry didn't match your boasting? I didn't want to be the Staryk's queen any more than I wanted to be his servant, or frozen into ice.

The purse he'd left was ten times as heavy as before, full of shining coins. I counted them out into smooth-sided towers, to try and put my mind into order along with them. "We'll leave," my mother said. I hadn't told her what the Staryk had promised, or threatened, but she didn't like it anyway: an elven lord coming to demand I give him gold. "We'll go to my father, or farther away," but I felt sure that wasn't any good. I hadn't wanted to believe in the Staryk at all, but now that I couldn't help it, I didn't believe there was a place I could run away that he wouldn't find some way to follow. And if I did, then what? My whole life afraid, looking around for the sound of footfalls in snow?

Anyway, we couldn't just go. It would mean bribes to cross each border, and a new home wherever we found ourselves in the end, and who knew how they'd treat us when we got there? We'd heard enough stories of what happened to our people in other countries, under kings and bishops who wanted their own debts forgiven, and to fill their purses with confiscated wealth.

So I put the six towers of coins, ten in each, back into the purse, and I sent Wanda for Oleg's sledge. We drove back to the city that very night, not to lose any of my precious time. "Do you have any more?" Isaac the jeweler demanded the moment he saw me, eagerly, and then he flushed and said, "That is, welcome back," remembering he had manners.

"Yes, I have more," I said, and spilled them out on the cloth. "I need to give back sixty gold this time," I told him.

He was already turning them over with his hands, his face alight with hunger. "I couldn't *remember,*" he said, half to himself, and then he heard what I'd said and gawked at me. "I need a little profit for the work that this will take!"

"There's enough to make ten rings, at ten gold each," I said.

"I couldn't sell them all."

"Yes, you could," I said. That, I was sure of: if the duke had a ring of fairy silver, every wealthy man and woman in the city needed a ring just like it, right away.

He frowned down over the coins, stirring them with his fingers, and sighed. "I'll make a necklace, and see what we can get."

"You really don't think you can sell ten rings?" I said, surprised, wondering if I was wrong.

"I want to make a necklace," he said, which didn't seem very sensible to me, but perhaps he thought it would show his work off and make a name for him. I didn't really mind as long as I could pay off my Staryk for another week.

"I only have three days," I said. "Can you do it that quickly?"

He groaned. "Why must you ask for impossibilities?"

"Do *those* look possible to you?" I said, pointing at the coins, and he couldn't really argue with that.

I had to sit with him while he worked, and manage the people who came to the stall wanting other things from him; he didn't want to talk to anyone and be interrupted. Most of them were busy and irritated servants, some of them expecting goods to be finished; they snapped and glared, wanting me to cower, but I met their bluster too and said coolly, "Surely you can see what Master Isaac is working on. I'm sure your mistress or your master wouldn't wish you to interrupt a patron I cannot name, but who would purchase such a piece," and I waved to send their eyes over to the worktable, where the full sunlight shone on the silver beneath his hands. Its cold gleam silenced them; they stood staring a little while and then went away, without trying to argue again.

I noticed that Isaac tried to save a few of the coins aside while he worked, as though he wanted to keep them to remember. I thought of asking him for one to keep myself; but it didn't work. On the morning of the third day, he sighed and took the last of the ones he'd saved and melted it down, and strung a last bit of silver lace upon the design. "It's done," he said afterward, and picked it up in his hands: the silver hung over his broad palms like icicles, and we stood looking at it silently together for a while.

"Will you send to the duke?" I asked.

He shook his head and took out a box from his supplies: square and made of carved wood lined with black velvet, and he laid the necklace carefully inside. "No," he said. "For this, I will go to him. Do you want to come?"

"Can I go and change my dress?" I said, a little doubtful: I didn't really want the necklace to go so far out of my sight unpurchased, but I was wearing a plain work dress only for sitting in the market all day.

"How far do you live?" he said, just as doubtful.

"My grandfather's house is only down the street with the ash tree and around the corner," I said. "Three doors down from the red stables."

He frowned a moment. "That's Panov Moshel's house."

"That's my grandfather," I said, and he looked at me, surprised, and then in a new way I didn't understand until I was inside, putting on my good dress with the fur and the gold buttons, and I looked down at myself and patted my hair and wondered if I looked well, and then my cheeks prickled with sudden heat. "Do you know Isaac, the jeweler?" I blurted to my grandmother, turning away from the brass mirror.

She peered at me over her spectacles, narrowly. "I've met his mother. He's a respectable young man," she allowed, after some thought. "Do you want me to put up your hair again?"

So I took a little longer than he would have liked, I suspect, to come back; then we went together to the gates and through the wall around our quarter, and walked into the streets of the city. The houses nearest were mean and low, run-down; but Isaac led me to the wider streets, past an enormous church of gray stone with windows like jewelry themselves, and finally to the enormous mansions of the nobles. I couldn't help staring at the iron fences wrought into lions and writhing dragons, and the walls covered with vining fruits and flowers sculpted out of stone. I admit I was glad not to be alone when we went through the open gates and up the wide stone steps swept clear of snow.

Isaac spoke to one of the servants. We were taken to a small room to wait: no one offered us anything to drink, or a place to sit, and a manservant stood looking at us with disapproval. I was grateful, though: irritation made me feel less small and less tempted to gawk. Finally the servant who had come to the market last time came in and demanded to know our business. Isaac brought out the box and showed him the necklace; he stared down at it, and then said shortly, "Very well," and went away again. Half an hour later he reappeared and ordered us to follow him: we were led up back stairs and then abruptly emerged into a hall more sumptuous than anything I had ever seen, the walls hung with tapestries in bright colors and the floor laid with a beautifully patterned rug.

It silenced our feet and led us into a sitting room even more luxurious, where a man in rich clothes and a golden chain sat in an enormous chair covered in velvet at a writing table. I saw the ring of fairy silver on the first finger of his hand, resting on the arm of the chair. He didn't look down at it, but I noticed he thumbed it around now and again, as though he wanted to make sure it hadn't vanished from his hand. "All right, let's see it."

"Your Grace." Isaac bowed and showed him the necklace.

The duke stared into the box. His face didn't change, but he stirred the necklace gently on its bed with one finger, just barely moving the looped lacelike strands of it. He finally drew a breath and let it out again through his nose. "And how much do you ask for it?"

"Your Grace, I cannot sell it for less than a hundred and fifty."

"Absurd," the duke growled. I had a struggle to keep from biting my lip, myself: it was rather outrageous.

"Otherwise I must melt it down and make it into rings," Isaac said, spreading his hands apologetically. I thought that was rather clever: of course the duke would rather no one else had a ring like his.

"Where are you getting this silver from?" the duke demanded. Isaac hesitated, and then looked at me. The duke followed his eyes. "Well? You're bringing it from somewhere."

I curtsied, as deeply as I could manage and still get myself back up. "I was given it by one of the Staryk, my lord," I said. "He wants it changed for gold."

"And you mean to do it through my purse, I see," the duke said. "How much more of this silver will there be?"

I had been worrying about that, whether the Staryk would bring even more silver next time, and what I would do with it if he did: the first time six, the second time sixty; how would I get six hundred pieces of gold? I swallowed. "Maybe—maybe much more."

"Hm," the duke said, and studied the necklace again. Then he put his hand to one side and took up a bell and rang it; the servant reappeared in the doorway. "Go and bring Irina to me," he said, and the man bowed. We waited a handful of minutes, and then a woman came to the door, a girl perhaps a year younger than me, slim and demure in a plain gray woolen gown, modestly high-necked, with a fine

gray silken veil trailing back over her head. Her chaperone
came after her, an older woman scowling at me and especially at Isaac.

Irina curtsied to the duke without raising her downcast
eyes. He stood up and took the necklace over to her, and put
it around her neck. He stepped back and studied her, and
we did too. She wasn't especially beautiful, I would have
said, only ordinary, except her hair was long and dark and
thick; but it didn't really matter with the necklace on her. It
was hard even to glance away from her, with all of winter
clasped around her throat and the silver gleam catching in
her veil and in her eyes as they darted sideways to catch a
glimpse of herself in the mirror on the wall there.

"Ah, Irinushka," the chaperone murmured, approvingly,
and the duke nodded.

He turned back to us. "Well, jeweler, you are in luck: the
tsar visits us next week. You may have a hundred gold pieces
for your necklace, and the next thing you make will be a crown
fit for a queen, to be my daughter's dowry: you will have ten
times a hundred gold for it, if the tsar takes her hand."

I LEFT TWENTY GOLD PIECES in the bank and carried the
swollen purse into the sledge waiting to carry me home. My
shoulders tightened as we plunged into the forest, wondering when and if the Staryk would come on me once more,
until halfway down the road the sledge began to slow and
stop under the dark boughs. I went rabbit-still, looking
around for any signs of him, but I didn't see anything; the
horse stamped and snorted her warm breath, and Oleg didn't
slump over, but hung his reins on the footboard.

"Did you hear something?" I said, my voice hushed, and then he climbed down and took out a knife from under his coat, and I realized I'd forgotten to worry about anything else but magic. I scrambled desperately away, shoving the heaped blankets toward him and floundering through the straw and out the other side of the sledge. "Don't," I blurted. "Oleg, don't," my heavy skirts dragging in the snow as he came around for me. "Oleg, please," but his face was clenched down, cold deeper than any winter. "This is the Staryk's gold, not mine!" I cried in desperation, holding the purse out between us.

He didn't stop. "None of it's yours," he snarled. "None of it's yours, little grubbing vulture, taking money out of the hands of honest working men," and I knew the sound of a man telling himself a story to persuade himself he wasn't doing wrong, that he had a right to what he'd taken.

I gripped two big handfuls of my skirts and struggled back, my boot heels digging into the snow. He lunged, and I flung myself away, falling backward. The crust atop the snow gave beneath my weight, and I couldn't get up. He was standing over me, ready to reach down, and then he halted; his arms sank down to his sides.

It wasn't mercy. A deeper cold was coming into his face, stealing blue over his lips, and white frost was climbing over his thick brown beard. I struggled to my feet, shivering. The Staryk was standing behind him, a hand laid upon the back of his neck like a master taking hold of a dog's scruff.

In a moment, he dropped his hand. Oleg stood blank between us, bloodless as frostbite, and then he turned and slowly went back to the sledge and climbed into the driving seat. The Staryk didn't watch him go, as if he cared nothing;

he only looked at me with his eyes as gleaming as Oleg's blade. I was shaking and queasy. There were tears freezing on my eyelashes, making them stick. I blinked them away and held my hands tight together until they stopped trembling, and then I held out the purse.

The Staryk came closer and took it. He didn't pour the purse out: it was too full for that. Instead he dipped his hand inside and lifted out a handful of shining coins to tumble ringing back into the bag, weighed in his other palm, until there was only one last coin held between his white-gloved fingers. He frowned at it, and me.

"It's all there, all sixty," I said. My heart had slowed, because I suppose it was that or burst.

"As it must be," he said. "For fail me, and to ice you shall go."

But he seemed displeased anyway, although he had set the terms himself: as though he wanted to freeze me but couldn't break a bargain once he'd made it. "Now go home, mortal maiden, until I call on you again."

I looked over helplessly at the sledge: Oleg was sitting in the driver's seat, staring with his frozen face out into the winter, and the last thing I wanted was to get in with him. But I couldn't walk home from here, or even to some village where I could hire another driver. I had no idea where we were. I turned to argue, but the Staryk was already gone. I stood alone under pine boughs heavy with snow, with only silence and footprints around me, and the deep crushed hollow where I had fallen, the shape of a girl against the drift.

Finally I picked my way gingerly to the sledge and climbed back inside. Oleg shook the reins silently, and the mare started trotting again. He turned her head through the trees slightly, away from the road, and drove deeper into the forest. I tried to decide whether I was more afraid to call out to him and be answered, or to get no reply, and if I should try to jump from the sledge. And then suddenly we came through a narrow gap between trees onto a different road: a road as free of snow as summer, paved with innumerable small white pebbles like a mosaic instead of cobblestones, all of them laid under a solid sheet of ice.

The rails of the sledge rattled, coming onto the road, and then fell silent and smooth. The moon shone, and the road shone back, glistening under the pale light. The horse's hooves went strange and quickly on the ice, the sledge skating along behind her. Around us, trees stretched tall and birch-white, full of rustling leaves; trees that didn't grow in our forest, and should have been bare with winter. White birds darted between the branches, and the sleigh bells made a strange kind of music, high and bright and cold. I huddled back into the blankets and squeezed my eyes shut and kept them so, until suddenly there was a crunching of snow beneath us again, and the sledge was already standing outside the gate of my own yard.

I all but leaped out, and darted through the gate and all the way to my door before I glanced around. I needn't have run. Oleg drove away without ever looking back at me. The next morning, they found him outside his stables, lying frozen and staring blindly upwards in the snow, his horse and sledge put away.

I COULDN'T FORGET AT ALL, that week. They buried Oleg in the churchyard, and the bells ringing for him sounded like sleigh bells ringing too-high in a forest that couldn't be. They would find me frozen like that outside the door, if I didn't give the Staryk his gold next time, and if I did, then what? Would he put me on his white stag behind him, and carry me away to that pale cold forest, to live there alone forever with a crown of fairy silver of my own? I started up gasping at night with Oleg's white frozen face looming over me, shivering with a chill inside me that my mother's arms couldn't drive away.

I decided I might as well try something as nothing, so I didn't wait for the Staryk to come knocking this time. I fled to my grandfather's house behind the thick city walls, where the streets were layered with dirty ice instead of clean white snow and only a handful of scattered barren trees stood in the lanes. I slept well that Shabbat night, but the next morning the candles had gone out, and that evening while I sat knitting with my grandmother, behind me the kitchen door rattled on its hinges, and she didn't lift her head at the noise.

I slowly put aside my work, and went to the door, and flinched back when I had flung it wide: there was no narrow alleyway behind the Staryk, no brick wall of the house next door, and no hardened slush beneath his feet. He stood outside in a garden of pale-limbed trees, washed with moonlight even though the moon hadn't yet come out, as if I could step across the threshold and walk out of all the world.

There was a box instead of a purse upon the stoop, a chest made of pale white wood bleached as bone, bound around with thick straps of white leather and hinged and clasped with silver. I knelt and opened it. "Seven days this time I'll grant you, to return my silver changed for gold," the Staryk said in his voice like singing, as I stared at the heap of coins inside, enough to make a crown to hold the moon and stars. I didn't doubt that the tsar would marry Irina, with this to make her dowry.

I looked up at him, and he down at me with his sharp silver eyes, eager and vicious as a hawk. "Did you think mortal roads could run away from me, or mortal walls keep me out?" he said, and I hadn't really, after all.

"But what *use* am I to you?" I said desperately. "I have no magic: I can't change silver to gold for you in your kingdom, if you take me away."

"Of course you can, mortal girl," he said, as if I was being a fool. "A power claimed and challenged and thrice carried out is true; the proving makes it so." And then he vanished, leaving me with a casket full of silver and a belly full of dismay.

I HADN'T BEEN ABLE TO make sense of it before: What use would a mortal woman be to an elven lord, and if he wanted one, why wouldn't he just snatch her? I wasn't beautiful enough to be a temptation, and why should boasting make him want me? But of course any king would want a queen who really could make gold out of silver, if he could get one, mortal or not. The last thing I wanted was to be such a prize.

Isaac made the crown in a feverish week, laboring upon it in his stall in the marketplace. He hammered out great thin sheets of silver to make the fan-shaped crown, tall enough to double the height of a head, and then with painstaking care added droplets of melted silver in mimic of pearls, laying them in graceful spiraling patterns that turned upon themselves and vined away again. He borrowed molds

from every other jeweler in the market and poured tiny flattened links by the hundreds, then hung glittering chains of
them linked from one side of the crown to the other, and
fringed along the rest of the wide fan's bottom edge.

By the second day, men and women were coming just to
watch him work. I sat by, silent and unhappy, and kept them
off, until finally despite the cold the crowds grew so thick I
became impatient and started charging a penny to stand and
watch for ten minutes, so they'd go away; only it backfired,
and the basket I'd put out grew so full I had to empty it into
a sack under the table three times a day.

By the fifth day, I had made nearly as much silver as the
Staryk had given me in the first place, and the crown was
finished; when Isaac had assembled the whole, he turned
and said, "Come here," and set it upon my head to see
whether it was well balanced. The crown felt cool and light
as a dusting of snow upon my forehead. In his bronze mirror,
I looked like a strange deep-water reflection of myself, silver
stars at midnight above my brow, and all the marketplace
went quiet in a rippling wave around me, silent like the
Staryk's garden.

I wanted to burst into tears, or run away; instead I took
the crown off my head and put it back into Isaac's hands,
and when he'd carefully swathed it with linen and velvet,
the crowds finally drifted away, murmuring to one another.
My grandfather had sent his two manservants with me that
day, and they guarded us to the duke's palace. We found it
full of bustle and noise from the tsar's retinue and preparations: there was to be a ball that night, and all the household
full of suppressed excitement; they knew of the negotiations
under way.

We were put into a better antechamber this time to wait, and then the chaperone came to fetch me. "Bring it with you. The men stay here," she said, with a sharp, suspicious glare. She took me upstairs to a small suite of rooms, not nearly so grand as the ones below: I suppose a plain daughter hadn't merited better before now. Irina was sitting stiff as a rake handle before a mirror made of glass. She wore snow-white skirts and a silver-gray silk dress over them, cut much lower this time to make a frame around the necklace; her beautiful dark hair had been braided into several thick ropes, ready to be put up, and her hands were gripped tightly around themselves in front of her.

Her fingers worked slightly against one another, nervous, as the chaperone pinned up the braids, and I carefully set the crown upon them. It stood glittering beneath the light of a dozen candles, and the chaperone fell silent, her eyes dreamy as they rested on her charge. Irina herself slowly stood up and took a step closer to the mirror, her nervous hand reaching up toward the glass almost as if to touch the woman inside.

Whatever magic the silver had to enchant those around it either faded with use or couldn't touch me any longer; I wished that it could, and that my eyes could be dazzled enough to care for nothing else. Instead I watched Irina's face, pale and thin and transported, and I wondered if she would be glad to marry the tsar; to leave her quiet, small rooms for a distant palace and a throne. As she dropped her hand, our eyes met in the reflection: we didn't speak, but for a moment I felt her a sister, our lives in the hands of others. She wasn't likely to have any more choice in the matter than I did.

After a few minutes, the duke himself came in to inspect her, and paused in the doorway of the room behind her. Irina was still standing before the mirror; she turned and curtsied to her father, then straightened again, her chin coming up a little to balance the crown; she looked like a queen already. The duke stared at her as if he could hardly recognize his own daughter; he shook himself a little, pulling free of the pull, before he turned to me. "You will have your gold, Panovina," he said. "And if your Staryk wants more of it, you will come to me again."

SO I HAD SIX HUNDRED gold pieces for the casket and two hundred more for the bank, and my sack full of silver pennies besides; a fortune, for what good it would do me. At least my mother and father wouldn't go cold or hungry again, when the Staryk had taken me away.

My grandfather's servants carried it all home for me. He came downstairs, hearing my grandmother's exclamations, and looked over all the treasure; then he took four gold coins out of the heap meant for the bank, and gave two each to the young men before he dismissed them. "Drink one and save one, you remember the wise man's rule," he said, and they both bowed and thanked him and dashed off to revel, elbowing each other and grinning as they went.

Then he sent my grandmother out of the room on a pretext, asking her to make her cheesecake to celebrate our good fortune; and when she was gone he turned to me and said, "Now, Miryem, you'll tell me the rest of it," and I burst into tears.

I hadn't told my parents, or my grandmother, but I told him: I trusted my grandfather to bear it, as I hadn't trusted them, not to break their hearts wanting to save me. I knew what my father would do, and my mother, if they found out: they would make a wall of their own bodies between me and the Staryk, and then I would see them fall cold and frozen before he took me away.

But my grandfather only listened, and then he said, "Do you want to marry him, then?" I stared at him, still wet-faced. He shrugged. "Sorrow comes to every house, and there's worse things in life than to be a queen."

By speaking so, he gave me a gift: making it my choice, even if it wasn't really. I gulped and wiped away my tears, and felt better at once. After all, in cold, hard terms it *was* a catch, for a poor man's daughter. My grandfather nodded as I calmed myself. "Lords and kings often don't ask for what they want, but they can afford to have bad manners," he said. "Think it over, before you turn away a crown."

I was tempted more by the power my grandfather had given me than the promise of a crown. I thought of it: to harden my heart a little more and stand straight and tall when the Staryk came, to put my hand in his and make it my own will to go with him, so at least I could say the decision had been mine.

But I was my father's daughter also, after all, and I found I didn't want to be so cold. "No," I said, low. "No, Grandfather, I don't want to marry him."

"Then you must make it better sense for him to leave you be," my grandfather said.

• • •

THE NEXT MORNING I ROSE, and put on my best dress, and my fur cloak, and sent for a sledge to carry me. But as I fastened the cloak around my throat in the sitting room, I heard a high cold jangling of bells drifting faintly in from the street, not the bells of a hired harness. I opened the door, and a narrow elegant sleigh drew up outside, fashioned it seemed entirely out of ice and heaped with white furs; the wolfen stag drew it, legs flashing, and the Staryk held the reins of white leather. The street lay blanketed by a thick, unnatural silence: empty even in midmorning, not another soul or sledge or wagon anywhere in sight, and the sky overhead gray and pearled-over like the inside of oyster shells.

He climbed out and came to me, leaving long boot prints in the snow down the walk, and came up the stairs. "And have you changed my silver, mortal girl?" he asked.

I swallowed and backed up to the casket, standing in the room behind me. He followed me inside, stepping in on a winter's blast of cold air, thin wispy flurries of snow whirling into the room around his ankles. He loomed over me to watch as I knelt down behind the casket and lifted up the lid: a heap of silver pennies inside, all I'd taken in the market.

He looked maliciously satisfied a moment, and then he stopped, puzzled, when he saw the coins were different: they weren't fairy silver, of course, though they made a respectable gleam.

"Why should I change silver for gold," I said, when I saw I'd caught his attention, "when I could make the gold, and have them both?" And then I untied the sack sitting beside the chest, to show him the heap of gold waiting inside.

He slowly reached in and lifted out a fistful of gold and let it drop back inside, frowning as he'd frowned each time: as though he didn't like to be caught by his own promises, however useful a queen would be who could turn silver to gold. What would the other elven lords think, I wondered, if he brought home a mortal girl? Not much, I hoped. I daresay in the story, the king's neighbors snickered behind their hands, at the miller's daughter made a queen. And after all, she hadn't even kept spinning.

"You can take me away and make me your queen if you want to," I said, "but a queen's not a moneychanger, and I won't make you more gold, if you do." His eyes narrowed, and I went on quickly, "Or you can make me your banker instead, and have gold when you want it, and marry whomever you like."

I PUT MY MONEY IN a vault and bought a house near my grandfather's; we even lent some of the gold back to the duke for the wedding. Isaac was busy for a month making jewelry for all the courtiers and their own daughters, to make a fine show at the celebrations, but he found time to pay visits to my family. I saw Irina once more, when she drove out of the city with the tsar; she threw handfuls of silver out of the window of the carriage as they went through the streets, and looked happy, and perhaps she even was.

We left the business back home in Wanda's hands. Everyone was used to giving her their payments by then, and she'd learned figuring; she couldn't charge interest herself, but as long as she was collecting on our behalf it was all right, and by the time everyone's debts had been repaid, she would have a handsome dowry, enough to buy a farm of her own.

I've never seen the Staryk again. But every so often, after a heavy snowfall, a purse of fairy silver appears on my doorstep, and before a month is gone, I put it back twice over full of gold.

This story was originally written for a 2016 anthology called The Starlit Wood: New Fairy Tales, *edited by Dominik Parisien and Navah Wolfe for Saga Press.*

COMMONPLACES

I love Irene Adler in all her many incarnations, but to be contradictory, I also often have a sneaking dissatisfaction with any one of them, starting with even her first appearance: there's a shape of a woman there I want to know and see, but I can't, quite, because her own author isn't seeing her truly. (I like to hope there are readers who feel that way about some of my own characters, someone who's become more real in their heads than I could get on the page.) So this is my attempt to write her into my sight.

My life is spent in one long effort to escape from the commonplaces of existence.
—SHERLOCK HOLMES, "The Red-Headed League"

THE NEWSPAPER IN LISBON CAME AT EIGHT AND went to Godfrey first, before he should leave for his office. "My wife is that treasure who does not require entertainment at the breakfast table," he liked to say of her to his friends; it would have been a little more accurate to say, Irene did not require the sort of entertainment she was likely to get out of Godfrey at the breakfast table, which did not very well meet the name.

She would have liked to take a section of the paper, but while Godfrey naturally obliged any such request, he would interrupt her in asking for pages back, that he might finish those items begun earlier. It was easier in the end to be patient, to let Godfrey keep the pages in neat order until he was done, while she spent her own breakfast sitting quietly in contemplation of her day and the small square of garden their cottage boasted. Her mornings when he had gone did not lack leisure.

"Sherlock Holmes is dead," he told her, before the maid had brought out the eggs, "at Reichenbach Falls."

She made absent expressions of dismay and shock, and when he had gone to his office, she read the story over three times: a bare paragraph describing the famous detective lost, a criminal mastermind claiming a final victim, his old companion left behind to give the report.

It was not much, and reading it over again did not make it grow longer. She already could have told the story over verbatim—years of practice from studying librettos—but even so she did not like to leave the paper on the table to be swept away; instead she carried it into the bedroom and put it into her bureau, and went outside to tend the roses. In twenty minutes she came back inside and read it once more, and then went out to the front stoop.

The street boys knew her, courtesy of a ball returned after a broken window without more than a calm request they should aim away from her house in future. They were happy to take a few pennies to fan out into the town for news for her. An hour brought her a slightly worn copy of *The Strand* with Dr. Watson's voice thick as old treacle on the page, full of studied melodrama and real grief.

At breakfast the next morning, she read it over and over again, while across the table Godfrey placidly read a fresh newspaper, full of different news.

THERE WAS NO REASON IT ought to have cut up her peace. She had not seen the man in two years and then had known him not at all: that he had once invaded her house in guise to rob her was not much foundation for affection, except what one might feel, she supposed, for a satisfying opponent one has bested. The story—of course she had read it—the story had been very flattering, but she had enough admirers to discount the value of another, even one who put her photograph above emeralds. And in any case, now he was dead.

The magazine went into the drawer with the newspaper, however.

Her mornings were of a settled round these days: what little management the little house needed, a trifle of work in the garden, a handful of calls received and returned. If her marriage had not made her wholly respectable, it had made her sufficiently so to permit her neighbors to indulge in an acquaintance which so satisfyingly allowed them to partake of just the least bit of notoriety, indirectly; to mention in whispers, at assemblies and balls, yes, that is her, the famous—

Irene tried not to think in such a way of them, those kind and stupid ladies who came visiting. Ordinarily she did not. She could not begrudge anyone a little excitement at so little expense to her, and they *were* kind: when she had been ill, last year—so wretchedly inadequate a word for that hollowed-out experience, tears standing in her eyes because she would not, would not let them run, not in front of the businesslike doctor speaking to Godfrey over her head, telling him prosaically they must be cautious, warning against another attempt too soon, while he washed his hands of the blood—

They had been really kind then, beyond polite expressions of sympathy: food appearing in those first few days when she could think not at all, and clean linen; Mrs. Lydgate and Mrs. Darrow coming by in the mornings with embroidery, sitting in perfect silence for hours while the window-squares of sun tracked a pathway across the sitting room. They had asked her to sing, a week later on, and when she had stopped halfway through "*Una voce poco fa,*" drooping over the pianoforte, they had taken up without a word a conversation about their unreliable maidservants, until she had mastered herself.

So she could not despise them anymore, because the kindness was real, as all the crowned glories had proven not to be; she knew better now, or thought she knew, how to value the treasures of the world against one another. But that week she found herself freshly impatient; she did not attend to the conversation in Mrs. Wessex's drawing room, until someone said to her, a little cautiously, "But you knew him, my dear, didn't you?"

"No," she said, "no more than the hare knows the hound."

"Well, it's a pity," Mrs. Ballou said, in her comfortably stolid way, without ever looking up from her knitting. "I'm sure I don't know what he was about, though, letting that dreadful man throw him off a mountain instead of calling the police, like a sensible man."

"Oh," Irene said, "yes," and taking her leave very abruptly went outside and stood in the street, half angry and half amused with herself, to be so schooled by a fat old dowager. Of course he was not dead.

She was not sure what to feel for a moment, but her sense of humor won out in the end, and she laughed on the doorstep and went home to throw the papers into the dustbin at last. There was an end of it, she told herself; it was the inherent absurdity of the story which had gnawed at her.

. . .

JOHN WATSON BELIEVED HIS OWN story, she was sure. He was, she thought, very much like Godfrey: the sort of man who would think it—not *romantic,* but rather quite ordinary *pro patria mori,* even if there were convenient alternatives to be had for the cost of a little reasoning. The sort of man who would trust in what a friend told him, unquestioningly, because to doubt would be faintly disloyal. Easy to fool such a man, and more than a little cruel to do so.

"Is something distressing you, my dear?" Godfrey asked, and she realized she was drumming her fingertips upon the writing table, while her correspondence went unanswered.

"I am only out of sorts," she said. "This wretched heat!" This was not a very just complaint: it was only the beginning of June, and lovely.

Two days later she took a train to Paris: alone, but for her maid. "If you would not mind waiting a week, I could tie up my affairs tolerably well," Godfrey said.

"You are very good, but in a week, I dare say the fit will have passed, and I will not want to go anywhere," Irene said. "Besides, I know you could not leave things in a state such as would leave you with an easy mind. No, I will fly away to Paris and repair my plumage, see some disreputable old friends and my very respectable singing-master, and come back just as soon as you have begun to miss me properly."

"Then you should have to turn around as soon as you had set foot out of the door," he said, gallantly.

She could be cruel too; perhaps that was what interested her.

. . .

IN PARIS, SHE LEFT HER maid behind in the hotel and went hunting. The whole enterprise was a shot at a venture, of course, but she thought either here or Vienna, and Paris was closer to Geneva. Irene spent the days sitting outside small cafés, legs crossed in neatly pressed trousers with her hair pinned back sharply under a top hat, sipping coffee and watching all the world as it passed before her table, noisy and vivid; watched women in elegant dresses going stately by like something from another life. Her nose was not yet used to the stench of the hansom cabs after so long in the quiet countryside; she felt herself set apart from it all, an observer by the side of the river.

When the lamplighters came around, she left a handful of coins and slipped away: to the Opéra, to the Symphony, where she bribed the ushers to let her in after the first act. Standing in the high tiers and off to the side, she studied the faces of the orchestras through a glass while below her Faust was carried away by demons, or Tchaikovsky's sixth tripped and glittered off the bows. Afterwards she went backstage with a bouquet of roses, instant camouflage against inquiry, and walked among the musicians to fish for accents.

On the fourth night she went to the Opéra-Comique, and the third violinist was a man with a narrow face, cheeks sallow and nose hawklike, who studied his music with more fierce concentration than a professional ought to have required.

She did not write to Godfrey that night: she spent it practicing beside the open window of her room, breathing in the warm, humid air of Paris, heads on the street turning up in the circle of gaslight below to look up as they went by.

Behind her, the maid unpacked the dresses from the traveling trunk and pressed them with a heated iron. In the morning, through an acquaintance, Irene presented herself to the director as Madame Richards from America, and sang just well enough to be placed in the chorus and considered a possible understudy for Rosette in *Manon*.

In her first rehearsals the next morning, she watched the violinist's shoulders. He did not turn from the music at all, but when she sang, one of fifteen voices, his head tilted a little, searching.

SHE DID NOT SPEAK TO him: he deserved, she thought, as much chance to escape as he had given her. But he was waiting for her when she came out of the stage door that evening, standing lean and straight beyond the waiting gaggle of boys who had brought flowers for the chorus girls. He was just out of the circle of lamplight, the brim of his top hat casting his face into shadow. She paused on the stairs, ignoring the handful of small bouquets offered to her consequence by those who, lacking some other object of affections, were considering whether to settle themselves upon her.

She smiled down at them and said in her full voice, undisguised, "Gentlemen, you are in my way." They let her through, not without a few looks after her, some a little surprised. But they were all boys, and the lovely young Mademoiselle Parnaud was directly behind her, so there were no eyes following by the time Irene reached him. She studied his face, curiously, as she had not had the opportunity to do before: he had handsome eyes, large and clear and grey, and his mouth was narrow but expressive.

"I have been insufficiently cautious, I find," he said, and offered her his arm. It was well muscled, if lean. They walked away together towards the Rue de Richelieu.

"I hope you do not have much cause for concern," she said. "If your nemesis indeed ended at the bottom of the Falls?"

"Yes," he said. "After I shot him, of course."

THEY HAD DINNER IN ANOTHER of the small anonymous cafés, sitting on the sidewalk with the noise of conversation and carriages around them. "Some of his lieutenants have escaped the net," he said, waving an impatient hand, long-fingered and pale, "but they are not of his caliber. They are all watching Watson, in any case."

"I suppose," she said thoughtfully, "that you will find that an excellent excuse to give him."

He looked at her sharply.

"It is not always easy to be adored," she said.

"No," he said. Then his mouth twisted a little, in wry amusement. "The only thing worse, of course—"

She nodded, and looked down into her coffee cup.

Her prince had taught her that lesson, with his jewels and his exclamations of surprise. He had never imagined she would take his engagement so badly. He had thought she was a woman of the world. He had thought she understood—and so indeed she *had* understood, after the fact: she had been loved only as a flower, set upon the mantel in a vase, inevitably to be discarded with the cloudy water.

Even in that first moment of harsh pain, she had not

regretted *him* in his person, not even on the rawest level—
his broad shoulders, his strong mouth. All her anger was to
have been so cheaply held, so easily cast off. She might have
dismissed it as his weakness, not hers; but she had chosen
him, after all.

She had taught *him* to regret *her,* though, and then she
had forgiven herself the mistake: she had been only a girl
then, not yet twenty, and after all she had learned quickly.
Only to be adored was, in the end, nothing; to be adored by
someone worthy, everything.

And oh, Godfrey was worthy, and she loved him, even if
something wild and errant in her still fought and struggled
against the necessary sacrifice of liberty and always would;
but she could not have him without it.

"How did you learn?" she asked, abruptly. "What taught
you—?"

"He married," Holmes said.

No need to ask who he meant, of course. "I encouraged
it," he added. "I wished that he were not necessary to me,
and so I convinced myself he was not; that I would do better
for solitude." He smiled, that wry look again. "I have had
more than enough leisure since to contemplate the irony of
having successfully deceived myself, who could scarcely be
led astray by the most dedicated attempts of all the criminals in London."

She did not ask him, of course, but there was a weary
regret in his face that made her quite certain the two of
them had never been lovers. He had thought of it, and rejected it, likely in defense of that same independence. Watson would have crossed that Rubicon for him, but he would
never have left, afterwards. A line from the story recalled

itself to her: *He never spoke of the softer passions, save with a gibe and a sneer*—some bitterness there, in Watson's words; he knew he had been refused, whether consciously or not. The marriage, Irene thought, had been some part revenge, and one startlingly complete, to have driven the man across the table into flight.

Irene had never before had the least cause to be grateful to that injustice which had made the sacrifice of her own virtue her own easiest road to independence, but at least she had never been tempted, afterwards, to think herself above such needs. "Will you go back?" she asked.

"Not while she lives," he said.

HIS ROOM WOULD HAVE BEEN untidy, but for the lack of possessions; no letters, no photographs, only a scattering of sheets of music on the windowsill and the dresser, and pieces of rosin for his bow left on the writing desk.

He was inexpert enough to confirm her suspicions, and taken aback by his own responses: a strange wrenched look on his face afterwards. She laughed at him softly, a greater kindness than pity, because he shook off the expression and came back into her almost fiercely.

Reputation had given her a dozen lovers, but in truth he was only the third to pass her bedroom door, and so very different from the others: thin and restless, and once he grew a little more sure of his ground, wholly without hesitation. It was splendid to feel she did not need to comfort or reassure, or indeed make any pretense whatsoever; she could interest herself only in her own pleasure, and in the freshness of the experience. She liked the hard planes of him, and the skilfulness of his hands, and his intensity: something almost of a fever running beneath his skin, which left a flush beneath the sharp-edged cheekbones.

In the morning she rose early and wrote Godfrey a letter from the writing desk, while Holmes slept on in the wreckage of the bed behind her, pale light through the window on his skin and the tangled white sheets; it was raining.

Paris is wet and beautiful in the spring as always, she wrote, *and I am glad that I came, but my darling, what is best is to know I have you to come home to, when I like the city have been watered at my roots. I feel myself again as I have not since last year. I am ready to be incautious again.*

"Commonplaces" was first published in The Improbable Adventures of Sherlock Holmes, *edited by John Joseph Adams, published by Night Shade, in 2009.*

SEVEN

It was inconsiderate of me to write a story called "Seven Years from Home" and also a story called "Seven": I apologize. I can't even claim that it was an accident; this was the second story of the two, and I recognized what I was doing at the time, but there wasn't any help for it. Sometimes you know a title from the beginning and sometimes you never know it and have to resentfully slap something on at the end, and in this case I knew it from the very first line.

This story is dedicated to Kathy Jane Tenold Speakman:
may her memory be a blessing.

NO ONE KNEW WHEN OR WHY THE CITY HAD FIRST been named Seven. There were ten walls running between six ancient towers that joined them into the city's five precincts, and four gates that went in and out of them. Seven was ruled by eleven: five councilors elected from the precincts, all women; five priests named by the temples, all men; and one king, to whom no one paid very much attention except when he had to break a tied vote, which the others made efforts to avoid.

Beneath the city ran thirteen mysterious tunnels carved by unknown hands. Once they had been the arches of bridges. Long since buried, they now carried the nourishing river under the city and out the other side to the wide ocean. Another city would have been named for that river, but instead it was the other way around: the river itself was called Seven's Blood, or just the Blood for short.

And whenever someone new came to the city, they always thought, incorrectly, that the city had been named for the seven great singing statues, although just like the river, their number had been chosen to grace the name instead.

By unwritten accord, nobody who lived in Seven ever corrected the visitors. It was how you knew someone was a fellow citizen, since you couldn't tell any other way. Among the people of Seven were the island cave-dwellers with their milk-pale skin, and brown fisher folk from the shores, and the deep-ebony farmers of the green fields that clung to the river before it reached the city, and travelers come on one of the thousand ships and boats and coracles that docked outside the walls every week. All those people had mingled furiously until there was not a feature or shade of skin or shape of brow or eye or chin that would let you distinguish a stranger who'd come through the gates five minutes ago from someone whose ancestors seven generations removed had lived all their lives in the city. Even accents differed wildly from one precinct to the next.

So no one told the strangers that Seven wasn't named for the statues. The seven of them stood at the gates that led in and out of the city. The Gate to Morning and the Gate to Evening and the Sea Gate each had two, and one stood alone at the Gate of Death. They didn't all sing at the same time, of course: even the ones that stood on either side of the same gate were angled differently into the wind, so it was rare for any two to sing at once, and if three or four were singing, it was time for the ships in the harbor to reef their sails and drop anchor and for the shutters to be closed so dust wouldn't whip into the houses. Elders told their grandchildren delightfully gruesome stories of the last great storm when all seven had sung at once.

They were made of the pale white clay that the river spilled out on the far side of the city, full of its effluvia. Broken bits of pottery and scraps of fabric mingled with human and animal wastes, flesh and bone and sludge and all the city's music. Clay-shapers had to work their hands over and over through every bucket they took, like squeezing fistfuls of flour and water, but there was a faint opalescent slick over the surface of that clay when it was fired that no one could mix or reproduce with glaze or paint. It was full of life, and therefore of death. No clay-shaper who put their hands to it wanted to work with any other, and none of them lasted more than five years before it killed them: a vein opened with a buried shard of glass or pottery, infections that festered, fevers that ate them away, or sometimes simply clay hunger that ran wild, so they worked day and night in their workshops until they fell down dead.

The statues had been meant, at first, to stop the city's clay-shapers dying. The law of Seven now decreed that the white clay could only be used to replace the statues. The desert and wind together ground them away little by little, and when a crack appeared, or the mouth and eyeholes gaped too wide to sing, or a surface was worn away to featureless smoothness, the council voted the honor of making a new one to the greatest of the city's clay-shapers. Once that shaper had finished their statue, they alone had the right to use the clay for the rest of their life, which was as a result generally short.

It happened once in a generation or so, and the fierce competition drove the rest to new heights. The craft of the great workshops grew ever more refined, and the ships carried away ever more delicate and fantastic vessels and cups and plates to all the distant reaches of the world. And whenever a statue cracked, and a new grandmaster was crowned, then for three years or four, sometimes five, a brief furious blossoming took place, and set the style for the next generation.

Kath was not the grandmaster of her generation: that was Hiron. He was unanimously elected to remake the left-hand statue at the Sea Gate, three years before Kath's marriage, and he died the year after it, of blood poisoning. Kath

herself was not even born to a clay-shaper family; she was
the daughter of a master ironsmith. But she married one of
the lower clay-shapers: a very good match. Her husband had
a small personal workshop where he made everyday pottery
for the lower classes: even the poor in Seven were proud of
the dishes they set on their table, whether or not they could
fill them. Unfortunately, he inconveniently died after father-
ing three children in the span of three years, with contracts
outstanding.

He had taught Kath how to throw a serviceable plate
and bowl and cup by then. After the three children were put
to bed, she closed the shutters and lit candles in his workshop and filled the orders. She claimed he had already made
them, they had only been air-drying before they went to the
kilns. The kiln masters were not supposed to allow anyone
not a member of the guild to fire their work, but they were
sorry for her, and the story was just plausible enough that
they accepted her pieces for firing. Afterwards she pretended that her husband had laid by a very large stock,
which miraculously matched what her buyers were looking
for, and the kiln masters kept letting her fill the bottom
rungs of their ovens.

But finally the end of her six months of mourning came
round, and the kiln masters turned to Grovin, the most
heartless of their number. He had neither wife nor child nor
even concubine; he cared for nothing except to preserve and
glorify the highest of the city's arts. He had fired every one
of the great Hiron's pieces, before the grandmaster had died;
it was rumored they had been lovers. Anyway, ever since he
had found out that his fellow masters had been letting the
widow's work through, he had been making increasingly

cold and pointed remarks about how the blowing desert sand wore away even the strongest porcelain. So they deputized him to ban her, and when she next approached pulling her week's wagonload, they all disappeared and left him to turn her away.

She had the baby in a sling across her front—Kath was far from a fool—and still wore her mourning gray. But Grovin paid no attention to the baby. He told her flatly, "Only a clay-shaper may use the kilns. Your husband is dead, and it is time for you to stop pretending to be what you are not and go back to your father's house."

There were six other unmarried daughters in her father's house. It had been crowded even before she had borne three children. "But, sir," Kath said, "surely you don't think an ironworker's daughter could make these?"

Grovin snorted, but when she threw the cover off her work, he looked, and then he looked again, and was silent. He bent and carefully took a piece out of the wagon, a small simple cup made for drinking vin, the strong liquor that the poor preferred. It was utterly contrary to the prevailing style, the one Hiron had set: Kath's piece had no ornament or decoration except a thin waving ridge that ran around the bowl just where the thumb might rest, inviting the hand to move the cup round as was traditional, tracing the endless line around.

The debate over letting her into the guild raged for seven days and nights, and was decided finally only because Grovin said flatly that he would fire her work even if no other clay-shaper came to his kiln as a result, and if he starved, so be it. They knew too well that he meant it. The masters of the clay-shapers' guild quietly agreed that the scandal would make more trouble than Kath would, so they let her in.

And indeed she didn't put herself forward; she continued to make only common, everyday pieces, and kept her prices low. But by the end of the year, there was a line at her door, and the poor reluctantly began to resell her older wares, because they could get too much money for them. Eventually she stopped taking advance orders: instead she made what she had clay to make and once a week opened her shop to sell whatever she had. Everything sold to the bare shelves.

The masters eyed her work uneasily. Hiron's statue at the Sea Gate was a marvel of the most delicate sculptural work; there was not a surface without ornament, and at its unveiling, a noble visitor from Wilsara over-the-sea had said—no one doubted it—that its song was as rich and complex and beautiful as the ten-thousand-voiced Great Chorus of the Temple of Thunder in that great city. For the last six years everyone had been striving to imitate and elaborate on his style. Kath's work seemed like a joke when one of her squat cups was put next to one of the grandmaster's triumphant fragile pieces, but if you looked at it too long, you began to feel the terrible sneaking suspicion that you liked the cup better.

Barely a month after she was let into the guild, the first few rebellious journeymen, mostly young men who liked to gather in taverns and argue loudly about art, began to imitate her style instead, and talk of the virtue of simplicity. While the fashion ought to have changed at some point, it was too soon, and too far. But no one knew what to do about it. A small group of the masters decided to go and speak to Kath and point out to her the hubris of setting up her own school, but the attempt foundered helplessly on the shoals of her solidity: her house full of yelling small children going in and out of the street playing, an untidy stack of her own pottery worth more than a chestful of jewels sitting dirty in the washtub, and Kath herself apologetically serving them tea with her own hands, because she explained the one maid was sick. It was impossible to accuse her of grandiose ambition, even as the masters held their mismatched cups as carefully as live birds, staring down at them and forgetting to drink until the tea was cold.

"So they've been to peck at you, have they?" Grovin said, that evening. He ate dinner at their house now. Kath had brought him home with her after she had learned he ate a dinner bought from a stall alone every night, disregarding his protests: he hated children, he hated women, he hated her cooking, and he hated company. He wasn't lying, he really hated all of those things, but whenever Kath threw a piece she liked very much, she kept it for home use—"That's your inheritance, so watch you don't break them," she told the children—and he did like great pottery, so after the first time eating off a blue-glazed plate that swelled from a faint shallow out to a thin edge, with small scalloped indentations all around the rim, he kept coming, and ate with his head bent over and staring down at whatever piece Kath was feeding him from that night, wincing and sullen at the noise around him.

"They don't mean any harm," Kath said. "I don't know what to say to them, though. I do what I like myself; that's all I know how to do. I couldn't do anything like Master Hiron's work without making a mash of it. But I told them so, and that I tell anyone who asks me as much, and they only looked glum."

Grovin knew the clay-shaper masters a great deal better than Kath did, and he knew perfectly well they did mean harm, by which *he* meant putting worse pottery into the world. "They'll make trouble for you," he said, but as it happened, he made the trouble, and worse.

Two days after the clay masters came to see Kath, the right-hand statue at the Gate of Morning began to hum softly, its voice going deeper and deeper until it was only just barely audible, a tickle of unease at the back of the listener's head. The clouds were already gathering over the sea, and the ships in the harbor were reefing their sails by the time the left-hand statue took up the song. Hiron's statue at the Sea Gate sang very frequently, but usually in a few thin, reedy voices; that night it was in full chorus, and even in the rain, some people had come out to hear it, although not quite as many as there should have been.

By the second night, no one was in the streets, or anywhere but huddled in the deepest cellars they could get to, and the seven voices of the statues could no longer be heard over the general howling of the wind. But when the ferocity was over, and everyone came blinking out into the washed-clean streets, a path of total destruction as wide as three streets had been inscribed across the city, as though some god had come out of the sea and walked straight through to the Gate of Death, the holy gate, and the statue there, less than a hundred years old, had been obliterated.

"Oh, shut up, you cowards, you all know it's got to be her!" Grovin shouted down impatiently, after the masters had all spent the first hour of their discussion very carefully not saying Kath's name. The kiln masters were allowed to come and sit in the gallery during the deliberations for a new grandmaster.

So were the journeymen clay-shapers, and after Grovin's shout, all of them burst out into clamoring, either in support or in violent opposition. Four fistfights broke out in the gallery and one on the floor. But that was exceptionally modest; there had been twelve, during the debate over Hiron's appointment. Even the ones who didn't *want* to name Kath—the very ones who had gone to lecture her, the previous week—had the uneasy sense that they had better. It seemed too pointed a message from the gods.

"But I can't," she said bewildered to Grovin, when he told her, smugly, afterwards. He stared at her speechlessly, and she stared back in equal incomprehension. "What would happen to the children? Anyway, I don't want to die just to work in bone clay. That's a thing for a fool young man to do, or a fool old one, not a sensible woman!"

"Your work will live forever while your children are dry in their tombs!"

"Unless my statue breaks after a hundred years," Kath said tartly, "and I'd rather live on in my children's hearts than a face of stone."

Grovin spent an outraged hour straight shouting at her, then stormed out finally in a rage and went straight to the Gate of Death, and the temple of the goddess outside it, which had just escaped the general devastation. It was very large and grand and mostly deserted; everyone wanted to bribe Death, but few wanted to court her. There was only one priest, who listened to Grovin's furious tirade and asked mildly, "What do you want?"

"I want her to make the statue!" Grovin said.

The priest nodded. "You ask for her death, then."

Grovin did hesitate for several moments. But then he said, "She's going to die anyway. Everyone does. But her work could live."

"All things come to the goddess in the end," the priest said. "But if you want to speed things up, you have to make fair return. A life, for a death."

Grovin hesitated again, but to do him what small justice he deserved, not as long as the first time. "Very well," he said, proudly and grandly, and three days later, the pains started in Kath's belly. The priest at the temple of Forgin—the god of surgeons and their tools, a favorite of ironsmiths—palpated her stomach and shook his head. "The mass is large enough to feel. A year, perhaps."

Kath walked out with Grovin and went home in silence, stricken. He didn't precisely feel guilty; he was still full of his own righteous sacrifice. But he did wait several hours, until after the children were in their beds and Kath had sat by them all for a long time. Only then, when she came back to the table and mechanically made the evening tea, he finally said, "Well, you'll do it now."

She looked up and stared at him with the teapot in her hand, still hollow, and then she paused—not quite as long as he had, in the temple—and then she put down the teapot and said to him flatly, "No. Not unless you marry me first."

Grovin stared at her. "What?"

"If you marry me and take the children as your own," she said. "Otherwise I won't."

"You have six sisters!"

"And they'll make it a fight over who takes my children in, for the chance of taking their inheritance, too," Kath said. "Marry me, and give the children a home, and I'll make the statue and work the white clay, as long as I can, to provide for them. Besides," she added, "they'll look after you in your old age," and Grovin almost opened his mouth to say that he wasn't going to *have* an old age, when he suddenly remembered the priest saying *a life for a death,* and understood only then, in real horror, that *this* was the price: he was indeed going to have an old age, and more to the point a long life of raising three small children, one of whom couldn't speak in complete sentences yet.

But he knew better than to try and go back on a bargain with the goddess, so the next morning he and Kath were married, in a quiet ceremony attended only by her family and a group of young journeymen who drank at the tavern around the corner from her house; they followed in delight to witness Grovin's doom: he was generally viewed with irritation by them all, for being a little too dedicated to art and showing up their own professed devotion.

Afterwards Grovin moved in with her: when she'd asked him to give her children a home, she'd only meant it in the legal sense. She'd already three months before bought the house next door to expand her workshop, so there should have been plenty of room, but the chaos of the household spilled into all the space available. Grovin put his small box down in the middle of a bedchamber that held a broken birdcage, a collection of small rocks, two rickety shelves, and six small boxes arranged behind little clay horses like a caravan, each one holding precarious towers of glorious glazed cups for cargo, one of which had already been chipped by the rough handling. He sprang to rescue them and looked around himself in almost savage despair, thinking of his own two-room house, scrupulously clean, with large cabinets against every wall, full of carefully spaced pottery, and his small cot in the middle of one room and his small table with its one chair in the other.

The next day, Kath went grimly to the clay fields, trailed by a ceremonial escort and a practical mule cart. Mostly when a new grandmaster first came to the fields, he spent a day alone in vigil, carefully sieving a few handfuls of the raw slip over and over to get the feel of it. Kath just had the two young men she'd hired shovel the slip into jugs and buckets until the cart was loaded up, and then drove back with it to the house. Two of her brothers-in-law, both ironworkers, had forged her five screens, going from one very coarse to one very fine, with large pans to go underneath them. The young men shoveled the clay on top of the coarse one and rubbed it through with wooden sticks, leaving behind a glittering deadly mess of pottery shards and pebbles, broken knife blades, chips of stone, frayed moldy rags. Whatever clay made it through into the pan, they rubbed through the next screen, and so on. Even the finest screen came out clogged with tiny gleaming slivers too small to tell if they had started as clay or iron or stone. When the last pan was full, they put the slip into a bucket and carried the screens and pans to the nearest fountain and washed them completely clean. Grovin followed and watched aghast as long trailing rivulets of precious white clay went running away into the gutters, along with all the detritus. He was not alone: the journeymen from the tavern were half-gleefully shocked in audience, and apprentices peeking in on their errands.

But the men Kath had hired were only laborers, and didn't care. They carried the clean pans and screens back to the workshop and rubbed the clay through a second time, and then a third. Three days later, after the clay was dry, Kath put on a pair of gloves made of very fine mail, and then another pair of thick leather and wool, and then a third of coarser mail, and went through the clay putting a handful at a time into a fresh bucket, poring over each one with the cold suspicion of someone eating a badly deboned fish. She only ended with three buckets of clay left out of the entire cartload.

She didn't begin with the statue, of course; she made a few test pieces. Grovin, sitting hunched in the kitchen trying not to watch the children playing roughly with three clay toy horses, spent the days in horrible thoughts: what if she wasn't good at working the white clay, what if it diminished her prosaic pieces, what if she had ruined the clay with too much sieving?

Finally she came out of the workshop with six cups and two bowls on a tray for him to fire, and they were ruthlessly unadorned, even compared to most of Kath's work. Everything was in the shape, and the shape was a little *too* simple, too stark, but Kath only said, "Fire them and we'll see," tiredly, and went to put dinner on with her hands unbloodied. When he brought them back after the first firing, she only made a simple bucket of clear glaze and dipped them three times, nothing more, and handed them back over.

But when he took them out of the kiln at last, he stood sweating and silent looking at them for a long time. The starkness was unchanged, and the glaze had dried clear, with an irregular crackling that interrupted and somehow brought forth the strange opalescent finish, and he picked up the first one before it was cool enough and burned his seamed leathery hands holding it, breathtaken, his eyes wet.

He carried the tray back to her house with a ceremonial air; not inappropriate, since the streets were full of supposedly loitering clay-shapers, who had all gathered to catch a glimpse. There was even a gathering of a dozen masters at the corner of Kath's street, all of them pretending they had accidentally run into one another. Grovin stopped beside them and they gathered around and handled the bowls and the cups in silence, turning them and passing them from one to the other, before reluctantly putting them back on the tray and letting him go into the house.

Kath looked at the tray and only nodded a little, still looking tired; she was sitting down, although it was the middle of the day, and she had a hand over her stomach. "It'll do," she said, and then she took one of the cups, mixed strong wine with water out of the jug, and drank it down.

In the meantime, several more cartloads of clay had come in, and been sieved and washed and dried and winnowed. She began on the statue the next day. The head was as long as Kath's arm from chin to crown, and almost faceless, only the slightest suggestion of the curve of chin and cheek, as if seen through a heavy veil. The mouth was the only opening, and that only a little, the surface of the clay caving softly into it as if a pocket of the veil had been breathed in. When Grovin saw it, he felt a stirring of unease, a guilty man who fears that his wife knows what he's been doing with his late evenings and is just waiting to make him sorry for it. "A woman?" he said, to cover it.

Kath said, "One I'm likely to know better soon," with a ghost of humor, and he squirmed.

"Only one copy?"

"Yes," Kath said. "If it doesn't come out, I'll make another."

While it dried, she went back to making cups and bowls and plates, a small steady stream piling up. The smaller pieces dried quicker; they were ready to go into the kiln along with the head. Every one of them came out well; the head came out cracked down the middle and stained with smoke. He brought it back dismayed, but Kath only shrugged and began on another copy.

It was four months before the head came out clean, and Grovin was in rising alarm by then. But Kath ignored his increasing hints. She made one head at a time, weeks to dry it out, and in the waiting she heaped up more cups and plates and bowls and pots and jugs, so many that they made walls inside the walls of her workshop, so many that they overwhelmed the hunger and purses of Seven, and to empty the shelves Kath sold chests full to sea captains taking them away to distant cities. Gold took their place, and then that went out again in chests: she bought houses for each of the children to inherit, and for each of her sisters, and paid to apprentice all their sons to clay-shapers.

But of the statue there was nothing, except one broken or flawed face after another. Grovin had a moment of intense relief when one fired without a crack, but as soon as he brought it out into the daylight, he knew it *was* wrong. He had to study it for ten minutes before he saw the flaw: a faint line running from the left eye down the cheek, where the glaze had fought with the opalescence instead of marrying it, but even before he found it, he knew.

He brought it back to Kath anyway, in desperation, hoping that she might at least move on before recognizing that it wouldn't do, but she only looked at him in surprise and then asked, "Are you feeling all right?" suspiciously, and made him drink a dose of one of the dozen medicines that now lined up on the high shelf above the table where the children couldn't reach. Then she went back into the workshop and started over yet again. That head joined the others, in their cracked and broken pieces, in the alley behind the house where Grovin had to go twice a day to collect the children from the courtyard. He disliked walking past them.

At last the seventh head fired perfectly, though, and when he brought it out he sagged in relief and then put his hands over his face and wept. He had spent six hours the night before walking up and down with one of the children crying on his shoulder with toothache. The night before that, he had spent five such hours, after first spending an hour lying awake listening to Kath doing the same, and thinking of how little work she would be able to do, until those thoughts drove him to get up and send her to sleep. The day before that, the oldest boy had knocked over a salt-cellar and smashed it into shards, and when Grovin had shouted in horror, the child burst into tears and Kath came running out of her workshop, hands wet with clay. Grovin had looked in past her shoulder just in time to watch a half-formed jug slumping into a formless pile on her wheel, like an undertow tide dragging away a jewel. He was very tired.

But when he took the head back to the house, Kath looked at it and sighed with something that wasn't quite relief. "Well, I'll go on, then," she said, and gave him another wagonload of small pieces to fire.

She did all the statue the same way, one piece at a time, over and over until it came out properly. The year went, and the stomach pains came, but she refused to be hurried. The temple physician shrugged when Grovin finally dragged her there. "It hasn't grown much. Another year, perhaps? Who can say." Kath only nodded and went back to her workshop.

The goddess grew slowly in the back alley, lying flat gazing up at the sky. Tuning the sound of the statue was ordinarily a vast and difficult aspect of the task, but Kath made no effort to do anything towards it as far as Grovin could see. The statue only occasionally made an unpleasant shrill whistling noise, like a kettle not quite boiling, when the wind ran into the opening at the bottom. The pitch changed only slightly as the body grew slowly down from the neck to the shoulders over the next year.

At the end of the second year, the priest of Forgin shrugged again, and sent them away with no promises. The statue crept towards its waist. Crate upon crate of bone clay dishes went out the front door. The young journeymen from the tavern had persuaded Kath to give them places in her workshop in exchange for doing her errands; they made dishes out of ordinary clay, but in her style. Grovin eyed them with disdain and refused to fire their pieces, except for one or two he grudgingly allowed as not entirely worthless. They were all annoyed with him, until one day they weren't, and began demanding that he tell them what was wrong with each piece they made, which annoyed him instead. But little by little they improved, roughly at the same rate as the statue grew.

The children grew also. At some point, Grovin couldn't even keep thinking of them as *the children,* as much as he tried to; now they were Shan, who came home from playing boisterous games every day in cheerful dirt he had not the least hesitation in marking all the dishes with, and Maha, who liked to put together mismatched plates whenever she was told to set the table, and Ala, who still didn't talk much and managed in her quiet obstinate way to get into the workshop every day. Grovin at last gave up and tolerated it because she didn't interrupt Kath's work. She only sat in a corner and watched, not her mother's work but her mother, as if she was trying to store up something she hadn't been told was soon to be gone.

Grovin had fed them and bathed them and told them bedtime stories of the hideous fates that awaited evil children who smashed breakable things, which they all loved so much that they demanded new ones every night, although they showed no signs of becoming more careful with the dishes as a result. He had grudgingly begun to teach Shan his letters, mostly to keep him sitting in one place for a while and away from the crockery, and Maha had begun to pick them up as he did.

Ala had no interest. But one morning Grovin came out and looked into the workshop: he measured his days by

whether Kath was well enough and sufficiently free from
distraction to get up and start working in the morning. She
wasn't there, but Ala was sitting at her table, playing with
scraps of clay as all the children often did, only she was playing with scraps of bone clay, and when he rushed inside, she
looked up at him and stopped him by holding up a thumb
cup, the first work of apprentices, which Kath often made
and encouraged her own journeymen to do, pressed out with
fingers and hands instead of on the wheel. Ala's cup was not
competent; her small fingers had left lumpy marks and visible fingerprints, and the rim was uneven, but it had something more than the charm of a child's work, which you liked
only because you loved the child, which Grovin resolutely
didn't. He would gladly have picked it from a shelf in some
cheap secondhand shop and put it on display next to a few
examples of the journeyman work of the same clay-shaper,
and then a single masterwork, to see the development of the
eye and hand and style. He took it from her hands very carefully and put it on the shelf with the drying pieces and led
her to wash her hands in the small basin Kath kept always
ready now, with a row of jugs the journeymen filled fresh at
dawn and a big slop bucket beneath to dump the water in
after every single washing. He a little reluctantly said, "You
must not touch the white clay again," as he made her first
soak her hands and wave them around in the basin before
bringing them out to be washed with the sludgy soap Kath
kept half dissolved in a dish on the counter.

"It's not the clay," Ala said.

It was as long a sentence as he had ever heard her produce, but he didn't care, so he wasn't paying much atten-

tion. "The bone clay," he said sternly again. "You must not touch it."

Ala looked up at him from the basin and said, "It's not the *clay* hurting Mama," with an effort that made it seem an accusation. Grovin flinched. He did not know what to say, but he was rescued: Kath came in, saw what he was doing, and in moments she was scolding and alarmed, and then Ala said again, "It's not the clay!" and burst into tears.

The whole morning was lost to soothing her: when she finally recovered and ran outside to play and yell, Kath spent an hour just sitting tiredly at the table, breathing deeply over a cup of tea. "Well, at least it's *not* the clay," she said finally, with a ghost of humor, and Grovin stared down at his hands as she pushed herself up and went at last into the workshop. He still wasn't paying attention to anything but his own guilt; it took him catching Ala with the bone clay a second time, two weeks later, making a roly-poly bliba figurine of the kind that the children of Seven loved to play with, round clay balls for arms and legs and head and belly. She didn't repeat herself, only stared at him mulishly after he finished lecturing, the figure on the table with its slightly tilted expression staring at him too, and in her silence, Grovin finally heard the words.

Hiron had been twenty-seven when he'd been chosen, ferociously proud and careless of his health the way only a healthy young man could be. He had never spoken a word of fear or hesitation to Grovin; the closest he'd ever said was, "They're usually giving it to dried-up old ancients. It's no wonder they die so soon. Anyway, no one can live forever," smiling, and he'd smiled even after he'd shown Grovin the hand of his statue, the intricate surface with its layers of small disks built up, tiny mountains like an army of bliba figures flattened out, and the palm stained dark brown with his blood, like a mirror of the white bandage wrapped around his own hand. It had been only three months after he'd begun. "A piece of glass," he'd said, still careless. "I didn't see it. It's nothing, a shallow slice, the priest says it'll be closed in a week."

The wound had closed only after three, and the scar never stopped being irritated and red. Both of Hiron's hands had been a battlefield of faint scar lines and half-healed cuts by the Festival of the Sun, and one of the other masters had even ventured, "Perhaps you should rest them a while." Grovin had eyed the man with irritation: at that very moment Hiron had been halfway through the magnificent breastplate, a marvel of delicate carving done at just the right stage of air-drying; he rose three times a night to check the sections, to be sure he didn't miss the chance.

Hiron had laughed a little, and said, "I'll rest them when the statue is done," but a month later, he had rested them sooner after all, because he spent a week vomiting and with the flux. Grovin hovered, feeding him soup and bread and wine with honey, miserably anxious: there were four pieces waiting for carving. Hiron tried to go to the workshop once, but his hands were shaking too badly; he scarred one piece beyond redemption, and then had to run staggering to the pot again anyway. After four days, Grovin looked in on the pieces that morning, then went back to his bedside and said, "It's no use, they're gone. You'll have to remake them when you're well again," and Hiron had wept a little before he turned to the wall and slept for the better part of three days.

His hands were healed a little more after the enforced rest, but he had a hollowed blue look to his face that hadn't been there before. He had been slower, afterwards; he only lost three pieces waiting for carving when feverish shakes laid him up two months later. He was sick three times during the rainy season, and listless; he was better once the weather dried out, but when the statue went up at last— after only eleven breakneck months of work—he came home from the dedication ceremony and lay down and was sick for a solid month with an illness no priest or physician or wisewoman could name or cure. Grovin brought a dozen through to look at him, spending the last of his own money to do it; Hiron had not sold a single piece since beginning to make the statue, and Grovin had not fired anyone else's work. Neither of them had ever put much of anything aside.

The landlord came by and apologetically said that he had to have the back rent, which wasn't to be had. Grovin had to sell four pieces of his prized collection, in anguish, although he managed to sell them to temples to be put on display, so at least he could go and visit them. "Never mind," Hiron said, consolatory. "The statue's done. As soon as I'm well, I'll sell some pieces, and you'll buy them back, if you really want to bother." Hiron himself had never had much patience for the work of other clay-shapers.

He did rise at last, thinner, and went back into the workshop, back to the clay. But he wasn't quite the same. Grovin swallowed it for a month, but he couldn't bear it; when Hiron tried to hand him one truly awful urn, finally Grovin burst out, "What are you doing? This looks like the work of those guildless imitators down by the docks, making trash to pawn off as the grandmaster's work. It's—*timid*."

Hiron had flinched, and then he'd smiled again, a little waveringly, and said, "You're always right, Grovin," and then he'd taken the piece and smashed it. His pieces improved after that, but there was still a thread of what Grovin called caution running through them, something withheld, for the next two years. Hiron wasn't sick quite as often, and once he was making pieces for sale, there was more money for food and firewood, although never quite enough to buy back Grovin's pieces. Hiron never brought in nearly as much as Kath with her crates full of dishes, and the money had somehow vanished more quickly even with only their two mouths to feed.

Then at the start of the fourth year, the blood-poisoning took hold. Hiron was feverish every evening, even when he felt well in the mornings. Everyone consulted could name it, of course; the symptoms were well known. There was no cure, except to stop working the bone clay. The grandmaster Ollin had even done so some two centuries before; he had died a year later in a plague and was still spoken of disdainfully among clay-shapers as having been justly punished for cowardice. Hiron and Grovin had insulted his name amongst themselves many times.

Hiron didn't stop working the clay. Grovin was a little afraid at first—not of that, but of another weakening in his work. But the timidity didn't return. Hiron's work bloomed instead, going abruptly larger and stranger and even more complicated and convoluted. The pieces he made had no purpose but display, and found few buyers, but Grovin gloated over them with brooding joy, firing them with immense care and almost alone in the kiln; he added in only grudgingly enough other goods to pay for the fuel, at rates so low that their shapers wouldn't complain about having their work treated dismissively and shoved to the sides. Hiron's pieces became still more wild as the fevers crept further and further into his days, figures that twisted and writhed as if against strangling bonds. He had long since stopped speaking of *when I'm better*. But he still never spoke of fear. Grovin took all the pieces that didn't go in the final sale and used them to decorate Hiron's tomb: a monument he considered greater than the statue itself, even if less refined tastes didn't appreciate it properly.

Hiron had lasted four years, in the end. Longer than most grandmasters. But the bone clay had been taking him from almost the beginning; in a long, slow feasting, not a quick slaughterhouse blow. Sitting in Kath's workshop, Grovin stopped lecturing Ala and instead looked down at her small, tender, unmarked hands. When Kath came in, he took her hands and turned them over, peering close: one small burn, from touching a cooking pot, and not a single cut, and her pains had not changed since the day they had first gone to the temple of Forgin three years before. She had been ill, now and again, but not with clay fever, or poisoning, or infections.

"Well, I'm not having *you* be the proof," Kath said to Ala, and sent her to sit in her room for punishment, and then she called in her journeymen and told them all that she'd let some of them knead the bone clay for her, if they were willing to try and see if any of them began to be ill. "But don't any of you do it if you have a child coming," she added, "and I won't have any bragging or teasing; it's not a joy worth dying for."

Grovin stifled himself before them, but when the journeymen had boiled out again in glee, he snapped, "It *should* be. That's what's wrong with their work: they don't care enough."

"If they don't care enough to die for it, that's as much as saying they've got sense," Kath said, washing her hands off, and for a moment he hated her.

"Do you feel nothing of your own art?" he said through his teeth. "I hardly know how you can make your work when you talk of it like a farmer, only worried about bringing your crop to market. I suppose there are birds that sing without understanding their own music—"

Kath startled round at him, surprised and hurt, but even as he stopped, she went indignant instead; she faced him and put her hands on her hips. "You love pottery because you've put your heart inside it," she said, sharp, "and you don't love the world because you've put none of yourself into any other part of it. Well, my heart's not shut up in a jar on a shelf. I understand my work, better than you. I'm making a thing out of the bones of the dead, and if it lives again, it's only because someone living loves it, even if it's just me myself. You can pretend, if you like, that a lump of baked clay means something on its own, even if no one touches it or looks at it or rejoices in it, and make that your excuse for not caring what any human being needs or wants. It's just another way of being selfish."

She swiped her wet hands off against her hips, back and forth, a decided gesture, and walked out of the workshop, back into the kitchen, with the shouting children. Grovin stood unmoving and blind there a long moment, and when he saw again, he had turned without realizing it towards the door, towards the faces of the goddess, blackened with smoke, cracked, misshapen; the goddess with her veiled face with its open mouth waiting, waiting to breathe and live.

"Seven" was first printed in Unfettered III: New Tales by Masters of Fantasy, *published by Grim Oak Press in 2019.*

BLESSINGS

The first fairy of my acquaintance was out of a Polish fairy tale, a mysterious and crotchety old woman in an enormous mushroom hat, handing out tiny bits of magic like breadcrumbs to lead a heroine into adventure and the doing of good. She's not in this story herself, but she certainly knows the wedding guests.

GRACE," THE DRUNK FAIRY SAID, "IS BY FAR THE BEST of the blessings."

She was drunk because her hostess, who herself had been blessed with hospitality—and a reasonably wealthy husband—had spent the months before her first child's birth in a fever of preparations, determined to obtain at least one blessing for her own offspring. She had brewed her own fairy wine out of blackberries and wild elderflowers that she and her ladies had picked in the woods, pricking many a finger in the process, and she had coaxed her husband to keep hunting until he managed to get three dozen pure white rabbits—"In winter!" he'd complained in exasperation—which had been stewed and baked into an elaborate pie. On the side of the room, the servants could be observed making the preparations to serve the final course, a fine white cake using a recipe of her own devising, made from fresh-laid eggs and newly churned butter, and dressed with candied flowers and even a ring of preserved orange slices. Even by fairy standards, it was an exceptional meal.

The fairy repeated, "By *far*," the remark delivered as a challenge, as she sat down again somewhat wobbly at the high table, and held out her wineglass to be refilled: she had just finished bestowing that very blessing on the small girl in the crib at the head of the room, and now could sit back to her meal in full enjoyment, with the smug consciousness of having amply repaid her hostess. Grace might not have been the most dramatic of the blessings, but it was indeed highly valued, being exceptionally open to interpretation, and rarely given to any child of such low rank—the mother was the daughter of a mere knight, and the father, despite his reasonable wealth, only a baron.

The five other fairies scowled at her. They too were all drunk and well fed, and the meal in their bellies was taking on the sour heaviness of an unpaid debt. They had all brought trinkets for the baby, of course, all the gift that could formally be expected by a low nobleman—which was why six of them had been invited in hopes of getting at least one blessing—but the feast had also exceeded what could formally be expected for their having deigned to grace the occasion. They could hardly refuse the cake, either—and didn't want to—and would have a lingering sense of a favor owed.

"Nonsense," a second fairy said. (I cannot, of course, tell you their names.) "Nonsense! Grace, for the child of a baron! Putting the cart before the horse." She pushed her own chair back and heaved herself out of it, marched up to the crib, and announced loudly, "Ever may this child's hands run bright with gold, and all the coffers of her house swell with riches!" She returned to the table and surveyed the others with a smugly superior lift to her chin. "Now that's a proper blessing."

She too held her glass out for more wine as a low pleased murmuring went around the room. Two blessings made a remarkable haul for a child of this rank, and wealth in particular was rarely given. It was too valuable to those who didn't have it—who often couldn't afford to properly feast fairies anyway—and too redundant to those who'd acquired it without mystical help. But at this rank of nobility, nothing could have been more ideal. The mother was beaming and delighted, already thinking of the excellent match her twice-blessed daughter would surely make, and the father not only delighted but relieved; he'd spent considerably more than he'd wanted to on the celebration, and he'd been worrying about how he'd repay the coin he'd borrowed to do it. But no one now would hesitate to lend money to him, and at very good rates. Even the guests smiled sincerely, rather than with envy; the parents, not being very important, had invited their friends and not their enemies to the christening of their child. The occasion had gone from ordinarily happy to auspicious, and all the company were pleased to be present. The musicians struck up another song with enthusiasm—rightfully expecting better tips—as the happy father waved a hand to them.

"Oh, wealth's all well and good," said the third, from out of the depths of her dark cloak. She was a shadowed fairy, and rather alarming even to her companions, but she lived nearer the father's house than any of the others, in a deep cave somewhere up in the mountains. The baron had known better than to slight her, of course, but his lady had gone beyond that, and sent the invitation with a personal note written in her own hand that they very much hoped to have the pleasure of her company, and a small package of sweet-meats. It was not the traditional sort of courting sent to shadowed fairies—the kind of lord who really wanted their attendance was more likely to send a gift of the knuckle-bones of plague victims—but the sweetmeats had been carefully made with rotted walnuts and pig's blood, and at the feast, the fairy had discreetly been served a plate of raw calves' liver dressed with a sauce of nightshade on a plate of tarnished silver. She had refused the fairy wine, but the hostess had quickly had a word with her steward, and a great goblet of steaming beef blood fresh from a newly slaughtered ox had been brought to the table, laced heavily with old brandy, and the fairy had drunk the entire thing down.

She now covered her mouth and belched out a thin trail of smoke. "Well and good indeed," she went on, "until someone takes it from you," and rose from the table in turn.

A hush descended as she went to the baby, her footsteps ringing ominously loud, and the parents began to look anxious: even if she hadn't been a shadowed fairy, three blessings was a little inappropriate for anything other than royalty. They looked still more anxious when the fairy stretched out a grey withered hand over the crib and intoned, "Let power come easily to her hand and there remain, and to her come dominion over the realms of men!"

The hush became silence. Three blessings was extravagant anyway, and power was a gift bestowed far more rarely even than wealth, as it involved a significant risk for the fairy in question. If two people blessed with the gift of power ever confronted one another, one fairy gift or the other would likely be proven false. (While I am not entirely certain what would happen to the losing fairy in this situation, I am assured it would be unpleasant.)

The remaining fairies could have left things well enough alone here, and should have, but as the shadowed fairy slouched deep into her seat again, she issued a small snort. "There, what's better than *that*? I'm surprised none of you twittering lot slapped a pretty face on her."

Fairies enjoy being taunted roughly as much as do boys

of twelve, and respond with as much maturity. The fourth fairy—who had just polished off her eighth glass of wine—sneered in heavy sarcasm, "Why would anyone do that? She'd be better off ugly as you instead!"

She instantly covered her mouth as the whole room gasped, but it was too late; the gift had flown. The mother made an abortive move towards the crib, her face falling, and the fairy looked abashed and guilty beneath the many censorious looks thrown her way. Looking around for a solution, she pointedly elbowed the fifth fairy, a spring fairy who would be half asleep for another two months anyway and under the influence was snoring gently away with her mound of grey-brown hair, dressed elaborately with vines of ivy, beginning to slide comprehensively off her head. "Wha?" the fifth fairy said.

"There's nothing like being *strikingly* ugly," the fourth fairy said, urgently, a hint that would have worked just fine on a fairy about half as drunk as this one.

"Go on, listen to you!" the soused fairy said groggily. "Strength! That's the best of them, everyone knows. Strength to the babe!" she added firmly, groping for her glass and toasting it in the crib's direction vigorously enough to splatter.

There was another round of gasps, broken up this time by tittering. The shadowed fairy shook with malicious cackles and the fourth fairy, glad to shift guilt over, snatched up a napkin and swatted the fifth, abusing her as the ivy came off the rest of the way. "You green-headed leaf peeper! Strength, for a girl! Get under the table with you!" as the first two fairies looked on and shook their heads in righteous disapproval.

Her twin sister, sitting on the other side, took offense both at the attack on her sister and at *leaf peeper*. "Much you should talk, handing out ugliness!" she said. "What's wrong with strength? Strong let her be, and see which does her more good, our gift or yours!"

"NO, THANK YOU," MAGDA SAID, graciously, and tuned out the formalities as the very relieved duke's son looked up—the first time he'd actually looked her in the face—and begged her to reconsider.

A doubled gift made all the others lean towards it; she couldn't have any of the ugliness of ill health, only the ugliness of brute strength. That was the only thing anyone saw when they looked at her, that she could pick them up and break them in half like giants did when mounted knights got too close, shelling them like lobsters. None of her features were ugly enough to stand out, none were nice to look at, and all together they made a bad painting without enough colors. But the proposals came anyway: she was destined to be rich and powerful, and she had six fairy godmothers looking after her interests.

She repeated her refusal, he gratefully promised not to trouble her any longer, and took himself away in a hurry. She had been left alone in the garden with him; as soon as he left, she tossed the embroidery hoop aside onto the bench and went to the back wall. She'd left her old bow and spare quiver there, tucked at the base behind a shrub. She slung them on, then jumped for the top, caught it easily and pulled herself easily over, and was free from her chaperone for the rest of the afternoon, which was the reason she'd agreed to entertain the proposal in the first place. She felt a little sorry for having alarmed the duke's son, who'd been decently polite about his courting, but at least she hadn't made him worry for long, and her mother would have made a fuss, otherwise.

She didn't risk her freedom by going to the stables for a horse. She jumped the moat behind the garden wall and jogged along the dusty track up into the Blackstrap Mountains on foot instead. It was a nice autumn afternoon, and only seven miles or so. It had been almost a year since the last time she'd managed to escape—her mother had kept closer reins on her since her sixteenth birthday—but she still knew the way. She stopped in the orchards to pick a good apple for herself to munch, and a few wormy and wizened ones to tuck into her good skirt, which she'd already tied up around her waist.

"I brought you some spoiled apples, Godmama," she said, poking into the mountain cave. "Withered and worm-eaten on the branch."

The shadowed fairy grunted in approval from the depths of the cave where she was stirring something noxious. "Put them on the bench there. What have you been doing with yourself all this time?"

"Courting," Magda said, succinctly, folding herself down onto the floor so she wouldn't knock her head on the roof of the cave.

"Courting, eh? Well?"

"I sent one away today," Magda said. "I don't remember his name. The Duke of Edgebarren's oldest son."

"Oh, a duke," the fairy said dismissively. "Don't you bother with a duke. He'll give himself the credit of it, when he gets anywhere, even if it's all your doing. Make it a knight or make it a king, that's my advice to you—if you do mean to saddle yourself with any of them."

She peered out of the hood, making it a question; her face was hidden too deep in the cowl to make out her features, but the cave mouth made a gleam of reflection in her eyes.

Magda considered: the duke's son made seventeen. Her mother was growing anxious, but Magda hadn't seen much to choose from among them. The ones whose ambitious fathers had sent them, who mumbled through their proposals without looking at her at all; the ones who put on false smiles as they looked up at her and pretended they liked feeling the weight of her hand in theirs as they led her through a dance. There *had* been a knight, and there *had* been a king, and neither of them saw anything to like when they looked at her, because the only strength they wanted in their house was their own.

Well, it had been a blessing, after all.

"I don't," she said, with decision.

"Just as well," the fairy said, nodding, and put down her stirring ladle. "You'd better come into the back, then. You'll be wanting a sword."

The first printing of "Blessings" was in Issue 22 of Uncanny Magazine, *May/June 2018.*

LORD DUNSANY'S TEAPOT

This story was written for the delightful anthology The Thackery T. Lambshead Cabinet of Curiosities, *where we were all asked to choose an item out of the mysterious Dr. Lambshead's cabinet, recovered after a fire, and to write about it. I cannot even make up a memory of how I came to drag in Lord Dunsany—an ancestor of Tolkien in the genre—and pawing through my old emails at the time has been no help, but after all, that loss of knowledge feels appropriate to the project.*

The teapot is unremarkable in itself: a roundbellied squat thing of black enameled iron, with the common nail-head pattern rubbed down low over the years and a spout perhaps a little short for its width; the handle has been broken and mended, and the lid has only a small stubby knob. Dr. Lambshead is not known to have used the teapot, which wears a thin layer of grey dust, but a small attached label indicates it was acquired at an estate auction held in Ireland circa 1957.

T HE ACCIDENTAL HARMONY OF THE TRENCHES PRO-
duced, sometimes, odd acquaintances. It was impossible not to feel a certain kinship with a man having lain huddled and nameless in the dirt beside him for hours, sharing the dubious comfort of a woolen scarf pressed over the mouth and nose while eyes streamed, stinging, and gunpowder bursts from time to time illuminated the crawling smoke in colors: did it have a greenish cast? And between the moments of fireworks, whispering to one another too low and too hoarsely to hear even unconsciously the accents of the barn or the gutter or the halls of the public school.

What became remarkable about Russell, in the trenches, was his smile: or rather that he smiled, with death walking overhead like the tread of heavy boots on a wooden floor above a cellar. Not a wild or wandering smile, reckless and ready to meet the end, or a trembling rictus; an ordinary smile to go with the whispered, "Another one coming, I think," as if speaking of a cricket ball instead of an incendiary; only friendly, with nothing to remark upon.

The trench had scarcely been dug. Dirt shook loose down upon them, until they might have been part of the earth, and when the all-clear sounded at last out of a long silence, they stood up still equals under a coat of mud, until Russell bent down and picked up the shovel, discarded, and they were again officer and man.

But this came too late: Edward trudged back with him, side by side, to the more populated regions of the labyrinth, still talking, and when they had reached Russell's bivouac he looked at Edward and said, "Would you have a cup of tea?"

The taste of the smoke was still thick on Edward's tongue, in his throat, and the night had curled up like a tiger and gone to sleep around them. They sat on Russell's cot while the kettle boiled, and he poured the hot water into a fat old teapot made of iron, knobby, over the cheap and bitter tea-leaves from the ration. Then he set it on the little camp stool and watched it steep, a thin thread of steam climbing out of the spout and dancing around itself in the cold air.

The rest of his company were sleeping, but Edward noticed their cots were placed away, as much as they could be in such a confined space; Russell had a little room around his. He looked at Russell: under the smudges and dirt, weathering; not a young face. The nose was a little crooked and so was the mouth, and the hair brushed over the forehead was sandy-brown and wispy in a vicarish way, with several years of thinning gone.

"A kindness to the old-timer, I suppose," Russell said. "Been here—five year now, or near enough. So they don't ask me to shift around."

"They haven't made you lance-jack," Edward said, the words coming out before he could consider all the reasons a man might not have received promotion, of which he would not care to speak.

"I couldn't," Russell said, apologetic. "Who am I, to be sending off other fellows, and treating them sharp if they don't?"

"Their corporal, or their sergeant," Edward said, a little impatient with the objection, "going in with them, not hanging back."

"O, well," Russell said, still looking at the teapot. "It's not the same for me to go."

He poured out the tea, and offered some shavings off a small brown block of sugar. Edward drank: strong and bittersweet, somehow better than the usual. The teapot was homely and common. Russell laid a hand on its side as if it were precious, and said it had come to him from an old sailor, coming home at last to rest from traveling.

"Do you ever wonder, are there wars under the sea?" Russell said. His eyes were gone distant. "If all those serpents and the kraken down there, or some other things we haven't names for, go to battle over the ships that have sunk, and all their treasure."

"And mer-men dive down among them, to be counted brave," Edward said, softly, not to disturb the image that had built clear in his mind: the great writhing beasts, tangled masses striving against one another in the endless cold dark depths, over broken ships and golden hoards, spilled upon the sand, trying to catch the faintest gleam of light. "To snatch some jewel to carry back, for a courting-gift or an heirloom of their house."

Russell nodded, as if to a commonplace remark. "I suppose it's how they choose their lords," he said, "the ones that go down and come back: and their king came up from the dark once with a crown—a beautiful thing, rubies and pearls like eggs, in gold."

The tea grew cold before they finished building the undersea court, turn and turn about, in low voices barely above the nasal breathing of the men around them.

IT SKIRTED THE LINES OF fraternization, certainly; but it could not have been called deliberate. There was always some duty or excuse which brought them into one another's company to begin with, and at no regular interval. Of course, even granting this, there was no denying it would have been more appropriate for Edward to refuse the invitation, or for Russell not to have made it in the first place. Yet somehow each time tea was offered, and accepted.

The hour was always late, and if Russell's fellows had doubts about his company, they never raised their heads from their cots to express it either by word or by look. Russell made the tea, and began the storytelling, and Edward cobbled together castles with him shaped of steam and fancy, drifting upwards and away from the trenches.

He would walk back to his own cot afterwards still warm through and lightened. He had come to do his duty, and he would do it, but there was something so much vaster and more dreadful than he had expected in the wanton waste upon the fields, in the smothered silence of the trenches: all of them already in the grave and merely awaiting a final confirmation. But Russell was still alive, so Edward might be as well. It was worth a little skirting of regulations.

HE ONLY HALF HEARD RUSSELL's battalion mentioned in the staff meeting, with one corner of his preoccupied mind; afterwards he looked at the assignment: a push to try and open a new trench, advancing the line.

It was no more than might be and would be asked of any man, eventually; it was no excuse to go by the bivouac that night with a tin of his own tea, all the more precious because Beatrice somehow managed to arrange for it to win through to him, through some perhaps questionable back channel. Russell said nothing of the assignment, though Edward could read the knowledge of it around them: for once not all the other men were sleeping, a few curled protectively around their scratching hands, writing letters in their cots.

"Well, that's a proper cup," Russell said softly, as the smell climbed out of the teapot, fragrant and fragile. The brew when he poured it was clear amber-gold, and made Edward think of peaches hanging in a garden of shining fruit-heavy trees, a great sighing breath of wind stirring all the branches to a shake.

For once Russell did not speak as they drank the tea. One after another the men around them put down their pens and went to sleep. The peaches swung from the branches, very clear and golden in Edward's mind. He kept his hands close around his cup.

"That's stirred him a bit, it has," Russell said, peering

under the lid of the teapot; he poured in some more water. For a moment, Edward thought he saw mountains, too, beyond the orchard-garden: green-furred peaks with clouds clinging to their sides like loose eiderdown. A great wave of homesickness struck him very nearly like a blow, though he had never seen such mountains. He looked at Russell, wondering.

"It'll be all right, you know," Russell said.

"Of course," Edward said: the only thing that could be said, prosaic and untruthful; the words tasted sour in his mouth after the clean taste of the tea.

"No, what I mean is, it'll be all right," Russell said. He rubbed a hand over the teapot. "I don't like to say, because the fellows don't understand, but you see him too; or at least as much of him as I do."

"Him," Edward repeated.

"I don't know his name," Russell said thoughtfully. "I've never managed to find out; I don't know that he hears us at all, or thinks of us. I suppose if he ever woke up, he might be right annoyed with us, sitting here drinking up his dreams. But he never has."

It was not their usual storytelling, but something with the uncomfortable savor of truth. Edward felt as though he had caught a glimpse from the corner of his eye of something too vast to be looked at directly or all at once: a tail shining silver-green sliding through the trees, a great green eye like oceans peering back with drowsy curiosity. "But he's not *in* there," he said involuntarily.

Russell shrugged expressively. He lifted off the lid and showed Edward: a lump fixed to the bottom of the pot, smooth white glimmering like pearl, irregular yet beautiful even with the swollen tea-leaves like kelp strewn over and around it.

He put the lid back on, and poured out the rest of the pot. "So it's all right," he said. "I'll be all right, while I have him. But you see why I couldn't send other fellows out. Not while I'm safe from all this, and they aren't."

An old and battered teapot made talisman of safety, inhabited by some mystical guardian: it ought to have provoked the same awkward sensation as speaking to an earnest Spiritualist, or an excessively devoted missionary; it called for polite agreement and withdrawal. "Thank you," Edward said instead; he was comforted, and glad to be so.

Whatever virtue lived there in the pitted iron, it was not more difficult to believe in than the blighted landscape above their trenches, the coils of hungry barbed black wire snaking upon the ground, and the creeping poisonous smoke that covered the endless bodies of the dead. Something bright and shining ought not be more impossible than that; and even if it was not strong enough to stand against all devastation, there was pleasure in thinking one life might be spared by its power.

THEY BROUGHT HIM THE TEAPOT three days later: Russell had no next of kin with a greater claim. Edward thanked them and left the teapot in a corner of his bag, and did not take it out again. Many men he knew had died, comrades in arms, friends; but Russell lying on the spiked and poisoned ground, breath seared and blood draining, hurt the worse for seeming wrong.

Edward dreamed sitting with Russell: the dead man's

skin clammy grey, blood streaking the earthenware where his fingers cupped it, where his lips touched the rim, and floating over the surface of the tea. "Well, and I was safe, like I said," Russell said. Edward shuddered out of the dream, and washed his face in the cold water in his jug; there were flakes of ice on the surface.

He went forward himself, twice, and was not killed; he shot several men, and sent others to die. There was a commendation at one point. He accepted it without any sense of pride. In the evenings, he played at cards with a handful of other officers, where they talked desultorily of plans, and the weather, and a few of the more crude of conquests either real or hoped-for in the French villages behind the lines. His letters to Beatrice grew shorter. His supply of words seemed to have leached away into the dirt.

His own teapot was on his small burner to keep warm when the air-raid sounded; an hour later after the all-clear it was a smoking cinder, the smell so very much like the acrid bite of gas that he flung it as far up over the edge of the trench as he could manage, to get it away, and took out the other teapot to make a fresh cup and wash away the taste.

And it was only a teapot: squat and unlovely except for the smooth pearlescent lump inside, some accident of its casting. He put in the leaves and poured the water from the kettle. He was no longer angry with himself for believing, only distantly amused, remembering; and sorry with that same distance for Russell, who had swallowed illusions for comfort.

He poured his cup and raised it and drank without stopping to inhale the scent or to think of home; and the pain startled him for being so vivid. He worked his mouth as though he had only burned his tongue and not some unprepared and numbed corner of his self. He found himself staring blindly at the small friendly blue flame beneath the teapot. The color was the same as a flower that grew only on the slopes of a valley on the other side of the world where no man had ever walked, which a bird with white feathers picked to line its nest, so the young when they were born were soft grey and tinted blue, with pale yellow beaks held wide to call for food in voices that chimed like bells.

The ringing in his ears from the sirens went quiet. He understood Russell then finally; and wept a little, without putting down the cup. He held it between his hands while the heat but not the scent faded, and sipped peace as long as it lasted.

The first publication of "Lord Dunsany's Teapot" was part of a 2011 anthology by Harper Voyager called The Thackery T. Lambshead Cabinet of Curiosities.

SEVEN YEARS FROM HOME

I read T. E. Lawrence's Seven Pillars of Wisdom *largely because of* Lawrence of Arabia, *curious about the real person beneath, and it was a strange experience. You can't believe almost anything he says, but I felt that I saw him clawing against the surface of his own life like watching a character in a horror movie groping frantically at a window, silhouetted hands moving. This is a story about someone like that.*

PREFACE

SEVEN DAYS PASSED FOR ME ON MY LITTLE RAFT OF A ship as I fled Melida; seven years for the rest of the unaccelerated universe. I hoped to be forgotten, a dusty footnote left at the bottom of a page. Instead I came off to trumpets and medals and legal charges, equal doses of acclaim and venom, and I stumbled bewildered through the brassy noise, led first by one and then by another, while my last opportunity to enter any protest against myself escaped.

Now I desire only to correct the worst of the factual inaccuracies bandied about, so far as my imperfect memory will allow, and to make an offering of my own understanding to that smaller and more sophisticate audience who prefer to shape the world's opinion rather than be shaped by it.

I engage not to tire you with a recitation of dates and events and quotations. I do not recall them with any precision myself. But I must warn you that neither have I succumbed to that pathetic and otiose impulse to sanitize the events of the war, or to excuse sins either my own or belonging to others. To do so would be a lie, and on Melida, to tell a lie was an insult more profound than murder.

I will not see my sisters again, whom I loved. Here we say that one who takes the long midnight voyage has leapt ahead in time, but to me it seems it is they who have traveled on ahead. I can no longer hear their voices when I am awake. I hope this will silence them in the night.

Ruth Patrona
Reivaldt, Janvier 32, 4765

THE FIRST ADJUSTMENT

I disembarked at the port of Landfall in the fifth month of 4753. There is such a port on every world where the Confederacy has set its foot but not yet its flag: crowded and dirty and charmless. It was on the Esperigan continent, as the Melidans would not tolerate the construction of a spaceport in their own territory.

Ambassador Kostas, my superior, was a man of great authority and presence, two meters tall and solidly built, with a jovial handshake, high intelligence, and very little patience for fools; that I was likely to be relegated to this category was evident on our first meeting. He disliked my assignment to begin with. He thought well of the Esperigans; he moved in their society as easily as he did in our own, and would have called one or two of their senior ministers his personal friends, if only such a gesture were not highly unprofessional. He recognized his duty, and on an abstract intellectual level the potential value of the Melidans, but they revolted him, and he would have been glad to find me of like mind, ready to draw a line through their name and give them up as a bad cause.

A few moments' conversation was sufficient to disabuse him of this hope. I wish to attest that he did not allow the disappointment to in any way alter the performance of his duty, and he could not have objected with more vigor to my project of proceeding at once to the Melidan continent, to his mind a suicidal act.

In the end he chose not to stop me. I am sorry if he later regretted that, as seems likely. I took full advantage of the weight of my arrival. Five years had gone by on my home-world of Terce since I had embarked, and there is a certain moral force to having sacrificed a former life for the one unknown. I had observed it often with new arrivals on Terce: their first requests were rarely refused even when foolish, as they often were. I was of course quite sure my own were eminently sensible.

"We will find you a guide," he said finally, yielding, and all the machinery of the Confederacy began to turn to my desire, a heady sensation.

Badea arrived at the embassy not two hours later. She wore a plain gray wrap around her shoulders, draped to the ground, and another wrap around her head. The alterations visible were only small ones: a smattering of green freckles across the bridge of her nose and cheeks, a greenish tinge to her lips and nails. Her wings were folded and hidden under the wrap, adding the bulk roughly of an overnight hiker's backpack. She smelled a little like the sourdough used on Terce to make roundbread, noticeable but not unpleasant. She might have walked through a spaceport without exciting comment.

She was brought to me in the shambles of my new of-fice, where I had barely begun to lay out my things. I was wearing a conservative black suit, my best, tailored because you could not buy trousers for women ready-made on Terce, and, thankfully, comfortable shoes, because elegant ones on Terce were not meant to be walked in. I remember my clothing particularly because I was in it for the next week without opportunity to change.

"Are you ready to go?" she asked me, as soon as we were introduced and the receptionist had left.

I was quite visibly *not* ready to go, but this was not a misunderstanding: she did not want to take me. She thought the request stupid, and feared my safety would be a burden on her. If Ambassador Kostas would not mind my failure to return, she could not know that, and to be just, he would certainly have reacted unpleasantly in any case, figuring it as his duty.

But when asked for a favor she does not want to grant, a Melidan will sometimes offer it anyway, only in an unacceptable or awkward way. Another Melidan will recognize this as a refusal, and withdraw the request. Badea did not expect this courtesy from me, she only expected that I would say I could not leave at once. This she could count to her satisfaction as a refusal, and she would not come back to offer again.

I was however informed enough to be dangerous, and I did recognize the custom. I said, "It is inconvenient, but I am prepared to leave immediately." She turned at once and walked out of my office, and I followed her. It is understood that a favor accepted despite the difficulty and constraints laid down by the giver must be necessary to the recipient, as indeed this was to me; but in such a case, the conditions must then be endured, even if artificial.

I did not risk a pause at all even to tell anyone I was going; we walked out past the embassy secretary and the

guards, who did not do more than give us a cursory
glance—we were going the wrong way, and my citizen's button would likely have saved us interruption in any case. Kostas would not know I had gone until my absence was noticed
and the security logs examined.

THE SECOND ADJUSTMENT

I was not unhappy as I followed Badea through the city. A
little discomfort was nothing to me next to the intense satisfaction of, as I felt, having passed a first test: I had gotten
past all resistance offered me, both by Kostas and Badea,
and soon I would be in the heart of a people I already felt I
knew. Though I would be an outsider among them, I had
lived all my life to the present day in the self-same state, and
I did not fear it, or for the moment anything else.

Badea walked quickly and with a freer stride than I was
used to, loose-limbed. I was taller, but had to stretch to
match her. Esperigans looked at her as she went by, and
then looked at me, and the pressure of their gaze was suddenly hostile. "We might take a taxi," I offered. Many were
passing by empty. "I can pay."

"No," she said, with a look of distaste at one of those
conveyances, so we continued on foot.

After Melida, during my black-sea journey, my doctoral
dissertation on the Canaan movement was published under
the escrow clause, against my will. I have never used the
funds, which continue to accumulate steadily. I do not like
to inflict them on any cause I admire sufficiently to support,
so they will go to my family when I have gone; my nephews

will be glad of it, and of the passing of an embarrassment, and that is as much good as it can be expected to provide.

There is a great deal within that book which is wrong, and more which is wrongheaded, in particular any expression of opinion or analysis I interjected atop the scant collection of accurate facts I was able to accumulate in six years of over-enthusiastic graduate work. This little is true: the Canaan movement was an offshoot of conservation philosophy. Where the traditionalists of that movement sought to restrict humanity to dead worlds and closed enclaves on others, the Canaan splinter group wished instead to alter themselves while they altered their new worlds, meeting them halfway.

The philosophy had the benefit of a certain practicality, as genetic engineering and body modification were and remain considerably cheaper than terraforming, but we are a squeamish and a violent species, and nothing invites pogrom more surely than the neighbor who is different from us, yet still too close. In consequence, the Melidans were by our present day the last surviving Canaan society.

They had come to Melida and settled the larger of the two continents some eight hundred years before. The Esperigans came two hundred years later, refugees from the plagues on New Victoire, and took the smaller continent. The two had little contact for the first half millennium; we of the Confederacy are given to think in worlds and solar systems, and to imagine that only a space voyage is long, but a hostile continent is vast enough to occupy a small and struggling band. But both prospered, each according to their lights, and by the time I landed, half the planet glittered in the night from space, and half was yet pristine.

In my dissertation, I described the ensuing conflict as natural, which is fair if slaughter and pillage are granted to be natural to our kind. The Esperigans had exhausted the limited raw resources of their share of the planet, and a short flight away was the untouched expanse of the larger continent, not a tenth as populated as their own. The Melidans controlled their birthrate, used only sustainable quantities, and built nothing which could not be eaten by the wilderness a year after they had abandoned it. Many Esperigan philosophers and politicians trumpeted their admiration of Melidan society, but this was only a sort of pleasant spiritual refreshment, as one admires a saint or a martyr without ever wishing to be one.

The invasion began informally, with adventurers and entrepreneurs, with the desperate, the poor, the violent. They began to land on the shores of the Melidan territory, to survey, to take away samples, to plant their own foreign roots. They soon had a village, then more than one. The Melidans told them to leave, which worked as well as it ever has in the annals of colonialism, and then attacked them. Most of the settlers were killed; enough survived and straggled back across the ocean to make a dramatic story of murder and cruelty out of it.

I expressed the conviction to the Ministry of State, in my pre-assignment report, that the details had been exaggerated, and that the attacks had been provoked more extensively. I was wrong, of course. But at the time I did not know it.

Badea took me to the low quarter of Landfall, so called because it faced on the side of the ocean downcurrent from the spaceport. Iridescent oil and a floating mat of discards glazed the edge of the surf. The houses were mean and crowded tightly upon one another, broken up mostly by liquor stores and bars. Docks stretched out into the ocean, extended long to reach out past the pollution, and just past the end of one of these floated a small boat, little more than a simple coracle: a hull of brown bark, a narrow brown mast, a grey-green sail slack and trembling in the wind.

We began walking out towards it, and those watching—there were some men loitering about the docks, fishing idly, or working on repairs to equipment or nets—began to realize then that I meant to go with her.

The Esperigans had already learned the lesson we like to teach as often as we can, that the Confederacy is a bad enemy and a good friend, and while no one is ever made to join us by force, we cannot be opposed directly. We had given them the spaceport already, an open door to the rest of the settled worlds, and they wanted more, the moth yearning. I relied on this for protection, and did not consider that however much they wanted from our outstretched hand, they still more wished to deny its gifts to their enemy.

Four men rose as we walked the length of the dock, and made a line across it. "You don't want to go with that one, ma'am," one of them said to me, a parody of respect. Badea said nothing. She moved a little aside, to see how I would answer them.

"I am on assignment for my government," I said, neatly offering a red flag to a bull, and moved towards them. It was not an attempt at bluffing: on Terce, even though I was immodestly unveiled, men would have at once moved out of the way to avoid any chance of the insult of physical contact. It was an act so automatic as to be invisible: precisely what we are taught to watch for in ourselves, but that proves infinitely easier in the instruction than in the practice. I did not *think* they would move; I knew they would.

Perhaps that certainty transmitted itself: the men did move a little, enough to satisfy my unconscious that they were cooperating with my expectations, so that it took me wholly by surprise and horror when one reached out and put his hand on my arm to stop me.

I screamed, in full voice, and struck him. His face is lost to my memory, but I still can see clearly the man behind him, his expression as full of appalled violation as my own. The four of them flinched from my scream, and then drew in around me, protesting and reaching out in turn.

I reacted with more violence. I had confidently considered myself a citizen of no world and of many, trained out of assumptions and unaffected by the parochial attitudes of the one where chance had seen me born, but in that moment I could with actual pleasure have killed all of them. That wish was unlikely to be gratified. I was taller, and the gravity of Terce is slightly higher than that of Melida, so I was stronger than they expected me to be, but they were laborers and seamen, built generously and rough-hewn, and the male advantage in muscle mass tells quickly in a hand-to-hand fight.

They tried to immobilize me, which only panicked me further. The mind curls in on itself in such a moment; I remember palpably only the sensation of sweating copiously, and the way this caused the seam of my blouse to rub unpleasantly against my neck as I struggled.

Badea told me later that, at first, she had meant to let them hold me. She could then leave, with the added satis-

SEVEN YEARS FROM HOME 243

faction of knowing the Esperigan fishermen and not she had
provoked an incident with the Confederacy. It was not sympathy that moved her to action, precisely. The extremity of
my distress was as alien to her as to them, but where they
thought me mad, she read it in the context of my having accepted her original conditions and somewhat unwillingly
decided that I truly did need to go with her, even if she did
not know precisely why and saw no use in it herself.

I cannot tell you precisely how the subsequent moments
unfolded. I remember the green gauze of her wings overhead perforated by the sun, like a linen curtain, and the
blood spattering my face as she neatly lopped off the hands
upon me. She used for the purpose a blade I later saw in use
for many tasks, among them harvesting fruit off plants where
the leaves or the bark may be poisonous. It is shaped like a
sickle and strung upon a thick elastic cord, which a skilled
wielder can cause to become rigid or to collapse.

I stood myself back on my feet panting, and she landed.
The men were on their knees screaming, and others were
running towards us down the docks. Badea swept the severed hands into the water with the side of her foot and said
calmly, "We must go."

The little boat had drawn up directly beside us over the
course of our encounter, drawn by some signal I had not
seen her transmit. I stepped into it behind her. The coracle
leapt forward like a springing bird, and left the shouting and
the blood behind.

We did not speak over the course of that strange journey.
What I had thought a sail did not catch the wind, but opened
itself wide and stretched out over our heads, like an awning,
and angled itself towards the sun. There were many small

filaments upon the surface wriggling when I examined it more closely, and also upon the exterior of the hull. Badea stretched herself out upon the floor of the craft, lying under the low deck, and I joined her in the small space: it was not uncomfortable nor rigid, but had the queer unsettled cushioning of a waterbed.

The ocean crossing took only the rest of the day. How our speed was generated I cannot tell you; we did not seem to sit deeply in the water and our craft threw up no spray. The world blurred as a window running with rain. I asked Badea for water, once, and she put her hands on the floor of the craft and pressed down: in the depression she made, a small clear pool gathered for me to cup out, with a taste like slices of cucumber with the skin still upon them.

This was how I came to Melida.

THE THIRD ADJUSTMENT

Badea was vaguely embarrassed to have inflicted me on her fellows, and having deposited me in the center of her village made a point of leaving me there by leaping aloft into the canopy where I could not follow, as a way of saying she was done with me, and anything I did henceforth could not be laid at her door.

I was by now hungry and nearly sick with exhaustion. Those who have not flown between worlds like to imagine the journey a glamorous one, but at least for minor bureaucrats, it is no more pleasant than any form of transport, only elongated. I had spent a week a virtual prisoner in my berth, the bed folding up to give me room to walk four strides back and forth, or to unfold my writing-desk, not both at once, with a shared toilet the size of an ungenerous closet down the hall. Landfall had not arrested my forward motion, as that mean port had never been my destination. Now, however, I was arrived, and the dregs of adrenaline were consumed in anticlimax.

Others before me have stood in a Melidan village center and described it for an audience—Esperigans mostly, anthropologists and students of biology and a class of tourists either adventurous or stupid. There is usually a lyrical description of the natives coasting overhead among some sort of vines or tree-branches knitted overhead for shelter, the particulars and adjectives determined by the village latitude, and the obligatory explanation of the typical plan of huts, organized as a spoked wheel around the central plaza.

If I had been less tired, perhaps I too would have looked with so analytical an air, and might now satisfy my readers with a similar report. But to me the village only presented all the confusion of a wholly strange place, and I saw nothing that seemed to me deliberate. To call it a village gives a false air of comforting provinciality. Melidans, at least those with wings, move freely among a wide constellation of small settlements, so that all of these, in the public sphere, partake of the hectic pace of the city. I stood alone, and strangers moved past me with assurance, the confidence of their stride saying, "I care nothing for you or your fate. It is of no concern to me. How might you expect it to be otherwise?" In the end, I lay down on one side of the plaza and went to sleep.

I met Kitia the next morning. She woke me by prodding me with a twig, experimentally, having been selected for this task out of her group of schoolmates by some complicated interworking of personality and chance. They giggled from a few safe paces back as I opened my eyes and sat up.

"Why are you sleeping in the square?" Kitia asked me, to a burst of fresh giggles.

"Where should I sleep?" I asked her.

"In a house!" she said.

When I had explained to them, not without some art, that I had no house here, they offered the censorious suggestion that I should go back to wherever I did have a house. I made a good show of looking analytically up at the sky overhead and asking them what our latitude was, and then I pointed at a random location and said, "My house is five years that way."

Scorn, puzzlement, and at last delight. I was from the stars! None of their friends had ever met anyone from so far away. One girl who previously had held a point of pride for having once visited the smaller continent, with an Esperigan toy doll to prove it, was instantly dethroned. Kitia possessively took my arm and informed me that as my house was too far away, she would take me to another.

Children of virtually any society are an excellent resource for the diplomatic servant or the anthropologist, if contact with them can be made without giving offense. They enjoy the unfamiliar experience of answering real questions, particularly the stupidly obvious ones that allow them to feel a sense of superiority over the inquiring adult, and they are easily impressed with the unusual. Kitia was a treasure. She led me, at the head of a small pied-piper procession, to an empty house on a convenient lane. It had been lately abandoned, and was already being reclaimed: the walls and floor were swarming with tiny insects with glossy dark blue carapaces, munching so industriously the sound of their jaws hummed like a summer afternoon.

I with difficulty avoided recoiling. Kitia did not hesitate: she walked into the swarm, crushing beetles by the dozens underfoot, and went to a small spigot in the far wall. When she turned this on, a clear viscous liquid issued forth, and the beetles scattered from it. "Here, like this," she said, showing me how to cup my hands under the liquid and spread it upon the walls and the floor. The disgruntled beetles withdrew, and the brownish surfaces began to bloom back to pale green, repairing the holes.

Over the course of that next week, she also fed me, corrected my manners and my grammar, and eventually brought me a set of clothing, a tunic and leggings, which she proudly informed me she had made herself in class. I thanked her with real sincerity and asked where I might wash my old clothing. She looked very puzzled, and when she had looked more closely at my clothing and touched it, she said, "Your clothing is dead! I thought it was only ugly."

Her gift was not made of fabric but a thin tough mesh of plant filaments with the feathered surface of a moth's wings. It gripped my skin eagerly as soon as I had put it on, and I thought myself at first allergic, because it itched and tingled, but this was only the bacteria bred to live in the mesh assiduously eating away the sweat and dirt and dead epidermal cells built up on my skin. It took me several more days to overcome all my instinct and learn to trust the living cloth with the more voluntary eliminations of my body also. (Previously I had been going out back to defecate in the woods, having been unable to find anything resembling a toilet, and meeting too much confusion when I tried to approach the question to dare pursue it further, for fear of encountering a taboo.)

And this was the handiwork of a child, not thirteen years of age! She could not explain to me how she had done it in any way which made sense to me. Imagine if you had to explain how to perform a reference search to someone who had not only never seen a library, but did not understand electricity, and who perhaps knew there was such a thing as written text, but did not himself read more than the alphabet. She took me once to her classroom after hours and showed me her workstation, a large wooden tray full of grayish moss, with a double row of small jars along the back each holding liquids or powders which I could only distinguish by their differing colors. Her only tools were an assortment of syringes and eyedroppers and scoops and brushes.

I went back to my house and in the growing report I would not have a chance to send for another month I wrote, *These are a priceless people. We must have them.*

THE FOURTH ADJUSTMENT

All these first weeks, I made no contact with any other adult. I saw them go by occasionally, and the houses around mine were occupied, but they never spoke to me or even looked at me directly. None of them objected to my squatting, but that was less implicit endorsement and more an unwillingness even to acknowledge my existence. I talked to Kitia and the other children, and tried to be patient. I hoped an opportunity would offer itself eventually for me to be of some visible use.

In the event, it was rather my lack of use which led to the break in the wall. A commotion arose in the early morning, while Kitia was showing me the plan of her wings, which she was at that age beginning to design. She would grow the parasite over the subsequent year, and was presently practicing with miniature versions, which rose from her worktable surface gossamer-thin and fluttering with an involuntary muscle-twitching. I was trying to conceal my revulsion.

Kitia looked up when the noise erupted. She casually tossed her example out of the window, to be pounced upon with a hasty scramble by several nearby birds, and went out the door. I followed her to the square: the children were gathered at the fringes, silent for once and watching. There were five women laid out on the ground, all bloody, one dead. Two of the others looked mortally wounded. They were all winged.

There were several working already on the injured, packing small brownish-white spongy masses into the open wounds and sewing them up. I would have liked to be of use, less from natural instinct than from the colder thought, which inflicted itself upon my mind, that any crisis opens social barriers. I am sorry to say I refrained not from any noble self-censorship, but from the practical conviction that it was at once apparent my limited field-medical training could not in any valuable way be applied to the present circumstances.

I drew away, rather, to avoid being in the way as I could not turn the situation to my advantage, and in doing so ran up against Badea, who stood at the very edge of the square, observing.

She stood alone; there were no other adults nearby, and there was blood on her hands. "Are you hurt also?" I asked her.

"No," she returned, shortly.

I ventured on concern for her friends, and asked her if they had been hurt in fighting. "We have heard rumors," I added, "that the Esperigans have been encroaching on your territory." It was the first opportunity I had been given of hinting at even this much of our official sympathy, as the children only shrugged when I asked them if there were fighting going on.

She shrugged, too, with one shoulder, and the folded wing rose and fell with it. But then she said, "They leave their weapons in the forest for us, even where they cannot have gone."

The Esperigans had several kinds of land-mine technologies, including a clever mobile one which could be programmed with a target either as specific as an individual's genetic record or as general as a broadly defined body type—humanoid and winged, for instance—and set loose to wander until it found a match, then do the maximum damage it could. Only one side could carry explosive, as the other was devoted to the electronics. "The shrapnel, does it come only in one direction?" I asked, and made a fanned-out shape with my hands to illustrate. Badea looked at me sharply and nodded.

I explained the mine to her, and described their manufacture. "Some scanning devices can detect them," I added, meaning to continue into an offer, but I had not finished the

litany of materials before she was striding away from the
square, without another word.

I was not dissatisfied with the reaction, in which I cor-
rectly read intention to put my information to immediate
use, and two days later my patience was rewarded. Badea
came to my house in the mid-morning and said, "We have
found one of them. Can you show us how to disarm them?"

"I am not sure," I told her, honestly. "The safest option
would be to trigger it deliberately, from afar."

"The plastics they use poison the ground."

"Can you take me to its location?" I asked. She considered the question with enough seriousness that I realized
there was either taboo or danger involved.

"Yes," she said finally, and took me with her to a house
near the center of the village. It had steps up to the roof, and
from there we could climb to that of the neighboring house,
and so on until we were high enough to reach a large basket,
woven not of ropes but of a kind of vine, sitting in a crook of
a tree. We climbed into this, and she kicked us off from the
tree.

The movement was not smooth. The nearest I can describe is the sensation of being on a child's swing, except at
that highest point of weightlessness you do not go backwards, but instead go falling into another arc, but at tremendous speed, and with a pungent smell like rotten pineapple
all around from the shattering of the leaves of the trees
through which we were propelled. I was violently sick after
some five minutes. To the comfort of my pride if not my
stomach, Badea was also sick, though more efficiently and
over the side, before our journey ended.

There were two other women waiting for us in the tree

where we came to rest, both of them also winged: Renata
and Paudi. "It's gone another three hundred meters, towards
Ighlan," Renata told us—another nearby Melidan village, as
they explained to me.

"If it comes near enough to pick up traces of organized
habitation, it will not trigger until it is inside the settlement,
among as many people as possible," I said. "It may also have
a burrowing mode, if it is the more expensive kind."

They took me down through the canopy, carefully, and
walked before and behind me when we came to the ground.
Their wings were spread wide enough to brush against the
hanging vines to either side, and they regularly leapt aloft for
a brief survey. Several times they moved me with friendly
hands into a slightly different path, although my untrained
eyes could make no difference among the choices.

A narrow trail of large ants—the reader will forgive me
for calling them ants, they were nearly indistinguishable
from those efficient creatures—paced us over the forest
floor, which I did not recognize as significant until we came
near the mine, and I saw it covered with the ants, who did
not impede its movement but milled around and over it with
intense interest.

"We have adjusted them so they smell the plastic," Badea
said, when I asked. "We can make them eat it," she added,
"but we worried it would set off the device."

The word *adjusted* scratches at the back of my mind
again as I write this, that unpleasant tinny sensation of a
term that does not allow for real translation and which has
been inadequately replaced. I cannot improve upon the
work of the official Confederacy translators, however; to encompass the true concept would require three dry, dusty

chapters more suited to a textbook on the subject of biological engineering, which I am ill qualified to produce. I do hope that I have successfully captured the wholly casual way she spoke of this feat. Our own scientists might replicate this act of genetic sculpting in any of two dozen excellent laboratories across the Confederacy—given several years, and a suitably impressive grant. They had done it in less than two days, as a matter of course.

I did not at the time indulge in admiration. The mine was ignoring the inquisitive ants and scuttling along at a good pace, the head with its glassy eye occasionally rotating upon its spindly spider-legs, and we had half a day in which to divert it from the village ahead.

Renata followed the mine as it continued on, while I sketched what I knew of the internals in the dirt for Badea and Paudi. Any sensible mine-maker will design the device to simply explode at any interference with its working other than the disable code, so our options were not particularly satisfying. "The most likely choice," I suggested, "would be the transmitter. If it becomes unable to receive the disable code, there may be a failsafe which would deactivate it on a subsequent malfunction."

Paudi had on her back a case which, unfolded, looked very like a more elegant and compact version of little Kitia's worktable. She sat cross-legged with it on her lap and worked on it for some two hours' time, occasionally reaching down to pick up a handful of ants, which dropped into the green matrix of her table mostly curled up and died, save for a few survivors, which she herded carefully into an empty jar before taking up another sample.

I sat on the forest floor beside her, or walked with Badea,

who was pacing a small circle out around us, watchfully. Occasionally she would unsling her scythe-blade, and then put it away again, and once she brought down a mottie, a small lemur-like creature. I say lemur because there is nothing closer in my experience, but it had none of the charm of an Earth-native mammal; I rather felt an instinctive disgust looking at it, even before she showed me the tiny suckermouths full of hooked teeth with which it latched upon a victim.

She had grown a little more loquacious, and asked me about my own homeworld. I told her about Terce, and about the seclusion of women, which she found extremely funny, as we can only laugh at the follies of those far from us which threaten us not at all. The Melidans by design maintain a five-to-one ratio of women to men, as adequate to maintain a healthy gene pool while minimizing the overall resource consumption of their population. "They cannot take the wings, so it is more difficult for them to travel," she added, with one sentence dismissing the lingering mystery which had perplexed earlier visitors, of the relative rarity of seeing their men.

She had two children, which she described to me proudly, living presently with their father and half siblings in a village half a day's travel away, and she was considering a third. She had trained as a forest ranger, another inadequately translated term which was at the time beginning to take on a military significance among them under the pressure of the Esperigan incursions.

"I'm done," Paudi said, and we went to catch up Renata and find a nearby ant-nest, which looked like a mound of white cotton batting, rising several inches off the forest floor.

Paudi introduced her small group of infected survivors into this colony, and after a little confusion and milling about, they accepted their transplantation and marched inside. The flow of departures slowed a little momentarily, then resumed, and a file split off from the main channel of workers to march in the direction of the mine.

These joined the lingering crowd still upon the mine, but the new arrivals did not stop at inspection and promptly began to struggle to insinuate themselves into the casing. We withdrew to a safe distance, watching. The mine continued on without any slackening in its pace for ten minutes, as more ants began to squeeze themselves inside, and then it hesitated, one spindly metal leg held aloft uncertainly. It went a few more slightly drunken paces, and then abruptly the legs all retracted and left it a smooth round lump on the forest floor.

THE FIFTH ADJUSTMENT

They showed me how to use their communications technology and grew me an interface to my own small handheld, so my report was at last able to go. Kostas began angry, of course, having been forced to defend the manner of my departure to the Esperigans without the benefit of any understanding of the circumstances, but I sent the report an hour before I messaged, and by the time we spoke he had read enough to be in reluctant agreement with my conclusions if not my methods.

I was of course full of self-satisfaction. Freed at long last from the academy and the walled gardens of Terce, armed with false confidence in my research and my training, I had so far achieved all that my design had stretched to encompass. The Esperigan blood had washed easily from my hands, and though I answered Kostas meekly when he upbraided me, privately I felt only impatience, and even he did not linger long on the topic: I had been too successful, and he had more important news.

The Esperigans had launched a small army two days before, under the more pleasant-sounding name of expeditionary defensive force. Their purpose was to establish a permanent settlement on the Melidan shore, some nine hundred miles from my present location, and begin the standard process of terraforming. The native life would be eradicated in spheres of a hundred miles across at a time: first the broad strokes of clear-cutting and the electrified nets, then the irradiation of the soil and the air, and after that the seeding of Earth-native microbes and plants. So had a thousand worlds been made over anew, and though the Esperigans had fully conquered their own continent five centuries before, they still knew the way.

He asked doubtfully if I thought some immediate resistance could be offered. Disabling a few mines scattered into the jungle seemed to him a small task. Confronting a large and organized military force was on a different order of magnitude. "I think we can do something," I said, maintaining a veneer of caution for his benefit, and took the catalog of equipment to Badea as soon as we had disengaged.

She was occupied in organizing the retrieval of the deactivated mines, which the ants were now leaving scattered in the forests and jungles. A bird-of-paradise variant had been adjusted to make a meal out of the ants and take the glittery mines back to their treetop nests, where an observer might easily see them from above. She and the other collectors had so far found nearly a thousand of them. The mines made a neat pyramid, as of the harvested skulls of small cyclopean creatures with their dull eyes staring out lifelessly.

The Esperigans needed a week to cross the ocean in their numbers, and I spent it with the Melidans, developing our response. There was a heady delight in this collaboration. The work was easy and pleasant in their wide-open laboratories full of plants, roofed only with the fluttering sailcloth eating sunlight to give us energy, and the best of them coming from many miles distant to participate in the effort. The Confederacy spy-satellites had gone into orbit perhaps a year after our first contact: I likely knew more about the actual force than the senior administrators of Melida. I was in much demand, consulted not only for my information but my opinion.

In the ferment of our labors, I withheld nothing. This was not yet deliberate, but neither was it innocent. I had been sent to further a war, and if in the political calculus which had arrived at this solution the lives of soldiers were only variables, yet there was still a balance I was expected to preserve. It was not my duty to give the Melidans an easy victory, any more than it had been Kostas's to give one to the Esperigans.

A short and victorious war, opening a new and tantalizing frontier for restless spirits, would at once drive up that inconvenient nationalism which is the Confederacy's worst obstacle, and render less compelling the temptations we could offer to lure them into fully joining galactic society. On the other hand, to descend into squalor, a more equal kind of civil war has often proven extremely useful, and the more lingering and bitter the better. I had been sent to the Melidans in hope that, given some guidance and what material assistance we could quietly provide without taking any official position, they might be an adequate opponent for the Esperigans to produce this situation.

There has been some criticism of the officials who selected me for this mission, but in their defense, it must be pointed out it was not in fact my assignment to actually provide military assistance, nor could anyone, even myself, have envisioned my proving remotely useful in such a role. I was only meant to be an early scout. My duty was to acquire cultural information enough to open a door for a party of military experts from Voca Libre, who would not reach Melida for another two years. Ambition and opportunity promoted me, and no official hand.

I think these experts arrived sometime during the third Esperigan offensive. I cannot pinpoint the date with any accuracy, I had by then ceased to track the days, and I never met them. I hope they can forgive my theft of their war; I paid for my greed.

The Esperigans used a typical carbonized steel in most of their equipment, as bolts and hexagonal nuts and screws with star-shaped heads, and woven into the tough mesh of their body armor. This was the target of our efforts. It was a new field of endeavor for the Melidans, who used metal as they used meat, sparingly and with a sense of righteousness in its avoidance. To them it was either a trace element needed in minute amounts, or an undesirable by-product of the more complicated biological processes they occasionally needed to invoke.

However, they had developed some strains of bacteria to deal with this latter waste, and the speed with which they could manipulate these organisms was extraordinary. Another quantity of the ants—a convenient delivery mechanism used by the Melidans routinely, as I learned—were adjusted to render them deficient in iron and to provide a home in their bellies for the bacteria, transforming them into shockingly efficient engines of destruction. Set loose upon several of the mines as a trial, they devoured the carapaces and left behind only smudgy black heaps of carbon dust, carefully harvested for fertilizer, and the plastic explosives from within, nestled in their bed of copper wire and silicon.

The Esperigans landed, and at once carved themselves out a neat half-moon of wasteland from the virgin shore, leaving no branches which might stretch above their encampment to offer a platform for attack. They established an electrified fence around the perimeter, with guns and patrols, and all this I observed with Badea, from a small platform in a vine-choked tree not far away: we wore the green-gray cloaks, and our faces were stained with leaf juice.

I had very little justification for inserting myself into such a role but the flimsy excuse of pointing out to Badea the most crucial section of their camp, when we had broken in. I cannot entirely say why I wished to go along on so dangerous an expedition. I am not particularly courageous. Several of my more unkind biographers have accused me of bloodlust, and pointed to this as a sequel to the disaster of my first departure. I cannot refute the accusation on the evidence, however I will point out that I chose that portion of the expedition which we hoped would encounter no violence.

But it is true I had learned already to seethe at the violent piggish blindness of the Esperigans, who would have wrecked all the wonders around me only to propagate yet another bland copy of Earth and suck dry the carcass of their own world. They were my enemy both by duty and by inclination, and I permitted myself the convenience of hating them. At the time, it made matters easier.

The wind was running from the east, and several of the Melidans attacked the camp from that side. The mines had yielded a quantity of explosive large enough to pierce the Esperigans' fence and shake the trees even as far as our lofty perch. The wind carried the smoke and dust and flames towards us, obscuring the ground and rendering the soldiers in their own camp only vague ghostlike suggestions of human shape. The fighting was hand-to-hand, and the stutter of gunfire came only tentatively through the chaos of the smoke.

Badea had been holding a narrow cord, one end weighted with a heavy seedpod. She now poured a measure of water onto the pod, from her canteen, then flung it out into the air. It sailed over the fence and landed inside the encampment, behind one of the neat rows of storage tents. The seedpod struck the ground and immediately burst like a ripe fruit, an anemone-tangle of waving roots creeping out over the ground and anchoring the cord, which she had secured at this end around one thick branch.

We let ourselves down it, hand over hand. There was none of that typical abrasion or friction which I might have expected from rope; my hands felt as cool and comfortable when we descended as when we began. We ran into the narrow space between the tents. I was experiencing that strange elongation of time which crisis can occasionally produce: I was conscious of each footfall, and of the seeming-long moments it took to place each one.

There were wary soldiers at many of the tent entrances, likely those which held either the more valuable munitions or the more valuable men. Their discipline had not faltered, even while the majority of the force was already orchestrating a response to the Melidan assault on the other side of the encampment. But we did not need to penetrate into the tents. The guards were rather useful markers for us, showing me which of the tents were the more significant. I pointed out to Badea the cluster of four tents, each guarded at either side by a pair, near the farthest end of the encampment.

Badea looked here and there over the ground as we darted under cover of smoke from one alleyway to another, the walls of waxed canvas muffling the distant shouts and the sound of gunfire. The dirt still had the yellowish tinge of Melidan soil—the Esperigans had not yet irradiated it—but it was crumbly and dry, the fine fragile native moss crushed and much torn by heavy boots and equipment, and the wind raised little dervishes of dust around our ankles.

"This ground will take years to recover fully," she said to me, soft and bitterly, as she stopped us and knelt, behind a deserted tent not far from our target. She gave me a small ceramic implement which looked much like the hair-picks sometimes worn on Terce by women with hair which never knew a blade's edge: a raised comb with three teeth, though on the tool these were much longer and sharpened at the end. I picked the ground vigorously, stabbing deep to aerate the wounded soil, while she judiciously poured out a mixture of water and certain organic extracts, and sowed a packet of seeds.

This may sound a complicated operation to be carrying out in an enemy camp, in the midst of battle, but we had practiced the maneuver, and indeed had we been glimpsed, anyone would have been hard-pressed to recognize a threat in the two gray-wrapped lumps crouched low as we pawed at the dirt. Twice while we worked, wounded soldiers were carried in a rush past either end of our alleyway, towards shelter. We were not seen.

The seeds she carried, though tiny, burst readily, and began to thrust out spiderweb-fine rootlets at such a speed they looked like nothing more than squirming maggots. Badea without concern moved her hands around them, encouraging them into the ground. When they were established, she motioned me to stop my work, and she took out the prepared ants: a much greater number of them, with a dozen of the fat yellow wasp-sized brood-mothers. Tipped out into the prepared and welcoming soil, they immediately began to burrow their way down, with the anxious harrying of their subjects and spawn.

Badea watched for a long while, crouched over, even after the ants had vanished nearly all beneath the surface. The few who emerged and darted back inside, the faint trembling of the rootlets, the shifting grains of dirt, all carried information to her. At length satisfied, she straightened saying, "Now—"

The young soldier was I think only looking for somewhere to piss, rather than investigating some noise. He came around the corner already fumbling at his belt, and seeing us did not immediately shout, likely from plain surprise, but grabbed for Badea's shoulder first. He was clean-shaven, and the name on his lapel badge was *Ridang*. I drove the soil-pick into his eye. I was taller, so the stroke went downwards, and he fell backwards to his knees away from me, clutching at his face.

He did not die at once. There must be very few deaths which come immediately, though we often like to comfort ourselves by the pretense that this failure of the body, or that injury, must at once eradicate consciousness and life and pain all together. Here sentience lasted several moments which seemed to me long: his other eye was open, and looked at me while his hands clawed for the handle of the pick. When this had faded, and he had fallen supine to the ground, there was yet a convulsive movement of all the limbs and a trickling of blood from mouth and nose and eye before the final stiffening jerk left the body emptied and inanimate.

I watched him die in a strange parody of serenity, all feeling hollowed out of me, and then turning away vomited upon the ground. Behind me, Badea cut open his belly and his thighs and turned him facedown onto the dirt, so the blood and the effluvia leaked out of him. "That will do a little good for the ground at least, before they carry him away to waste him," she said. "Come." She touched my shoulder, not unkindly, but I flinched from the touch as from a blow.

It was not that Badea or her fellows were indifferent to death, or casual towards murder. But there is a price to be paid for living in a world whose native hostilities have been cherished rather than crushed. Melidan life expectancy is some ten years beneath that of Confederacy citizens, though they are on average healthier and more fit both genetically and physically. In their philosophy a human life is not inherently superior and to be valued over any other kind. Accident and predation claim many, and living intimately with the daily cruelties of nature dulls the facility for sentiment. Badea enjoyed none of that comforting distance which allows us to think ourselves assured of the full potential span of life, and therefore suffered none of the pangs when confronted with evidence to the contrary. I looked at my victim and saw my own face; so too did she, but she had lived all her life so aware, and it did not bow her shoulders.

FIVE DAYS PASSED BEFORE THE Esperigan equipment began to come apart. Another day halted all their work, and in confusion they retreated to their encampment. I did not go with the Melidan company that destroyed them to the last man.

Contrary to many accusations, I did not lie to Kostas in my report and pretend surprise. I freely confessed to him I had expected the result, and truthfully explained I had not wished to make claims of which I was unsure. I never deliberately sought to deceive any of my superiors or conceal information from them, save in such small ways. At first I was not Melidan enough to wish to do so, and later I was too Melidan to feel anything but revulsion at the concept.

He and I discussed our next steps in the tiger-dance. I described as best I could the Melidan technology, and after consultation with various Confederacy experts, it was agreed he would quietly mention to the Esperigan minister of defense, at their weekly luncheon, a particular Confederacy technology: ceramic coatings, which could be ordered at vast expense and two years' delay from Bel Rios. Or, he would suggest, if the Esperigans wished to deed some land to the Confederacy, a private entrepreneurial concern might fund the construction of a local fabrication plant, and produce them at much less cost, in six months' time.

The Esperigans took the bait, and saw only private greed behind this apparent breach of neutrality: imagining Kostas an investor in this private concern, they winked at his venality, and eagerly helped us to their own exploitation. Meanwhile, they continued occasional and tentative incursions into the Melidan continent, probing the coastline, but the disruption they created betrayed their attempts, and whichever settlement was nearest would at once deliver them a present of the industrious ants, so these met with no greater success than the first.

Through these months of brief and grudging détente, I traveled extensively throughout the continent. My journals are widely available, being the domain of our government, but they are shamefully sparse, and I apologize to my colleagues for it. I would have been more diligent in my work if I had imagined I would be the last and not the first such chronicler. At the time, giddy with success, I went with more the spirit of a holidaymaker than a researcher, and I sent only those images and notes which it was pleasant to me to record, with the excuse of limited capacity to send my reports.

For what cold comfort it may be, I must tell you photography and description are inadequate to convey the experience of standing in the living heart of a world, alien yet not hostile, and when I walked hand in hand with Badea along the crest of a great canyon wall and looked down over the ridges of purple and grey and ochre at the gently waving tendrils of an elacca forest, which in my notorious video-recordings can provoke nausea in nearly every observer, I felt the first real stir of an unfamiliar sensation of beauty-in-strangeness, and I laughed in delight and surprise, while she looked at me and smiled.

We returned to her village three days later and saw the bombing as we came, the new Esperigan long-range fighter planes like narrow silver knife-blades making low passes overhead, the smoke rising black and oily against the sky. Our basket-journey could not be accelerated, so we could only cling to the sides and wait as we were carried onward. The planes and the smoke were gone before we arrived; the wreckage was not.

I was angry at Kostas afterwards, unfairly. He was no more truly the Esperigans' confidant than they were his, but I felt at the time that it was his business to know what they were about, and he had failed to warn me. I accused him of deliberate concealment; he told me, censoriously, that I had known the risk when I had gone to the continent, and he could hardly be responsible for preserving my safety while I slept in the very war zone. This silenced my tirade, as I realized how near I had come to betraying myself. Of course he would not have wanted me to warn the Melidans; it had not yet occurred to him I would have wished to, myself. I ought not have wanted to.

Forty-three people were killed in the attack. Kitia was yet lingering when I came to her small bedside. She was in no pain, her eyes cloudy and distant, already withdrawing; her family had been and gone again. "I knew you were coming back, so I asked them to let me stay a little longer," she told me. "I wanted to say goodbye." She paused and added uncertainly, "And I was afraid, a little. Don't tell."

I promised her I would not. She sighed and said, "I shouldn't wait any longer. Will you call them over?"

The attendant came when I raised my hand, and he asked Kitia, "Are you ready?"

"Yes," she said, a little doubtful. "It won't hurt?"

"No, not at all," he said, already taking out with a gloved hand a small flat strip from a pouch, filmy green and smelling of raspberries. Kitia opened her mouth, and he laid it on her tongue. It dissolved almost at once, and she blinked twice and was asleep. Her hand went cold a few minutes later, still lying between my own.

I stood with her family when we laid her to rest, the next morning. The attendants put her carefully down in a clearing, and sprayed her from a distance, the smell of cut roses just going to rot, and stepped back. Her parents wept noisily; I stayed dry-eyed as any seemly Terce matron, displaying my assurance of the ascension of the dead. The birds came first, and the motties, to pluck at her eyes and her lips, and the beetles hurrying with a hum of eager jaws to deconstruct her into raw parts. They did not have long to feast: the forest itself was devouring her from below in a green tide rising, climbing in small creepers up her cheeks and displacing them all.

When she was covered over, the mourners turned away and went to join the shared wake behind us in the village square. They threw uncertain and puzzled looks at my remaining as they went past, and at my tearless face. But she was not yet gone: there was a suggestion of a girl lingering there, a collapsing scaffold draped in an unhurried carpet of

living things. I did not leave, though behind me there rose a
murmur of noise as the families of the dead spoke reminis-
cences of their lost ones.

 Near dawn, the green carpeting slipped briefly. In the
dim watery light I glimpsed for one moment an emptied
socket full of beetles, and I wept.

THE SIXTH ADJUSTMENT

I will not claim, after this, that I took the wings only from
duty, but I refute the accusation that I took them in treason.
There was no other choice. Men and children and the el-
derly or the sick, all the wingless, were fleeing from the continuing hail of Esperigan attacks. They were retreating deep
into the heart of the continent, beyond the refueling range
for the Esperigan warcraft, to shelters hidden so far in caves
and in overgrowth that even my spy-satellites knew nothing
of them. My connection to Kostas would have been severed,
and if I could provide neither intelligence nor direct assistance, I might as well have slunk back to the embassy, and
saved myself the discomfort of being a refugee. Neither alternative was palatable.

 They laid me upon the altar like a sacrifice, or so I felt,
though they gave me something to drink which calmed my
body, the nervous and involuntary twitching of my limbs and
skin. Badea sat at my head and held the heavy long braid of
my hair out of the way, while the others depilated my back
and wiped it with alcohol. They bound me down then, and
slit my skin open in two lines mostly parallel to the spine.
Then Paudi gently set the wings upon me.

I lacked the skill to grow my own, in the time we had; Badea and Paudi helped me to mine so that I might stay. But even with the little assistance I had been able to contribute, I had seen more than I wished to of the parasites, and despite my closed eyes, my face turned downwards, I knew to my horror that the faint curious feather-brush sensation was the intrusion of the fine spiderweb filaments, each fifteen feet long, which now wriggled into the hospitable environment of my exposed inner flesh and began to sew themselves into me.

Pain came and went as the filaments worked their way through muscle and bone, finding one bundle of nerves and then another. After the first half hour, Badea told me gently, "It's coming to the spine," and gave me another drink. The drug kept my body from movement, but could do nothing to numb the agony. I cannot describe it adequately. If you have ever managed to inflict food poisoning upon yourself, despite all the Confederacy's safeguards, you may conceive of the kind if not the degree of suffering, an experience which envelops the whole body, every muscle and joint, and alters not only your physical self but your thoughts: all vanishes but pain, and the question, is the worst over? which is answered *no* and *no* again.

But at some point the pain began indeed to ebb. The filaments had entered the brain, and it is a measure of the experience that what I had feared the most was now blessed relief; I lay inert and closed my eyes gratefully while sensation spread outward from my back, and my new-borrowed limbs became gradually indeed my own, flinching from the currents of the air, and the touch of my friends' hands upon me. Eventually I slept.

THE SEVENTH ADJUSTMENT

The details of the war, which unfolded now in earnest, I do not need to recount again. Kostas kept excellent records, better by far than my own, and students enough have memorized the dates and geographic coordinates, bounding death and ruin in small numbers. Instead I will tell you that from aloft, the Esperigans' poisoned-ground encampments made half starbursts of ochre brown and withered yellow, outlines like tentacles crawling into the healthy growth around them. Their supply-ships anchored out to sea glazed the water with a slick of oil and refuse, while the soldiers practiced their shooting on the vast schools of slow-swimming kraken young, whose bloated white bodies floated to the surface and drifted away along the coast, so many they defied even the appetite of the sharks.

I will tell you that when we painted their hulls with algae and small crustacean-like borers, our work was camouflaged by great blooms of sea day-lilies around the ships, their masses throwing up reflected red color on the steel to hide the quietly creeping rust until the first winter storms struck and the grown kraken came to the surface to feed. I will tell you we watched from shore while the ships broke and foundered, and the teeth of the kraken shone like fire opals in the explosions, and if we wept, we wept only for the soiled ocean.

Still more ships came, and more planes; the ceramic coatings arrived, and more soldiers with protected guns and bombs and sprayed poisons, to fend off the altered motties and the little hybrid sparrowlike birds, their sharp cognizant eyes chemically retrained to see the Esperigan uniform colors as enemy markings. We planted acids and more aggressive species of plants along their supply lines, so their communications remained hopeful rather than reliable, and ambushed them at night; they carved into the forest with axes and power-saws and vast strip-miners, which ground to a halt and fell to pieces, choking on vines which hardened to the tensile strength of steel as they matured.

Contrary to claims which were raised at my trial *in absentia* and disproven with communication logs, throughout this time I spoke to Kostas regularly. I confused him, I think; I gave him all the intelligence which he needed to convey to the Esperigans, that they might respond to the next Melidan foray, but I did not conceal my feelings or the increasing complication of my loyalties, objecting to him bitterly and with personal anger about Esperigan attacks. I misled him with honesty: he thought, I believe, that I was only spilling a natural frustration to him, and through that airing clearing out my own doubts. But I had only lost the art of lying.

There is a general increase of perception which comes with the wings, the nerves teased to a higher pitch of awareness. All the little fidgets and twitches of lying betray themselves more readily, so only the more twisted forms can evade detection—where the speaker first deceives herself, or the wholly casual deceit of the sociopath who feels no remorse. This was the root of the Melidan disgust of the act, and I had acquired it.

If Kostas had known, he would at once have removed me: a diplomat is not much use if she cannot lie at need, much less an agent. But I did not volunteer the information, and indeed I did not realize, at first, how fully I had absorbed the stricture. I did not realize at all, until Badea came to me, three years into the war. I was sitting alone and in the dark by the communications console, the phosphorescent afterimage of Kostas's face fading into the surface.

She sat down beside me and said, "The Esperigans answer us too quickly. Their technology advances in these great leaps, and every time we press them back, they return in less than a month to very nearly the same position."

I thought, at first, that this was the moment: that she meant to ask me about membership in the Confederacy. I felt no sense of satisfaction, only a weary kind of resignation. The war would end, the Esperigans would follow, and in a few generations they would both be eaten up by bureaucracy and standards and immigration.

Instead Badea looked at me and said, "Are your people helping them, also?"

My denial ought to have come without thought, leapt easily off the tongue with all the conviction duty could give it, and been followed by invitation. Instead I said nothing, my throat closed involuntarily. We sat silently in the darkness, and at last she said, "Will you tell me why?"

I felt at the time I could do no more harm, and perhaps some good, by honesty. I told her all the rationale, and expressed all our willingness to receive them into our union as equals. I went so far as to offer her the platitudes with which we convince ourselves we are justified in our slow gentle imperialism: that unification is necessary and advances all together, bringing peace.

She only shook her head and looked away from me. After a moment, she said, "Your people will never stop. Whatever we devise, they will help the Esperigans to a counter, and if the Esperigans devise some weapon we cannot defend ourselves against, they will help us, and we will batter each other into limp exhaustion, until in the end we all fall."

"Yes," I said, because it was true. I am not sure I was still able to lie, but in any case I did not.

I was not permitted to communicate with Kostas again until they were ready. Thirty-six of the Melidans' greatest designers and scientists died in the effort. I learned of their deaths in bits and pieces. They worked in isolated and quarantined spaces, their every action recorded even as the viruses and bacteria they were developing killed them. It was a little more than three months before Badea came to me again.

We had not spoken since the night she had learned the duplicity of the Confederacy's support and my own. I could not ask her forgiveness, and she could not give it. She did not come for reconciliation but to send a message to the Esperigans and to the Confederacy through me.

I did not comprehend at first. But when I did, I knew enough to be sure she was neither lying nor mistaken, and to be sure the threat was very real. The same was not true of Kostas, and still less of the Esperigans. My frantic attempts to persuade them worked instead to the contrary end. The long gap since my last communiqué made Kostas suspicious: he thought me a convert, or generously a manipulated tool.

"If they had the capability, they would have used it already," he said, and if I could not convince him, the Esperigans would never believe.

I asked Badea to make a demonstration. There was a large island broken off the southern coast of the Esperigan continent, thoroughly settled and industrialized, with two substantial port cities. Sixty miles separated it from the mainland. I proposed the Melidans should begin there, where the attack might be contained.

"No," Badea said. "So your scientists can develop a counter? No. We are done with exchanges."

The rest you know. A thousand coracles left Melidan shores the next morning, and by sundown on the third following day, the Esperigan cities were crumbling. Refugees fled the groaning skyscrapers as they slowly bowed under their own weight. The trees died; the crops also, and the cattle, all the life and vegetation that had been imported from Earth and square-peg forced into the new world stripped bare for their convenience.

Meanwhile in the crowded shelters the viruses leapt easily from one victim to another, rewriting their genetic lines. Where the changes took hold, the altered survived. The others fell to the same deadly plagues that consumed all Earth-native life. The native Melidan moss crept in a swift green carpet over the corpses, and the beetle-hordes with it.

I can give you no firsthand account of those days. I too lay fevered and sick while the alteration ran its course in me, though I was tended better, and with more care, by my sisters. When I was strong enough to rise, the waves of death were over. My wings curled limply over my shoulders as I walked through the empty streets of Landfall, pavement stones pierced and broken by hungry vines, like bones cracked open for marrow. The moss covered the dead, who filled the shattered streets.

The squat embassy building had mostly crumpled down on one corner, smashed windows gaping hollow and black. A large pavilion of simple cotton fabric had been raised in the courtyard, to serve as both hospital and headquarters. A young undersecretary of state was the senior diplomat remaining. Kostas had died early, he told me. Others were still in the process of dying, their bodies waging an internal war that left them twisted by hideous deformities.

Less than one in thirty, was his estimate of the survivors. Imagine yourself on an air-train in a crush, and then imagine yourself suddenly alone but for one other passenger across the room, a stranger staring at you. Badea called it a sustainable population.

The Melidans cleared the spaceport of vegetation, though little now was left but the black-scorched landing pad, Confederacy manufacture, all of woven carbon and titanium.

"Those who wish may leave," Badea said. "We will help the rest."

Most of the survivors chose to remain. They looked at their faces in the mirror, flecked with green, and feared the Melidans less than their welcome on another world.

I left by the first small ship that dared come down to take off refugees, with no attention to the destination or the duration of the voyage. I wished only to be away. The wings were easily removed. A quick and painful amputation of the gossamer and fretwork which protruded from the flesh, and the rest might be left for the body to absorb slowly. The strange muffled quality of the world, the sensation of numbness, passed eventually. The two scars upon my back, parallel lines, I will keep the rest of my days.

AFTERWORD

I spoke with Badea once more before I left. She came to ask me why I was going, to what end I thought I went. She would be perplexed, I think, to see me in my little cottage here on Reivaldt, some hundred miles from the nearest city, although she would have liked the small flowerlike lieden which live on the rocks of my garden wall, one of the few remnants of the lost native fauna which have survived the terraforming outside the preserves of the university system.

I left because I could not remain. Every step I took on Melida, I felt dead bones cracking beneath my feet. The Melidans did not kill lightly, an individual or an ecosystem, nor any more effectually than do we. If the Melidans had not let the plague loose upon the Esperigans, we would have destroyed them soon enough ourselves, and the Melidans with them. But we distance ourselves better from our murders, and so are not prepared to confront them. My wings whispered to me gently when I passed Melidans in the green-swathed cemetery streets, that they were not sickened, were not miserable. There was sorrow and regret but no self-loathing, where I had nothing else. I was alone.

When I came off my small vessel here, I came fully expecting punishment, even longing for it, a judgment which would at least be an end. Blame had wandered through the halls of state like an unwanted child, but when I proved willing to adopt whatever share anyone cared to mete out to me, to confess any crime which was convenient and to proffer no defense, it turned contrary, and fled.

Time enough has passed that I can be grateful now to the politicians who spared my life and gave me what passes for my freedom. In the moment, I could scarcely feel enough even to be happy that my report contributed some little to the abandonment of any reprisal against Melida: as though we ought hold them responsible for defying our expectations not of their willingness to kill one another, but only of the extent of their ability.

But time does not heal all wounds. I am often asked by visitors whether I would ever return to Melida. I will not. I am done with politics and the great concerns of the universe of human settlement. I am content to sit in my small garden, and watch the ants at work.

Ruth Patrona

"Seven Years from Home" was first printed in an anthology edited by George R. R. Martin and Gardner Dozois called Warriors, *published by Tor Books in 2010.*

DRAGONS & DECORUM

Back many years ago, I did a Temeraire fanart contest, which turned into the anthology Golden Age and Other Stories, *where readers sent me their art and I chose a set of winners to get either drabbles or short stories written. Laurie Damme Gonneville sent in a sketch of Captain Elizabeth Bennet and her dragon Wollstonecraft, and this story leapt into my head almost entirely complete.*

I don't have a favorite book, but I have owned seven different copies of Pride & Prejudice, *because in those dark days before ebooks, whenever I ran out of books on vacation without a good bookstore nearby, I would paw over whatever limited stock was in range and almost always decide that I would rather re-read* Pride & Prejudice *than whatever else was available.*

WELL, MR. BENNET, SUCH DREADFUL NEWS," his lady said to him one day. "The Seventh Wing is come to Meryton. Whatever is to be done?"

"I do not see that anything can be done," Mr. Bennet said. "The Admiralty are most unreasonable, to be sure, but I believe they insist on safeguarding the nation. We will have to endure not being bombarded by the French in the night."

"Oh! Pray do not joke about such a thing, and you must know I am speaking of Elizabeth: what is to be done?"

Miss Elizabeth Bennet did not ordinarily occasion any great maternal anxiety. Indeed, Mrs. Bennet contrived tolerably well not to think of her second daughter at all, save to pronounce her "comfortably settled, with her uncle," and very occasionally to write the girl a long, badly-spelt letter detailing the most recent of her woes and nervous maladies. The object of these missives responded with brief and encouraging notes which a more careful reader than her mother might suspect were written without any reference to the original.

Mrs. Bennet was of a family less respectable than her husband's. Her elder brother was indeed an officer in the notorious Aerial Corps, though himself gentlemanlike in his manners and respectably married. Having achieved the rank of first lieutenant, the elder Gardiner did not look further, and as officer to one of the Chequered Nettles stationed in London, enjoyed there a settled family life. They naturally did not move among the better circles of society, and displayed a distressing lack of concern for it.

Meanwhile, with her husband's estate entailed upon a distant cousin, and having produced five daughters dowered with little more than an inclination to be handsome, Mrs. Bennet early began to consider herself justified in indulging an anxiety for their future. Her fretful concerns occasionally found in her brother an audience, and drew him at last to bring forward a hesitant offer couched in vague terms, of a form of support which he might perhaps be able to offer one of his nieces.

Her answering raptures made him cautious. "Pray do not be so enthusiastic, my dear sister," he said with high alarm. "I must speak with my brother, first," and insisted on closeting himself at length with Mr. Bennet without any further intelligence.

"I am sure you have the best uncle in the world," Mrs. Bennet informed her eldest daughters, Jane and Elizabeth then being thirteen and ten years of age respectively, and considered old enough to bear their mother company in the sitting room of a morning when no more entertaining visitors had presented themselves. Her good opinion was a little shaken, shortly thereafter, when Mr. Bennet disclosed to her the full nature of her brother's proposal. But she was possessed of that happy sort of character which was very soon able to discard such considerations as danger and hard use and loss of respectability, when these were weighed against the certain and immediate satisfaction of having one of her beloved children taken off her hands. After only a brief hesitation she renewed her approbation, and pressed her husband to accept.

This was no less than to sacrifice one of her daughters to the Aerial Corps, to be trained as a captain for some peculiar and recalcitrant breed of dragon which refused male handlers. "I would not suggest it for a moment, my dear sister," Lieutenant Gardiner said that evening to his sister and brother-in-law, as they sat together in the drawing room after dinner, "save that there are two Longwing breeding pairs currently at work and a third to come shortly. We confidently expect to have a new beast to harness every other year for the next decade, and there is a sad lack of coming candidates. My niece is quite certain to make captain, if she have any aptitude for the work."

"Oh! A captain in the Corps!" Mrs. Bennet said. "I am sure it would be a splendid thing for any of the girls."

"And which of the girls would you propose?" Mr. Bennet said, in his dry way, having been silent for most of the evening. Mrs. Bennet was not so unnatural a mother as to be equal to the question.

The next afternoon, the two elder Miss Bennets had the questionable pleasure of accompanying their father and uncle to the covert at Meryton, where a courier-dragon had brought him on his visit, and of seeing the beast themselves. Jane shrank away in alarm from the inquisitive Winchester, which had thrust its head forward to inspect the ribbons on her gown, but Elizabeth, already independent-minded and bidding fair, in her mother's opinion, to be a difficult girl, after only a few shrinking moments asked if she might safely pet the creature.

"I do not mind at all," the dragon answered her, "—you might scratch my cheek right there beneath the harness; there is an itch I cannot get at conveniently."

Too young to be much surprised at being addressed by a dragon, she industriously squirmed a small hand beneath the leather harness and scratched away heedless of the inch-long fangs near-by, to the dragon's loud appreciation. Her uncle directed a significant glance at her father over her head. Three weeks later she willingly departed under his aegis for the training grounds in Scotland, and so was lost to her parents and to respectable society.

But she had done well in her new profession, and her uncle's promise had lately been fulfilled: since the spring, she had been *Captain* E. Bennet, of the somewhat scandalously named Wollstonecraft, and her last letter to her parents had announced her assignment, with her newly trained dragon, to the Seventh Wing.

"I am surprised, my dear," Mr. Bennet now answered Mrs. Bennet. "I have heard you lament the distance between you and your daughter any time these past nine years. Surely this must be an occasion for rejoicing."

"Of course I am excessively glad to see dear Elizabeth again," Mrs. Bennet said. "But if she is to be in Meryton, she cannot fail to meet the rest of the village in the street from time to time. Whatever will they think? It cannot do the other girls any good."

"You are quite right. We must make our sentiments on the matter perfectly plain. We will give a ball for her in two weeks, and invite the neighborhood."

Mrs. Bennet objected in horror and at length. Mr. Bennet was unmoved. He was of a capricious and sardonic nature, which delighted in human folly. Elizabeth had been his favorite for her quick wit, even as an unformed child, and he had really regretted her loss. His consent to her departure for the Corps had only been obtained, though he had never avowed it, from a peculiar fear of the sorrow which might be her lot if she *did* marry to secure her future, unlike his wife's concern for the reverse.

That same peculiarity in his character now induced him to insist upon an occasion which promised to give pleasure to no-one directly concerned, as Captain Bennet's reaction on receiving the brief note which informed her of the honor to be done her more nearly resembled her mother's than anything else.

"Whatever am I to do?" she demanded of her interested dragon, who was peering over her shoulder at the letter.

Wollstonecraft offered no assistance, merely advising her with great enthusiasm to purchase a dress and jewels. "You are sure to meet a tall and handsome stranger," she added, "who will fall madly in love with you." The dragon had in her first year already developed a great taste for gothic literature, which led her to view an eligible lover as a desirable sort of prize; and had given her a highly inaccurate notion of the usual course of a ball.

"What a strange creature you are," Captain Bennet said, although with a caress of the long and deadly snout beside her which belied her words. "Nothing could be more inconvenient, if it were in the least likely to happen."

"I do not see why not. You are very pretty, all the aviators say so."

Wollstonecraft spoke with immense satisfaction, much to Captain Bennet's mingled mirth and dismay. "They are not thrown much in the way of pretty girls, you know," she answered her dragon, laughing. "I am afraid we cannot consider them reliable authorities."

She could not easily excuse herself from the pleasure of the occasion, not even on the grounds of duty, for the station at Meryton was, she knew very well, a mere way-station where little action was to be expected. She was young, and her dragon even younger, and only necessity had made her a captain and formation-commander with so little experience to her credit. In her rear-officer, Captain Winslow of the Parnassian Vindicatus, she had a twenty-year veteran who was entirely competent to answer any small French incursion without her. The prospects for any larger action were so insignificant as to bar consideration. She could not say it was impossible for her to leave her post for a single night.

Having resigned herself to suffering a ball in her honor, Captain Bennet was not so without vanity that she did not wish to appear to advantage. She was a little better equipped for this task than most young women of the Corps, having been received home at Christmastime, and having besides spent a good deal of time in the society of her uncle's family: one of his own daughters had also gone to the Corps, but the other had preferred to remain in the domestic sphere, and had just lately married a promising young officer. And to provide a more immediate advantage, her sister Jane braved the terrors of the covert to escort her to the town seamstress.

"My dearest Jane," Captain Bennet said, embracing her sister, "how well you look! I must be very glad to have gone to the Corps. I would certainly have required a great deal of fortitude otherwise to be always outshone by my sister. Here, this is my darling Wollstonecraft: is she not lovely?"

"Oh! Yes," Miss Bennet said, trying to smile despite trembling: only a very partial spirit indeed could have applied the epithet to Wollstonecraft, who added to the usual glaring orange eyes of a Longwing a slightly lengthened and vicious-looking snout framed between the yellowed spurs of bone whence the deadly acid came. Her upper teeth protruded around her lower jaw, producing an overhang rather like stalactites, and these were dangerously serrated. "Lizzy, she will not—she will not bite, will she?"

"Of course I will not bite," Wollstonecraft said, "unless a French dragon should try and come this way: and in that case, I should spit, and not bite them, most likely. So you are Elizabeth's sister? I am very pleased to meet you. Pray will you be sure that Elizabeth buys a very nice gown? I am fond of purple, myself, and I think she would look excellently well in it."

Captain Bennet withdrew to her small private cabin to exchange her trousers and coat for a walking-dress, and shortly the sisters walked out of the covert and into the town arm in arm. "So tell me more of this Bingley fellow of yours," Captain Bennet said. "All I know from my mother's last letter is he has five thousand a year and danced with you twice at the assembly, and that I am to wish you happy at any moment; and from yours, only that he is somewhere between sixteen and eighty years of age."

"Oh!" Jane cried, coloring a little, "I do wish—I do wish that our mother might express herself with a little more circumspection. Of course she was writing to you, my dear Lizzy, and no one could ask her to be anything less than frank, but I fear she has led you astray. Mr. Bingley has been—is—extremely civil, but nothing more than that."

"Is he handsome?"

"Anyone would call him handsome, I think. His manners are all that is pleasing, and I will say that he is the most charming gentleman of my acquaintance. But that is all."

"Oh, that is all, is it! I see my mother has understated the case, for once," and from this conclusion Elizabeth refused to be moved by her sister's continuing protests. "Unless he is a great fool, he must love you, for he will not find anyone half so beautiful and so good-natured anywhere in the world, so if your heart is won, I must count you as good as lost. I can only hope he deserves you, dear Jane."

She thus found herself glad of the ball after all, for its offering her the opportunity of looking Mr. Bingley over more closely. Perhaps as a natural consequence of her now-settled independence, she had begun to think herself a protector of her sisters. Well aware of their mother's single-minded devotion to their establishment, and privately mistrustful of her parent's judgment, she feared to see Jane pressed to enter into a situation which could not give her true happiness.

But on this score she was soon relieved from care. The night of the ball arrived, Mr. Bingley was presented to her early in the evening, and she rejoiced to find him as Jane had described him, an amiable young man with easy and unaffected manners, ready to please and be pleased by his company. "Miss Elizabeth Bennet!" he cried, plainly not even noticing that she had mistakenly shaken his hand, rather than merely giving him her fingers to touch. "I am delighted to make your acquaintance at last. I understand you have been from home long?"

"I have made my home with my uncle these last nine years, sir," Elizabeth said—not untrue, if one considered the

Corps their mutual home—"and am only lately settled in Meryton, for a time."

"Well, I am very glad to hear it," Mr. Bingley said, with every appearance of meaning his words. "I know it will not fail to give your sister the greatest pleasure, and I hope we will see a great deal of you, as long as you are here."

His warmth was amply recompensed by the cold bare civility of his sisters. "Your uncle is an aviator, I understand," Miss Caroline Bingley said to Elizabeth, with an air of very faint incredulity, as though she did not care to believe it.

"He is," Elizabeth said, and added with a little pardonable malice, "we have several officers, in our family." She had endured a great deal of hissed whispers from her mother before the party on the need for secrecy, and the deadly danger to her sisters' reputations if her own profession should become known to the company.

She was armored against incivility, however, by the knowledge that a dragon waited eagerly for her to return and give a full accounting of the gowns and jewels worn by every lady present. She did not feel unequal to her company: her gown was silk, her hair had been done up by her mother's maid, and without attaching any great importance to the fact, she was comfortably aware she was in good looks.

She could not help but take a certain small satisfaction in having the young gentlemen of the neighborhood seek an introduction, and solicit her hand in one dance after another. But Captain Bennet was enough her father's daughter to laugh at herself for this vanity, and to be amused rather than piqued when she overheard Mr. Bingley's particular friend, a Mr. Darcy, describe her scornfully to that gentleman as "tolerable, but not handsome enough to tempt me," when Bingley would have presented him to her as a partner.

Others did not take the remark so lightly, however. "Oh!" Wollstonecraft said, her scarlet eyes widening when this incident had been recounted to her, in the spirit of sharing a joke. "If only I had been there! I should have given him a sharp lesson. *Tolerable,* indeed! My beloved Elizabeth, you must have been the most beautiful lady there, I am sure of it. Although," she added broodingly, "I do wish you had agreed to buy some jewels."

"No, my sister Jane was that," Elizabeth answered, with real satisfaction, "and my family are not rich enough for me to go about buckled in jewels: a fine thing it would look for me to be in diamonds, and my elder sister with a string of pearls."

"Diamonds," Wollstonecraft sighed.

Elizabeth laughed. "I am very content with my ball, in any case. Jane has found herself a charming young man, I believe, who may be the only person in the world as amiable and accommodating as she is herself. They are very well matched. As for Mr. Darcy, I am told by my mother that he is past bearing with, and if she can say so, considering that he has a splendid estate in Derbyshire and ten thousand a year, that paints him a very monster indeed. I can well support the burden of his disapproval."

She thought herself done once more with society, having endured this trial, but events were not to permit her so easy an escape. Having made arrangements to enjoy a country walk with her sister three days hence, Captain Bennet was disturbed to receive a short and ill-written letter from Jane early upon the prescribed morning with her excuses: she was at Netherfield Hall, and too ill to leave the house.

"She must be at death's door to write me such a letter. I think I had better have a look in on her," Elizabeth said to Wollstonecraft. "Will you mind if I have Pulchria lift me over? We cannot go stampeding all Mr. Bingley's game, and the lawn of Netherfield Hall is not large enough for you." This was nearly true, but Elizabeth also thought it ill-advised to take Wollstonecraft anywhere she might encounter the unfortunate Mr. Darcy. The dragon had not ceased to mutter with indignation. "I will come back tomorrow midmorning, at the latest."

"Of course not," Wollstonecraft said, after a moment of visible struggle. "But I will just have a word with Pulchria," she added, "in case you should see that Mr. Darcy," confirming Elizabeth's concern.

Pulchria, a Grey Copper, was one of their rear-wing dragons, and only six tons; neither she nor her captain had any objection to the short jaunt. Captain Bennet was shortly deposited upon the lawn, and walked up to the house in front of an alarmed audience whose presence was betrayed only by the twitching of curtains in the windows. Thinking not at all of her appearance, she had worn her one other walking-dress, sadly outmoded, and her Hessian boots beneath, which had kicked up a great deal of mud onto her hem by the time she reached the door.

Mr. Bingley received her with great generosity and warmth despite having been called from his breakfast table by a dragon at the door. The civility of his welcome was not matched by the rest of the scandalized party, who answered her own very perfunctory greetings with a few cold syllables, and as soon as Mr. Bingley escorted her to her sister's room, they were quick to exclaim over her behavior. "Well, Mr. Darcy," Miss Caroline Bingley said to that gentleman, "I am sure you would not wish to see your sister astride a dragon, or presenting such a peculiar appearance."

"Certainly not," Mr. Darcy said, but as his astonishment caused his gaze to follow Captain Bennet as long as she was in sight, this response did not much satisfy Miss Bingley.

Quite unaware of this exchange, Elizabeth was disturbed to find Jane very poorly indeed, and the doctor, who was attending her, unsparing in his concern. "I am afraid I do not know the first thing about nursing, but if you can write me out instructions, I will see it done," she said to that gentleman, and took herself back down to the sitting room, where Mr. Bingley had returned.

"Thank you, sir," she said, in response to his sincere expressions of hope for Miss Bennet's speedy recovery, "but I am afraid Jane is not well at all. However, if you will be so good as to lend me a few of your older maidservants, I trust we may contrive to pull her through the wind."

She addressed Mr. Bingley, unconsciously, with the calm certainty which she was used to use with her own officers and crew. She had been encouraged in that mode early in her training by one of her commanders, Captain St. Germain of Mortiferus. "You're too slight, m'girl," that officer, who suffered not at all from the same complaint, had said, "and too pretty. You shan't be able to bellow the fellows down as Roland or I can do; so you must make it sound there ain't any question they will do as you wish." At first hard-won, by now that assumed air of authority had become second nature in any circumstance where she felt herself in command, and she had not the least hesitation in taking charge of her sister's care even in Mr. Bingley's house.

Mr. Bingley himself did not take notice of her manner: he was too intent upon promising her any assistance she required, and directing his housekeeper to meet her requests at once. But Mr. Darcy regarded her across the room with renewed surprise, and as soon as Elizabeth had gone again, Miss Bingley once more cried out upon her. "What an abominable air of independence!" she said. "I declare I am ready to sink with shame on her behalf. It must be this excessive association with aviators. I would almost say it has destroyed her respectability."

"I think it shows a very great consideration for her sister," Mr. Bingley said, protesting, but he was quickly sunk beneath a storm of opposition from his sisters.

Elizabeth would have returned scorn for scorn, if she had known anything of Miss Bingley's remarks. But she was quite preoccupied, all the rest of the day, with her sister's care. Miss Bennet was far more ill than she had wished to acknowledge even to herself, and her fever proved stubborn enough to hold until early in the evening. The third ice-bath at last broke it, and she was eased into bed weary but with slightly better color.

"There," Elizabeth said, "you begin to look more like yourself, dear Jane. I think we have turned the corner, but I will not leave you until the morning. I hope Wollstonecraft will forgive me, but I am determined to bivouac at the foot of your bed tonight."

"Dearest Lizzy," Jane said drowsily, "I am so very grateful to have you, although I ought not say so, for I know you are neglecting your duty for my sake. But you must go down for dinner."

"I hope not. They cannot want me, and I have nothing to wear."

"You shall wear my clothes. Our mother sent some things for me, when she learned I could not leave directly. Pray do, sister. I cannot be easy in my mind when I have already so abused Mr. Bingley's hospitality."

Reluctantly, Captain Bennet went down in her borrowed gown and slippers, to face a company as unwelcome to her as she was to them. Mr. Bingley she thought better and better of, every moment, but of his sisters and friend she thought less and less. By nature independent-minded, her training and the company of aviators had increased her sense of scorn for condescension and the forms of polite society, when these were unaccompanied by real accomplishment and warmth.

"I hope dear Miss Bennet is better?" Miss Bingley asked her with a thin cold politeness, but as this was followed in close succession by her turning away and pressing Mr. Darcy for his opinion on the ragout of rabbit which had just been offered him, Captain Bennet was very little inclined to view it as evincing any real sentiment.

Her brother's inquiries, when they had retired to the drawing room, were more eager and more sincere. He repeated several times his hope that Miss Bennet should be wholly well soon, his determination she should not leave one moment sooner than this event, and his pleasure in Elizabeth's own company.

"Thank you, sir," Elizabeth said, touched by his kindness, although she could not feel herself a happy addition to the party. She did not play whist, and had to avow a lack of familiarity with the poets on whom Miss Bingley, with an air of great condescension, inquired for her opinion; and when Mr. Hurst expressed, with a grunt, his dour certainty of Bonaparte's coming across the Channel one of these days, she was unable to refrain from answering with quick scorn, "Not while Mortiferus and Excidium are at Dover."

"Eh? Who?" Mr. Hurst said, and she was recalled to her own indiscretion.

"The Longwings stationed at the covert there," she said as briefly as she might, belatedly conscious she had arrested the attention of all the company.

"You mean the dragons, I suppose," Mr. Bingley said, eager to pursue any line of conversation which should make his guest more comfortable, unaware that she would really have preferred any other. "I am ashamed to say I do not know the first thing about them. Are Longwings very large?"

Elizabeth could not refuse to answer, although she feared to betray herself at any moment. "Middle-weight, sir," she said reluctantly, "but they are vitriolic—they have venom."

"They can't poison all the French coming over," Mr. Hurst said, with a snort.

"A Longwing's venom is capable of working through six inches of oak in ten minutes. A drop will kill a man at once. Bonaparte cannot come across with less than a hundred dragons, if that would even do, so long as we have Long-wings on the defense."

Captain Bennet spoke decidedly and with pride. Although she would have been sorry to embarrass Jane, not even that consideration could outweigh her loyalty to the

Corps. But she was conscious of putting herself forward, and she took the pause which her response brought as an opportunity to escape to the other side of the room and pretend to be perusing the books on the shelf there.

This brought her nearly to Mr. Darcy's elbow, where that gentleman sat writing a letter, and in a minute Captain Bennet became aware that he had paused in his work and was sitting back in his chair, looking at her as though he meant to address her. She glanced at him with open inquiry, wondering why he did not speak, before she recollected that she ought not have taken notice. But by then he had flushed a little and rose to join her politely, much to her dismay.

"I suppose you are fond of Vauban," he said, naming one of the authors on the shelf she regarded.

"I find he relies too much on mathematics, sir; in my opinion Coehoorn is more useful, as a practical matter," she answered, thoughtfully, before she recollected too late again that she ought know nothing of fortifications, and supposed that he had been meaning the remark as a jest at her expense.

Mr. Darcy, who had merely cast upon anything to hand on which to make conversation, was unaware of the sentiments he had provoked: he only recognized that her color heightened and her eyes were remarkably brilliant. "I have not made a study of such matters myself," he said, and then was silent.

"I begin to fear you must think us very useless creatures, Miss Elizabeth Bennet," Mr. Bingley called to her from the table. "And I cannot defend myself against the charge, but I assure you Darcy is a very sober fellow—at school he was forever at his books."

"And bent upon studies more natural and appropriate to your station in life," Miss Bingley said to Mr. Darcy, quick to interject herself into the conversation in his defense. "I am sure Miss Elizabeth will agree with me, will you not? After all, we cannot all be aviators."

"By all means," Captain Bennet said, still in a temper, which this sly remark did not improve. "It is not everyone who can occupy themselves with the business of defending the nation."

She was sorry directly she had spoken; if Mr. Darcy and Miss Bingley chose to be uncivil, the same behavior was not pardonable on her part, having imposed herself upon her host. "The management of a great estate must be as difficult as that of dragons," she added hastily, to take the sting from her words, "and as necessary," and offered Darcy a slight inclination of her head, as she would have made to a fellow-officer whom she had accidentally offended.

Darcy answered it in kind, and with Jane as her excuse, Elizabeth shortly made her escape from the drawing room, feeling an equal share of mortification and disdain. "I must confess to you, dearest Jane," she said, when she sat beside her sister once again, "as wretched as I feel to have so exposed myself to your friends, and on your behalf for having so awkward a sister, I cannot but be profoundly grateful for the good fortune which gave me my escape from a life of such intercourse. How can it be supported! Such idleness, mingled with such insipidity! I should far rather face a volley of rifle-fire than endure many more nights of like company."

. . .

WITH JANE ON THE MEND, Elizabeth had intended to return to the covert at the first hour of the next morning, but this aim was frustrated, when she woke, by a cold rain falling. She did not think the conditions so very bad; she would have set forth glad only for the loan of a cloak, and spoke of asking, but Jane expressed so much astonishment at the idea of her walking a few miles in spring rain that Elizabeth was forced to realize she would cut an even more peculiar figure with her company if she were to insist upon leaving the house straightaway.

"I must send a word to the covert, then," she said, giving it up, and scribbled a few hasty lines to be read to Wollstonecraft. She enclosed the letter to Captain Winslow, and carrying it downstairs looked for a servant to take it—a great nonsense, she thought, that any domestic might be sent to Meryton with a note, and she forced to remain indoors, as though she would dissolve in a mild shower for having been born a gentleman's daughter.

She encountered Miss Bingley downstairs and stopped briefly to assure that lady of her sister's improving health. "We will of course take ourselves out of your way at the first opportunity," Captain Bennet said. "You must long be wishing your house to yourselves, and I am sorry the rain must keep us here."

Miss Bingley said all that was polite and necessary, with no great enthusiasm, and glancing at the letter said, "May I be of service, Miss Elizabeth? You are writing to your uncle, I suppose?"

"No, my uncle is gone to London," Elizabeth said. "But I should be obliged to you if someone might take this letter to Meryton, for Captain Winslow."

Miss Bingley looked briefly as astonished as if Elizabeth had asked for the moon and then with wooden face put out her hand and said, "If you please."

Elizabeth wondered a little, but thinking little of Miss Bingley's sense, and caring less for her opinions, she did not investigate her reaction; she merely handed over the note, and returned to Jane's room to bear her company and chivvy her into swallowing a little more broth and bread.

Jane was so much improved that by the noon hour, she was able to rise and dress. Elizabeth saw her escorted downstairs, and sheltered from draughts in a place by the fire in the drawing room. The rest of the company joined them shortly thereafter, with sidelong glances at Elizabeth which she did not understand. "My dear Miss Bennet," Miss Bingley said to Jane, "how happy I am to see you so much better. We must have a private word, if the rest of the company can permit it."

Elizabeth could hardly ignore so forceful a hint; she took herself to the other side of the room, relieved to be pursued only by Mr. Bingley, who also bore a curiously anxious look, but spoke to her civilly, until Jane raised her voice from the fire and said, "Lizzy, pray, is this your letter?"

"Good God!" Elizabeth cried, seeing the note in Jane's hand, "Miss Bingley, I depended upon you to have it sent. They will have missed me at the covert this hour and more."

"If you do not scruple to acknowledge it," Miss Bingley said, rising from her chair with color in her cheeks, "I shall not to say that I wonder at your effrontery in attempting to make me your accomplice. As a guest in this house, you ask me to send an illicit letter for you to a gentleman unconnected with you in any way—"

"Impertinent nonsense," Elizabeth said sharply, and turning to Mr. Bingley, "Sir, you must get your cattle in the stables at once, and tied, if you do not want them to spook: there will be a dragon here for me at any moment."

"A dragon for you?" Mr. Bingley said, in plaintive confusion, but Elizabeth was already hurrying for the door, and stopped only long enough to turn back and kiss Jane's cheek, and beg her to forgive the abrupt desertion.

Mr. Darcy, standing by the door, followed her into the corridor with a sharp frown on his face. "Miss Bennet!" he said, and when she paid him no attention and continued towards the front of the house, he caught up to her quick strides. "I cannot understand your behavior," he said, "—it admits of no respectable characterization. At the very least, you owe your host an explanation."

"What I owe my host," Elizabeth said, without slackening her pace, "is to keep his house from being torn down about his ears—oh, damn and blast it all, there she is."

They had come into the gallery, and with the rain slackening and the clouds thinning, Wollstonecraft's shadow showed dark on the grounds outside, the enormous outspread wings throwing a rapidly increasing blot. Elizabeth gave over trying to find her way to a door and instead dashed to the nearest large window. Climbing awkwardly to the sill, she managed to unhook the two heavy panes and throw them open to the air, while Mr. Darcy stared up at her with astonishment.

"Wollstonecraft!" Elizabeth called, waving a hand madly, and with impatience thrust away Darcy's arm: he had climbed up beside her and was trying to restrain her, and for a moment she thought she would have to knock him down.

Wollstonecraft's answering roar shook all the panes as she descended on the grounds and thrust her head towards the window.

"Elizabeth, Elizabeth," she said, "—you did not come! You are quite well? You are not hurt?" She twisted her head to present one enormous and coldly slitted orange eye to Darcy, who to his credit did not immediately flee the scene, but stood with his arm still outthrust to shield Elizabeth from the jaws before her, although his face had gone pale. "Who is that gentleman? Have they kept you here?"

"No, no, my dear!" Elizabeth said hurriedly, "I wrote you a letter, only it went astray: pray don't be alarmed. We must be back to the covert at once, though. Do give me your leg to get up."

Wollstonecraft drew her head away from the window with a low grumble of dissatisfaction. "As long as you are with me again, and you are quite well." She put out her fore-leg to let Elizabeth climb out of the window and into her grasp, making a protective cage of her talons. "Is that Mr. Darcy?" she added, suspiciously.

"That is quite enough: I cannot have you snap at him," Elizabeth said, with alarm.

"I will not *snap,* but before I go away, he *shall* say that you are not merely tolerable, and that he is very sorry to have been so ungentlemanly and rude."

She swung her heavy head back towards the open window; Mr. Darcy, still fixed upon the sill, stared up at the cold look bent upon him, at first only bewildered by such a reproof, coming from such a corner; then he understood the words and flushed deeply. He said awkwardly, "I beg your pardon, Miss Bennet—"

"*Captain* Bennet," Wollstonecraft hissed, angrily.

"Pray will you be silent, you miserable creature," Elizabeth said despairingly. "You will have us in the soup directly. Mr. Darcy, I beg your pardon for her abominable manners, and hope that you will pay no attention to her; she is in a temper and does not know what she is saying. We must go! Pray make my apologies; good-bye."

She kicked Wollstonecraft as hard as the slippers would allow, and with a final grumble the dragon withdrew from the house and took herself back aloft. "Well," Elizabeth said aloud to herself in consolation, as the wind tore at her thin and useless gown, which she was sorry to take away with her in exchange for a pair of good boots and a sensible dress, "at least I will never have to look him in the face again."

ALTHOUGH THE NAME PEMBERLEY HAD a vaguely familiar ring, Elizabeth was too weary, after the dreadful defeat and the long flight from London, to search her memory; she wanted only to put Wollstonecraft down somewhere, and get her formation some sort of fodder to share out for the night. The couriers were flying between the retreating formations with assignments: they were each of them being ordered to one large estate or another, and granted liberty to hunt deer.

They landed upon a broad and beautiful greensward, in the last hours before sunset. Vindicatus laid down the four cannon he carried with a deep sigh of relief; the middle-weights and light-weights set down their two or one apiece, and Elizabeth slid from Wollstonecraft's back with only a silent pat to her neck. The crews busied themselves creating some kind of order out of the general confusion, and Elizabeth nodded to Rowling, her ground-crew master, who told off a few men to the great house high up on the hill, for supplies.

"Do you think you could hunt for everyone, my dear Wollstonecraft?" she asked, low: she hated to ask for more, after Wollstonecraft had been aloft all day, but she alone of the dragons in their company had not been burdened with cannon, kept free to maneuver in case the French beasts should catch them. They had been detailed off by Admiral Roland to cover the Corps' retreat.

"Of course," Wollstonecraft said stoutly, and took herself into the forest; in a little while she came back with five limp deer, and all the dragons tore into the lean frames without any hesitation. "I have eaten another," Wollstonecraft said, licking her chops clean of blood, "and there is a lake just over the hill when we are thirsty: and oh! Elizabeth! The loveliest house imaginable."

"I will go and have a look, Winslow, if you have no objection," Elizabeth said, wanting badly to wash her face, and when she had gone up and rinsed her mouth and spat, she took off her flying hood and patted down her blown hair. She looked across the water, tiredly, at the great golden expanse of Pemberley House standing there, as wide across as the lake itself, it seemed to her, and almost dream-like after the fury and struggle of the day. And as she stood there, the master of the house came out of the wood around the edge of the lake, walking swiftly towards the encampment, and halted when he saw her.

Captain Bennet stared at him blankly and said without thinking, "Mr. Darcy!"

"Miss Bennet," he said, in equally instinctive answer,

then stared at her. She was in flying-gear, of course: trousers, Hessians, her long leather coat with the split tails and her sword and muskets belted at her hip.

"Were you coming to the camp?" she said after a moment. "We can walk down together."

He fell into step with her, silenced momentarily by the very number of questions provoked by her appearance. He had not forgotten Miss Elizabeth Bennet in the intervening three years, and indeed had long wished to see her again, and to demand of her some rational, if not respectable, explanation for the incident which she had caused at Netherfield Hall.

He knew that the elder Miss Bennet had confided some explanation to Mr. Bingley in apology for the scene which had been visited upon his house, and the confusion of his stables. But Bingley refused to communicate that explanation, having received it in confidence; he could only say he was himself perfectly satisfied, and that Miss Elizabeth Bennet had acted as she ought. Yet his character was sufficiently complaisant and generous to have made Darcy doubt this conclusion exceedingly, and to continue to desire a confrontation with the guilty party.

He knew he was to blame for having so enthusiastically pursued the society of the Bennets, in seeking that confrontation, that he had neglected to preserve his friend from the danger of that same society. Darcy had gone to half-a-dozen assemblies and house parties where Miss Elizabeth Bennet might have been expected to appear. Finding her gone on one excuse after another, he had brooded on her absence without attention for the progression of Bingley's courtship. When Darcy had finally been roused to alarm, Bingley, emboldened by Miss Jane Bennet's confidence, had already persuaded himself of his place in that lady's affections, and he refused to be moved therefrom by all the entreaties which Darcy and his sisters could make. Darcy could afterwards only console himself for this failure by considering that the lady was as admirable in every other regard excepting her connections as she was lamentable in those, and that the match was already proving a remarkably happy one.

But the Seventh Wing had departed for Edinburgh even before the wedding, and in so doing had put an end to all hope of further intercourse between Mr. Darcy and Miss Elizabeth Bennet. Not, however, an end to his thoughts of her. The mode of her departure from Netherfield Hall might have been sufficient to fix her in his memory as a figure of scandal, but without his wishing it so, another feeling also had secured her place as a woman of whom he had not ceased to think, and against whom he found himself comparing all others of his acquaintance.

From time to time, against his will, he recalled as plainly as though he stood there in the gallery again her slim figure standing upon the broad window-sill, heedless of the rain and wind which billowed the thin gown against her body and tore her hair loose—recalled her arm outstretched to calm the savage beast bending towards her, and felt her once more slip away from beneath his grasp as she stepped into its talons. He had struggled again and again to conquer the unruly sentiment which made so disreputable a scene nevertheless impossible to forget, without success.

He had tried to persuade himself that he was shocked, more than any other emotion; when this effort failed him, he settled it with himself that he only acknowledged her courage, as one might admire a worthy foe—he had struggled himself not to be unmanned in the face of the dragon. But he looked at her again now in the twilight, and before they reached the camp he halted and said abruptly, "Miss Bennet!"

She looked at him with some apprehension. He said, "Forgive me—I would speak as the friend of your brother Mr. Bingley, as he is not here; I hope you know that any protection I may offer you, on his behalf, I would be honored to do. I hope you will come to the house and stay with us as long as you wish. My sister is presently at home with her companion, a widow of respectable character, and I will take the liberty to extend her invitation with my own."

We may well be astonished at such a leap from condemnation to welcome, if we disregard the power of Mrs. Bingley's assurances, Bingley's own certainty, and an as-yet-unnamed feeling in Mr. Darcy's breast, which had joined forces to defend Elizabeth's character in his mind. He knew enough, more than he wished, of Mrs. Bennet, and recalling her want of scruple began to wonder if perhaps her vulgar determination to see her daughters settled had sacrificed Elizabeth to some evil position. What this might rationally be, he could not conceive, but his suspicions were formed by dimly remembered fairy-stories of childhood, in which dragons figured as the devourers and gaolers of innocent maidens.

Elizabeth was entirely unaware of the direction of his thoughts. Having fled his society in lively dread of the consequences of having betrayed the respectability of her family, she had never considered that a brief exchange during a rainstorm, with a hissing dragon for accompaniment, might not have conveyed to Mr. Darcy a full and accurate understanding of her circumstances and her role in the Corps. She answered him therefore without any of that ordinary caution which she might have used to conceal her position, from one she did not think aware of it. "I am very sensible of the kindness of your invitation, Mr. Darcy—I beg your pardon most sincerely that I must refuse. I cannot leave Wollstonecraft or my men out in the cold."

"Your men?" Mr. Darcy said, but they had reached the camp, where a fresh courier had landed, and Captain Winslow turning addressed Elizabeth and said, "Dispatches, Captain Bennet," as he gave them to her.

"Thank you, Captain Winslow," she said, and broke the seal to read them quickly. "Gentlemen, the scouts have swept the countryside behind us, and it is confirmed that Marshal Davout has fallen off our tails," she said, to the general nods and relief of her formation-captains, who had gathered close around her to hear the news. "The Corps is falling back on Kinloch Laggan. Our orders are to hold here for the moment as a rear position, and secure our own supply as best we can."

She gave a few further orders to that end, and then turned to Mr. Darcy, whose stares she once more misunderstood. "Mr. Darcy," she said, "will you be so good as to walk with me a moment," and taking his arm guided him back out of earshot. He yielded to the pressure of her hand, made unresisting by surprise. She saw that surprise, but misjudged its source. "You must be wondering, sir," she said soberly, "and I shall not attempt to conceal the evil news; there can be no hope of doing so for long. The worst you can imagine is true—Dover is lost—London lost."

Although Elizabeth had misunderstood his looks, her

news repaired her mistake: Mr. Darcy was not of a character to dwell upon his own confusion, when he had just received intelligence of so staggering a blow to his nation; all his questions were forgot at once, and he cried, "Good God!" in real horror.

Elizabeth shared that horror. She had lately been stationed with Wollstonecraft on the northern coast, an isolated posting she knew very well she had brought on herself by speaking too frankly to the Admiralty of her sentiments at the recent demotion of Admiral Roland. A frantic courier-message had brought them to the battle of the Channel too late to do more than bear witness to its conclusion: fifty thousand men already landed with a hundred French dragons circling for cover above them; and she was now fresh from the newest disaster outside London, where Napoleon had nearly snapped his jaws shut about the entire British Army.

Her spirits were badly bruised, but she was conscious of her duty not to spread demoralizing sentiments; with an effort she rallied herself to add, "I am sorry indeed to be the bearer of such news, but I will leaven it, if I may, by assuring you that hope is not lost; our forces have by and large escaped Bonaparte's trap, and when we have regrouped, I have every confidence in our eventual victory. Which indeed," she added, with a burst of resentment she could not contain, "might not have been so dreadfully forestalled, if only Admiral Roland's advice had been heeded—but I must say no more. I fear, sir, that we have put you out."

"As if any such concern should weigh with you, under these circumstances. You shall have everything it is in my power to provide; and I renew my offer, Miss—Captain

Bennet," Darcy corrected himself, not without an involuntary questioning note, which no power could have repressed entirely, "not merely for yourself but of course your—your officers, to quarter with me; I am certain shelter may be contrived for all your men."

"I am afraid the greater difficulty will be in feeding the dragons," Elizabeth said, as they came through the trees around the lake, and found Wollstonecraft sitting raptly on the shore with Pulchria and Astutatis, one of their Yellow Reapers, all of them gazing across the water at the enormous house with all its windows lit up brilliantly, the warm stone capturing the last rays of the sun and shining against the deepening twilight behind it.

"Oh! Elizabeth!" the dragon said, swinging her head about. "Come and look with me. Have you ever seen anything so beautiful? It might all be made of gold. What is that place?"

Mr. Darcy had long nursed, along with his memories of Elizabeth, a painful consciousness of what he considered the failure of his courage, when last confronted with a dragon. He had indeed deliberately come out to greet the aviators on this occasion from an intention to allow himself no such weakness, and was doubly glad in front of Miss Bennet to find himself equal to answering the monstrous creature, "That is my house, Pemberley."

Wollstonecraft rolled one fiery orange eye towards him and exclaimed, "Why, that is Mr. Darcy," followed in a moment by, "Your house?" in tones of rising astonishment.

• • •

"ELIZABETH," WOLLSTONECRAFT SAID, A WEEK later, "I have thought it over at great length, and I suppose I had better forgive Mr. Darcy after all."

"I should hope so," Elizabeth said. She had been surprised and gratefully so by the welcome which Darcy had extended to their formation: she had not looked for anything but the most unwilling and reluctant cooperation from any landowner on whom they had been summarily imposed, and from Darcy in particular would have expected every effort to avoid intercourse with the scandalous aviators settled upon his grounds. Instead he had thrown wide his house to all of them: he had even presented Elizabeth to his own sister, despite any attempts on her part to demur. "I beg your pardon, Mr. Darcy," she had said, "but I cannot get myself up in a dress when at any moment we may have to go aloft."

"Captain Bennet," he said, "I assure you that my sister will not censure your attire; no one could, when you wear it in the course of your duty."

Elizabeth had been moved although unpersuaded, recalling Miss Bingley's refinements upon Georgiana Darcy's perfect deportment and exquisite manners. However, she could not refuse when so pressed, and the introduction being accomplished, had soon understood that Miss Darcy was taken aback only by painful shyness, and was in any case too much in awe of her older brother to disapprove of anyone whom he presented to her.

"Do you really ride a dragon?" Georgiana had dared to ask her, in little more than a whisper.

"There is nothing more delightful, if you have a head for it, and are dressed for the heights," Elizabeth had said, already easy enough with her company to be incautious, and added without thinking, "I should be happy to take you up of a morning, if you like, once the scouts have reported the roads clear."

Almost at once she had recalled to herself the unsuitability of this suggestion. But even to this Mr. Darcy had not objected. He had given her officers dinner every night, and she had been astonished to find him so affable and warm a host with them as to make all his guests easy, even though as aviators they were nearly all of them unaccustomed to polite society and a table of the sort which he laid before them. He had not blinked to be addressed from five seats away, nor when the officers had handed around the dishes among themselves, while his unhappy footmen tried without success to dart in between and recapture them.

Most vitally, he had laid out from his own stores the oats that necessity now prescribed for the dragons' meals, and had insisted they make free not only of his deer but also of his handsome herd of cattle. He had made a point of coming to the covert daily to hear the reports of the scouts, and to share what intelligence his own servants and tenants had brought him of the surrounding countryside. By his correspondence with other men of property, of his and his late father's acquaintance, he had even arranged similar assistance for half-a-dozen other formation companies and some two dozen couriers, to the material assistance of their communications and spying upon the French operations.

"I should hope so," Elizabeth went on now, "when he has been so invaluable to us: I could wish some gentlemen of the Admiralty would behave half as well as he has." She thought with approval of Darcy's visit that morning; they had walked together through the covert, and he had spoken in a sensible way to Vindicatus, whose massive size might pardonably have given pause to any person not accustomed to dragons.

"I have flown over all his grounds, now, when we have not been patrolling," Wollstonecraft said, "and they are delightful in every particular. Do you know, Elizabeth, there is a ruined castle here, which I have been informed dates to the ninth century and is rumored to contain *buried treasure,* and atop that rise to the north where that little cage sits," meaning by this an elegant folly large enough to entertain a party of six, "you will find a charming plaza built entirely of Italian marble, ideal for sunning oneself: it has a magnificent prospect over the entire countryside. As for the house, nothing more could be asked: if only I might go inside! But really I cannot imagine there is anything within to compare to the pleasure of looking upon it from without. I should not tire of the sight all my days. And I believe you once said he has ten thousand a year?"

"You mercenary creature. Are these the qualities which have won him your pardon?"

"Well, it is hard to imagine him such a paltry fellow, when he has so many beautiful things, and he has behaved so prettily since we came, that I am willing to grant he has learned his lesson. Perhaps he was only ill, when he spoke so slightingly of you before; he may have had some trouble with his eyesight at the time."

Elizabeth only hummed idly in answer; she was preoccupied with her reports, which indicated that the French foragers were making grievous depredations against the countryside to the south, and so thought nothing more of this conversation; to her regret. For on the next occasion which offered, several days later, when Mr. Darcy had come to the covert to bring them several handsome bullocks from his herd, Wollstonecraft cornered the gentleman and demanded if this were not indeed the case.

"Wollstonecraft!" Elizabeth said, despairingly. "What Mr. Darcy will think of you,"—of us, she privately thought, with a dismay sharper than she would have liked.

But Darcy stammeringly said, "I cannot claim to have been ill at the time, madam; only gravely mistaken, for it is some time since I have considered Captain Bennet one of the handsomest women of my acquaintance," and having delivered this astonishing speech, he at once colored, then bowed and very abruptly departed, leaving behind a deeply satisfied dragon and a deeply distressed captain, who said to the former, "Oh, for Heaven's sake, Wollstonecraft, pray stop prancing. Can you not see this is the most dreadful situation imaginable?"

CAPTAIN BENNET WOULD HAVE BEEN glad to forget the incident entirely; that being beyond her power, she would have been satisfied only to pretend that it had never happened. She was not insensible to the compliment of Mr. Darcy's admiration, nor could she fail, with such explicit proofs made her, to see that admiration working in all his exertions on behalf of herself and her formation. That it must have overcome all the sentiments which had, she knew, opposed him to his friend Bingley's match with Jane, and to any close association with aviators, was only a further testament to its extent.

If her own feelings towards Mr. Darcy had remained unchanged, she might have been little troubled by knowing of
his. But those feelings were wholly altered: disdain become
respect, dislike become affection. She had come to consider
him a man to be relied upon, and one whose company
brought her pleasure. And she could not help but recognize
that she had indulged in that pleasure, with the excuse of
their circumstances, far past the bounds of propriety. Mr.
Darcy had called upon her every day; she had welcomed his
visits and encouraged them. She had been often alone in his
company. He was not a fellow-officer, and their intercourse
could not be defended as a matter of duty. It had only
seemed so impossible that Mr. Darcy should love her, that
she had never considered whether her behavior might be
giving rise to sentiments which could never be answered.

"I do not see why not," Wollstonecraft said, madden-
ingly. "Only think, Elizabeth, how splendid it should be to
have you the mistress of Pemberley!"

"And what use do you suppose I should be to Pemberley
or its master, when the Corps must send us to London, or
station us in Dover after God willing we have chased Napoleon off our shores?" Elizabeth said. "Besides, you absurd
creature, he may have fallen in love with me, but he cannot
mean to marry me; I am a serving-officer, not a respectable
gentlewoman." She had never before counted her reputation
any real cost. She still did not really regret it now, but was
conscious of a faint pang which served to make her wary of
her own feelings. It must be for the best that Mr. Darcy
would never propose to her. She could only have given pain,
in making him a necessary refusal. She hoped that he would
say no more, and resolved to avoid being alone in his com-

pany henceforth, and to delegate to her officers the necessary discourse between the covert and the house.

These hopes were frustrated, the next day, when walking
to the lakeshore after the morning's patrol, as had become
her custom, she accidentally encountered Mr. Darcy lingering in a small copse of trees along the path. She hesitated,
and nearly turned back; but he caught sight of her and coming near held out a folded and sealed letter, which she received on instinct. "Captain Bennet, I hope you will do me
the favor of reading that letter," he said, and bowing took his
leave.

Elizabeth wanted almost nothing less than to read the
letter; she carried it back to her small bivouac as gingerly as
an incendiary, and considered whether it ought not be put
on the fire at once. But curiosity was too strong to be overcome. She opened the envelope and read, in a clear strong
hand,

Captain Bennet:

I beg you not to fear, on opening this letter, that it
should contain the further expression of sentiments,
which if not grossly offensive, could nevertheless offer
you neither pleasure nor satisfaction. The demands
of honor alone could justify laying this missive before
you, and it has been formed in no expectation of any
reward save the comfort of having made a deserved
apology to one on whom, I fear, I have inexcusably
encroached. While I hardly claim to be owed your
attention, I do sincerely request it, and hope that you
will grant it from generosity of spirit.

That my behavior towards you has been such as
to raise expectations in the eyes of the world, if not
in your own breast, I have been unpardonably late to
recognize. The dreadful circumstances attendant on
your arrival at Pemberley, which must have been your
own foremost concern, I cannot claim as an excuse.
Indeed, the fear that you may have been impelled
by a sense of duty to endure unwanted attentions
has formed no small part of my anxiety to deliver
this letter to you. If this be the case, I must beg your
pardon, while offering you my assurances that these
shall never be renewed, and that those small efforts
on my part which have only been my due, not to you
but to our nation and our King, shall not slacken as a
consequence.

My sense of your own character, however, and
of your forthrightness and courage, has leavened this
particular fear. I trust I have not been so insensible
as to force my company upon you unwilling, and still
more do I trust that you would have acted swiftly,
had I indeed made myself disgusting to you. Yet this
should not render me blameless—indeed, the opposite. The charge that I had attempted to insinuate
myself into the affections of a lady the close connection of my nearest friend, and forced to remain in
my sphere by the exigencies of war, should hardly be
leavened by my having succeeded in that indefensible
object.

Nor can I pretend to have given no thought to the
obstacles which my family and position should lay
in the way of my making the only honorable answer

to having so grossly trespassed upon your feelings, should I have done so. You know too well, I think, that I was at pains to detach my friend Bingley from your sister. That want of connection, and the considerations of propriety, which he wisely refused to regard as an obstacle to his achieving the hand and heart of a lady worth winning, weighed too long and too heavily upon me. I have lately had cause to regret my folly in this regard, seeing in their happy union that best and most desirable outcome which any man might hope for.—Or envy.

Only when I had exposed my feelings to you so outrageously, yesterday afternoon, was I forced to set aside the last of my selfish concerns. It seemed to me then that I had nothing more to do but decide upon the mode of a declaration whose substance was demanded by my honor. I am ashamed to say that it was only in attempting to form that declaration in accordance with the respect I feel for you, that I discovered the impossibility of doing so.

In my self-centered preoccupation, I had neglected to contemplate those obstacles which your position should place before your receiving with pleasure the addresses of any gentleman. Having at last done so, I was struck with their inescapable force. That you should desert your dragon in the hour of our country's need, or worse yet remove her from the fray, must be unimaginable, an act very near treason, and even to propose that you should do so an insult which no person of spirit could easily endure.

I am well aware this explanation is a paltry one.
It is little defense to say that pride and vanity have
been my distraction. If I had sooner shown the proper
consideration for your situation, I should not now find
myself obliged to choose how to offend one whom
I both esteem and admire. I can only say that I may
justly be reproached for anything but a lack of sincere
feeling. My folly has not been self-interested, and I
hope I have injured no-one worse than myself in its
commission. Only one answer can be made, and that
is to assure you that if by any act now or henceforth
I may make amends for my behavior, I shall be yours
to command. I have nothing more to say but God
bless you, and to hope you will pardon me for styling
myself,

Your Most Obedient Servant,
FITZWILLIAM DARCY

CAPTAIN BENNET HARDLY KNEW WHAT to make of her letter.
That Mr. Darcy should have so far overcome his pride as to
wish to pay his addresses to her, in spite of the material objections to the match which she herself had viewed as an
impassable bar, would alone have surprised her; that he
should have refrained not for the sake of his reputation but
for that of her own honor as an officer, was so astonishing as
to nearly make her doubt her own understanding. The letter
had to be read again. But the meaning did not alter on a
second reading, or a third, except for the more inconceiv-

able. Indeed Mr. Darcy had contrived, while not soliciting her hand, to offer his own; the conclusion could be understood in no other way.

It now remained only for Elizabeth to be gratified that she had inspired so fervent an emotion, and to be sorry for the pain she had unintentionally given. These must be the boundaries of her own feelings on the matter. Anything else was impossible. She knew it well. If she read the letter three times more, and folded it away into the inner pocket of her coat rather than burn it, that was only a gesture of sympathy. Her mind dwelt on particular phrases only to extract their full meaning—a small vanity, nothing more. *One whom I both esteem and admire*—there was an encomium indeed! Only the most insensible creature in the world could read those words without a stirring of emotion.

Elizabeth found she must stop herself from bringing the letter out again. "This will not do," she said, and took out her dispatches from that morning, instead. But her mind refused to manage the ciphers properly, still bent upon the puzzle of another text. "I will go flying," she said.

Wollstonecraft was nothing loath to accommodate her wish, but when they were once in the air, insisted on speaking to Captain Bennet only of the many beautiful features of the grounds and the good qualities of their master, all unaware of the pain she was giving. "There is that tower I believe I mentioned to you," she added. "Mr. Darcy tells me it is a hunting lodge: I believe it is larger than many another person's house. Look, there he is; we will go and say good morning."

Too late Elizabeth reached for the speaking-trumpet: Wollstonecraft had already banked deeply left, descending in a rushing wind that blew away Elizabeth's shout of protest. Mr. Darcy was indeed not far from the hunting lodge, riding alone. He and his alarmed horse looked up at the same time, and the poor beast bolted out from under him.

"Whyever did it run?" Wollstonecraft said, aggrieved, looking after the horse. "I did not mean to eat it; and if I *had* meant to eat it, I could certainly catch it, whether it ran away from me or no."

"You ought to know by now a horse will run when you come down behind it; that is not a cavalry-mount, with a hood and blinders. Mr. Darcy! Are you very hurt?" Elizabeth called down anxiously, unlatching her carabiners, and slid down Wollstonecraft's side to find that gentleman dazed and with the breath knocked out of him, and a badly wrenched knee.

"I can do very well, Captain Bennet," he said in a voice sufficiently thin of air to belie his words, and tried to stand.

"You cannot at all," Elizabeth said, bracing him just in time to prevent a collapse: the leg did not wish to bear his weight. "Whatever were you thinking?" she said to Wollstonecraft. "We must get him inside the house."

"I am sure that need be no great difficulty," Wollstonecraft said, and with her talons pried open the large front door for them, leaving the iron locks hanging from the torn door-frame. "Now it is open. Here, I will put him inside."

Mr. Darcy submitted with more courage than grace to being gathered up in a Longwing's talons. When Wollstonecraft had deposited him more or less intact upon the floor of his entrance hall and Elizabeth had joined him there, with her help he levered himself onto a sofa draped with holland covers in the parlor just off the hall, and then said, "Thank you, Captain Bennet; if you will send word to the house when you have gone back to the covert, I would be grateful."

Elizabeth struggled with the natural instinct to accept this hint, and thereby put a period to a scene which could only be full of awkwardness; but guilt and practicality restrained her. "I cannot desert you in this state when we have been the cause of your injury," she said, and returning to the doorway called to Wollstonecraft to fly back to the covert, and send for help. She turned back into the parlor reluctantly. Mr. Darcy had stretched out his injured leg, bracing the knee, and he had fixed his gaze resolutely upon the fine prospect outside the window, with a degree of attention better merited if a troop of Bonaparte's soldiers had been crossing the lawn.

They neither of them spoke, until the silence had been prolonged beyond any reasonable duration between two people who had neither of them any occupation, and Elizabeth's sense of the ridiculous came slowly to her rescue. "Mr. Darcy!" she said at last. "I suppose we could not have found ourselves in a more awkward situation. We must consider it an opportunity to display our characters. I fear to expose my own as wretchedly forward, but I will venture to speak. I hope you will permit me to thank you for the letter you gave me."

Darcy did not look at her all at once, but turned his head in such a way as to direct his gaze near her feet, and then lifted his eyes in one swift movement to her face, as though fearing what expression he should encounter. But Captain Bennet only smiled, or tried to, although conscious more than ever that her feelings were far from what they ought to have been. Darcy's reserve was not equal to concealing his suffering, given this much leave to express it; his looks betrayed him, and she could not see his unhappiness without wishing almost to share it.

"The only thanks which ought pass between us," he said, nearly inaudibly, "must be mine, if you should accept my apologies."

"None are necessary. I beg you not to repine any further. My situation is so peculiar, so unworldly one might even say, that even the most refined sense of decorum might fail as a guide. I am very sensible of the consideration that you have shown for my honor, and sorry that my own caution should have failed me. It is so many years since I gave over all thoughts of marriage, and in comparison to the unsettled situation of my sisters, and the burden of our mother's hopes, I little regretted it then."

"*Then?*" Mr. Darcy cried, with a meaningful emphasis upon the word.

Elizabeth colored and was silent. It was now her turn to feel she had betrayed herself. To give Mr. Darcy encouragement, when she could give him no hope, was cruelty; to permit herself to desire what must be forever beyond her reach an indulgence she could not afford. But alas! these rational conclusions did as much good to stem the tide of passion as might be expected from the usual efficacy of such measures.

"Captain Bennet," Darcy said, "—Elizabeth," and struggled to his feet, only to nearly overbalance himself again. She went swiftly to him. His arm leaned across her shoulders; her hands were pressed to his side, bearing up his weight. They looked into one another's faces.

Darcy's restraint failed him. "Elizabeth, will you—"

"I cannot," she said, cutting him short. A calm clarity, heretofore only experienced in the moments directly before battle, had settled upon her. Her own choice was made; now honor demanded she make plain the limits of what she might offer him. "I cannot marry you."

Darcy flinched and would have drawn away. Elizabeth reached her hand for his cheek and turned him back, and deliberately raised her chin. He trembled against her in understanding. For one moment longer he lifted up his eyes, gazing blindly towards the window; then he closed them, and bent his head to meet her lips.

CAPTAIN BENNET RETURNED TO THE covert late that afternoon in great disorder of spirit. She had known that the Corps might one day ask her to sacrifice her virtue, in hopes of producing an heir to her captaincy; and she had been bluntly and forthrightly educated on the practicalities by Captain St. Germain. "And I won't tell you not to in the meantime," that officer had added, "because that is of no use; this ain't a nunnery we are living in. Only be cautious about it, and never take one of your own officers to bed."

None of this excellent advice had prepared Elizabeth for the particular evils of her present situation. She had accepted with calm resignation the loss of her reputation and the approval of the world; she had long known she would receive no respectable offers of marriage, and hoped only for an amiable, gentlemanlike arrangement with a fellow-officer, when the time came. But these sacrifices she had learned not to regret. That a gentleman had wished despite every barrier between them to bestow upon her hand and heart, and that she should suffer at refusing him, was a grief for which she had never looked.

"And to such an offer!" she cried to herself, alone in her small tent and looking once again through tears at the fatal letter, "—to such a gesture, I have offered in return only the lowest, most vulgar expression of feeling; in exchange for the honor he has done me, I have only stained his, with no hope of ever repairing the spot. What have either of us gained by it, but uneasiness and worse regrets? And yet, when this is all I may ever have of him—"

Reflection did not ease either Captain Bennet's pain or her guilty conscience. She passed an uneasy night, wondering alternately when next she would have the power of being alone with Mr. Darcy, and hoping for the strength of will to avoid another such encounter; she slept only fitfully, towards the hours of the morning, and roused with difficulty at the sound of a throat cleared outside her tent. She gathered herself hurriedly, and coming outside found her first lieutenant, Cheadle, awaiting her urgently with a fresh dispatch.

She broke the wafer and read the message. Mingled relief and regret: she felt at once that a hand had been stretched forth to save her, only a little too late. "Mr. Cheadle," she said, "pray send to Captain Winslow and the other captains. Admiral Roland requires us at Folkestone without delay. It seems Bonaparte means to try another crossing, and we must be there to stop him."

LIEUTENANT GARDINER'S LONDON ESTABLISHMENT WAS familiar, comfortable, and quiet; an ideal setting for a wounded soldier, and the careful and affectionate nursing of her aunt

Gardiner shortly saw Elizabeth past the crisis of the feverish wound she had taken at the battle of Shoeburyness. But it left her with cause for regret at her surroundings: there was little remaining to distract her heart from its unfortunate occupation.

When Napoleon had been trampling the fields of Britain, and she and Wollstonecraft had nightly to scour the Channel for any sign of French ships trying to bring over more soldiers for his army of conquest, she might thrust Mr. Darcy from her mind with some success. Lying in a peaceful bedroom, with a view over the small garden tenanted by no-one more exciting than her youngest cousins, who furthermore had been abjured to keep quiet to avoid disturbing the convalescent, the matter proved considerably more difficult.

In vain did Elizabeth order herself to forget. The worst danger to her health past, consideration for Wollstonecraft's anxiety had won her the liberty of leaving her bed and going to the covert for a visit, once each day, but this having been accomplished, Captain Bennet was ordered back to her bed with very little to do, and all of that sadly uninteresting and faded. She had always been used to find diversion in many places, but now books slipped out of her hands and slid to the coverlet with their pages unturned; trays were carried away with only a few mouthfuls taken; and she answered with so much distraction and restlessness, when her aunt sat with her, that Mrs. Gardiner began to be afraid for her health, and speak to Lieutenant Gardiner of calling in a physician.

But Admiral Roland came to her first, a fortnight after the battle, with a better medicine. "Bennet, you have a listless air," she said, with her blunt kindness. "The hole those

Frenchmen put through your side has healed nicely, so I dare say you had better get back to your duties: it will only be light work for a while now, for all of us. In any case," she added, "you will need to be on your feet next Thursday week. They are going to make you Knight of the Bath: it will be in tomorrow's *Gazette*."

Elizabeth had at first to overcome the most extreme astonishment at this news before she was able to express the sentiments of gratitude and delight natural to any young officer in like circumstances. We may well suppose these increased by her complete lack of anticipation of the honor to be bestowed upon her.

"No, you may thank General Wellesley," Admiral Roland said, when Elizabeth attempted to thank her. "The Admiralty would be delighted to go on pretending we don't exist, except when we are in the air, but he has no notion of brooking it, and you may well imagine the lot of them are ready to give him anything and everything, at present."

Such an interesting piece of news could not fail to lift Captain Bennet's spirits—and Admiral Roland's prescription was eagerly seized upon; as soon as her visitor had gone, Elizabeth rose from her sickbed and dressed in haste, meaning to go and share the news with Wollstonecraft. But she had no sooner finished tying her neckcloth when one of the servants came to her room, wide-eyed, to inform her that a *lady* had called upon her, and demanded to see her at once.

"A lady?" Elizabeth said, in some puzzlement.

It was indeed a lady: the card upon the salver read *Lady Catherine de Bourgh*, whose name was only dimly familiar—some struggle was required before Elizabeth recalled that Mr. Darcy had an aunt, of that name. "But whatever can have brought her to see me?" Elizabeth said, wondering also at the lack of propriety in Lady Catherine's coming to call upon a stranger in so insistent a manner, without any introduction to establish the acquaintance. But she could not refuse a relation of Mr. Darcy's, and though wishing nothing more than to be gone, she shifted her clothing once more to put on a morning-dress, and descended to greet Lady Catherine.

She found that noblewoman, dressed with far more grandeur than was appropriate to the occasion and the hour, standing stiffly by the mantelpiece in the sitting room and inspecting with a disapproving expression the handful of small watercolors displayed upon the walls therein, which were not fashionable but merely the handiwork of Mrs. Gardiner's children. "Ma'am," Elizabeth said, and only just remembered to curtsey, instead of bow.

"You are Miss Elizabeth Bennet?" Lady Catherine demanded. Elizabeth admitted it. "I am Lady Catherine de Bourgh—I am, indeed, the aunt of Mr. Fitzwilliam Darcy, and his nearest living relation. Having said so much, I fancy I can have left you in no doubt of the cause which has compelled me to approach you."

"Your ladyship is quite mistaken," Elizabeth said, with increasing reserve; she could not wish but to like any of Mr. Darcy's relations, but it was impossible to excuse the brusqueness of Lady Catherine's manner. "I cannot in the least account for the honor of your visit." But no sooner had Elizabeth spoken than she forcibly recalled the terrible extent of French depredations in the final weeks of the war, and alarm made her forget decorum—she took a step into the room and cried out, "Mr. Darcy is not—your nephew is well?"

But Lady Catherine only colored with anger. "Let it be understood at once, Miss Bennet, that I will brook neither impertinence nor insincerity," she said. "You will not claim the right to make such an inquiry of *me*, while denying me my rights to demand an accounting from you."

Reassured that she could not have received this answer, as peculiar as it was, if Mr. Darcy had been seriously injured, Elizabeth had now only to be baffled. "Your ladyship must excuse me from willfully provoking any such charge. I can only assure you once again of my very sincere confusion, and urge you to speak plainly."

"Very well, Miss Bennet," Lady Catherine said. "My character has always been of a forthright nature, and if you will insist upon evasions, I will meet them with frankness. My daughter and I were forced by the invasion to leave our home in Rosings Park, and seek a refuge with my nephew at his home in Derbyshire. We found him very altered. He would not at first confess the cause, but when I had questioned the servants, I learned that Pemberley had lately been compelled to house a host of dragons and aviators, and that *you yourself,* Miss Bennet, had formed one of their number, and were, indeed, serving as an aviator yourself.—Well? Do you deny this shocking report?"

"I do not," Elizabeth said, her temper rising at the tones in which Lady Catherine uttered the name of *aviator.*

"And you avow it so brazenly! That you have sunk so entirely beneath reproach!"

"If I could consider myself to have done so, in serving

my King, I might indeed feel shame," Elizabeth said. "But I cannot, and if your ladyship means to speak insultingly of the Corps, I must beg to be excused from any further conversation."

"Not so fast, if you please!" Lady Catherine said. "You shall not escape me so easily. I have not come to reproach you for staining your own character and reputation, which must be the business of your own family, but that of a gentleman of irreproachable honor and ancient family—I am speaking of my own nephew."

Halted by this accusation, too close to those she had leveled against herself, Elizabeth did not immediately quit the room, and Lady Catherine seized upon the opening thus afforded her to press home her attack. "My inquiries further uncovered the most appalling intelligence, surely a scandalous falsehood, that through the association thus unavoidably thrust upon him, you had practiced upon him—you had enticed him—to such lengths that he was on the point of making you—*you*—an offer of marriage.

"I could not insult my nephew so far as to broach the subject with him. I knew it must not be the truth—I knew he would never commit so great an offense against the propriety and reputation of his family. But I have been resolved to confront you, as soon as the unsettled state of the countryside should allow it, and to make plain to you that your wiles shall never achieve this disgraceful alliance. Now what have you to say for yourself?"

"Nothing whatsoever, to one so wholly unconnected to me, and who has not scrupled to offer me every form of insult," Elizabeth said, and only the very strongest feeling for Mr. Darcy prevented her from giving a harsher answer. "Your ladyship must excuse me; I can endure no more." She left the room without waiting for another word, shutting the door firmly behind her, and ran directly upstairs to her room, where she paced the narrow confines of her chamber in great disorder of spirit, as conscious of guilt as Lady Catherine might have wished, if from a very contrary motive.

That Lady Catherine thought only of her nephew's reputation in the eyes of the world, and cared nothing either for his virtue or for his happiness, was manifest, and her ill-bred insults invited no answer but scorn. But Elizabeth could not ignore that *she,* too, had safeguarded only the first, and wounded both of the latter. Mr. Darcy had been willing to set aside the opinions even of those nearest to him, whose opprobrium he must have known to expect. He had not counted insurmountable all the practical difficulties which the match would entail, nor should he have. How many women endured with courage long separations from their husbands, gone to sea or covert, and counted the joy of irregular reunions a sufficient recompense?

She had not matched that courage. She had chosen certain misery and vice for both, from the hollow motive of preserving his uncertain chances of future happiness, and her freedom from obligation. But what were those chances? That Mr. Darcy might be expected to marry a woman of superior wealth and rank than herself, was hardly to be doubted. But he had never yet shown himself inclined to do so. That his wife might be expected to devote herself to his interests was equally certain, but he had not made an offer to a woman who could do so. Observers might be amazed that with all his advantages, Mr. Darcy had made a choice so little calculated to improve his comforts in life. But surely she had no right to choose decorum over honesty, and make her duty an excuse to avoid the censure of the world.

In sudden decision, she put off her gown, and dressed again in her flying-gear. A chair bore her to the gates of the covert, where Wollstonecraft eagerly called a greeting as soon as she had come into view. "You are dressed for flying," the dragon said joyfully. "Are you better today at last, dear Elizabeth?"

"I am, my dearest," Elizabeth said. "I am quite well, and I mean to prevail upon you to take me up—indeed, I hope you will not mind taking me so far as Derbyshire."

"To Derbyshire!" Wollstonecraft said, her slit pupils widening orange a moment. "Oh! I should be delighted. Perhaps you have heard from Mr. Darcy?"

"I have not," Elizabeth said, in repressive tones, but Wollstonecraft only gave a knowing nod of her head.

"You are quite right, of course we must call upon him," the dragon said. "It would never do to neglect the acquaintance. Perhaps he has not yet heard of our victory."

"Scheming creature," Elizabeth said, affectionately, and went to speak with Captain Winslow and to acquaint him with her design of going north for a few days; having left the formation in his excellent hands, and having spoken with her first lieutenant and her ground-crew master, and visited her wounded men, she felt herself at liberty to set forth, and went aboard, well bundled against the chill, which if it were not as appropriate in Wollstonecraft's opinion as having set forth in a diaphanous muslin gown and an excessively long and draughty cloak, at least was surer of safeguarding her health.

The flight was not sufficiently long as to tire Elizabeth,

after her long weeks of rest, but entirely long enough to make her anxious for the reception she might find. That Mr. Darcy's heart was likely to be fickle, she did not in the least fear; but it did not seem to her unlikely that he might have thought better of his intentions. "If he should reproach me with having shown an unpardonable indifference to his honor and my own, how might I defend my conduct?" she privately asked herself, as Wollstonecraft stretched her wings, and found no satisfactory answer. But she felt strongly that she owed him the chance to renew his addresses, even at the risk of learning he no longer wished to do so.

Wollstonecraft came down upon the far shore of the lake, with its beautiful prospect upon Pemberley, at Elizabeth's request; she desired at once the chance of composing herself better during the walk towards the house, and to give ample warning of her arrival. But the second aim made the first impossible; when she was only halfway around the circuit of the lake, a break in the trees permitted her to see the master of the house leaving by a side door, and coming quickly along the very path she walked, before he was once again hidden from view. The remainder of the walk did nothing to soothe her spirits. Every step drew her nearer to a final confrontation, and she was sure he was only beyond the next tree or shrub many times before he at last appeared, his hands clenched by his sides and the expression of his face grave and drawn.

He started when he saw her, and instantly cried, "You are very pale—you have been ill," with so much alarm that Elizabeth forgot her first embarrassment in assuring him she was well, and wholly recovered. "But you *were* wounded," he said, low, and she had to confess it; somehow her hands had come to be clasped in his, and he stood with his head bowed over them, and Elizabeth could be stifled no longer.

"Mr. Darcy," she said, "I hope you know I would never reproach you, if you had thought better of the sentiments which you expressed to me, this past December." His head lifted, as she spoke, and he fixed his gaze upon her so intently as to make her avert her own eyes, to maintain her countenance. "My duty remains unchanged, and with it every obstacle in the way of my having the power to offer any man a respectable or a comfortable home, nor have I possessed for years a character which might be compromised in the eyes of the world in such a way as to lay demands upon any man to repair it. But nevertheless I cannot permit the answer which I gave you, on the occasion of our last meeting, to stand. I am ashamed of having made it. No further word will pass my lips upon this subject, but I would not have you think I do not esteem and value you more deeply than any other gentleman of my acquaintance."

"Captain Bennet!" he said. "—Elizabeth!" Although he was too much surprised to express himself very fluently, he did not long leave her in any doubt of his desires and by what means he felt she might best ensure his happiness. A small bench was to be found among the trees a little further along the path, overlooking the lake, and to this place they repaired and sat a long while together, discussing the arrangements for their future. They agreed upon it that Mr. Darcy would shortly take up residence in his house in London, where they would marry, and that they should together wait upon Mr. Bennet at Longbourne the following day, to acquaint her family with their intentions and seek their consent to the match.

"But I am afraid you must first apply to another authority: I certainly cannot marry without Wollstonecraft's permission," Elizabeth said, her spirits now restored enough to laugh, and they went arm in arm to the dragon waiting expectantly at the end of the path.

"Yes, Elizabeth may marry you, if she likes," Wollstonecraft said in judicious and somewhat lofty tones, but when Mr. Darcy had parted from them, to return to the house and share his happiness with his sister, before Elizabeth should join them for dinner, Wollstonecraft very nearly knocked Elizabeth down with a congratulatory nudge, and said gleefully, "And you *shall* be married by special license, of course. Oh! Elizabeth! I do not think there can be a happier dragon in all the world."

"Dragons & Decorum" was originally published in the anthology Golden Age and Other Stories *by Subterranean Press in 2017.*

CASTLE COEURLIEU

The late Barbara Tuchman is one of my favorite historians. This story was heavily inspired by A Distant Mirror, *her wonderful book about the Black Plague and the fourteenth century in medieval Europe, which also planted some of the seeds of* Spinning Silver. *The donjon of Castle Coucy meets the Tower of the tarot deck.*

ISABEAU CAME TO CASTLE COEURLIEU AS A GIRL OF TWELVE, and its lady: she had been married two weeks before to the Comte de Coeurlieu, who was thirty-two and very large, with an always-angry hatchet face slashed and pierced through the left cheek where he had taken a crossbow bolt at the battle of Leprans, full six years ago. She had been excited beforehand: she knew it was a grand match, beyond her family's deserts, and he was famous; he had won a tournament in disguise as a young man, although he was too great a seigneur to have exposed himself so, which was very romantic. But she recoiled a little when she met him, and her voice quavered when she spoke her vows to the middle of his chest.

But he looked down at her afterwards, from his great height, and said not unkindly, "I am for the war in Grosviens. You will go to Coeurlieu, my lady, if it pleases you," and she said with relief, "As it pleases my lord."

Alone then Isabeau came to Coeurlieu. She was not overly impressed by castles, having lived in many, even great ones, but when the carriage crept out of the woods and climbed steadily up the winding road, she could not look away from the ancient donjon rising enormously, a flinty grey that looked nothing like the warm golden stone of the rest of the walls.

"The Duc de Niente built the castle round it, three hundred years ago," Jerome told her, as they sat on one of the outer walls looking upon it, kicking their dangling heels as they ate the quincebread they had stolen from the kitchens. He was the Comte's son, by his previous wife who had died two summers before, and thirteen, but the plague had caught him glancing as a child. He had survived, but his whole right side was weak: he could not hold a sword. So he had been put to be a magister instead, but he hated to read and write, and in the three days since she had come, he had escaped his tutors six times on the excuse of making her new home known to her.

"Everyone knows there's no use to the lessons," he said, matter-of-fact, when she a little timidly asked if he would not be punished, meaning would she not be punished, too. "It will be six years more before I can go to war even to hurl stones. And I won't live so long. It's been eight years since the last plague."

Isabeau nodded. "My mother and my nurse died last time." She remembered her mother not at all, and her nurse vaguely, a warmth suddenly gone out of her life, but that was why the Comte had taken her, with her dowry of only two small castles. Those the plague had passed over, it most often passed over again, and she had lived crying in her room for a whole day and night cuddled to her nurse already dead in the bed beside her. So many people had been dying that no one had remembered to look for her until they came to bring her to her mother's funeral the next morning.

But the plague always came first for those it had marked the last time, and it would come again, soon. So she followed Jerome when he led her to the kitchens and past the table where the cook's sweating third assistant had just brought the quinces from the oven sticky and gleaming in their pastries, and no one stopped them. They carried their stolen prizes out onto the wall, to eat, and to look out the arrow slit at the carts crawling up and down the road to the castle, going in widening circles down the hill and escaping into the countryside, and sometimes they looked instead within, at the life of the courtyard bustling around in the looming donjon's shadow.

"If you are inside, and you close the doors, nothing can get in," Jerome said. "In my grandfather's day, Magistra Pia set fire and wind and half a mountain of stone against it, and all she did was make the walk," pointing to the long irregular stripe of black stone set into the courtyard, leading to the donjon doors. The walk looked much stranger than the tower itself, so polished that the clouds moved in slow reflected billows across the surface, and perfect shades walked upside down beneath everyone who crossed it on their way through.

"Why build other walls, then?" Isabeau asked with interest. The donjon was so enormous it could have held everyone who lived in the castle, all within, and an army besides. It seemed a waste to put anything more around it.

"Strange things happen at night, or when the doors are shut," Jerome said in portentous tones. "And not all who go within come out again."

It was by far the most interesting thing that Isabeau had ever heard of, that she could see with her own eyes and touch with her own hands. She had only heard of war from the jongleurs, singing the clash of swords and the storm-fires raised by the great magisters, and once when she had been eight years old, she had been living in Castle Rouge-Bois and there had been a unicorn sighted in the forest. All the knights and grown ladies had gone out to chase it, and she had run up to the highest tower to watch them ride out in dazzling array, and from there saw one tiny glimpse, on a distant hill, of a white beast darting into the trees. She had never told anyone of it because hers had been the second sighting, and a unicorn was never seen thrice, so everyone came back disappointed with no great horn to make a cup for the king's grace. But the donjon did not run away or vanish. It stood there grey and stolid and nevertheless wondrous, surrounded with as many stories as there were bricks in the castle walls built round it.

Father Jean-Claude, the priest who took her daily confession, was persuaded to put aside his Bible and tell her that one hundred years ago, the rash and boastful Sir Theolian Ogre-Killer had gone into the tower, his squire reluctantly behind him, vowing he would suffer whatever adventure came unto him in that place. But he passed all the day and night loudly carousing, and nothing either strange or wondrous befell him. At last he grew impatient and made to leave, but when he opened the doors to go forth, he found only darkness without, unbroken by any gleam of lantern or sound of human voices. His squire cried out, "My lord, let us not tempt God's mercy, but close again the doors," but Sir Theolian said, "Fie, coward," and seized sword and lantern and set into the dark. His footsteps died away at once, although for a long time after his light might yet be seen receding in the distance.

But his trembling squire knelt and prayed to God for deliverance, and in the midst of his prayers, he heard the bells ringing for dawn, and raising his head saw that sunrise had come into the windows. When he opened the doors and came forth to the courtyard, he there found the same host assembled who had seen Sir Theolian go within, and not the span of a candle's mark had passed. No sign of Sir Theolian was ever from that day heard or seen by mortal man, and so did God rebuke pride and vainglory. But the squire was greatly chastened and took holy orders and became St. Anselm of the Tower, and ever after told the story to warn others from sin.

And Father Jean-Claude triumphantly took Isabeau to see a small hut built against the side of the tower, beginning to collapse now from pilgrims breaking off parts of the branches. The saint's cot still lay within, the coverlet slowly rotting, although his remains were kept in the chapel in a golden casket.

Isabeau liked that story, although she liked better the one the old woman told her, who sat carding wool in the courtyard: In the old days, the crone said, before the castle had been built, and there was only the tower, and its doors stood open to the world—no one could tell Isabeau when the tower had been built, itself, or what man had made it— in the old days, when there had only been the nameless village now called Coeurlieu down at the bending of the river where the old mill still stood, there had been a girl called Beau-Mains who brought her father's flock of sheep every day to graze upon the green hillside round the tower doors. But she was sullen to be set to this duty, because she wished never to work, and only to keep her hands fine and soft, so she did not mind the sheep very well. And so one afternoon in warm summer she slothfully fell to sleep upon the hill and started up only as the sun was going down, and found her flock all gone missing with their bleating voices coming faint from within the walls.

She was afraid of the tower, but she feared more the sharp switch that her mother would use on her back if she came home without her sheep, and so she went foolhardy or brave within. She climbed the stairs round and round and up and up, calling, hearing always the sheep answering her from afar, until she came out upon the roof and found them there with the first stars coming out in the night sky.

They followed her down again. But the great halls had gone very dark, and the stairs went round longer than they ought, and though she walked a long time, she did not come to the ground again. The sheep were docile and huddling close around her legs, as though they feared some wolf or beast, and whenever she turned round and counted them, the number had changed: there were always more.

She began to fear her own flock, even as they clustered round her ever more closely. She shivered and wished mightily that she had paid more attention to her sheep, and could recognize them one from another, and pick out the strange ones, but then to her even greater alarm, one of them she did recognize: as a child she had taken a fancy to one lamb, small and gentle and white, and had fed it by hand, and called it Snow, and loved it, until by mistake her father had butchered it for the village Maying. She had wept for a week.

She wept now with horror as Snow came and butted her hand, and yet she still petted the soft nubbly head for comfort, and said, "Snow, Snow, which way shall I go?" and when

she came to the next landing, which ought have been the
ground and yet was not, the lamb baaed softly and turned
from the stairs and out into the darkness of the hall.

Beau-Mains and her flock followed the little lamb,
which seemed almost to be shining in the dark, until she
came to a door which ought not have been there, in a wall
which did not curve but ran straight as long as the light
reached to either side. Inside she found a table with four
small boxes lying open, and in each a great colored jewel as
large as her fist: the first of red like blood, the second of
browns and deep yellows like mingled shades of earth, the
third a virulent green, and the last as clear as water over
stones. She gasped with delight and snatched the jewels up,
putting them into her apron, and Snow went onward to a
door behind the table.

Beau-Mains followed the lamb, and came into another
room, where inside stood another table with four larger
boxes lying open, each full of coins as is a cup of water: the
first of brass, the second of silver, the third of gold, and the
fourth of some strange black metal which she had never
seen. Beau-Mains would have filled the rest of her apron
only with gold, but the lamb butted her until she grudgingly
took a few coins from each box, as much as the thin fabric
would hold, and followed Snow to a third door.

In the third room there were four great stone coffins of
four great lords, their faces and their swords carved into the
stone and their names upon the sides. Beau-Mains was only
a peasant girl and could not read the letters, but she looked
upon them in silence and knew them for seigneurs of high
birth, for they were tall and comely and well armored. And
in each stone coffin there was a hollow above the lord's

heart, which was made of like shape to the jewels she had found, and upon the eyes of each lord there were carved two stone coins like in size to the coins she had found. Not without a longing look, Beau-Mains put in each hollow one of the jewels, and on the eyes of each lord two of her precious coins, and with the meager handful which was left to her she followed after the lamb through the final door.

And here at last Beau-Mains found herself once more on the floor of the tower, with the great doors standing open ahead of her, but alas! She was not alone in the hall. A terrible beast stood there with a great collar round its neck chained three times to the wall: a vast coiling serpent with its maw directly at the door, its eyes red and its teeth yellow and brown with old bloodstains. It moved and writhed restlessly, and it cast its eye rolling over Beau-Mains and her flock, and it saw them and snorted steam and hunger from its fearsome nostrils. The chains restrained the beast so it could not come at them, though it strained at their limits, but neither could she come to the door, but that she would go so close the beast could devour her.

Now once more the little lamb made its soft bleating noise, and from the flock around Beau-Mains, a great many of the sheep came apart to stand with Snow, and among them Beau-Mains recognized a few others which she knew also had gone to butchering, or been taken by wolves. And the lamb led its portion of the flock away from Beau-Mains, towards the writhing beast, and Beau-Mains hid her face and put her arms round the sheep that remained to her, burying her head against their wool, so she might not hear the savage feeding.

When the sound of devouring had ended, Beau-Mains

lifted her tearstained face from her sheep, and saw that the great beast had gorged and fallen to sleep, and now slumbered with its wet maw shut. On soft feet she led her flock past its red teeth and through the doors and out upon the familiar hillside, and as soon as they were out together they ran and ran and ran all the long way home. And there Beau-Mains would have been whipped by her mother for being late, and for her gasping sheep, and also for telling stories, but from her apron Beau-Mains took out her handful of coins: brass, and silver, and gold, and one coin of strange cold black metal which the smith's forge could not melt, nor his hammer break, and so her tale was known for true, even though the next morning, when the villagers with pitchforks and spears went warily to the tower, they looked within the tower and found neither beast, nor lords, nor chests of gold and silver, but only the sun shining through the round circle in the roof.

This story Isabeau loved better than any other about the donjon, both for Beau-Mains, and for the coin of strange cold black metal, which Jerome showed her: it was in the castle's treasury, in a small chest of wood, and when she touched it with her own fingertip she could feel it taking the warmth from her flesh with a delicious shiver. She did not mind that there were three other tales of the coin quite unlike the story of Beau-Mains, although she rejected scornfully the one which suggested the coin had not come from the donjon at all, but instead had been brought from the East some two centuries before, which was plainly ridiculous: two such miracles could not be in so much proximity and yet unrelated.

"We can go in, if you like," Jerome told her. "It's all right for as long as there's no star in the sky." He took her through the doors and pointed up: in the very center of the ceiling, there was a large ring of metal open to the floor above, and when she stood directly underneath it and looked up, she saw a round circle of blue sky visible through a succession of such openings, just as in the story of Beau-Mains.

There were no doors or chambers within. Each floor was one vast great echoing chamber, so far across that when Isabeau raced Jerome from one end to the other, she was breathless and gasping by the time she reached the other side. The wide stone stairs were twice as deep as the length of her own foot, big enough to hold the mailed foot of a knight, and they climbed two vast spiraling swoops up the inside of the tower walls until they passed through to the next floor above. A narrow walkway of stone circled halfway up the chamber, like a balcony looking down upon the window, and arrow-slit windows stood at every tenth step along it.

The second floor was just the same as the first, but the windows were larger: she could have stood upon the sill and stretched to her toes and reached the length of her fingers and still the top of the window arch or the sides would have been beyond her. The third was a little less high, and there was only one turn of the stairs, and no walkway: the windowsills stood at the height of her chin, and you could stand upon a box and fold your arms and rest your head upon them and look out for seven leagues in any direction over the folds and rolling waves of the countryside, like an ocean of green and grain, halted for one instant of time.

Then to the roof, where the wind whistled thin and strange in her ears, and the world below seemed more removed than it ought to have been. There was a pool upon the roof, which caught rainwater, and long golden fish swarmed in its dark depths, which no one could catch: she and Jerome tried with nets, but the fish always dived away into the dark, and though they put their arms and their long nets as far down as they could go, there was no sign of them, although as soon as they drew out, the fish came back to the surface.

But mostly they stayed on the third floor, where no one came. During the hours of daylight, there were four pages stationed on the roof to keep a look-out in all weathers, who at every hour had to answer the distant call rising up through the circle: *What comes to Coeurlieu?* and much woe did they get if they did not report a wagon-train or a carriage or a visitor riding to the castle, who came in by the gates later. Meanwhile the knights on the day's watch saved themselves the stairs, and sat round their table on the ground floor comfortably drinking and playing cards, or very occasionally training; in winter, they made the great circle a riding-school. And the second floor was filled with stores, though nothing of essential worth. But the third floor was all but empty: not as useful for a look-out, and too many stairs to climb up and down every day. No one came to look for them there, or objected.

She soon grew used to the endless stairs and the endless country outside the windows. Jerome taught her to read there, the two of them lying on their stomachs on the sun-warmed stone looking over his hated books: Isabeau had been taught her letters, but never much more. He even taught her a few magister's charms, enough to make small chips of rock hop like frogs and catch the sun in a mirror that would shine for a few minutes. She had never had a friend before. She had lived always with girls either too much older or younger; she did not like to look after little ones, and the elder had not paid much attention to her. She had been trained more or less by a succession of noble ladies, sent from one castle to another as her father gained a higher place for her, and she had a little talent for cards and embroidery, which won her a little share of society and praise. But now the frame and the fabric lay forgotten more often than not.

By the time the letter came, near midsummer, she could read it for herself: the Comte had helped the king break the siege of Grosviens, and he was coming home. "God save my good lord and bring him swiftly," she said, sadly, handing the letter back to Father Jean-Claude, who had brought it to her. She knew she had not done her duty. Her husband would come home and she would have nothing to show him for her time, but that she had learned to read, which she ought have done sooner, and the distraction of his heir.

She hurriedly began to embroider a cloak with the yellow flowers of the Comte's coat of arms on long green vines, at least to have a gift which might please him, though so little work would not show her very industrious. When Jerome tempted her again to put it aside and come wander with him, she looked out the window and imagined to herself that she saw the Comte emerge from the woods upon the road, and refused. Jerome sighed but kept company with her, and even turned the pages of his books occasionally when she reproached him.

The vines grew and the flowers bloomed, all along the border, and then she decided to risk beginning the great donjon on the center of the back. She rose with the first

348

NAOMI NOVIK

light good enough to see her needle, and in the evenings in her own bedchamber bent late over the sewing with smoky candle-light. The tower climbed, its windows stitched in black and the stones in silver thread, until all that was left to sew was the Comte's flag streaming from the battlements on the roof, which she could not do until the next merchant brought her the blue thread for which she had waited two weeks already. She set the frame down frowning, and then Jerome sat up from his books and looked at the heap of the cloak in her lap and said slowly, "My father has not come yet."

They climbed the stairs to the roof of the donjon to look out at the countryside: no sign of a company anywhere, only a single rider far distant, raising a small cloud of dust at his heels. The wind tugged at her hair beneath her coif, and she put her arms round herself, strangely cold, though the summer sun beat strong and hot upon her skin.

The rider came to Couerlieu before the sun went down: the plague had erupted in Blens, between here and Grosviens, and many roads were closed: the townsfolk had heaped barricades of burning brush across them, to try and fend off death. The king had desired the Comte to stay with him in Mont-Sauvage, and therefore the Comte commended the castle and his lady to Sir Gaubard, the stolid old knight of forty-three who was the chatelain. Sir Gaubard gave orders at once to have the road to the castle closed, and to send men down to Coeurlieu town to receive messengers and supply, which would be brought halfway up the mountain, there to wait three days, before they ascended the rest of the way. The plague would come anyway, of course; the plague came everywhere.

Jerome took the news in silence, and afterwards hid himself in such wise that Isabeau could not find him. She did not see him until the next day, when standing on the walls in the evening, she heard the plague bells tolled in town, faint but clear, with three notes struck to mark three deaths. She turned away and saw him crossing the courtyard with a sack over his shoulder and a walking-stick, going into the tower, and no one halted him.

Isabeau stood a moment, afraid, and then she went down the stairs to the courtyard and ran after him, in time to see him climbing to the second floor of the tower. She pursued, calling his name, but he did not turn; he climbed on swiftly, and by the time she had reached the second story, he had disappeared onto the third, and the round circle of sky was grown deep violet blue, although there were yet no stars.

She looked down. The doors stood open, but if she climbed a few steps further, she would no longer be able to see them. A heavy silence lay upon the air within. Everyone had gone out of the donjon, as they did every night when the bells rang for vespers. It was her duty to go out, too. Jerome might stay, just as he might neglect his tasks and lessons, because there was no use to him. But she knew that when she came to look for him in the morning, he would forever be gone: diving deep into dark like the golden fish, no matter how she tried to grasp him.

There were day-candles in small niches along the stairs, and by chance one had been blown out sometime early in the day. She pried it from the puddled wax at its base and lit it from one of the dying stubs, and with it in her hands climbed timidly higher, calling Jerome's name softly. Her voice seemed to press against resistance, and he did not answer. She reached the third floor, familiar and yet gone strange: outside the too-high windows she could see only dark, and long shadows hid the curving wall, dancing over the floor to the tune of the sputtering lights. She climbed onward.

Icy air struck her in the face as she pushed open the door to the roof, full of the unexpected wrong smell of snow and winter. "Jerome, are you here?" she called. No answer came. Above her head the stars shone high and infinite and unfamiliar, and the horizon was a circle of solid dark all around, with no rolling shadows of hills or trees breaking into the smooth bowl of the sky. She walked quickly around the full circle of the battlements and came back to the door, panting clouds. A thick layer of ice had grown atop the pool, the fish pale ghosts moving beneath it. There was no sign of Jerome.

It was too cold to stay outside. She pulled the door open and crept back inside to warm herself, and then halted and huddled back against the doors. All the dying candles had grown back to life, golden light shining out of the niches onto the turning stairs. But the air at her back was now cold as on the roof itself, and growing steadily colder. She put down her own candle, and shivering went slowly down the stairs with the chill following her. Air streamed white from her lips as though her soul was slipping from her body with every breath.

She reached the third floor. Her fingers were grown almost numb. The candles all stood tall and unflickering as if they had been freshly lit, but they only made circles of light which did not touch one another, or the walls. She darted from one island of candle-light to another until she came

close enough to dash to the window-seat where she and Jerome had passed their afternoons, where she had left her
embroidery forgotten. The cloak still lay on the stones, with
the frame fixed round the top of the tower where no banner
yet flew. But she had sewn the tower against a green hillside
marked with white sheep. Now it stood only on a circle of
black, and the border was all of knotted white stars in a pattern she had never made.

She held it in her hands, afraid, but she was too cold.
She undid the frame and wrapped the cloak, meant for a tall
man, around herself sideways twice. The warm thick wool
muffled the chill. She looked for Jerome's books, too, but
they were gone: perhaps he had come taken them. But he
had left his paper and ink, and after a moment she knelt
down and laboriously wrote *I am here Isabeau* with many
blots and left the sheet upon the ground weighted with her
frame.

She did not call Jerome's name anymore. The stillness of
the tower lay upon her too heavily. She hurried back to the
stairs and started down again. She would wait by the doors
for sunrise, she told herself, and resolutely did not think of
Beau-Mains climbing endlessly, and the dreadful devouring
beast. And indeed for her the stairs continued descending
ordinarily, and though few candles were kept lit on the second floor, she could see enough as she came down towards
it to know that it was still *there,* and not vanished.

Isabeau could not help but think of an apple in honey, or
a handful of nuts: she had not eaten her dinner, silent with
the empty place at table where Jerome ought to have been.
But the sacks and barrels and boxes of the stores had become strange lumpy shadows, and she remembered unwill-

ingly that the angry reeve had driven all the kitchen boys mercilessly for a whole day last month, because someone had turned round all the stores and they had to be put back into order; and only four days ago, sixteen barrels of preserved plums had been found devoured overnight with no one to admit to the act.

She reached the landing, where the stairs plunged onward towards the ground, and for a moment was relieved: she could see the doors, and they stood open. But then she realized—the doors stood open, although they ought to have been closed and barred for the night long since. And while she stood there irresolute, she heard a heavy footstep somewhere on the stairs below her, loud, with the rasp of chainmail rings on stone.

Another step came, and another: climbing. She turned away, her heart pounding like a rabbit, and went out among the stores, sliding her feet one after another slowly ahead of her through the dark, as though her pointed toes would warn her of unsteady ground. She groped past the barrels and sacks, and finally hid behind a stack of boxes as the footsteps grew loud and nearby.

They paused upon the landing and then came onto the floor. Isabeau stayed crouched and shivering. The footsteps were slow and dragging a little, the mail scraping against the stone. They stopped and she heard a creaking sound, a wordless deep grunt, and she jumped involuntarily at a loud crack of splitting wood: he was opening a box, or a barrel. He began to eat: loud smacking sounds, slurping, and she pressed her hands over her ears trembling. He kept eating a long time, making small grunts and panting for breath when he paused long enough to get any.

At last he finished and she heard him push up from the barrel, the wooden rim thumping against the floor as it wobbled with his weight coming off. He stood breathing heavily. She shut her eyes and pressed herself to the side of the box and prayed silently that he would go away, go on higher up the stairs.

He moved. She held her breath listening: the heavy dragging steps began to recede. He was going back to the stairs. She hesitated and then crept slowly forward on her hands and knees, as silent as she could be. She didn't want to see him at all, any part of him, but she still more desperately wanted to know whether he went up or down.

She crawled to the very edge of the boxes and knelt up and edged her cheek out past it until her eye came clear and she could see towards the stairs. He was a hunched shadow framed in the light of the landing, a gleam of silver mail along the edges of his body. His back was turned to her: his long hair was stringy grey and the pate nearly bare, and dreadfully she saw upon his neck a swollen black lump, and the ends of his dangling wet fingers were blackened as with soot.

He paused a moment and began to turn his head slightly. She pulled back out of sight, clenching her hands. His footsteps went onward, and when she dared one more glance around, his heels were vanishing up the stairs.

She sat down in the dark where she was and hugged her knees to herself under the cloak, listening in relief as his steps went dying little by little away. She still did not move for a time, waiting to be sure, and then at last she crept back out—she did not look into the opened barrel—and darted a quick look up the stairs. She saw no sign of him, gratefully, and she set her foot upon the steps to go down the rest of the way.

And then far-off she heard a voice, strange and croaking-harsh, almost a gargle, say, "*Isabeau.*"

She froze upon the steps, shaking. The line she had written to Jerome—

The footsteps were coming back. Again and closer the voice said, "*Isabeau,*" and she fled away and down, clutching up her skirts to go more quickly, her heels skidding down the edges of the steps, scraping her shins against them. On the ground were all the racks that the knights used in their work, the piled hay bales and the tall cut lances heaped; she would hide, she would hide. Her soft leather shoes were quiet, he did not know where she was. She would hide, and pray for morning, and the sun would come and save her.

She slipped and fell and nearly tumbled over the edge, biting her lip not to cry out. The footsteps were rasping one after another above her. "*Isabeau,*" the gargle said again: hungry. She went quicker, desperate, until she sprang off the stairs onto the floor. The doors stood open, but outside there was only an endless, impenetrable dark, unbroken even by the stars. She stood hesitating, trembling, and then she pulled her thin linen coif off her head and threw it into the doorway, so it fell just across the line of the dark, with the ties trailing.

She fled for the bales draped with cloth, hiding herself beneath, and lay there and caught her gulping breath, her hand pressed over her mouth to muffle the sound. She could see thinly through the weave of the coarse cloth, where the candles made their pools of light, and when his feet came down from the landing she saw them come. The cloth blurred him to a faceless lurching, the scrape of his feet and the heavy wet sound of his own breath.

He reached the floor, and his head turned towards the doors. He did not move at first. In the thick close stuffiness she shut her eyes and prayed, her lips moving soundless against her palm, and then she opened her eyes and saw him in the doorway, bending to take her coif. "Isabeau," he crooned over it, pressing it to his face. Muffled through the cloth, there was something almost familiar in his voice, as though she had heard it before; but then he went lurching out the doors, into the dark, and the dark swallowed his footsteps as though he had never been.

She shut her eyes a moment more in gratitude, trembling, and then threw off the coarse, hay-smelling cloth and scrambled out meaning to flee back to the roof; she stood up in a gold-glitter cloud of hay dust, pinching a sneeze down behind her hand with her eyes squeezed shut, and when she opened her eyes, she halted. The old knife-scarred table where the knights played their idle cards was in front of her, and three queens sat round it, with coins and cards heaped between them. They turned their heads and looked at her.

She did not think of running. There was no use in running, of course, but it was not only that there was no use. If the other had seen her, she would have run until there was no more running, no matter how useless. But they were not like him. Terror and calm nestled together in her belly, but she took the folds of her skirt and she curtseyed to them low, and said, "God give you all grace, noble ladies," and the one in the middle, tall and pale and clad in black, answered her, "And to you, my lady."

They were all strangely beautiful and strangely alike:

their faces might have been cut from stone by a sculptor making copies, long and graven and unlined, and each of them wore upon her breast a jewel strung on a chain: one golden-brown and yellow like tiger's-eye, one the deep red of blood, and the one in the middle, who faced her, a jewel clear as water.

"Come and play," the red-jeweled one said to her. There was one seat empty at the table, and cards left before it.

"She has no stake," the yellow-jeweled one said. They were different at a closer look: her face and lips were narrower, her cheeks hollowed and gaunt, and her hands where they came from her sleeves were so thin the bones strained against the skin.

The other scowled at her across the table. "I am tired of waiting while our sister goes roaming upon the world."

Isabeau wished to say she did not know the game; she wanted to excuse herself. But on the discard heap, the king of coins stood face-upwards, and it was Sir Gaubard: his frowning anxious face painted so real to life he might have been caught up out of the world and put into it whole. She held up the fold of her cloak so the tower would show, and timidly brought it to the table and held it out. "Will this serve?"

The yellow-jeweled sister eyed it hungrily. The sister in the middle nodded once, and gestured to the empty chair opposite her. Isabeau sat down with them and picked up the cards. The air had warmed; she was not cold anymore. Now her hands shook because she lifted faces she knew with every card from the hand before her: the old sour cook on the nine of coins, Father Jean-Claude with his cross as the ten of cups; a groom who liked to sing on the four of spades. There were so many she could barely hold them all.

"The play is yours," the red-jeweled one said. Isabeau hesitated, and then took a card from the deck: it was Estienne, one of the younger knights, on the nine of swords. The queens all watched her, silently, as she worked it in among the others. She hesitated and asked softly, "Must I discard?"

They all inclined their heads. She looked down at her cards and blinked away stinging. They were crammed so close in her small hands that the faces were covered, and she could only see the suits and numbers. And yet there was a face upon each one. She could not take one out.

The red-jeweled queen shifted impatiently and made a loud sigh, and with a sharp jerk Isabeau pulled out the lonely six of coins and threw it out onto the pile before she could look too close at the young man upon it: she thought his name was Lucien, and he was an apprentice to the smith.

The play went round and round. New cards marched into her hands, threatening to spill over: more than there ought to have been, and sometimes it seemed to her that she already held a card of the same markings, but when she looked into her hand, she could not find it. Sometimes she drew a card and laid it on the discards straightaway; she made herself a rule she would not give away one in her hand unless the new was better, to make it less of a choice. But she was too quick at cards not to know that this card would bring her closer, and that one further, and which was the best to throw away.

The red-jeweled queen played impatiently: she drew cards and sometimes threw them out again a few turns later,

as though she had changed her mind, and she liked swords
best; the yellow-jeweled queen greedily snatched her card
from the deck as soon as the turn was hers, and frowned
long and lingering before she had to discard each one, grudging. Between them, the queen in black velvet played steadily,
without much passion; she took her cards and laid the discards down almost to a measured pace.

They had already been playing a long time when Isabeau
drew the king of cups: Jerome with a golden goblet in one
hand and a book open upon his lap. She put him at once
into her hand, pushing the card in quickly near the knave
with Father Jean-Claude upon it, which she had not yet
been able to bring herself to discard, on the excuse that she
had the ten of cups as well, and some little hope of the nine.
But she had a sharp painful sense that she had seen the
queen of cups thrown out already in play by one of the others, and two of the other kings were already gone.

As if to taunt her, the nine of cups came on the very next
turn: Sister Brigitte, who led the singing every Sunday, and
so she and the priest were safe on either side of old retired
Magister Leon, who slept in the north tower and rarely ever
came down to dinner. But the king of cups continued to
stand alone as the turns crept onward, and on every side the
others were shifting their cards as though their hands were
nearly formed. And then Isabeau took from the deck the
king of swords, and it was her husband, with his stern
marked face and his kind eyes.

Of the swords she had now the knave and the ten and
the nine, so she put him beside them, and threw out the
very last of the solitary cards she had saved, a three of spades

with a little boy who tended goats upon it: she did not know his name, but she remembered his grinning pride: she had been sitting high up on the castle wall with Jerome when his mother had told him he might take the herd out alone for the first time. She looked away.

The yellow-jeweled sister drew a card and her hungry eyes brightened; her lips curled with satisfaction as she put the card into her hand and threw out another. She looked over with that thin smile as the play continued on, and Isabeau did not need to be told that she had nearly finished. The play came round to her again. She reached out a trembling hand and drew a card from the deck with her own face upon it, a queen, and where the suit ought to have been only a jester's star.

The yellow-jeweled queen was drumming her fingers impatiently. The game was done: Isabeau had to make one hand, or the other. She swallowed and chose, and laid down her cards with her face looking out from between Jerome and Father Jean-Claude, making the long line of cups, and she put the Comte's card last upon the high heap of the discards.

She wiped away tears as the yellow-jeweled queen threw down her cards scowling, and the red-jeweled queen sighed and tossed her own atop the discard heap as well: the Comte vanished beneath the cascade. They rose from the table and walked out the doors and into the dark, their long trains whispering over the floors until they were engulfed. Across from her, the last of the queens with her black clothes and her clear jewel gathered the heap, and held out her hand for the rest of the cards.

Isabeau hesitated with her hands spread over them, protective, but the queen said, cool and implacable, "All the cards are mine in the end. Only fools forget it."

"Yes, Your Majesty," Isabeau whispered, and gathered them together, and gave them over.

The queen put the deck into a velvet bag that hung from her silver belt and rose from the table. "Go to the roof and shut the door, and do not open it again until morning," she said. "And never again seek this place. You have given the beast your scent, and he will find you the next time if you do."

Isabeau shivered. "Is it—Sir Theolian?" she dared to ask.

"It is your friend," the queen said, dreadfully. "And it is the knight as well, and the others before them. They came to take shelter from me, and when they found me here, they fled into the dark, and still there they hide. But I am there, too."

Isabeau swallowed and looked at the coins heaped before her in piles of silver and gold and cold black. "May I—may I ransom Jerome?"

"For a little while." The queen picked one black, cold coin from the heap and held it out. Isabeau closed her hand round it, and by the time her fingers had curled shut, the rest had rattled away into the air, vanishing, so she could again see the pale cuts in the wood where hands had carved *Bastien likes pigs* and *Melisende has my heart* and a rough picture of a strutting cock with enormous plumes with the name *Philippe* beneath it.

"Go," the queen said, and Isabeau climbed shakily from the chair and made her curtsey, and then she flew up the stairs with the coin still clutched tight in her fist, without stopping, until she was on the roof with the door shut behind her, and she took down the pole with the banner of Coeurlieu and barred it too. Then she wrapped herself tightly in her cloak and huddled against the small shelter of lee of the battlements to wait for morning, and then, though she did not remember sleep, she was waking in a sweat, the sun halfway up the sky and pounding down upon her in the heavy wool.

She found Jerome on the third floor, sprawled limply asleep amidst the scattered heap of his books, the note she had written him crumpled in his hand, and when she shook him he jerked up with a staring look of fear and horror and caught her arms too tight. He held on trembling for a few moments, and then he said, hoarsely, "You did come. I thought I heard your voice, but I couldn't find you. Is it morning? I didn't think the morning would ever come again."

"Yes," Isabeau said. "Yes, and it's already growing late. Let's go outside."

"Castle Courlieu" was first published in Unfettered II: New Tales by Masters of Fantasy *by Grim Oak Press in 2016.*

THE LONG WAY ROUND

Whenever I get asked how I develop some part of my books—
a magic system, a fantastical species, some invented history—
the answer is always that I never do it in advance. Every story
and every novel starts for me with a first line that makes me
want to know more myself, about the characters revealed in
that line and the world taking shape around them, and I find
out more about them one line at a time, making small deci-
sions as I go that gradually accumulate until I know the rules
of the world, until I know the people I'm talking about, and
then I go back to the beginning and clean up all the places
where I've gotten something wrong.

But what I love about fantasy—which is after all the super-
set of fiction, and not the other way around—is that in fantasy, I
have the full power to control the stage, to build as much of the
set as I want, and increasingly I've wanted to use that power to
build a very large one, an entire world full of its own history, and
tell a story in that setting. But the only way I know how to dis-
cover that world is to tell myself stories about it.

That's my current project, under the working title of Folly, *and this is one of the stories I've been telling myself about it. I expect several of the details in it to be wrong, and the world may be completely different by the time it finishes taking full shape, but I hope you won't mind coming on this journey of discovery with me, even if it does turn out to be a convoluted route.*

WHAT IF WE WENT THE LONG WAY ROUND INstead, next time?" Aston said.

Tess, still stewing, pushed her hair out of her face and looked over in surprise. Her brother was sitting perched on the prow of the main hull, throwing seed shells at the bowfish like a boy. He hit another one of them on its bright green nose, but the bowfish kept right on surfing the wave ahead of the ship, gleefully jump jump jumping out of the froth, wriggling their tails with delight at the speed. They loved the *Plucky* with unswerving devotion, despite the net waiting to catch dinner: the same way that Aston loved all of his worst and most ridiculous ideas.

When one of his ideas landed in her boat, Tess always picked them up and gave them a good look, mostly before throwing them straight back. But this one she would have liked to keep on board, even though she knew she couldn't. "Go around Syrac?" she said, wistfully, although their father had taught her better when she'd asked him the same question as a girl of twelve. *Better half your profit gone to the smiling thieves than all of it gone to the belly of a krake,* he'd told her.

But he'd sighed after he said it, and she was still smarting herself, enough to give it a moment's real thought. The strutting boy who'd come over this morning from the shakeboat couldn't have been more than thirteen, but he'd been practicing hard to be an officious prick of thirty. "You *do* have a revenue chit, I trust?" he'd said, speaking in High Syracian instead of water tongue, and to Aston instead of her, although his eyes had been at the right level to be staring directly at the sailmaster's badge on her neck cord; the top of his head had just barely cleared her chin. "I'll need to see into your hold as well, of course."

But his shakeboat had been six times the length of the *Plucky,* and the marines on either side of him had been full-grown men with hard professional eyes, so Tess had to bite her tongue. She'd silently got out the lockbox from the main hull to get the chit—the one that had indeed cost them half the profit they'd make on the spices and truesilk packed into their hold. The boy had peered at it hard, front and back, as if he'd been hoping to find a fake, and he'd made them open up every last sack they had stowed so he could inspect them, even though he could see it was just the two of them for crew.

And then while he'd been watching them pack everything up again, disappointed, he noticed the gold medal hanging on the mast, the one they'd won a week ago in the Old Syrenac races, and he'd had the gall to keep them at anchor for another hour of good wind just to make them show him how Aston's swing-sail worked. Not that the Syracian boy didn't need the lesson; looking at his rigging, his poor galleymen were probably rowing twice as hard as they should have needed to.

So it wasn't any mystery to her why Aston was asking the question. The southern route looked so easy on a chart, too, at least for a proper sailmaster of Ester. *She* wasn't an incompetent twat who didn't know how to rig a sail for a Cauldron tailwind. But the reason no one went south around Syrac was because that was where the big krakes went, anytime one of them finished eating all its spawn-mates and had to give up living in the Cauldron and go to the ocean valleys to keep growing. And if you went sailing over their heads, they came up and smashed your boat, because they remembered being hunted themselves, at spawning time, and they resented it.

For a moment, though, Tess looked at the gold medal, hanging in its pride of place again on the mainmast, and let herself think about the idea. Not one boat in ten would make it, but they'd just finished proving that the *Plucky* was faster than any hundred other boats. The leanest, hungriest krake couldn't go more than ten licks, and the *Plucky* could have made an easy twelve even if her sails *had* been rigged by an incompetent twat. But the winds sometimes died away to nothing in the far south, and krakes sometimes hunted together . . .

But before Tess could work herself up to letting out her own sigh and saying no, Aston said, "No!" in tones as indignant as though *she* were the one having an unreasonable idea. "Go around Syrac? I'm not having my boat smashed by a krake!"

Tess rolled her eyes. "So what *do* you mean?" she said, and then—only because she *knew* her brother and his terrible and ridiculous ideas—she realized. "Go the *long* way round? Across the *Empty*?"

"Why not?" Aston said, sitting up bright-eyed and tossing his handful of uneaten seeds out into the sea, and Tess groaned and laid herself out flat on the narrow deck between the hulls like a beached starfish with nothing to do but accept its suffering.

WHY NOT WAS HER LEAST favorite pair of words in the entire world, and had been ever since Aston had got old enough to speak. It was no use to ask him *why* back; most of the time he didn't have an answer. The why was so deep in him that he couldn't explain himself. All he could do was ask her *why not* until she ran out of reasons, or found one so good that it silenced him—or until a different and even worse idea came leapfrog over the head of the first one and took its place.

She could tell from the beginning that this was going to be one of the really bad ones, impossible to dislodge. "But really, why not?" Aston asked that very night after dinner, looking at her anxiously even as he bent over the side to rinse the bowfish bones out of his bowl. Aston didn't actually like the arguments—if you could call them that—any more than she did. He just couldn't let the ideas go, once they came into his head.

Whenever Tess had tried complaining to Mother, when they'd been little, she'd always just said comfortably that there wasn't any help for it, because Aston had been born on the blue night. Tess didn't swallow that excuse for a moment. Three other children had been born on the blue night in Port Ester. One had died of spots at seven, one had drowned at fifteen, and the barrel-maker's daughter Wilma had never been troubled by an idea, good or bad, in her life. No: the terrible ideas were all Aston's own, and at the moment, Tess felt as strongly as she ever had that he ought to have been taught to keep them to himself.

"*Why not,*" she said bitterly. "Why not sail round across the Empty, just to skip the shakeboats. Why not sail up to the moon and back down from there instead? The last time someone tried it from the Minnows, they made it two thousand miles of blue water without so much as a speck of land. Even if it *could* be done, we'd be at sea for five months!"

"Not in the new ship," Aston said, which only made it better. Use all the money they had in the world to build the new ship, a *trading* ship, and take it on a wild sea-flight all around the empty side of the world.

The money, Aston didn't say, even while he was looking at her eager as a seal, that they'd just won in Old Syrenac, racing the boat he'd built her against the best shipbuilders and crews in the world—which had been his *last* mad and stupid idea. Tess snarled under her breath and stormed off to sit alone on the ama to work out the reason that would let her shut him up.

It *was* a ridiculous and terrible idea. She could have taken the *Plucky* anywhere in the world that mattered: there were five continents tucked close round the Cauldron Ocean, the Hearthlands of the world gathered in a circle around their swirling pot full of trade currents, and she knew how to get to all of them, any time of year. The hundred little ports of Ester, the great city-kingdoms of Syrac; she could get them to Gos or Shon or even Hameland, if Aston had wanted to hunt walrus.

She didn't even know if you *could* get around the long way. In Syrac, the followers of the Endless One and the followers of the Lord of Rivers had fought three holy wars over whether the ocean went on forever or whether it went curving over the top of the world and poured away into the underworld—at least, that was their excuse for fighting. One of the hairy men from Hameland had once told her, with enormous assurance, that if you just kept going into the Empty, you found the place where it turned up and became the sky.

She did know all of those were nonsense, because if you were a fisher in Ester, every spring you saw the spirit-cups from Shon come bobbing in from the east, after they'd been thrown in the sea, by whoever it was who lived all the way over on their western coast. "Messages to the dead," Father had told her, the first time she'd spotted a string of them going by; he'd let her scoop some of them out of the water and look at the beautiful messages inside that she couldn't read. One had been written in gold ink that glittered in the sun; another didn't have words at all but a tiny little painting. She'd sealed them back up carefully with a paste of glub fat and put them back in, to keep going round.

So the Empty went all the way round the world, and if a spirit-cup could float across it, a boat could too. But that didn't mean people could. They *had* sailed out a good long way, in both directions. The spices in their stowage, the ones she'd bought in the market in Old Syrenac, came from an island called the Yellow Pebble, far out west from Gos. Whether it was a thousand miles west or two thousand depended on who was telling the tale. And in that same market, she'd sold twenty jars of brined penky eggs from the Minnows, which were five hundred miles east from Ester.

Tess had never met anyone from the Yellow Pebble, but

she knew for certain sure that Minnows sailmasters were as good as they came. Some of them would sail all the way to Port Ester just if they'd had an especially good catch of sunfish, the way you might take a quick run up the coast to Springwell one day because you wanted sweet oysters. They had a dozen aleshop tales they were happy to tell you, for a drink, of men who'd tried to sail east to Gos, tales full of monstrous storms and smoking water and not a square inch of land anywhere to be found, and that was how she knew it was at least four thousand miles of ocean to cross and maybe more, without fresh water, without a living soul to meet, without a single chart.

But the one and only thing that the councils, barons, and priests of the six portenas of Syrac agreed on amongst themselves was that anyone sailing past any of their high towers had to pay their monstrous duties, and if you didn't, and a shakeboat caught you without a chit, they'd take your entire cargo and maybe some blood along with it. So the Minnowmen kept trying, and surely the sailors of Gos had tried too. And since none of them had ever made it, in either direction, the only sensible conclusion was that it couldn't be done.

Except . . . none of them had been sailing one of Aston's ships. "I'm *thinking* about it," she told Aston flatly, when he tried again the next night over their grilled bowfish and breadfruit. "*You* think about how you're going to build us that tradeship."

"I don't need to, I already know," Aston said, which was a lie. What he meant was, he knew about a quarter of the way in, and he'd work out the rest of it when he got there.

"No," Tess said. "If you want me to think about this,

you're going to think about *that*. You're going to build it in your head, start to finish. No realizing halfway through that you need some other wood, or that you want to change round all the rigging. We could afford that on *Plucky*, we can't afford it on . . ." She paused, and Aston said, "Blue," without a pause, as if he was just finishing the sentence for her with something he already knew.

"Blue?" Tess said, a little warily. Maybe he was just thinking of all that blue water, but she didn't like that she'd just been thinking about the blue night. She wished she still had a bowfish bone to break and throw over the ama.

"That's her name," Aston said, with simple finality. He'd bend like a reed in the wind for anything except his boats. "All right. You think about getting across the Empty, and I'll think about *Blue*. Fair bargain."

And he went on and did it, the rest of the trip, perched on the top of the heap of sacks, drawing pictures with wriggler ink on scraps of fishskin and spare sailcloth, muttering to himself and getting angry as he turned up mistakes and had to go back and change things. So Tess was stuck keeping her side of the bargain, too, thinking about how much of a tradeship's stowage they'd have to use for supplies, and how much they'd save on the duties, and coming up with numbers she didn't like: they were too good.

So she and Aston were both irritated the rest of the way home, and sailed into Port Ester so grouched up that they'd forgotten all about winning the race. It took them by surprise when they passed the first ship they knew, a deepwater fisher called *Pellina,* and her crew spotted the gold medal flashing in the sun and started to cheer them wildly. They tacked round and followed them all the way into harbor. There was a flotilla of three dozen boats trailing behind *Plucky* when they finally came in, and the docks were filled with people cheering and waving handkerchiefs for them, from the boats that had gone racing in ahead to spread the news. They both got hoisted on shoulders in the crowd and paraded through the streets and all the way up the slope to the Lordstow, where the High Lords declared a festival in their honor.

Tess woke up in the middle of the night starving— a feast given by the High Lords wasn't always as substantial as it seemed to be while you were eating it, and this one had appeared to feed half of Port Ester with suspicious speed— and found Aston at the hearth already cooking a pot of old rice, the only thing they had in the house, cold and empty after three months with no one in it. They ate it straight out of the pot down to the bottom and then sat yawning together, without saying a word, and finally Tess said, "All right. We'll try."

IT TOOK A YEAR TO build *Blue*. First, Aston had to get married. He sighed a bit, but there wasn't any other way of getting a real proper big shipbuilder's dock. There were only thirty of them in Port Ester, jealously guarded, and they couldn't have bought one just for money even if they'd *had* the money. The only reason they could get one at all was because *Plucky* had won the Old Syrenac races, so now old Master Loth, who'd only been pretending to build ships on his dock for the last six years, would let Aston marry his niece Vinna, and use the dock himself.

Tess wasn't much more enthusiastic than Aston about

the idea. Vinna liked to be very fine, and she'd often turned up her nose at them when she'd been a shipbuilder's niece and they'd been grubby fisher's kids running around the docks. But that would be all right, really, because Vinna wasn't a sailor and she wouldn't want to go out on the sea herself. So Aston and Tess would be able to carry on the same way they had ever since she'd been nine and he'd been five and he'd first rigged them up a raft and sail, cobbled together out of driftwood and her old dress, and she'd taken it out in the bay and they'd come home with three fish netted, and sold them for twopence to spend on candy.

Now they'd come home with a medal of gold, which went on the mantel in Loth's big fine house, and ten sacks of truesilk and twenty bags of spices, which Tess sold for more money than they'd ever had in their entire lives all together, and then spent right away again on buying two giant logs of lirenwood to be hauled down out of the hill forest for the hulls.

The week after the wedding, Aston disappeared with his hired log-finders up into the forest, and Tess took *Plucky* out with the first two prospective crewmen. She sailed with them eastward, past the tip of Ester and just into the Empty, to see how they did for a week without sight of land, and also to learn more of the Empty herself. She hadn't sailed those waters much before, and she had more experience than most. She'd only been fifteen when Father had started taking her out past the eastern end of Ester to teach her how to sail hard winds and a mountain coast, so she could get her own master's rank from the sailing guild. He'd already been sick by then, the stomach pains coming more and more often, and he'd wanted to make sure she had her badge before he died.

So she knew that as soon as you came around Thorn Point, the winds and waves coming in grew broad shoulders and another row of teeth. It was like coming out of a bay into blue water, only the bay you started from was already blue water. Even when the sky was clear, the wind was still as strong as a storm brewing. The first time she'd come out here, Father had made her swing so far out from the cliffs before she made the turn that they'd seen a true deep krake breaching the surface maybe ten miles further south, erupting straight up with its enormous maw wide open and living waterfalls of green wrigglers spilling out to either side down its long neck and body. The crash when it landed again had come over the sea to them like a sound of distant thunder.

Tess still remembered every minute of that sail. It had been a fight the whole way up and down the Toothpick Mountains, the wind and sea trying to carry her onto the shore the entire time, constantly having to shift the rigging to keep to the course she'd plotted. Father had told her he wasn't going to help, but he'd been gripping the bench so hard, to keep from going for the ropes himself, that he'd left nail marks on the underside of the wood. She knew that because her own fingers found them now: she'd taken the old familiar bench from *Gullwing* to put into *Plucky,* and this time she was the one sitting, letting her hired hands keep to the course, watching to see if they could do it and how well. It felt almost like Father was there again, sitting alongside her.

Over the next three months, she took different crewmen

out for the same sail, over and over. When she'd found six men who didn't leave her with splinters under her finger-nails, she started taking them out still further into the Empty, and they found the wide westward-flowing current that was marked on all of the charts she'd dug up of the route to the Minnows. The water was warm and sparkling-clear, and full of sunfish so big they could have hoisted them as sails. They caught a netful, and when they did hoist the sails for home, the current below and a steady ferocious wind at their backs sent *Plucky* flying home so fast that the fish were still fight-ing by the time they came into harbor.

That was what first made Tess think of going to Gos the ordinary way, through the Cauldron—even though that would mean having to buy a revenue chit after all for that part of the journey—and sailing on west from there, instead of try-ing to go against that current. She didn't know whether she'd find a wind ready to blow them straight west the whole way, but she did know for certain that she'd find it on *this* end. If they came around and were running short on water or food, that last boost could make all the difference between reach-ing home hungry and sick and not reaching it at all. Even if they had enough supplies, they'd still be *tired*; the kind of tired that made it hard to row and hard to keep your spirits up. She'd rather have *home* on the far end of the journey, and familiar waters to sail through.

It was a good plan—as good a plan as you could have for anything this stupid. But it also made the journey go real in her head. After that, it wasn't just something she was think-ing about anymore, it was something coming, something they were going to *do*.

And *Blue* was becoming real at the same time, too. Aston

and his new journeymen were at the work morning and night, only their feet visible beneath the gigantic lirenwood hulls, eighty feet long each, and the tapping noises echoing from the hollowing inside were like a flock of strange birds pecking away. The bright lemony scent of freshly cut inner lirenwood filled the air all around them, so strong that even in the hottest days of summer, not a single bitey was anywhere to be seen.

Blue was so big that she made *Plucky* look like a new chick next to its osprey mother, hatching in backwards order. Half of Port Ester stopped by to watch her being built, especially once Aston started to fire-shape the thinned hulls, moving in and out of them as if he was dancing, the bronze coal-holder in his gloved left hand, one of his shaping blocks on the three middle fingers of his right hand, with his thumb and little finger on either side to feel when the lirenwood had gone just soft enough to shape, and just cool enough to let go again. Most shipbuilders working on a tradeship would do fire-shaping with big carved blocks the full height of the hull, and teams of men to hold them, but Aston did all of it himself little by little, so Tess saw the glowing red-orange light dancing on the docks every time she sailed back into port, late at night, beckoning her home.

He shaped both the hulls completely from end to end, and then he sanded them, and then he shaped them again and sanded them again, two more times, until they looked finished to any sensible person's eye, and then he waited for a perfectly clear dawn and did a final sanding pass over both of them, with his anxious journeymen wiping off the dust and rubbing in the first coat of oil right behind him. The long whorls of the wood glowed in alternating rings of deep purple and paler brown, like the shapes on a sea-chart, showing you where the safe harbors lay.

A FEW WEEKS LATER, THEY put the hulls in the water for the first time and put on the first bars of the deck between them, and then they strung up the sails that had been made out of the one sack of truesilk that Tess hadn't sold, giving the osprey her wings. Several of the shipbuilding masters had come to watch. Vinna moved among them proudly with a tray of her sour-plum dumplings, which had reconciled Aston to marriage after the first formal courting visit, and then they went aboard, and Tess formally asked Aston for the name of the ship, and then he ceremonially passed the handle of the rudder over to her. She gave the order to make sail, and took them out for a turn around the harbor, *Blue* slicing through the calm waters as sweet and easy as if she were no bigger than *Plucky*.

That evening, a messenger came down from the Lord-stow to call on them. Aston was still out fussing over *Blue,* but Tess was home going over the books, trying to work out how much money they could spend on the outward-bound cargo, and how much she'd have to pay for the revenue chit. She'd been buying up small batches of fermented breadfruit for the last six months, whenever she could get a good price for it, and she had a couple of sea grannies in town working at making her journey-cakes of dried smallkrake, glub fat, and sour berries: the smallest food she could carry. She'd bought six enormous cask gourds, lined with wax and seal-skin, to hold their water and catch the rain. She planned to pack the rest of her hold full of the wool rugs and woven cloth that were luxuries in Shon, and sell them to merchants in Gos. If they made it to the Yellow Pebble, she'd trade there for truesilk and spices.

She was halfway through some figuring when the knock came, and she overheard Vinna opening the door and lost the thread of the numbers when she heard a man say coldly, the way no one in Port Ester would ever speak to a ship-builder's wife, "I am here to speak with Intessa Roh," and she looked up and gawked at the grand personage on the threshold. It was an actual sorcerer, in a short robe of thin green truesilk, with long dangling mustaches.

Tess had to sit across from the sorcerer waiting wood-enly while Vinna made the tea, exchanging stares in formal silence. It was hard to say who was more appalled. The sor-cerer kept forgetting to meet her gaze, distracted by the hor-ror of being in their sitting room: a grand chamber with three chairs and a bench and a fireplace made of dead lirenwood, taken from a ship made by Loth's great-grandfather that had stayed in service so long that the hulls had finally gone com-pletely hard and couldn't be shaped back into trim.

Even the sorcerer didn't turn up his nose at the dump-lings, though; they vanished entirely before the second cup was poured, and Tess won the contest of dismay hands-down when the man wiped his mouth and informed her, austerely, "My master, High Lord Ferantis, has sent me to inform you that you and your brother will dine with him to-night."

Tess had no idea what to make of it. The High Lords did condescend to feast some of the guildmasters and bankers, every once in a while, and at the summer solstice they threw open the gates of the Lordstow and held a great festival for all of Port Ester, anyone who'd climb up the heights. But that was as far as socializing went, at least up on the hill—although of course the lords and their children often came down to the port and entertained themselves in one way or another.

There wasn't really much in common between the High Lords and their subjects. Most Estermen lived on the shores and got their living from the sea in one way or another. The High Lords were the survivors of the torlaks; they'd come to Ester fleeing from Syrac after they'd been chased out of the portenas during the Night of Blood. They'd brought gold and silver and treasure to a country full of shepherds and fishermen, and they'd built themselves great houses up on the cliffs that they stuffed with books and weirds. They ruled in a very offhand sort of way: they demanded taxes, but otherwise they mostly spent their time quarreling with each other over magery and who was the best wizard, and other things no sensible person cared about.

But when they did bother to tell anyone on Ester what to do, you did it, because if you didn't do what a High Lord asked you to do nicely, the next day you'd do it after all, with no asking required. They couldn't *do* anything with their magic on its own: they couldn't shift the weather; they couldn't make fire or put it out; they couldn't heal or build or grow or anything useful in the world. But they could slip sideways into your mind and push and prod and poke until they got you to do what they wanted, and maybe afterwards you'd still be the same person, but maybe not.

No one on Ester had much liked them coming in and taking charge, but at least the wizards had learned something of a lesson after they'd been chased out of Syrac by the mobs. They had made a Council of Lords to rule them, and if one of them started to go really wicked, like the mad tor-laks had, back in Syrac, the rest of them stopped him. And after the High Lords had come to Ester, they'd put a stop to the sea-raids: their magic *was* good enough for that. They could get into the heads of the rakers from the Shells as easy as into those of any other men, and make them beach their smallkrakes to die thrashing on the shore. So now the rakers went for the portenas instead, and that was enough to make the High Lords worth putting up with.

And if, once in a while, one of them did something espe-cially alarming—such as swamping your town for a night with a wave of mysterious blue light that none of them would ever explain—they'd pay off anyone who was ever actually hurt with gold. That was how Father had been able to buy *Gullwing.* Tess had it bright and clear in her mind, her first two memories linked together: kneeling at the attic window staring at the blue wave rushing down the hill and yelling as it burst in through the window and came pouring over her and down the ladder into the room where Mother was labor-ing to bring Aston into the world, on its way to cascading out into the sea and vanishing over the horizon. And then the next morning—it had really been two weeks, but in her head, the time between had vanished—Father taking her by the hand onto *Gullwing,* and telling her, "This is our boat now, Tessy," and the big white wave of the loose sail over-head, snapping crisp in the light breeze.

But even if the High Lords weren't so awful that men had to band together and run them off, for a long time they still hadn't been *Estermen.* Estermen liked to say that half their blood was salt sea water, and as far as the High Lords were concerned, sailing wasn't much above scrubbing floors. It was where their fish came from, and the trade goods they wanted to buy, and that was all. And so it had stayed, for the better part of two hundred years, until Guildmaster Poltas of the shipbuilders had started the boat racing festival in Port Ester at New Year's, just like the famous races that were still held in Old Syrenac every year.

The High Lords all still thought of Syrac as the only civilized place in the world, and also they loved squabbling even more than they loved their mostly useless magic. Ever since, for the last fifty years, the whole pack of them and their wives and children and cousins were down in the harbor for the race every time, sponsoring boats and betting furiously against each other and scheming to make this or that favorite win. It had started to close the distance, a little.

So it wouldn't have surprised Tess very much to have one of the High Lords take *some* notice of them. For the last two years, all their scheming hadn't made any difference to the boat races. The *Plucky* had won every one so handily that it had been a bit disappointing to everyone by the end. Tess and Aston hadn't even been taken out drinking after the last race; they'd just bought some fried fish and beer for supper and gone home for an early night. That was when Aston had said, "We could take her to Old Syrenac, for the New Year races," over the dinner table, stirring the little pile of silver prize money with his finger, and when Tess had said, "No, we couldn't!" he'd said, "Why not?" and they'd come back with the gold medal.

But medal or not, lowfolk weren't asked to dinner with a single lord. She didn't even know *how* the lords took their meals on ordinary nights. They had to eat somehow, but surely they didn't gather round the enormous feast tables all the time. So she said, "Sir, we'll do as he commands, of course, but I'll tell you right now we won't have any idea how to go on," although she saw poor Vinna cringing behind the door at her boldness. But when the seas were high, you had to run straight into the waves and take them head-on, if you didn't want to be rolled over.

"Lord Ferantis is not interested in examining your *manners*," the sorcerer said, primly, which didn't make Tess feel much better, since it did imply he meant to examine something *else*. It wasn't comfortable to be examined by the High Lords. No one much liked to bring them a court case; it wasn't hard to decide who was in the wrong when you could force both sides to tell you the truth, but sometimes the forcing itself left a strangeness in the mind that didn't heal for a long time, if ever.

But there wasn't any help for it. If she and Aston didn't go on their own tonight, they'd go tomorrow without meaning to; they'd find themselves at the gates of the Lordstow, the world gone blurry and confused around them, and it would stay that way a long time too. So a boy was sent to the docks to get Aston in from the ship, and Vinna dragged Tess into her room to be put into the louppa she'd worn for her wedding, the silk pants billowing out from the gold cuffs buckled below her knees, and the chest wrap tying her breasts down like coconuts being packed for a long journey in the hold before the gorgeously embroidered tunic went on over. "I'll tear it or stain it!" Tess said, protesting.

"What does that matter!" Vinna said fiercely. "If he thinks you're pretty, he might not pull your brains out of your ears, or Aston's," and that was sensible, so Tess endured it. But as soon as they were shown into Lord Ferantis's hall, and he rose to greet them, it was immediately clear that he was ten times prettier than she would ever be, and the only person in the room who cared was her idiot brother.

The Lordstow was less a castle than it was a walled town, a great festival courtyard at its center with a leaping fountain and thirty-six townhouses surrounding it, each one putting forth a face of palatial splendor, and the enormous Hall of Lords filling up the entire northern end. Lord Ferantis's house was fourth from the corner on the east. Dinner was served in an elegant marble-floored dining room on a table not much bigger than their own, but made of gorgeous teakwood inlaid with bone and gold. Lord Ferantis didn't ask them any questions about *Blue* or the upcoming journey during the meal; instead he asked them in a deep and musical voice for stories of their past sea voyages, where they'd gone, what the discomforts and challenges had been. He looked no older than twenty, his face smooth and unlined; surely he had some magic going to keep him looking so young.

Aston didn't say a word more or less than he would have otherwise, meaning none. But he kept staring at Ferantis and his beautiful cheekbones and long straight nose and full mouth in exactly the way he'd spent the last ten months staring at the lines and curves of his ship taking shape. Lord Ferantis thankfully didn't seem to notice, but Tess forgot to be nervous for herself or the plans for the journey with something so much worse to fear. All she wanted was to tell Ferantis anything he wanted to know, and then steer her brother out of here before he ran himself onto the shoals. She talked more than she would have otherwise, as if she could turn his rudder away from disaster with words. Lord Ferantis listened, his long fingers delicately twisting a glass of wine back and forth, the sides of the cup at once clear and iridescent, catching the light and making the red wine shimmer strangely.

The dishes were cleared. He rose and led them into a sitting room crammed with books, books covering every single wall to the height of a mast, and sitting before the fire he said, "You've been very kind to indulge my questions," as if they'd done it out of generosity, and not because they'd been commanded to appear. "I expect you've been wondering why I've been asking them. There's been a great deal of debate among the lords about your prospective voyage. Many consider it merely a foolish enterprise, of course. But some of us see . . . remarkable potential."

"Yes?" Tess said, remembering to be nervous after all.

"All of Ester chafes at Syracian domination," Lord Ferantis said, which was more than Tess would have said. "But so long as they control the waters of the Cauldron, there's no easy path to escape it. The portenas and their privateers reap the benefits of our people's work, and their duties are so enormous that we are forced to limit our own to nearly nothing, to keep our shippers from losing money. If your voyage *did* succeed . . . much in the world could change, and very quickly."

"We'll do our best," Tess offered, hoping that was what he wanted.

"But there's some concern among the proponents of this idea," Lord Ferantis went on, as if she hadn't spoken. "They fear that you can't afford to let this journey fail."

"If it does, we'll just keep trying until it works," Aston

said, speaking for the first time—and missing the point entirely.

"They think we'd lie about it," Tess told him, sharply, and then said to Lord Ferantis, "M'lord, we're expecting it to fail. No one's ever sailed across the Empty before. There's no chart to go on, and we don't know how big it is. If our supplies run too low and we still don't know where we are, we'll have to turn back. But Aston's right; if it doesn't seem hopeless, we'll try again. We'll just raise more money before we try the trip again, so we don't need to take on as much cargo, and can carry more water instead."

Ferantis was studying them both, a gleam in his eye. "It seems that I've asked the right question for the wrong reason. You're planning to carry a cargo, even though you could use the space for supply, and improve your chances."

"Well, we can't afford *that*," Tess said. "We need to pay our crew, and buy supplies, and we've a loan to pay off for the materials to build *Blue*."

"How much?" Ferantis said.

Tess stared at him, realizing too late what he was about to offer her. But if the High Lords paid for them to go and find a long way round, then they *wouldn't* be able to afford for the journey to fail. "M'lord," she said slowly, trying to think her way through, "anyone *else* making the trip will need to carry a cargo, too, or else there's no use for the route."

"Once you've found there *is* a way, we can worry about making it a quicker one," Ferantis said. "Now: *How much?*" There was just a hint of steel in his tone.

"Seven silver for the crew, fifteen for supplies, twelve for the interest," Tess said, grimly. He'd just make her, if she didn't tell him. "We had to borrow three hundred silver."

"I'll cover the expenses," Ferantis said. "And you'll have five hundred silver, if you make it back around."

She swallowed around a dry mouth. "That *would* be a good reason to lie, m'lord," she said.

"It would," Ferantis said. "Which is why I'll be coming with you."

"What?" Tess said, in horrified dismay, as beside her Aston straightened up with the sunrise of a new and even more terrible idea than any he'd ever before managed in his life taking shape behind his eyes.

TESS GAVE UP ALL CAUTION entirely and spent the next three weeks desperately trying to persuade Lord Ferantis not to come. She even finally bluntly told him he'd have to come out on the *Plucky* with her, to see if he could stand it, hoping he couldn't. "I've personally sailed in the races," Ferantis said mildly. He didn't seem to be fussed when Tess talked to him like a person, even though Vinna still blanched every time she overheard it, which she *did,* because Lord Ferantis now came down in person, every single day, to look over *Blue* and the preparations, and to talk to Tess—and her still-besotted brother.

"The races are in the bay, or in the Cauldron," Tess said. "We'll be in the Empty. It won't be the same at all."

"I could come too," Aston said, popping up behind her.

"No, you couldn't!" Tess snapped at him. "You're needed on *Blue*!" He looked at her disappointed, but he had the sense to know that if he'd dared ask her *why not,* about *this,* he'd get three earfuls and she'd shove him off the dock besides.

Ferantis only looked amused, like he was watching japers perform for him on stage, and said, "All right, master navigator. We'll go out tomorrow, then."

Tess had a moment of hope when she took *Plucky* out past the Toothpicks. The wind and the current were at odds today, a heavy spitting bank of clouds low on the horizon to the northeast promising trouble and cold wet, and almost at once they were going up and down like rocking horses, if the horse had slammed you back and forth so hard your teeth clacked. She'd put Ferantis in the sleeping berth towards the back, where the ride would be less bouncy, but he still looked startled and queasy, holding on tight to the lifelines inside.

Even when she got them further out into what she already thought of as the smooth sailing of that broad current, the surf was still choppy by Cauldron standards. When she finally settled down, satisfied, they were still rolling smoothly over a five-foot swell, and Ferantis was sitting with his eyes shut and his fingers pressed to his forehead, his mouth tight. Tess waited until he blinked them open and looked at her, and she said, "It'll be a month at least, just like this, without a glimpse of land," and waved her hand out at the wide empty blue around them.

And Ferantis said, "Yes, I see." He made a low thoughtful noise deep in his throat. "I've been amiss. I didn't want to do any active prying—unusual talents can be disturbed too easily, and you and your brother are too valuable to take such a risk," he added, alarmingly. "But you've been trying so assiduously to keep me off, I assumed that you were afraid that if I were along, I'd force you to keep going beyond what you thought was safe. But instead you're afraid of having a sick and delirious wizard aboard."

Tess had been afraid of having an outraged wizard aboard, or far worse an encouraging wizard aboard, but now that he'd said it, she was afraid of the *other* things, too. "I'd say the same to any landsman, m'lord," she said. "When I was hiring for the crew, I didn't even bother talking to any sailor who hadn't been to Gos and back. Sailing for pleasure, it's not the same as being a fisher out on the sea a week at a time, and fishing isn't the same as a trading journey of a month. This will be worse than either. Likely we won't even see land for months. I don't know for certain how Aston and I will do ourselves."

Ferantis nodded, and then dashed all her raised hopes and said, "Well, Mistress Roh, you can set your mind at rest. I *will* come with you. And if our spirits wear out before our supplies, my magic will renew their strength."

THE ONLY THING THAT GAVE Tess any comfort as they set out was the last lingering chance that Ferantis would think better of it by the time they reached Gos. She deliberately told the men that they would sail straight there, without putting into any harbor, to have practice at living for three weeks at sea before they went on into the Empty. And then she took Aston aside and told him through her teeth that if he so much as gave Ferantis a wistful glance, she'd leave *him* in Gos, and he could work his passage home as a common hand on someone else's ship.

"Tess," Aston said, tentatively.

"Not a *word*," she said, flatly. "Vinna's got a baby coming!"

"She doesn't mind," Aston said.

"What?" Tess said, in horror; if he'd been stupid enough to breathe a word about it to anyone *else*—

"I told her I only wanted the dock, when I asked her to marry me," Aston said. "I didn't think it was fair to pretend. She asked if I'd give her children, and keep her and them like I'd promise, and she said she didn't mind otherwise. And I have!"

"She didn't mind when she thought her rival was a *ship*!" Tess said, but Aston was unperturbed.

"She won't mind *this,* either," he said, and Tess was forced to admit—to herself, not to Aston—that he was right. Vinna *would* be glad to look the other way if her husband caught himself a High Lord. The High Lords married each other's daughters or occasionally the daughters of their sorcerers, but every so often they did take a lover from the low-folk, and it was perfectly understood that if they did, the liaison would of course last only as long as the lord liked, but when it was over, the lover would have a handsome house in the best quarter of town, and a great many expensive gifts, and be treated with respect and welcomed into the highest circles of port society. So Vinna wouldn't mind; she and her children would reap all those rewards.

"Well, I *do* mind," Tess said flatly. "Do you think I'm taking on any of the crewmen because I like their looks? It's going to be hard enough at sea for months without anything like that going on. I mean it, Aston. If you won't give me your word not to start anything, you're not getting on *Blue,* and if you don't keep it all the way to Gos, I'll leave you there."

Aston gave her a wounded look, but she didn't budge this time, and after a moment he heaved a small sigh and promised.

For what good it did. Aston *did* keep his word all the way to Gos, where they did find a navigator to the Yellow Pebble, and he even kept it all the way there, to the dusty golden island with the shrubs covered in tiny pungent ashk seeds and peppercorn clusters; vines dangling big pods just like peas that they called sippo, which dried to a fragrant smoky-sweet flavor like something between the smell of toasted sugar and burning hickory chips. The hull was crammed with green coconuts and preserved breadfruit, but Tess filled every nook and cranny with small sealskin bags packed full of spices, and then she talked to all the navigators on the island, and paid one of them silver for a chart that showed the five thousand miles west that *they'd* sailed. The only decently sized bit of land anywhere on it was called the Isle of Death: far to the north, off the western coast of Shon, and the navigator told her that the same folk who threw the spirit-cups into the sea each winter also took condemned criminals to that island and left them there to die, so they wouldn't have blood on their own hands. After she put that chart next to the chart she had from the Minnows, she shook her head and went back to the tavern where Ferantis had taken the entire top floor for his chambers, and in his sitting room told him bluntly, "It's no use, m'lord. We won't make it."

She showed him and Aston, laying the two charts next to one another. The trouble was that familiar great current, marked as clear on the ocean as the Long Wolf's tail was in the sky. She hadn't the slightest doubt that it was good information, either: it was on all three of the charts she'd seen here, on all five of the Minnows charts she'd seen, and every navigator on either side had told her about it. And she'd felt it herself: that broad expanse of swift-moving water, rushing along—surely the same current that brought the spirit-cups west, and finally broke apart on the coast of Ester to go swirling into the Cauldron.

"But it would seem to me that such a current would only speed our journey, if indeed it flows westward the whole way," Lord Ferantis said.

"It will," Tess said. "But not enough." She put the charts together, and showed him the line of the current—and the disjunction, where the two currents were far apart. "These charts make eight thousand miles of blue water just to start. And they don't line up, so there's more water between them. I think at least a few hundred miles, and I'd guess more, because why shouldn't it be more?"

"From the west coast of Shon to the east coast of Ester is seven thousand miles, the sages say." Lord Ferantis said. "You're suggesting that the Empty is larger than the Cauldron and all the Hearthlands put together."

"If it was small, someone would have sailed it before," Tess said. "And we can cram in enough food and water for a couple of months, but even if we get lucky with rain and fishing, we'll still have to turn back after six weeks at the most. If we made two hundred miles every day, which we won't, we'd only cover eight thousand miles." She paused, seeing Ferantis scowling at the charts as if he wanted to make *them* mind him, the way he could force a man to do. "You're paying, m'lord, so we'll still try it if you want to," she added. "We can improve the charts, and if we manage to make landfall on some of these little islands along the way, we can plant some of our coconuts and breadfruit. In ten years, if they grow well, those islands will be places on the way where someone could replenish stores. But I'll tell you straightaway that we won't make it all the way across on what we can carry."

She left him frowning and dissatisfied. And because High Lords weren't used to being told they couldn't have their way, what Ferantis did, afterwards, was to call Aston back up to his rooms. He poured him a drink of some potion, and coaxed him to lie down on the bed, and rested his fingers on Aston's brow and asked him whether she was telling the truth.

So Aston kept his word, every last bit of it; he wasn't the one who started it. Ferantis did, when he peeked inside Aston's head and fell headlong into the blazing idiotic idea that Aston was still clinging to like a barnacle. His grip on it wasn't in the least dislodged by Ferantis trawling through his brain, even though it ought to have been. They didn't leave the room for three days afterwards, and meanwhile, downstairs and overhearing the delightedly shocked whispers of the tavern servants being ordered to bring them food and wine, Tess could have pulled all the hair from her head in fury and worry.

She didn't feel any better about it when they finally emerged with Ferantis wearing the bewildered expression of a man who'd been caught in a southsummer storm for three days and nights and had no idea where he was anymore. When she dragged the information out of Aston about what had happened, and then shouted at him for an hour about going to bed with a man who'd tried to turn his skull upside down and shake it out like a sack, Aston had the gall to tell

her that Ferantis had done it very *carefully*, and then added
that Ferantis had told him that when a wizard did it that way,
instead of some more aggressive sorts of prying, then whatever the other person felt or thought could pass over to him,
if it was strong enough. "So it's not really his fault either,
Tess," Aston said earnestly.

"It ruddy well is!" Tess said, but there wasn't any con-
vincing Aston, and the only thing Ferantis meant to be
ashamed of was that he'd fallen in love. Apparently having
ordinary feelings of the heart was unseemly for wizards, who
were supposed to be above such matters—though still allowed to entertain themselves below them, apparently—and
he'd been unenthusiastically preparing to marry some other
wizard's daughter to get his hands on a larger library, much
like Aston had married for his dock.

Instead now it *was* love, at least for the moment. Tess
didn't believe for an instant that it was going to last—and if
it *did* last, that would only make for a worse mess, because
the last place Aston belonged was in the middle of the kind
of scheming and wrangling that apparently went on among
the High Lords, who from everything Ferantis let slip made
the jealous guildmasters of Port Ester, toothy sharks one and
all, seem like glubs by comparison. He'd mentioned once,
all idly, that he'd had to kill three other men with his mind-
magic just to be named one of the High Lords and to inherit
his own father's house.

But for the moment Ferantis was just as sickly besotted
as Aston was, despite also being terrified at the idea that
anyone might notice. It was just as well he hadn't realized
that everyone on board had noticed, and just as well that
she'd hired a crew of six sensible men who all understood

instantly without being told that they were meant not to know, and that knowing would be unhealthy.

Ferantis insisted on setting out at once, in what Tess could have told him was a misguided attempt to jolt himself out of it. She could have told him, but didn't, because at least at sea, the two of them would have a harder time of it finding ways to spread the information any further. She also hoped they might not keep fucking, but that was a thin and faded hope which didn't last the first night back out on the water, listening wide-awake to the deck creaking as Aston sneaked out of his berth and to the captain's cotch they'd built at the back of the deck, where Ferantis slept.

At least Ferantis did believe her now, about the crossing, and even more than he ought to have, as if he'd picked up *that* from Aston too. If Tess had told Aston it was fifty thousand miles across the Empty, he'd have swallowed it with total unquestioning faith. In his head, she was the authority on everything in the world that mattered except for shipbuilding, and even there she was still the authority on what they could *afford* to build. Tess hadn't thought of Ferantis as a young man before; he was a *High Lord,* with magic to twist men's minds into knots if he wanted to use it, and she'd assumed that he kept himself looking young with spells. But now, watching him thrashing helplessly around his own feelings like a netted wriggler in midair, she asked him when he'd been born, and discovered to still more dismay that actually he was barely a year older than Aston; he wouldn't even have been of age yet, down in Port Ester.

"And they made you fight for your father's place, as a boy of eighteen?" Tess said, appalled.

"No one *made* me," Ferantis said. "There's only thirty-six

seats in the High Lords' Chamber. When one comes vacant, any qualified man may present himself to contest for it. But if I'd waited, it would have been another ten years or more perhaps, before another one of the old ones died, and in the meantime, whoever took the seat could claim my father's house and turn us out."

Tess was even more appalled. Except after another few days at sea, it came out in bits and pieces that what Ferantis meant by *turn them out* was, he and his siblings would have had to give up the townhouse in the Lordstow and go home to their villa just outside Westshore, a beautiful port town on the western coast of the Cauldron that was nearly as big as Port Ester, and he himself would have had to endure the indignity of serving another High Lord as a sorcerer if he wanted to keep using magic. It was the sort of fate that could only look intolerable to an eighteen-year-old boy. His mother had died some years before, and the father evidently hadn't bothered to teach his son any sense before he'd followed her.

And Ferantis had won his stupid fight, so he hadn't bothered to acquire any sense on his own since. The more dribdrabs of information that came out of him, the more worried Tess became. When he'd said that there was a contingent of High Lords who were interested in the crossing of the Empty, really he'd meant there were three other lords besides him who had bothered to give it more than a curious thought, and he'd made a fuss at the others to get the money out of the treasury. He hadn't been prying into Aston's head just for amusement: he'd staked his *own* reputation on their making it across, and if they didn't, he'd lose an unhealthy amount of his standing, which evidently was precarious enough to begin with.

"But what does that *mean*?" Aston asked him. "If you're all equal, in the High Lords' Chamber, then what difference does standing make?"

They were lying in the captain's cotch together, late in the evening with the stars and the Big Sister overhead, talking low enough to imagine that no one else could hear them, but the wind was at their stern, carrying the words forward, and Tess was sitting perched out on the front of the starboard hull, putting her hand into the water to feel the currents, to mark them on the new chart she was making.

"We're not really equal. Everyone has a single vote, but there are parties, and the men who lead those parties are the real powers," Ferantis said. "And they're always looking for a chance to have one of their followers take another seat. They were all disappointed when I won. They'd like to impeach me, to get it free again. If they could convince enough others to vote with them . . . ."

Even sitting downwind, Tess could hear the evasion in his tone, and Aston did too. "And then . . . you'd have to stop using magic?" he asked, pressing.

Ferantis was silent a long dark moment, and then he said, low, "No. If you're impeached . . . they put you to death. They don't want anyone trying for revenge. They'd put my brother to death, too; give my sister in marriage to a sorcerer, someone too old to sire children, to spend her life as a servant. They'd share out our lands . . . ." He stopped talking on a gasp; then added, as if he was trying to convince himself, "It takes an eight-tenths vote, so it's hard. There has to be a good enough reason, or most of the lords won't vote for it. No one likes when it's done. But . . . my father already diminished our family's standing badly. He just barely survived an impeachment vote himself, and he never managed to re-store his reputation before he died. That's why I was trying to do something important, something that would increase the power of Ester and my family both. But if I fail in-stead . . ." He trailed off.

Aston said, "Tess will get us across if anyone can. And if she can't . . . we'll think of something else."

That came out of his mouth after seven weeks and three days at sea. Tess thought they'd crossed nearly four thou-sand miles of ocean by then. The chart she'd bought on the Yellow Pebble had been good for the most part until now, but she hadn't managed to find a single one of the tiny atolls they'd marked, and now she was sure she was past the end of it. She'd started her own chart four days ago, wriggler ink on fishskin, and she was trying to keep the *Blue* in the wide westward current, but even that was starting to give her trouble, getting weaker, being broken up into patches of water with different temperatures, sometimes streaks of cold and sometimes bursts of warmer water. The wind had been com-ing from unexpected sides, once or twice blowing head-on into her face.

Tomorrow she would have to tell everyone they were going on short rations. They had five days more sailing be-fore they'd have to turn back, at best, and then Aston would start trying to think of *something else* to save his lover. Tess stewed over it the whole rest of her night's shift, and didn't even bother rousing the second watch; why shouldn't some-one get some sleep?

The worst thing was that she already knew exactly what Ferantis should do. He should fall over the side of the ship in a rough sea and die a brave adventurer, giving his enemies the open seat they wanted. Then his family would be allowed to go on living, and *he* could go on living, too, an anonymous scribe or bookkeeper on Yellow Pebble. And then Tess would have to sail back to Port Ester alone, to keep Aston's word to Vinna, because *he'd* stay behind, too.

Oh, she knew she could take Aston with her if she wanted. She had a fistful of debts he owed her: the four years she'd fed him and paid their bills, going out alone for weeks to fish them enough to live on and buy supplies while he dreamed and worked on his first real ship. He wouldn't refuse, if she called them in. But she wasn't a bank. There was too much chance Aston would end up *happy,* on Yellow Pebble. And she wouldn't break her heart. She'd have *Blue* and *Plucky,* and with them to grow on, she'd have a full-fledged trading company soon enough. She'd be fine, and Vinna would be fine, and the baby wouldn't know the difference. She'd have them both to love, and to need her. So she wouldn't have enough—not quite enough—of a reason to give Aston, when he asked her *why not.*

But it would be a breaking up of the life they'd imagined and worked for all these years, and inside her belly was an angry pair of krake jaws that wanted to snap and tear at him for imagining himself a different one. He'd be gone as clear as if he'd truly died. You couldn't send regular messages to someone on Gos to begin with, and they wouldn't be able to risk someone finding out the secret of Ferantis's disappearance.

And it felt worse that he was casting it aside to reach for a life that she'd refused for herself. Father had started there, before he'd taught her blue-water sailing instead. He'd tried to persuade her to let him make a match for her, three times, with three good men. She hadn't longed for any of them, but she'd mostly said no because she hadn't wanted to leave Aston alone with his dreams, a hanger-on in her house. So there was that much justice in her anger. Aston hadn't had to *ask* her to choose him, to choose their little family of two. And now he was going to choose a stranger instead, a selfish and thoughtless one, unless she put a leash around his neck and dragged him the other way behind her like a whining dog. It wasn't fair, and that was the truth.

But it was a truth she could only use to make it easier to let him go, and not to keep him. When he was gone, she'd have to let herself know that Aston was selfish and thoughtless, too, and that he'd been so at her expense, all these years. That didn't matter when they were together, and she had the joy of his spark, his quickness, the lightning-flash of him—like riding a fast-sailing boat before a high wind, knowing her hand on the tiller kept it flying, the magic they'd made together on the sea. But once she didn't have that joy anymore, the memory of it would fade like a storm clearing away over the horizon, almost impossible to imagine once it was gone and the ocean lay smooth and clear again all around you.

She'd remember more clearly all the things that would still be with her: the dangerous and heavy work and the thick calluses it had built up on her hands and beaten into her salt-rough and reddened face; the regret for the paths she hadn't followed and the husband and children she'd never have. She wasn't too old to have them, but she was, because she had learned too well not to let herself get carried away. She'd never be foolish enough to trust a man with everything that was now hers, everything she'd built with years and drudgery.

All those hard things she'd given without return would pay her back in ease: they would let Aston fade away into a bittersweet past, only a shadow at her side in another life. She would be unselfish, this one more time, and if he let her, that would tip the balance between them over too far, and some of the love would go slopping out, like a too-full cup tipped sideways by a heaving sea. And then she wouldn't break her heart, and if he did, that wouldn't be her trouble anymore.

But that knowledge only made it harder now. It hurt worse to think of losing Aston that way, twice over: losing him and losing her own love for him. But that was the only way she could lose him. She could feel it happening already, before he'd even asked her *why not.* Just imagining him asking, knowing that he would, was sending a little bit of the love leaking out over the sides. Because yes, it *was* Ferantis's fault, but it was Aston's, too. She'd asked him to let go of this idea in every way she could, and he'd refused.

She sat in the bow brewing anger inside her the whole rest of the night, shifting the sails over and over in irritation whenever the wind came unexpected and slapping at her face, which it did a dozen times, as if to go along with her mood. When Aremus got up at dawn and said, "Mistress Tess," she snapped, "What?" in a flat-out surly way, before she could roll her tongue back into her mouth. "Sorry, what?" she said over again, in apology, and Aremus said, with a jerk of his chin, "What is't?"

"What's what?" she said, and then she saw the black speck against the paling sky. She took out her spy-glass, the old heavy one made of bronze, with the guild stamp from the glassmakers of Meles. The sailing guildmaster had given it to her, ceremonially, when they'd seen the *Blue* off. He'd told her, "No ship that's left Port Ester with this glass hasn't come back, Mistress Roh. Don't be the first."

She opened it to its full length and squinted through, sweeping back and forth until she found the speck: a bird. One that looked like a gullbird but with black wings and white tips, flying east. She put down the glass and stared, and then looked to find it again, and instead spotted two others, also flying, and in the next ten minutes, before the sun was even fully up, she'd seen a dozen, all flying the same way: out to sea, for their breakfasts, the way they always did in the mornings. And *out to sea* could only happen from land.

She took out the old charts, her heart pounding with hope, and tried to make them fit together, anywhere along their way. She couldn't manage it; the great current sat there enormous and implacable across them both, and wouldn't line up. But perhaps the Minnows chart was wrong, or maybe the current shifted with the seasons; the Cauldron currents were different during summer and winter. Maybe they were the same chart after all, the same five thousand miles of ocean, or close enough. She could have made a mistake about the stars.

Or if she hadn't, if the stars and the charts were correct, then maybe she'd been right to start a new chart, and there was an island of decent size between them. If the Empty had to be ten thousand miles across, she couldn't have asked for a better place for one to be. If it had gullbirds, maybe it had water, or coconuts at least. It even seemed likely, the more she thought about it. She'd never heard that they had black gullbirds in the Minnows. She'd never heard of black gullbirds at all.

She didn't say anything, and Aremus and Jowly, who were solid navigators themselves, if still officially journeyman-rank, didn't say anything either. There was no sense tempting fate by talking about it out loud. So Aston had no idea, and Ferantis even less. But she spent the whole day looking for land in every way she knew how. She wasn't chasing the big current anymore; she was feeling the pattern of the swells, looking for anything that might point her way towards land—they weren't any help; by midday the swells were all over the place, and she couldn't get any sense of direction from them—and staring at the infuriatingly cloudless sky. She'd already decided that if the big current came back together for her, she'd assume she'd missed the island and turn round and try again, maybe a little further south. But she saw more birds flying all morning, a dozen at least, and the wind at their backs was picking up, almost like a sea breeze blowing; they had to be close.

And then late in the afternoon she spotted the first thickening on the horizon of what might have been a cloud-bank, due east. Throwing caution and her sails to the wind, she sent *Blue* leaping on ahead towards it, hoping to get a clear sighting before the night came on. For once, reckless-ness was rewarded: in an hour the clouds had climbed fully up into the sky, and she was sure that she saw a reflection of land, tinged green and brown, on their underside. Jubilation was thick in her throat, and she almost said something, but made herself swallow it. Another hour might bring them in sight of the actual land, she thought. She'd be patient.

Half an hour later, she sighted the second cloudbank,

east and further north, also reflecting colors; at least sixty miles north of the first, at a guess. Aremus and Jowly were standing next to her, staring as the clouds came up over the horizon and then looking over at her, as if they wanted to be sure they weren't imagining something that wasn't there. Twenty minutes later they saw a third bank, far to the south, and an hour later she said, "Reef the sails, and put over the sea-anchor," as great clouds of birds started to come flying in, some right over their heads—gullbirds and sagbeaks and ospreys and a dozen other kinds of sea-birds she'd never seen before to put a name to, with bellies full of fish, going home.

"What is it, Tess?" Aston asked her, anxious.

"We'll sight land tomorrow morning," she said.

He drew a breath, turning with wide dawning joy towards Ferantis, who said sharply, "The Minnows? Or another island, somewhere we can get more water?"

"It's not the Minnows," she said. "And getting water won't be our trouble. Sailing round is going to be our trouble."

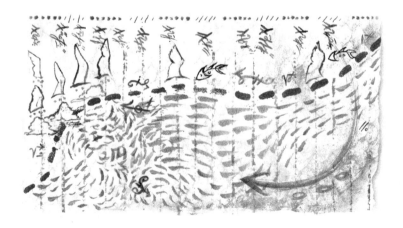

. . .

IN THE MORNING SHE STARTED the cautious approach, as grudging with sail as a miser with his silver. The currents and the winds were as wild as horses, coming at her from every direction, and the tide kept trying hard to carry her in faster than she wanted to go. She hated every inch of sea-ground she had to give with no idea of the coast ahead. There could be cliffs as sheer as the Toothpicks about to start poking up over the horizon, with nary a bay or a cove to shelter in.

But what first came over the horizon wasn't a mountain. She had no idea what she was looking at when the smooth round top of it began to come into view. An hour later, with the whole towering thing fully visible—dwarfing the tall trees all around it, maybe a hundred feet tall or more—she still didn't know, but everyone on board was staring at it too. It was standing on a high promontory that just hooked around the southern end of a gigantic bay as beautiful and wide as the Harbor of the Mother in Portena Leraba: water smooth as silk, curving inland. As inviting a place to land a ship as you could have asked for, on a shore you didn't know—only they'd have to sail past the thing to get in.

It wasn't just that there *was* something built. This wasn't a barren scrap of rock with a few coconut trees and maybe a spring; this island was a place big enough for people to live in. The land kept on running north and south as far as the glass could show her, and there were those cloudbanks, too. It might easily be bigger than the Yellow Pebble. Tess wouldn't have been surprised to find that big bay full of fishers, and a town covering the shore, and why not a palace or a monument? But half the strangeness was that there wasn't a sign of any of those things. The whole shore was deserted. There wasn't even a break in the trees around the structure; they'd grown up clustered tight around it, and there were plenty of big ones: as if it had been abandoned a century ago and more.

And the other half of the strangeness was the thing itself. The torlaks of Old Syrenac had built enormous temples that were still standing a thousand years and more, even now after they had all been chased out to become High Lords in Ester instead: polished marble with the small pyramid houses at the top, climbing into the sky like stairways to the home of the gods. She'd gone upriver to see one of them when she and Aston had been in the city for the races, and it had been so huge she'd called it impossible. But she'd been wrong: it *had* been possible. She could imagine how it had been built, and why: the years, the money, the army of laborers, the quarried stone, and the pride and greed that had spent them.

This thing, she couldn't even put a name to what it was, and she couldn't think of any reason anyone would have wanted to, either. The part they'd seen first, half of them had called it a tower, and the other half had called it a mast, and as they got closer, half of them had switched round to call it the other, but they still hadn't all settled on one or the other. It was round, and skinnier than a tree trunk, too narrow for stairs to be inside and too tall for anyone to reasonably climb, but it was too big to just be a pole.

And as they'd come closer, the other part had come into sight: halfway up the pole-tower, there was another part jutting straight into the air, impossibly. It wasn't just a platform;

at the end, there was a deep section, at least the height of a man if not more: it looked like a big dipping cup, the kind you would use to scoop gutbait out of a pail or flour out of a sack. The closer they got, the less sense it made. The whole thing should have tipped over, and if you *could* have built it, and kept it up, why would you? It looked like something a child would draw in sand on the shore, or try to build out of twigs, but all made of some kind of metal that looked as smooth as polished silver, and changed all the colors that reflected in it to their opposites. The temple in Old Syrenac had shown some sign of the years: the gold plates stolen, the paint worn away, the stones crumbled. There wasn't so much as a smudge of tarnish or rust upon this pole or the jutting platform. It might have been built fresh yesterday, only who'd built it, and where were they?

So of course the first thing Ferantis wanted to do was go and have a look at it. "How close can you get us?" he demanded, staring at it fervently from the front of the deck.

"Do you think it will be more than a day's climb, to get up there?"

Tess didn't even want to sail past in sight of the place, and she knew her crew all felt the same exact way, even though not one of them had said a word. None of them were so religious that they hadn't got on board to sail across the Empty, but it didn't take a fanatic to worry that they'd come to one bad place or another. This didn't seem much like the abode of demons that the River Gospels talked about being on the underside of the world, but after all, no one had ever come back from there to report. And it *could* have been the paradise home of the Endless, with all that shining blue water and the thick green forests, but even if that wasn't a hell, no one of much sense really wanted to *meet* their god, at least not early and uninvited.

But she could see plain enough that if she just told Ferantis *no,* he'd tell her *yes,* and make it stick. "We'll have to wait until the morning, and then it'll be another day to make landfall somewhere safe," she said, to buy herself time and her crew some steadiness.

Six days later, though, she was standing grimly by, watching Ferantis put his hands on the thing, and the only saving grace was, she'd left Aston behind with *Blue.* She'd known better than to leave anyone else behind: there wouldn't have been a ship to sail away on, by the time they'd got back.

"Going up there is a stupid thing to do," she'd told Ferantis bluntly on the shore, with all the men listening, and pointed to the mountains they could now glimpse to the west, a handful of sharp blue peaks, soft and misty with distance even on a clear day. "This isn't an island, not even a big one. It's *land*. We've sailed past the end of the chart I got in Yellow Pebble, but only *just* past the end, and I don't believe that in a thousand years of sailing, no one's ever found this country. If there are people here, they're unfriendly, and if there aren't, there's a reason. You want to learn more about whatever that thing is, you should come back here with seven ships packed with soldiers. And you can live to do that, if we go now and sail for home."

But Ferantis had been unmoved, and he'd told her, cool and final as if he were standing in the Lordstow, "Mistress Roh, I understand your anxieties, but I've already done a scrying, and I can assure you that there is no thinking being anywhere nearby but ourselves. I think you don't give yourself and your brother enough credit. We sail on the finest ship ever built, under the hand of the finest navigator—and with the bravest crew," he'd added, with a grand gesture sweeping over six wooden-faced men who'd all been considering whether they could club him to death before he could scramble their brains, "and I'm certain we *are* the first to find this country."

"Then who built *that*?" she demanded, and he had the gall to say, "Perhaps it is a natural formation," which he wouldn't have cared about in the first place. When he saw her expression—she couldn't control the outrage—he at least amended his words to say, "Or I should say, we are the first in a long time. Look around yourself—look at that untouched forest, even on this magnificent shore. Whoever once lived in this place, they've abandoned it and left behind their greatest monument. Surely fate has led us here, to find this one miraculous—" He stopped, having to try to think of a *word* for the thing, because it made so little sense, before he decided and went on, "—edifice. It would be folly to go without trying to learn more of it."

If it hadn't been for Aston, Tess would just have let Ferantis haul up the nets he was busy throwing, and then sailed for home in the morning when they found him on his bedroll with his skull staved in, and no one to point a finger at. Instead, she took a deep breath and told the men, "Go by twos. Get some firewood, and see if you find anything that looks like good eating, and come back before it gets dark. I'll have a stronger word with his lordship," and when they'd all left, she told Ferantis flatly, "The only folly around here is yours, and they all know it. And they *also* know that the other High Lords won't miss you if you don't come home. Unless you want to be dead before morning, then when those men come back, you'd better give them a good and bright reason to go up there, and I *don't* mean by putting claws into their brains. I need them to get us home again, if you don't get us all killed."

Ferantis looked abashed, and when the men came back, he'd announced that when they returned to Ester, each one of them would get ten times their pay, and in gold instead of silver. Tess had taken them all aside herself also and said, "We'll stay well back and let him poke at it if he wants to, and if he's blasted for his pains, we'll head down and go straight home."

She still hadn't dared leave any of them behind. Aston had argued for going up himself, and her staying behind, but she wasn't having that, either. "You haven't got a chance of keeping those men in line," she said, without a moment's hesitation, when he tried to say *why not* to her, as if for once he didn't know perfectly well. "They know you're in love. They won't trust you, and *I* don't trust you either."

So she was up here with all of them behind her, crouched a hundred yards back from the leg of the dipping-cup pole, peering down the narrow path Ferantis had clumsily hacked through the brush to get himself up to the base. Her whole back was tense, taut as a line in a gale, and she and all the men drew back as Ferantis put his hands on the surface— and nothing happened.

Nothing kept on happening, for the next five hours. Ferantis touched the pole, spoke to it, sang to it; he tried to cast spells on it. He tried to write on it with ink, which ran straight off; he hit it with a stick and with a rock, both of which clanged faintly but didn't do anything else, not even leave a mark. By the end of it, even Jowly, who was a follower of the Endless and had spent the first hour praying in quiet desperation, had just dozed off in boredom. The weather was hot and sticky and it was dim and quiet on the damp forest floor, full of the reassuring ordinary smell of leaf and mold. They were sitting under a bunch of trees that didn't look quite like lycca trees but dripped the same pink-colored sap, so much so that after a couple of hours, Pinharo absently picked himself a big chew off one trunk and didn't even realize he'd done it for ten minutes, after which Aremus suddenly said, "D'you put that in your mouth?" and Pinharo froze staring at them as they all stared back, and then he took it out and looked at it and then said, "Guess I'm already dead if it's poison," and put it back in, and added, "Good flavor."

Finally Tess said, "All right, stay here, I'm going to get

him," and walked down the path to where Ferantis was standing at the foot of the dipping-cup pole with his face red and sweaty and twisted up in frustration. She didn't like the thing any better when she was up close to it. It *was* a tower, and bigger than she'd realized; they'd just been so far away that it had looked skinny, but the only real way it was skinny was by comparison to its height. The pole was as big around as a three-hundred-year lirenwood, wider than *Blue*'s deck, and it came straight up out of the ground. Ferantis had tried to dig down around it; he'd gone almost four feet down, and it just kept going into the earth. "It won't *answer* me!" he burst out to her furiously.

Tess eyed him. "You thought it would?" She couldn't understand how. She felt in her bones, in the popped knuckles of her left hand that ached when heavy weather was coming, that this thing was nothing to do with them.

Ferantis made a wild stormy wave of his hands. "I can *feel* it. It's just—*ignoring* me!"

She stared at him. "Are you saying it's *alive*?"

It seemed that she'd asked him a difficult question. "No," he said finally, wavering, but he sounded unsure. "But it *does* have a mind. It does!" he added, more to himself than her. "It has—*something*! Something that moves in it like thought, like—*hunger*—"

"And you're trying to *wake it up*?" Tess said, through her teeth, and Ferantis paused.

"No, I don't mean— It's not hungry for *us*," he said, a little too quick, avoiding her eyes. He was *lying*. He didn't have any damned idea what it was hungry for, and here he still was, doing his best to throw fresh red meat into krake waters.

Tess lost her temper and said, "You stupid, selfish *twat*," and he jerked and stared at her, shocked as if no one had ever spoken to him honestly in his entire life. "We sail across the ocean and run straight into this mad thing that doesn't make any sense at all, and you don't know a damned thing about it except it's huge and *hungry,* but you've been poking at it all day, trying to make it answer you? The only answer you're likely to get is being eaten, and you'll deserve to be, but we don't!" He flinched back, his eyes widening. "But you don't give a smallkrake's spit about us, do you? You don't even care about your *own* life, you're so busy grabbing after the nearest next thing you think you want, without bothering to ask yourself if there's any *sense* to it, if it matters more than what you've already got—"

"Just like *him!*" Ferantis blurted at her, with the air of someone trying to defend himself; he was staring at her so hard and unblinking he might have been trying to bore holes into her skull, and Tess stopped, pressing her mouth tight.

"Yes," she said flatly. "Just like my brother. But he's doing it because he thinks you love him. And maybe I'm just as much a fool as he is, but at least Aston's not a worthless greedy glub who doesn't care about anyone else at all. Because he's always *asked me.*"

She turned and walked away from him, half expecting to be turned around, half expecting to feel something taking hold of her brain and body, but it didn't come, and before she was halfway down the track, she heard Ferantis come after her. He followed her and the men all the way back down the long hot trail, through the sweating trees, and back to where Aston was waiting, anxiously, with a fire going and fish roasting on spits, and *Blue* with the edges of her reefed sails fluttering in the wind.

. . .

THE NEXT MORNING TESS GAVE the order to pack up. They filled up all their gourds and casks with sweet water; there were a dozen streams that ran into the bay, and likely turned into a river further inland. They loaded all the emptied spaces in the hold with fresh fruit they'd found, and meat they'd quick-smoked. The fruit was small and round and harder than unripe mangoes, but when you got through the skin, the pale green flesh yielded to a bite, crisp and sweet and sour. The meat had come from a thing like a small deer with long legs and a cloud of spindly antlers, which Jowly had seen eating some of the fallen fruit. He'd shot it with an arrow, and he and Pinharo had carried it back. Ferantis didn't say anything or argue; he just went on board, and Aston looked between the two of them and didn't ask Tess what had happened.

She sailed them back out of the bay into the mess of tangled currents, looked over her shoulder at the clouds massed to north and south both, and told Jowly, who'd had the best luck, "Toss a silver: tree we go north." When he opened his palm, the fish was facing up, so she turned south instead.

Two days later, the crew were all rubbing Jowly's head and patting his back to borrow some of his luck: that morning, the coast had turned sharply westward, and a good strong current was carrying them along; Tess didn't tempt fate by saying it out loud, but she thought it might even be their old friend the wide current, coming back together again.

But five days later, while they were eating their dinner, Aremus said, "What's that?" and they looked and saw something shining on the coast somewhere up ahead. Tess brought out the glass and stared through it blankly: the coast was curving south again, and somewhere halfway down the curve stood a small cone-shaped building, gleaming red.

They sailed past it the next day. It wasn't red after all. It looked like nothing more than one of the long coconuts that grew on the islands near Gos, with the top cut off to make a drinking cup, and turned upside down, only it was made of some kind of black stone, cut in facets like a gigantic gemstone and polished so bright it had been catching the colors of the sunset. It wasn't anything like the dipping-cup pole, except that it didn't make any more sense, and it was just as isolated, standing all alone at one end of a long sandy strip of beach. There wasn't any sign of anyone around it, either.

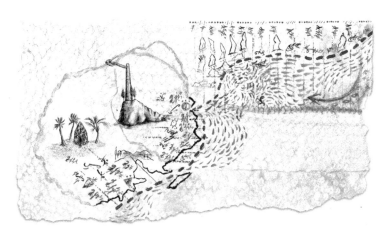

But unlike the dipping-cup pole, this thing had a *door,* or at least an opening in the side. Ferantis stared at it as if he'd been at sea for three days without fresh water and turned to her and said, "If you make landfall along the shore, I could go and look at it alone," and he didn't say *why not,* but that was what he meant.

It didn't seem like it could be worse than the first one; at least it was much smaller. Tess let Ferantis off on the shore a mile east of the hut. Aston watched him through the glass the whole way as he trudged down the sand to the hut and went inside. He had to duck to go in the opening; the whole hut was barely ten feet tall.

Tess wouldn't have been surprised to see the opening close up around him like a pair of jaws snapping shut, but instead he came out again after three hours and came back to the ship with his face in such a knot that Tess knew he hadn't been able to get any more of an *answer* out of this one, either.

Six weeks later they were still sailing west, and they'd seen another five of the follies, as they'd come to call them: all different, all absurd, all of them abandoned and silent. It stopped feeling like a hideous chance had brought them so close to the first one; the things were all over the place. Ferantis wasn't even asking to go look at them anymore, and Tess wasn't worrying about them either; she was more worried about their course. The current had petered out again, and she'd seen two thick cloudbanks to the south of them, hinting there was *more* land over there, just out of sight. She had the bad feeling she might be sailing inland, instead of around the southern edge of what had to be a *continent.* She was pretty sure by now that it was bigger than Syrac; maybe even bigger than Shon. Huge mountains had reared up on the coastline alongside, so tall their tops were wreathed in snow and clouds, and she didn't see any end to them.

When the storm clouds gathered up ahead of her in the west four days later, a thick bank of dark grey crackling with lightning spidery through them, she decided and turned south, away from them and from the land. If she ran into *another* coastline, it would mean they'd gone the wrong way into a gulf, and there would be nothing for it but to turn around and go back out again.

But when she did find another coastline, it wasn't on the opposite side, it was to the west, running north–south, with a whole new line of jutting mountains tall and spiky like a fortress wall along it. The coastline was mostly sheer walls of rock, but they passed one pocket of a valley that came green all the way down to the water. Another folly made of brilliant white clay sprouted halfway up the slope, like a mushroom the size of a boat shed, with seven round windows and a flock of enormous things like woolly goats with round horns eating the grass around it, unconcerned. She made landfall with no objections, and they had roast roundhorn for dinner below the mushroom folly, with Ferantis glaring up at it resentfully. After dinner she stitched another piece of fishskin parchment onto the map that she was drawing, while he went and mucked around with the folly just as uselessly as before.

It took another month of sailing, slow and cautious, following the coastline around curves and divots and promontories, stars she'd never seen heaving up over the horizon after others that were out of season, as if they really had got into the underworld. They'd gone so far that the wind had ice upon it, like trying to sail to Nelboiya in winter, and they were shivering all day, running through their food quick. She'd just begun thinking in dismay if she'd have to turn

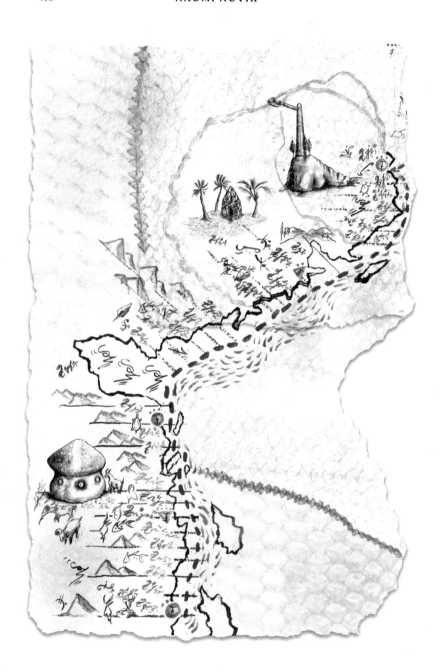

around after all, and sail all the way back north and then try
to find them a way round in that direction. On her map the
continent was now twice the length of Shon and still growing.

Finally the coastline turned westward, but to follow it,
she had to creep slowly through a narrow strait between jag-
ged cliffs, and it was a week sailing the half-frozen coastline
before it finally started leading them north again. They saw
another five follies, and still not a single person anywhere,
although once when they landed, they got run off the shore
by an angry beast something like an overgrown cross between a walrus and a barca that had decided two tusks just
weren't enough, so it would add on an extra pair below, and
also why not some bony plates for good measure. The thing
had been lolling on the sand sleepily like nothing more than
a delicious mountain of blubber waiting for the knife, but
when Jowly had tried to get it with an arrow, first of all a
good shot had bounced right off its back, and then it had
stood up furious on four thick legs and charged them so fast
that they'd just barely pushed *Blue* off in time to keep it
from leaping onto the deck. It paced them along the coast
bellowing hoarse challenges for the whole next hour, until
she gave up on another landing and turned back out to sea.

There was a two-day heartbreak of sailing into a bay
whose mouth was so large she hadn't been able to see the
other side until she'd sailed into it, but when Aremus had
taken four soundings in a row all going shallower, she'd
turned and got them out of it. But at least when they sure
enough found the coastline on the other side, it had turned
north again by that night. She let herself think that maybe
she'd made the turn around the end of the continent at last,

and found her way back out into the Empty. She even dared to try sailing further west, out into blue water.

That, of course, was when they sighted krakes. She knew they were there before she saw them; for half a day, the soundings kept getting deeper and deeper, and then they just stopped finding the ocean floor altogether. When Pinharo dipped in his fishing net, there were three green wrigglers in there among stringy trailers of seaweed. "Oh, crog it all," Tess said, and took them back closer in to the coast, giving up all her westward progress. There wasn't any other choice: when skinny Des went up to the top of the mast that morning, he could see a long streak of green in the water not five miles of sea away: masses of wrigglers. At least she could squeeze them for more ink, which it looked like she was going to need.

The wind almost died as they slogged on northward, alongside that green ocean valley they kept sighting every morning. She had to scrabble after every breath of the land and sea breezes she could get, endless tacking—oh, she missed *Plucky's* swing sail—and all of them taking turns paddling to make a quarter of the miles they could have with a good wind, creeping along until she began to think they'd gone nearly as far north as they'd had to come south. And then, to her exasperation, she saw cloudbanks to the west reflecting still *more* land. An island, she told herself, but the clouds stayed alongside all day. She would have been sure they were in another bay, if it hadn't been for the ocean valley; she'd never heard of one being anywhere but open ocean.

The next morning, Des whistled the sharp warning note from up on the mast, and they all stopped and watched the krake, just lazily coming up and swimming almost directly parallel to their course, its mouth wide open for breakfast: it was one of the really big ones, its maw big enough you could have sailed a Syracian barge straight into it without hitting the teeth on either side. It didn't breach, but it rolled, lifting a big side flipper out of the water as if it were waving at them, and then down smack into the water again with a sound like a thousand men clapping all together at once. The ripple hit them a few minutes later, lifting *Blue* up and gently down again.

Ferantis panicked and asked what they were going to do and how they could get away, and all the sailors immediately told him in great seriousness that they had to cover themselves in a paste of fish guts, for the smell made the krakes keep away, and handed him a pot that Pinharo had been saving hopefully. Tess glared at Aston hard to keep him quiet, and Ferantis got far enough to scoop up a handful and smear it halfway up his arm, then looked around at them all with an odd squinting expression and then stopped with his mouth in an O of shocked indignation. Everyone laughed, and then Tess said to him, "It's your first krake sighting. Now we dunk you over the side to wash it off, and then you're a true man of the sea," and held out the loop of rope, and he stared in her face and then a little uncertainly took it and put it on, under his arms, and let them dunk him three times. They brought him up dripping, and all joined in to towel him off with spare sailcloth—a bit roughly, perhaps—and then Tess poured everyone a tiny glass of goat's-milk brandy out of the small flask she kept in her box, and they toasted him and all sang "The Krake Hunter" together, and Ferantis's expression wavered between liking it and worrying that some other High Lord would pop up and catch him liking it.

Having a first-krake ceremony was always good for raising the mood, and Tess was even more glad to have given
the crew a chance to get back at Ferantis a little *without*
blood coming into it. They were all more cheerful, and she
needed them in good spirits: she still had to get round that
ocean valley, and who knew how long it went? And even
once she did, it would be another two months of blue-water
sailing to get home, if she was lucky, which she didn't have
any reason to expect to be.

But they'd finally reached the end of their bad luck.
The next morning, Des reported that the streak of wriggler
green had gone thinner; by the end of the week, it was all
gone, and the soundings were coming back more shallow.
The straits they were in narrowed, and when they sighted
the coastline to the west she crossed over to follow that one
instead as it started curving back away. The wind started
picking up, coming almost straight from the east, strong and
eager, and it felt so much like the wind off the coast of Ester
that she couldn't help but hope it would carry them to the
open ocean, and all the way home.

Three days later, all the coastline to be seen anywhere
was lying comfortingly to the south. The soundings had
gone deep again, but not too deep, and when she put her
hand in the water, she felt it stirring against her fingers,
down there deep: the pull of the wide ocean current. She
didn't tempt fate. "We'll make landfall tomorrow, for a few
days, and take on fresh water and supplies," was all she
told Aremus, but her crew knew her by now; they were in
a holiday mood when they dropped the anchor, and the
next morning as she piloted them in, it only seemed like
another lucky sign when the sun lit up a folly on the hill

above the shore: a curving shape of dusty blue stone like the swell of a wave before it crested, twice as tall as a man's height in the middle.

Ferantis didn't bother to go look at it this time, but Tess did, walking all the long way up the hill from their fire. She had a feeling of wanting to go up and say goodbye to the place, somehow. Maybe the follies had lost some of their fearful strangeness, from seeing so many of them, or because she now had the comfort of seeing the way home out ahead of her. Or maybe it was just *this* folly that seemed more friendly: as she got closer, she realized it wasn't made of stone at all, but sea-glass, if you could get huge curved panes of sea-glass. It wasn't all one piece, but big sections in different shades of blue, held together with strips of silvery metal, and in two or three layers, so the blues all washed into one another.

This folly was hollow, too. Tess walked slowly around it. At one end she found the wave sliced off into an oval opening, wide and inviting. The sunlight was streaming in through the glass, making the inside of it an underwater world of blues shimmering over one another, like diving in warm shallow water on a sunlit day. She almost held her breath as she stepped in, as if she were going under the surface, and the blue light washed over her, weightless and half familiar.

She stood there a while in the rippling endless blue, a cool breeze flowing in through the folly, until she heard Ferantis catching his breath on a gasp. Tess turned back. He was in the opening staring at her, his face stricken, and Tess said, slowly, "Your father—what did your father do? To almost be thrown out—"

But standing in the endless rippling beauty of the light,

she already knew, even before Ferantis whispered, "The blue night."

"He *made* the blue night?" Tess said. "Why? What was it *for*?"

"He was trying to find a way to invest conjuration with material—" Ferantis cut himself off with a helpless jerk of his hand, like trying to explain rigging to an inlander in ordinary words. "The high magic only works on the mind," he said abruptly. "I can make you think you're eating a banquet, but if it's sand underneath, you'll still die of hunger. And the copper arts work only upon the body, and only in its limits. My father was trying to create a new kind of magic that would let him change what was *real*, not just what you think. It's what we're *all* trying to do," he added. "All of us in the Council, all our research—ever since the Night of Blood, when our ancestors fled Syrenac, it's what we're all looking for—"

"So that the *next* time a mob comes for you, too big to master all their minds, you'd just be able to sweep them into the sea," Tess said.

"It's not just for that!" Ferantis said. "Can't you imagine everything we could do? Feed the hungry—master the weather—build great citadels!" he added, with a burst of fervent energy, and Tess understood then why he'd been so desperate to get at the follies, to find some way to use them: whoever had built these strange, mad, beautiful places, they'd had the kind of magic he was after. The kind that all the High Lords wanted, and were hungry for.

She took a deep breath and came back out of the blue to face him in the sunlight, in the open air, like surfacing out of a wave that had swept overhead and passed her by. "All *they* did, once they had it, was build nonsense castles in the air," she said, jerking her head at the folly. "And now all of them are gone. Maybe *they* starved trying to eat sand, or glass, or stone." Ferantis's face had gone surprised and uncertain, and Tess shook her head. "Whoever made these things, they were fools. The kind of fool you'd like to be, and Aston, too, throwing the whole world over the side to keep chasing a dream. You haven't even given a thought to what we've found that *really* matters, have you?"

"What?" he said, bewildered, looking into the folly again, at the beautiful beckoning shimmer of blue light so much like the flood of magic his father had spilled useless away into Port Ester like a pot boiling over, because he hadn't been satisfied with the magic he already had.

Tess reached out and took him by the chin and turned his head away from it and towards the long green stretch of thick shaggy green forest going up the hills behind the folly. "Look there. Do you know what those trees are?"

"Lirenwoods," Ferantis said immediately, like something he'd learned in a book, and only looked puzzled back at her, still not understanding.

"*Full-grown* lirenwoods," Tess said. "It takes two weeks to find one big enough for a hull these days on Ester, and that's if you hire good log-finders, who know the sheltered valleys where the big ones grow. We're running out of them. But I can see six prime ones just standing here. Aston could set up a workshop right on this shore and build a whole fleet of boats as easy as kiss your hand." Ferantis blinked at her. "And that's one landfall we've made. As for feeding the hungry—those roundhorns we ate two weeks ago were better eating than goats. Pinharo can't stop talking about the lycca chew he found near the dipping-cup pole. There were unripe sippo pods growing near that twisted-up tower we saw on the eastern coast. Good growing land all over. We've found a whole continent abandoned, bigger than Shon and Syrac put together, with not a single person in it. And it's *already* real. What more do you want? A second world to live in? You can't have both of them at once."

FERANTIS STILL LOOKED BACK AT the folly three times as they walked back to camp, but more time passed between each glance, and by the time they reached the fire, he'd stopped and was frowning deep in thought. He'd asked her questions about the continent, how big it was, how long it would be to sail here from Ester the short way round, already starting to think about numbers. As soon as they got to camp, he asked to see her chart, and to have her explain the symbols to him, and everything she'd marked; he even sat down with it and took out a box full of inks in small jars and a set of tiny brushes, and started on adding color, and little pictures of the follies they'd seen, in a careful hand.

"Aston's up the hill," Jowly told her, after Ferantis got stuck in and stopped asking her questions. Aston had gone to look at the lirenwoods, of course; she ought to have expected it. She nodded and went to find him. He wasn't right at the edge, he was further into the trees, sitting dreamy-eyed just gazing up at a truly monstrous lirenwood, at least twice the size of the ones that had gone to make *Blue*, and when she came, he said, hushed, "Do you see it, Tess? How beautiful it'll be?"

"No," she said, "but I'm glad that you do." He turned and smiled at her, and reached to take her hand.

"*He* will be, too," he said. "He will, Tess, really. He's so quick. He told me what you said to him. He knew it was true, and he didn't want it to be. He just needed—" He moved his hands, the way he did when he was shaping a hull, taking the finest wood he could find and coaxing it to bend into something beautiful.

She sighed a little, but after all, her brains weren't scrambled, and Ferantis hadn't made any of them do anything, and now he *wasn't* going to have to squirrel himself away on the Yellow Pebble, a thousand miles from home, and take Aston with him. "I suppose he's not a glub," she allowed, grudgingly, and Aston beamed up at her.

"You'll have him, won't you?" he said.

"What?" Tess said, confused.

"And we'll all go up the hill and live with him, and his brother and sister," Aston explained, with his earnest air. "Vinna will be so happy. And you *do* want children of your own," and Tess stared at him as she understood what mad idea he'd taken on now. It did make perfect sense—for *him*. Of course now he'd got his beautiful new thing in order, he wanted her steering its course. "He needs us," Aston added, *us,* just as if he'd never, not once, thought of leaving her behind: and he wouldn't have, would he; he'd never have bothered to think it through and see anything he wouldn't accept up ahead.

Her eyes were smarting a little. "You want me to *marry* him?" she said with love and exasperation both flooding back in.

"Well," Aston began.

"No!" Tess said. "No, no—"

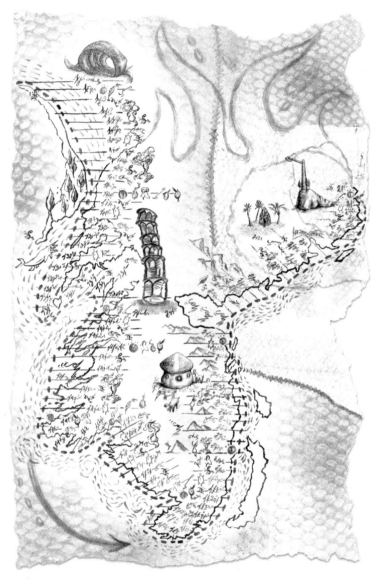

A map of the first Long Journey, wherethrough the Abandoned Lands were discovered, with notes upon current and wind and coastline as could be gathered during the passage, and upon some of the follies there encountered, by the hand of Intessa Roh, Master Navigator of the Sailing Guild of Port Ester.

ABOUT THE AUTHOR

NAOMI NOVIK is the *New York Times* bestselling author of *A Deadly Education, The Last Graduate,* and *The Golden Enclaves,* the award-winning novels *Uprooted* and *Spinning Silver,* and the Temeraire series. She is a founder of the Organization for Transformative Works and the Archive of Our Own. She lives in New York City with her family and six computers.

naominovik.com
X: @naominovik
Instagram: @naominovik

ABOUT THE TYPE

This book was set in Fairfield, the first typeface from the hand of the distinguished American artist and engraver Rudolph Ruzicka (1883–1978). Ruzicka was born in Bohemia (in the present-day Czech Republic) and came to America in 1894. He set up his own shop, devoted to wood engraving and printing, in New York in 1913 after a varied career working as a wood engraver, in photoengraving and banknote printing plants, and as an art director and freelance artist. He designed and illustrated many books, and was the creator of a considerable list of individual prints—wood engravings, line engravings on copper, and aquatints.